In Love wi...

From pennies to pearl... the Rush sisters are swept off their feet by their handsome bosses!

Sisters Patience and Piper Rush might not have
had much growing up but they *always* had each
other, through good times and bad.
Now, oceans apart, can they find comfort,
safety and acceptance in the arms of their
drop-dead-gorgeous bosses?

In June 2015...
Patience finds herself falling for the
man of her dreams in
A Millionaire for Cinderella

And

In September 2015...
Piper's heart is captured by her brooding
Parisian boss in
Beauty & Her Billionaire Boss

Only in Mills & Boon® Cherish™!

BEAUTY & HER BILLIONAIRE BOSS

BY
BARBARA WALLACE

Published in Great Britain 2015
by Mills & Boon, an imprint of Harlequin (UK) Limited,
Eton House, 18-24 Paradise Road, Richmond, Surrey, TW9 1SR

© 2015 Barbara Wallace

ISBN: 978-0-263-25166-1

23-0915

Harlequin (UK) Limited's policy is to use papers that are natural, renewable and recyclable products and made from wood grown in sustainable forests. The logging and manufacturing processes conform to the legal environmental regulations of the country of origin.

Printed and bound in Spain
by CPI, Barcelona

Barbara Wallace can't remember when she wasn't dreaming up love stories in her head, so writing romances for Mills & Boon® Cherish™ is a dream come true. Happily married to her own Prince Charming, she lives in New England with a house full of empty-nest animals. Occasionally her son comes home, as well.

To stay up-to-date on Barbara's news and releases, sign up for her newsletter at www.barbarawallace.com.

To Pete—Your patience and support are a gift for which I can never say thank you enough.

And to M.G.—for giving someone that dose of common sense when we most needed it.

CHAPTER ONE

THERE SHOULD BE a law against a man looking so good in a tuxedo. Staring at the man asleep in the chair, Piper felt an appreciative shiver. Monsieur Frederic Lafontaine had shed his jacket and untied his tie, yet he still looked like a million dollars, what with the way his shirt pulled taut across his linebacker-sized shoulders. She had to start using his dry cleaner. The guy must have been sprawled here for hours, and yet his clothes didn't have a single wrinkle. Piper's uniform wouldn't last five minutes. In fact—she ran a hand down the front of her black skirt—it hadn't.

Then again, she didn't have cheekbones that could cut glass or thick brown hair that begged to be touched, either. Maybe perfection came in bundles.

Taking a deep breath, she touched his shoulder and tried not to think about the broad muscles beneath her fingers. Eight months of working for the man, and she still hadn't shaken her attraction. "Monsieur? You need to wake up. It's after seven o'clock."

When he didn't respond, she shook his shoulder again, this time a little more aggressively. The motion did the trick. Slowly, his eyes opened, and he blinked unseeingly. "You fell asleep in the chair," she told him.

"Oh." His voice was thick with sleep, making it deeper and rougher than usual. "What—what time is it?"

"Seven fifteen."

"What?" He bolted to his feet, arms akimbo, his right hand connecting with the cup of coffee Piper set on the end table only seconds before. The cup took flight, sending coffee over everything.

"Dammit!" he hollered as the hot liquid splashed his shirt. He immediately started pulling at the cloth, lifting it from his skin. "How many times have I told you, you must tell me when you put something within reach? You know I can't see anything put to the side."

It was hard to say much of anything seeing as how he jumped up before she had a chance to open her mouth. "I'll get you a towel."

"Don't bother." He'd already yanked the shirt free from his waistband. "Clean up the rest of the spill before it stains the carpet. I'm going to take a shower." He turned to head upstairs.

"Wait," Piper called.

Moving this time before he could speak, she scooped up the cup from where it had fallen on the carpet, half an inch from the toe of his shoe. "You were going to crush it," she said, holding the china teacup in front of his face.

If he appreciated her heads-up behavior, he didn't say so. "Tell Michel when he arrives that I will be ready shortly. And make sure my briefcase is by the front door. *On the left*," he added with emphasis.

As if she would leave it somewhere else. Piper bit back the sarcastic response. She learned a long time ago that some fights weren't meant to be won. Arguing with a man who was wearing hot coffee on his stomach was definitely one of those fights. Instead, she waited until he'd stalked his way upstairs, then treated herself to a glare in his direction. It would serve him right if she moved his bag to the right just to spite him. Because goodness knows the world might end if the briefcase was on the wrong side of the doorway.

Not that she would actually move the thing. Put out or not, she wasn't so petty that she'd pick on a blind man—or half-blind man as the case may be. Truth was, nitpicky as they were, monsieur's "rules" served a purpose. When she took this job, it was made very clear his limited field of vision required everything in the house to be just so. Chief on the list was that nothing should be set to the side without his knowledge. His lack of peripheral vision might cause a mishap, he'd explained. Most of the time, the system worked. There were times in fact, such as when he crossed the room with his slow, purposeful strides, that Piper forgot the man had trouble seeing.

After double-checking on the briefcase—which was on the left as always—she headed for the utility closet. "So goes another fun-filled day in Paris," she said as she marched into the kitchen for her cleaning supplies. Naturally, the coffee had fallen on the handmade Persian carpet. That meant instead of using the nice handy carpet-cleaning machine in the closet, she had to get the stain up with water and a vinegar paste.

This was not how she expected her year abroad to go. Her year here was supposed to signal the start of a new and exciting life. The wonderful moment when she stopped being dumpy Piper Rush and became Piper Rush, chef extraordinaire who dazzled the culinary institute with her skills and enthralled French men with her American wit. In short, the complete opposite of her life in East Boston.

She should have known better.

Didn't take long for her to realize that Paris was exactly the same as Boston, only in French. Which actually made it worse than Boston. Despite spending hours shoulder to shoulder with a dozen other people, she hadn't made a single close friend. Everyone was too busy trying to impress Chef Despelteau. In a way, you'd think the fact that she couldn't impress the man if she tried would help her cause, but no. Yesterday, after she didn't use enough confit to brown her chicken, he declared her cassoulet flavorless and spent ten minutes lecturing her on the importance of taste, even when making "peasant food." All her classmates did was snicker. City of Lights, her foot. More like the City of the Unfriendly.

Even Frederic barely paid attention to her, unless there was an errand to run, or she needed to wake him up. He was too busy lecturing at the university or heading off to some fancy social event.

The perpetual loneliness she fought to keep under wraps threatened to wedge free. She had to swallow to keep it from rising up and choking her. God, what she wouldn't give for someone to talk to. *Or to go home.*

Out of habit, her hand reached for the cell phone

tucked in her apron only to leave it behind. It was still the middle of the night in Boston. Her sister, Patience, would still be asleep. Patience—the only reason she was sticking things out to completion. Her sister was convinced Piper was living the dream, and considering how much Patience had sacrificed so Piper could actually have a dream, she didn't dare disturb the fantasy. Besides, her sister had issues of her own. She and her boss's nephew were doing some kind of back-and-forth that had Patience on edge. The last thing she needed right now was a whiny baby sister burning up the data package complaining because her year abroad wasn't all sunshine and roses.

She carried her supplies into the salon, pausing when she reached the front window. A few blocks away, the Eiffel Tower loomed tall, reminding her she really had no right complaining. She might be lonely, but she was a lonely person living in luxury. Instead of monsieur's mansion, she could be living in some ratty apartment battling roaches for breakfast. Or worse, living on the streets. Been there, done both. She didn't feel like doing either again.

If only she had someone to share Paris with, then things wouldn't be so bad. It wasn't going to happen, though. If she hadn't found a kindred spirit yet, she wasn't going to. She was simply going to have to suck things up, the way she always did.

Speaking of sucking, she had a carpet to clean. Staring at the stain darkening the beige carpet, she sighed. This better not be a sign of how the rest of her day was going to go.

* * *

Frederic winced as he peeled the wet shirt from his body. Not because the liquid stung his skin, although it did, but because he was appalled at his behavior. Yelling at his housekeeper that way. Like a child throwing a tantrum. Didn't he swear he would never be that way? Become one of those angry invalids who took their bad moods out on others? Yet the first time he spills a drink, he lashes out. Embarrassment was no excuse.

What did he expect, falling asleep in the salon like that? It was the last glass of Bordeaux. Knowing the way alcohol went to his head and made him overly pensive, he never should have indulged. Last night found him sitting for hours, watching the tower's twinkling lights, his mind a sea of morose thoughts.

The dampness from his shirt found its way to his palms. Resisting the urge to hurl the garment across the room, he draped it on top of the duvet for Piper to find later. He stripped off the rest of his tuxedo as well, making sure he returned the suit and his shoes to their assigned places in the closet. Oh, but for those days when undressing meant toeing off your shoes wherever you stood and tossing your clothes in a heap.

Obviously, last night's moroseness hadn't subsided. Why else would he be bemoaning a past that he couldn't get back? After all, he'd come to terms with his failing eyesight long before it started to steal his peripheral vision. From the moment the doctors first told him his retina was degenerating, in fact. He knew full well that one day the tunnel through which he viewed the world would close completely, leaving him blind. He'd accepted his fate and framed his life in anticipation. And when the time came, he would shoulder the burden alone, the way a person should. He wouldn't drag others down with him. A promise that, until this morning, he'd done a very good job of keeping.

He owed his housekeeper a very large apology.

When the employment agency first recommended the American culinary student, he thought the idea ridiculous. A temporary resident? She'd be too distracted by studies and sightseeing. But as it turned out, Piper was nothing short of exemplary. Today aside, she did her job quietly and unobtrusively. In fact, the two of them could go days without crossing paths. Precisely the kind of help Frederic preferred.

Today's mistake with the coffee was as much his fault as hers. She no doubt set down the cup to wake him, not expecting him to stand up so quickly.

He would definitely apologize.

Unfortunately, there wasn't time right now. Leaning in close, he read the time on his nightstand clock. With luck, he could shower and make his first class in plenty of time. Whether or not his morning began poorly didn't matter to his superiors at the university. They expected him to deliver his lectures on time, regardless. This evening, then. Before the symphony. He would find Piper and explain that he overreacted. Then they would both forget this morning ever happened.

Staining the carpet turned out to be the high point of the day.

First, cleaning the rug took longer than planned. In

addition to the major stain, there were a dozen or so tiny spots that needed blotting. It took her forever to find them all, so by the time Piper finished, she was running late. Chef Despelteau was less than thrilled to see her slip through the door five minutes into his lecture.

Now this.

"Uninspired," Chef Despelteau pronounced. "Your spices, they do not dance, they plod. I expect my students to produce magic in the kitchen, not…" He dropped his fork back onto the plate with an expression that was usually reserved for walking around landfills. Shaking his head, he moved on, his silence letting everyone know Piper wasn't worth more of his time.

"…so pathetic. Why is she even here?"

The whispered comment drifted from the stovetop across the aisle. Apparently whoever said it didn't care if anyone heard him. Why should he, when the whole class was thinking the same thing?

Keeping her shoulders square, Piper stared straight ahead and pretended she didn't hear a thing. That was the number one rule. Never let them think they were getting to you. Never lose control. Never let them see you cry. Crying only gave the bullies power. Let them whisper behind her back all they wanted; she would not give them the satisfaction of seeing so much as a twitch.

She succeeded, too. All through Chef Despelteau's final remarks, through the Métro ride home, and even into the house. She managed to last until she saw the living room carpet and the faint brown ring reminding her she'd failed that task, too. Letting out the coarsest obscenity she knew, she broke down.

Screw cooking school. Tossing her bag in the chair, she stomped into the kitchen. Screw monsieur, too. Him and his impossible-to-clean carpeting. Screw Paris with its beautiful buildings and sidewalk cafés and shops she couldn't afford. She hated them all.

Carbs. She needed carbs. Yanking open the refrigerator door, she grabbed a wedge of cheddar cheese and an onion. Creamy, gooey macaroni and cheese, that's what this pity party needed. *How's that for peasant food, Chef Despelteau?*

Now if she would only stop crying. Sniffing back a fresh batch of tears, she grabbed the cheese grater and took to demolishing the cheddar to a shredded pulp.

"There you—"

"What now?" she snarled. What else could she add to her list of mistakes today?

Frederic blinked in shock. Great. Yelling at her boss. That's what she could add. Because, of course.

Horrified, she turned back to the cheese. "I mean, about this mor—morn…" The tears were back. She scrunched her face trying to stop them.

A paper towel floated in front of her face.

"Is everything all right?"

Why'd he have to sound nice, too? It made things worse. "Fine." Taking the paper towel, she wiped her cheeks and blew her nose.

"You don't look fine."

"The cheese is making my eyes water."

"I see. It must be quite pungent."

Piper ignored the comment, choosing to wipe her nose again instead. "Did you need something, monsieur?"

A tentative smile worked its way across his features. Afraid to set her off again, probably. "I wanted to apologize for losing my temper this morning. The coffee, it was not your fault."

No, it wasn't, she wanted to say. She didn't. Since he apologized, the least she could do was be gracious in return. "I should have known better than to put a cup where you couldn't see it."

"And I should know better than to behave like a brat," he countered, one-upping her. "It's rude to blame others for my shortcomings."

Piper wasn't sure she'd call partial blindness a shortcoming, but she accepted the apology anyway. If she didn't, the two of them might spend all night exchanging regrets. "Thank you," she said with a sniff. The man would never know that his "I'm sorry" had just beat out the coffee stain as the day's bright spot.

"Do you need another paper towel? I would offer you something nicer, but I'm not a handkerchief person. A napkin perhaps?"

That made her smile, picturing him retrieving a napkin from the linen closet. "Thanks, but I'm okay now." There remained a slight pressure behind her eyes trying to push out tears, but she could keep that under control. A quick splash of water and she'd be fine.

"Are—" She took one last swipe at her nose. "Are you in for the evening?" As if she didn't already know the answer. Frederic was seldom "in." His evenings were one big social engagement. How one person could squeeze so much activity into a week, she didn't know.

Just as she expected, Frederic shook his head. "I

have tickets for the symphony. I came home to change my shirt is all."

Meaning he would be home late, as usual. "I'll make sure to leave the foyer light on before I turn in."

"Thank you." He turned to leave only to pause. "Why don't you take the evening off as well? Some time with friends might make you feel better."

Sure it would, if she had friends to go out with. "I…" Thankfully, the *beep* of an incoming message on her cell phone saved her from having to make up some embarrassing lie.

"Sounds like your friends have the same idea," Frederic said.

She reached into her pocket, smiling when she read the message on her screen. "It's my sister," she told him. Why she felt she needed to tell him that, she didn't know.

"You have a sister."

A question as much as a statement. Surely he knew. Then again, he might not. This was the longest conversation they'd ever had.

"She works as a housekeeper back in Boston."

"Ah, so cleaning is a family business."

"More like a family situation we both fell into." From his expression, she could tell he didn't get the joke. No surprise. It wasn't very clear, or funny. "She wants to video chat."

"Sounds like you've got something to look forward to."

"Yeah." Piper smiled. Talking to Patience would definitely make her feel better.

"I'm glad." And for the first time she could remember, he gave her a warm, genuine smile. "I'll leave you alone so you can talk. Good night."

"Good night." To her horror, she almost said "Don't go" instead. Her loneliness was out of control if a smile could make her slip up like that.

Piper waited until she heard the front door shut before going to get her computer. Her apartment sat at the back of the house. Technically, it was more like a suite of rooms—bedroom, bathroom and sitting room—but they were still nicer than anything she could afford on her own. They also came with kitchen privileges and monsieur's kitchen was a dream come true even for an *uninspired* cook like her.

It was into the kitchen that Piper carried her laptop. Patience specifically said video chat, which meant she was planning on a nice long conversation. By putting the laptop on the counter, Piper could cook while they talked. It would be almost like home.

Almost.

A few keystrokes later, Patience Rush's face appeared on screen. Took the older woman about two seconds to frown. "Your eyes are all red and puffy," she said. "Is everything okay?"

Wow, was that the question of the night or what? Maybe she should have looked in a mirror to see how awful she actually looked. "I was chopping onions," Piper replied. At least it was more believable than blaming the cheese.

Too bad her sister didn't let the lie slide as easily as her boss had. "Onions, huh? You sure?"

"Yes, I'm sure."

Patience arched a brow. Her form of mother guilt. It worked every time.

"Okay," Piper admitted, "*maybe* I was thinking about home a little bit too."

"Oh, sweetie, I miss you, too. But hey, a couple more months and you'll be back in Boston bragging to everyone you know how you're a fancy French chef. Do you have any idea how proud I am of you?"

"I do," Piper replied, the familiar knot starting to twist in her stomach. She got the heavy unsettled feeling every time Patience started gushing about her great Paris adventure.

"So what is it that has you video chatting me in the middle of your day?" she asked, changing the topic. Her sister seemed especially bubbly today. A big difference from the last few phone calls. Her image on the screen glowed and not from computer glare either.

"What? A girl can't miss her baby sister?"

"A girl can definitely miss her baby sister." Same way the baby sister could miss her. Piper blinked back some fresh tears. "But usually you text. I know you've got a lot on your plate."

"Never too much for you."

"Awww." Sweet as the sentiment was, Piper wasn't buying. Not with the way her sister's eyes were sparkling. "Seriously, what do you want?"

"I have a favor to ask."

"I knew you wanted something." Although what kind of favor could Piper do from halfway around the world? Send someone a souvenir? "What do you need?"

"I need you to pay a visit to someone there in Paris."

"Who?"

Piper listened as her sister explained. The favor was for Piper to visit the sister of a dead artist named Nigel Rougeau.

"Hey, isn't your boss's cat named Nigel?" she interrupted. Patience was always telling stories about the big Maine coon cat.

"The cat's a namesake," Patience replied. "Nigel was Ana's lover in the seventies." Ana being the little old lady Patience worked for.

Her sister went on to explain a very tragic story involving Ana and the painter. "There's a small chance that one of the paintings Ana posed for still exists," she said.

"And you want me to talk with Nigel's sister and find out for you."

"If anyone knows if one of Nigel's paintings survived, it would be someone in his family."

True enough. Especially if Nigel and his sister were as close as she and Patience were.

"I think she'd find talking to you a lot less intimidating than a private detective."

"I am definitely unintimidating," Piper replied. More often than not, she was the one intimidated.

"So you'll do it?"

"Of course." A couple hours of her time was nothing. In fact, it would break up the monotony. "I'll call her tomorrow and see if she'll meet with me. Maybe you'll luck out and there'll be a big old painting of Ana hanging in her house."

"Wouldn't that be something," Patience said with a

laugh. "Stuart and I will be glad for any information you can find out."

"Stuart, huh?" That was a new development. Until recently, Patience's descriptions of Stuart Duchenko leaned more toward the suspicious jerk variety. Putting down her knife, she leaned close to the screen. "How are things going with the two of you? Is he still cool with, you know, the club?"

"Seems to be," Patience replied.

"See? I told you he'd understand. It's not like you went to work in that place because you liked dancing naked on tables." It was the same reasoning Piper used on herself whenever the teasing at school got to be too much to bear. Of course, she never told Patience about what the kids used to say. Her sister was embarrassed enough.

Case in point, the wince crossing Patience's face right now. "Of course I didn't, and you were right. Stuart says he understands."

"Wait—what do you mean 'says he understands'? Don't you believe him?" There was a note of reluctance in the comment Piper didn't like.

"No, I believe him. Stuart's been great."

"Then what's wrong?"

"Nothing." Patience shook her head.

Nothing came with a very dreamy sigh. No way was Piper letting the reaction go by unnoticed. "Patience? What aren't you telling me?"

"Um…"

Son of a gun, her sister was red as a tomato. There was only one thing that would make her blush that deeply. "Oh my God! Is something going on between you and your boss?"

"He's not my boss," Patience said quickly. "He's my boss's nephew."

She was splitting hairs and they both knew it, which was why Piper asked, "What exactly is the difference?"

"About the same as between you dating *your* boss and you dating his next-door neighbor."

"Pul—leeze." Like that was a good example. "The only neighbor I've met is an eleven-year-old boy, and my boss doesn't even…"

"Doesn't even what?"

Notice I'm here. That's what Piper was going to say, anyway. Only he had noticed tonight. Absently, she ran a knuckle down her cheek as she remembered his kind gesture.

"Piper?"

"Sorry," she said, shaking off the memory. "I lost track of what I was about to say. And *you* still haven't answered my question. Are you dating Stuart Duchenko?"

There was a definite darkening to her sister's blush. "For now, yes."

A different kind of heaviness took up space in Piper's stomach. The same uncomfortable feeling she used to get as a kid when waiting to be picked for dodgeball. She was always left for last.

Ignoring the sensation, she pushed her lips into a smile. "No way! That's great! I'm so happy for you." She was, childish reaction aside. She had no reason to feel anything *but* happy, really. It was just her pity party making its reappearance.

"Don't go making a big deal," her sister was saying. "The two of us are having fun together, that's all. It's nothing serious."

The sparkle in Patience's eyes said otherwise, but Piper kept the thought to herself. Patience would admit the truth soon enough.

The two of them talked and joked while Piper worked and for a little while, her loneliness receded.

"Why aren't you making some fancy French dish?" Patience asked as she was putting the casserole in the oven.

"Because I felt like macaroni and cheese. Would you feel better if I called it *macaroni au fromage*?"

"A little." From her chair on the other side of the world, her sister frowned again. "Are you sure you're all right? You mentioned your boss earlier. Is he still treating you okay?"

Once again, a paper towel and a smile flashed before Piper's eyes. "He's treating me fine."

"That sounded weird."

"What do you mean?"

"The way you said 'fine' with a long sigh."

Piper rolled her eyes. As if her sigh could be any longer or dreamier-sounding than the ones her sister made. "How should I say it? He treats me fine. We hardly see each other." Today's encounters notwithstanding. "Not everyone socializes with their boss, you know. I meant Ana," she added quickly before Patience got the wrong idea.

"So long as he isn't giving you a hard time."

"I swear, he isn't."

They talked a little longer, mostly about silly stuff. Patience told a few stories about Nigel the cat and about how things were going with Stuart. Piper lied about how well school was going. By the time they said goodbye, she'd cooked and eaten her casserole. She would have said that the night was exactly what she needed, except that as soon as she turned off the computer, her melancholy returned stronger than ever.

"It's Hollywood's fault," she said to the Eiffel Tower a little while later. "All those movies making Paris look so wonderful. Leading a woman to hope life might be more magical under French skies."

There was a smudge on the glass. Breathing some fog on the pane, she wiped at it with her sleeve. Patience would be horrified by her casualness. Her sister took cleaning very seriously.

Maybe if she tried a little harder. Gave more effort in class, learned to appreciate her surroundings more. Maybe then she could work up the enthusiasm she was supposed to feel for this adventure. Right now, she only felt tired. The carbohydrates were kicking in. Merging with her sad mood and killing what was left of her cleaning ambitions.

Discarding her plans to dig out the cleaning supplies, she sank into a nearby chair. The same one she found Frederic sleeping in this morning, she realized. Outside, the tower twinkled mockingly. Leaning her head back, she watched the lights dance. They were beautiful, weren't they?

"Easy chair to fall asleep in, no?"

The voice close to her ear was deep and rough. Piper jumped to her feet. Grabbing the first thing she could find, she whirled around ready to attack.

Frederic raised his hands in mock surrender. "I'm sorry. I didn't mean to scare you."

"You didn't…" Considering she was wielding a pillow as a weapon, she gave up the argument. "I wasn't expecting you home so early, is all." It was early, right? *Please say it was early.*

"My date wasn't feeling well, so we left the concert at intermission." His eyes narrowed, as if zooming in on her. Too late, Piper realized she still wore her chef's jacket instead of her uniform. "You were working hard?"

"No. I mean, I planned to but I…"

"I am joking."

"Oh." Thank goodness the lights were dim and he couldn't see how red her cheeks were.

"If I recall, I suggested you take the night off to relax. I'm glad you did." He crossed to the window. Hands clasped behind his back, he stood looking out at the tower.

One of the things Piper had noticed while working for Frederic was the way he concentrated so intently on whatever he was doing. Walking. Looking out the window. Some of the focus she attributed to his bad eyes, but lousy vision didn't explain the power behind his movements. He moved with such deliberation. As though nothing could deter him from the action at hand. The guy could give Chef Despelteau a run for his money when it came to laser glares, that's for sure. She could only imagine what it was like to be one of his students.

Or one of his dates, for that matter.

All of a sudden she realized those slate-colored eyes were looking at her. He'd said something, and she missed it. Again, she thanked the dim lighting for protecting her from bigger embarrassment. "I'm sorry, what did you say?"

"I asked if you were enjoying your year in Paris so far."

You mean her crying jag earlier didn't give him a clue? "It's a beautiful city."

"That it is. Have you done much sightseeing?"

"A little." When she first arrived and was still in her starry-eyed phase. After a couple weeks, however, solo sightseeing lost its luster. "Between class and work, I haven't had much time."

"That is too bad. You should make sure you see as much as possible. You never know when you'll have another chance."

"I'll try to remember that." For some reason, Piper felt as though he was talking about more than sightseeing. Or maybe fatigue was making her read too deeply between the lines. For all she knew, this was his normal way of making conversation. He approached everything else with intensity; why wouldn't he approach talking the same way?

Regardless of the reason, the exchange left a hum in the air that made her antsy. Piper couldn't help thinking how crisp and elegant he looked in his summer suit.

Meanwhile, she was growing more aware of her wrinkled jacket by the second. Not to mention the smell of onion and cheddar cheese clinging to her fingers.

Suddenly, she needed some space. Setting down her pillow, she announced, "I'm going to finish cleaning the kitchen." The kitchen was spotless, but she needed some kind of excuse. Then, whether because of the thickened atmosphere or something else, she added, "I'm really sorry, too, about my meltdown earlier."

"Already forgotten, Piper. I hope whatever caused your distress is gone by tomorrow."

"I hope so, too." Not very likely, but a girl could hope. She went to say good-night, but Frederic had already turned his back to the room, his attention once again on the scene outside his window.

Must have been a trick of the shadows. Standing there with his hands behind his back, he suddenly looked alone and far away. *Maybe I'm not the only lonely person in Paris.* The thought was in her head before Piper could stop it.

Frederic Lafontaine, lonely. Sure. Now she knew she was tired.

CHAPTER TWO

THE NEXT MORNING, Piper called Marie Rougeau-Montpelier and introduced herself. To her surprise, the elderly woman said she would be thrilled to meet with her, especially once Piper mentioned her brother's art-work. She invited Piper to visit after lunch. The appoint-ment meant skipping a day of class, but Piper didn't really mind. A day off, in fact, might do her some good. Help her get her head back into the game.

Marie's address, which turned out to be a luxury tower near La Défense, the business district just out-side the city, was easier to find than she expected. Not wanting to ring the woman's bell before she was ex-pected, Piper found herself wandering around La Grande Arche, the city's twentieth-century version of the Arc de Triomphe. It was the perfect summer's day. Not too hot, not too cold. Being lunchtime, the square was filled with people. Business executives sat on nearby steps soaking up the sun while tourists and others lounged on the grass in the nearby park. Piper strolled the perimeter and watched as they laughed and chatted with each other. Was this what Frederic meant when he told her to see as much of the city as possible?

Thinking of her boss made her insides sag. He was nowhere to be found when she woke up this morning. That didn't surprise her, he was nowhere to be found most of the time, but Piper sort of hoped that after last night, the routine might have changed. She still couldn't shake the image of him staring out his salon window. Looking so solitary and distant. So *alone*.

There's a word for what you're doing, you know. Projecting or connecting, something like that. Whatever the word, she needed to stop. Just because she was in another sad mood didn't mean her boss was too.

Her feet hurt, protesting having to wear sandals after months of wearing sturdy shoes. She looked around for a café where she could give them a break. There was one on the corner with a maroon-and-white awning that wasn't overly crowded. Helping herself to one of the empty rattan chairs that lined the sidewalk, she had just pulled out her cell phone when she heard a familiar-sounding voice ordering an espresso.

No way. She looked to her left. Even with aviator sunglasses covering his face, she recognized Frederic's profile instantly.

He was alone. At least the chair across from him was empty, and judging from the way his long legs were stretched out to claim the table's real estate, he wasn't expecting a guest to arrive anytime soon. Piper's eyes traveled their length, from his wingtips to the muscular thighs that disappeared beneath the tablecloth.

In contrast to last night, today he looked the picture of ease.

Must be nice to feel so confident instead of having to fake it all the time. And to be that good-looking. Patience was always saying that being beautiful wasn't all it was cracked up to be. Piper wouldn't know. She was never someone people thought of as beautiful. When the guys in high school made fun of Patience's job, they did so with a glaze of lust in their eyes. No one's eyes ever glazed for Piper.

Just then, as though sensing her stare, Frederic turned in her direction. Piper started to shrink back into the shadows, then caught herself and waved instead. He didn't wave back.

She was about to take offense when she realized she wasn't in his field of vision. Smoothing her skirt, she walked toward his table.

"Bonjour, monsieur," she greeted with a smile.

The sound of an American accent jarred Frederic from his thoughts. He knew of only one person who spoke French with an accent like that. Blinking out of his fog, he found a whirl of yellow and red in his line of sight. Lifting his eyes, he saw a familiar brunette head. "Piper? Where did you come from?"

"Two tables over. I waved, but you weren't paying attention."

She was being polite. They both knew he didn't wave because she wasn't sitting in his field of view.

"Lost in thought," he replied, continuing the pretense.

"I'm not bothering you, am I?" Piper's question brought him back.

"Not at all. I'm killing time after an appointment is all." Yet another pointless meeting with his ophthalmologist. He went every few months simply to hear that his eyes were still diseased.

"And you?"

"Killing time before an appointment, actually."

Sitting back in his chair, Frederic found himself wishing he'd been paying attention when she approached. Whenever he saw Piper at the apartment, she wore either her chef's jacket or that awful maid uniform that was the antithesis of every French maid fantasy ever written. This sundress, however... The bright colors definitely suited her better. Plus, there was an expanse of flesh around her shoulders he didn't normally get to enjoy.

"Are you meeting a classmate?" he asked. A date would certainly explain the dress. Why he was suddenly intrigued by her social life, Frederic wasn't sure, except that the memory of her crying by the kitchen counter refused to leave him. He found it odd, an attractive American—and she was attractive as that expanse of skin attested—spending her evenings in Paris alone.

"I'm supposed to meet with someone at the Rose d'Arms," she said. "It's a retirement home a block or so from here."

"Looking for a surrogate grandmother?"

"Hardly," she said with a laugh. A very pleasant-sounding laugh, too. Like bells. "I'm doing a favor for my sister."

"At a retirement home?"

"It's a long story. I won't bore you with the details. I really just stopped by to say hello. I'll let you get back to whatever it was you were…"

"Please. Stay. We can kill time together."

"Are you sure?"

There was hesitancy in her voice. Frederic couldn't blame her. Eight months of hardly talking, and now here they were on their third conversation in two days. "I wouldn't have offered if I wasn't sure," he told her. "There is no reason for the two of us to sit at separate tables when we are both by ourselves. Besides, you have me intrigued."

The café had arranged the tables as so many cafés in the city did, with the seats side by side so that patrons could enjoy the view. As Piper slipped into the seat beside his, Frederic was struck by an aroma of vanilla and spices that made his mouth water. "Did you bake today?" he asked.

"No. I skipped class. Why?"

"No reason." Who knew a person could smell delicious? "Tell me this long story of yours."

Piper took a deep breath. "Apparently, Ana, my sister's boss, lived with an artist here in Paris in the seventies and posed for a bunch of paintings. Her greatnephew, Stuart, is hoping to surprise her with one as a gift, so Patience asked me if I would talk to the artist's sister to see if any of his paintings survived."

"Doesn't your sister realize there are easier ways to track down an artist's work? If he is well-known…"

"This is where it gets complicated."

She paused while the waitress brought his espresso and she placed her order.

"Complicated how?"

"The artist died in an accident a long time ago. According to Ana, he would have been huge—like Picasso huge—but then Theodore Duchenko went and bought up..."

"Wait..." Frederic needed to go back a step. "Did you say Theodore *Duchenko*?"

Piper nodded. "That's right. Patience works for his sister, Ana Duchenko."

Unbelievable. Duchenko Silver was world renowned. Frederic knew curators who gushed over adding a piece of the famed Russian silver to their collections. As for the late Theodore Duchenko, the man had been considered one of the most ruthless tycoons of the twentieth century. "You're saying that you're trying to track down a portrait of Ana Duchenko."

"Not just a portrait. A nude," Piper replied. "Nigel painted a bunch, and they were supposedly pretty racy, which is why..."

"Duchenko wanted them destroyed," he finished for her. "This is astounding. The Duchenko name, it is... well, let us say that if a portrait still exists, the significance in terms of pop culture alone would be immeasurable."

"I don't think Stuart cares if the painting has any kind of value—he just wants to give his aunt back a piece of her history. The way my sister tells it, Ana truly loved the man."

The waitress returned with her café au lait. "It's all very tragic, really," Piper said, taking a sip.

Tragic but exciting. Frederic found his curiosity piqued in a way he hadn't felt in years. Not since his university days. "There is nothing like the thrill of discovering a new artist," he told her. "The euphoria, it hits you like a…" The sexual metaphor was too crude to share with a woman. He settled for saying "There are few pleasures like it. I envy you."

"The whole thing is probably a long shot."

"Perhaps," he said, reaching for his drink. It quite probably was, in fact. "But long shot or not, the chase is always exciting."

"Want to come with me?"

Frederic set his cup down with a *clink* so he could focus his gaze on her. "Pardon?"

"You just said you envied my going on the hunt. Besides, I don't know anything about art. What if there's a giant painting of Ana hanging on this woman's wall? How will I know if it's worth Stuart's money?"

And she thought *he* was the best person to evaluate? "You just said the painting wasn't about value."

"It isn't." There was silence as she shifted in her chair. When she spoke again, Frederic heard a change in her voice. It became lower, with less spark. "Never mind. It was only a suggestion."

"No, I'd love to join you." Unsettled by the sadness he thought he heard in her voice, he spoke without thinking.

The smile worked its way back into her voice. "Awesome! I'll finish my coffee and we'll go."

A visit to a retirement home, Frederic said to himself as he sipped his espresso. *To meet with an old woman. No harm in that.*

Why, then, did he feel as if he was getting involved in something more?

There wasn't, of course, an undiscovered painting hanging in Marie's apartment. Only a very tall, pinched-looking woman wearing a velvet tracksuit. She greeted the two of them with a wide smile. "A professor. How exciting," she gushed, squeezing his hand. "Please come in."

"I knew you'd be a hit," Piper murmured as she stepped inside.

Frederic grinned in response. His insides were feeling the thrill of the hunt.

While he still wasn't entirely sure why Piper had asked him to come along, he'd decided to embrace the opportunity. Who knew when another chance would cross his path? Or, for that matter, come with such an attractive package. Piper was far enough into the room that he could finally see her figure. She had curves a sculpture would love. Soft and supple. The kind meant to be traced by a person's hands.

That's it. He was getting rid of the maid's uniform.

"What period do you study, Professor?" Marie was asking. The older woman was already limping across the sitting room en route to the bookcase.

"Medieval. Pre-Romanesque mostly."

"Nigel would have called you stuck in the past, but

then he prided himself on being antiestablishment. We all did back then. Please, have a seat."

She gestured to a sofa barely large enough to deserve the label. Feeling overly large, he perched on the edge of the seat and wondered how a woman Marie's height could ever sit comfortably. The cushion dipped and Piper sat beside him. Vanilla and spice teased his nostrils again. It was like walking into the most pleasant bakery on earth every time the woman sat down.

"He had such promise, my brother. My mother used to brag he knew how to paint before he could walk. An exaggeration, I'm sure. Come to think of it, though, I can't remember a time when he wasn't drawing or painting or something."

Reaching up, she pulled out what looked like a large plastic binder and opened it up. "This is him here," she said. "Five years old and he'd already won his first competition."

She set the album on Frederic's lap. The old photo was too small and blurry for him to focus much on, but he leaned forward and pretended all the same. Piper leaned in as well, her left knee knocking against his as she shifted angles. Frederic sucked in his breath at the awareness shooting up his thigh. Even with two layers of material, he felt every bump and bone pressed against him.

"Impressive," he murmured. Although he wasn't sure if he meant Nigel's childhood art or Piper's knee.

"He could have done so much," Marie said. "We all told him to stop riding that motorbike, but he was stubborn." A crack worked its way into the end of her voice.

"I'm sorry," she said, pressing a fist to her lips. "It's been a long time since I've talked about Nigel at all."

"We're sorry if we're bringing up bad memories," Piper remarked.

"That's all right. They aren't all bad. In some ways, I think Nigel wanted to die young. He once told me that art only reached the masses once you were gone."

"I could name a few living painters who might disagree," Frederic replied.

Her resulting smile was watery, but strong. "I never said his theory made sense. In the end, it didn't matter anyway, because his work never reached anyone."

Because Theodore Duchenko ordered it destroyed.

"That is why we're here," Piper said. "My sister works for Ana Duchenko."

Every ounce of humor disappeared from Marie's face. "That family destroyed my brother," she said, stiffening. "I was only a child, but I remember how my parents cursed Theodore Duchenko and the rest of them."

To her credit, Piper didn't stiffen in return. He always thought how a person reacted when challenged said a lot about them. His housekeeper, it appeared, knew how to stand tall. "From what I hear, Theodore Duchenko deserved cursing," she said. "What he did was awful."

"It was an outrage. Ruining my brother's life, decimating his art all because he was afraid his family would be embarrassed." The rest of her rant disappeared in a soft mutter.

"For what it's worth, Ana never spoke to her brother again because of what he did."

Marie stopped muttering. "She didn't?"

"No. My sister says Ana blames her brother for Nigel's death as much as you do. She never married, either."

"Because of Nigel?"

"She loved your brother very much."

This was the part of the story that made Frederic uncomfortable. Love stealing a young heiress's future. The idea of a life stolen out from under you struck a little too close to home.

Marie was back at the bookcase, a long purple silhouette whose head was cut off in darkness. "I only met her once," she was saying. "Nigel brought her to Sunday dinner and told us all she was his muse. My parents were not happy. I remember my father whispering that Ana 'looked expensive.'" Frederic could picture the scene. Nigel, their starving artist son, walking in with his wealthy seventeen-year-old lover.

"I know that Theodore tried to destroy all of Nigel's paintings." Piper's knee brushed Frederic's again as she shifted in her seat. His entire leg felt the contact this time. "We're hoping, though, he might have missed one or two."

"If one existed, don't you think my family would have kept it?"

"Perhaps there was a sale he made before Theodore arrived in France," Frederic suggested. "Or a gift he gave to a friend."

Marie shook her head. "I have no idea. The only paintings left of Nigel's that we have are a couple small landscapes he did for my mother while he was in art school."

"It's all right," Piper replied. "We figured it was a long shot."

Perhaps, thought Frederic, but she had clearly hoped. Her disappointment was palpable.

Whenever one of his students felt let down, he made a point of reminding them life was full of disappointments.

Right now with Piper, all he wanted was to squeeze her hand. Reassure rather than remind. It was definitely not like him.

Marie was still talking. "To be honest, even if a portrait of Ana did survive, I'm not sure my parents would have kept it. They didn't want anything to do with the Duchenkos."

"No," Piper said. "I don't suppose they would."

"My brother did have a friend who might know. He owned an art gallery in the Marais. A very successful one, I believe. His name was Gaspard."

Frederic looked up. "You don't mean Gaspard Theroux?"

"Yes, that's him."

"You know him?" Piper asked.

"Galerie Gaspard Theroux is one of the most respected galleries in Paris."

"Gaspard and Nigel were very close. If he is still alive, he might know whether any of Nigel's early Ana studies sold."

"I'll tell you one thing," Frederic said as they were walking across the square a short while later. "If Gaspard represented Nigel's work, he must have been very talented. The gallery is known for discovering the best rising talent in Europe. I've bought a couple pieces from Gaspard's son, Bernard. He doesn't have quite the same eye as his father, but he does well."

Piper didn't care how good an eye the guy had. All she cared about was that her search hadn't reached a dead end. It took her by surprise just how disappointed she was when Marie first said the paintings were gone. The repeated stories of Ana and Nigel's love affair had gotten to her.

She turned so she could get a better view of the man walking beside her. Inviting Frederic to join her was a total impulse. He sounded so animated when he was talking about Nigel's work being a significant discovery. Plus, she liked the idea of his company in case Marie wasn't as friendly as she had sounded on the phone. There wasn't a woman of any age who wouldn't like seeing a man who looked like Frederic on her doorstep.

Now as it turned out, he turned out to be an invaluable resource. "I don't suppose you know if Gaspard Theroux is still alive, do you?"

"He is, but he has had health problems the past few years. His mind…" Frederic gestured with his hands as to say he didn't know.

That's what Piper was afraid of. She combed her fingers through her hair with a sigh. At least she had a place to start. "Maybe his son knows something. What did you say his name was?"

"Bernard."

"I'll give him a call tomorrow." Maybe his father kept records from those days.

"Good luck. Bernard is not the easiest person to reach. He tends to ignore people who aren't serious collectors. Even his gallery is open by appointment only."

Great. How was she going to get an appointment? Make a pest of herself until he called back?

Or… An idea struck her. "He returns your phone calls, doesn't he?"

"Of course. We've done business for years. Are you asking me to call Bernard for you?"

"Would you? It might make him more willing to talk with me. Then, if the painting gets discovered, you can take partial credit."

Frederic laughed.

"What?" Piper had heard him laugh before, but never with such a teasing tone. In spite of his sunglasses, the smile lit up his face. She liked how he threw his head back, too, as if tossing the laugh toward the sky. "You don't want credit?"

"On the contrary, recognition is always welcome."

"Then what's so funny?"

"Nothing."

Something amused him. Was it her? If so, why didn't she feel a knot in her stomach, the way she usually did when people laughed at her? Instead, she had a warm squishy feeling running all through her.

"Will you call Bernard?"

"Yes, I will. As soon as I get back to the university."

"Thank you! You're awesome." She was so glad she asked him along today. Finally a good day in Paris. She threw her arms around his neck and hugged him.

It didn't dawn on her what she had done until she

felt the corner of his belt buckle against her rib cage. With heat shooting to her toes, she released her grip, and prayed her face wasn't as flushed as it felt.

"Um…thank you," she stammered.

"My pleasure," he replied. Piper thought she saw a hint of a smile as he spoke, but double-checking meant looking into his face. Considering her skin was on fire, staring at the cell phone he was now dialing seemed a safer bet. "As enjoyable as this afternoon has been," she heard him say, "I have a faculty meeting I need to attend. Should I have Michel drop you off at the house?"

Meaning sit with him in the backseat of his car? "That's all right, I'll take the Métro." Another safe bet. "I want to stop at the farmers' market, anyway."

"Suit yourself. I'll let you know what Bernard says."

Piper watched as he headed to the same café where their afternoon started, moving with his usual careful, deliberate grace. Clearly, her hug affected only one of them. But then, did she really expect otherwise?

CHAPTER THREE

WHEN SHE RETURNED from class the following day, Frederic was waiting in the main salon. "We've got a meeting with Bernard in half an hour," he said. "The car is on the way."

"We?" she repeated, making sure she heard correctly. This was the first they'd spoken since she rushed off last night, and considering her overreaction to his hug, there was a good chance she misheard. "You're coming?"

"I have to. I'm invested in the search now. Plus, Bernard has a painting he thinks I might be interested in."

"Oh." So she hadn't heard wrong. Her stomach gave a tiny bounce at the discovery. "I'll go get ready."

She rushed through the kitchen, unbuttoning her jacket as she went. Frederic worked fast. Sure, he said he would call yesterday, but she fully expected to be dropped in priority when he got to his meeting. *He did say he was invested*, she reminded herself. Still, the idea that her errand stayed atop his to-do list left her strangely flattered.

Yesterday's yellow dress was on the back of her chair.

Her one good summer outfit. She'd foolishly assumed she'd be shopping in Paris.

Better than jeans and a T-shirt, she reminded herself while slipping the dress over her head. The skirt was wrinkled from yesterday, but serviceable. Only Frederic would know she was wearing the same outfit. Assuming he even paid attention to what she wore. Grabbing her sandals, she hurried back to the salon.

"That was fast," Frederic remarked when he saw her. He, she noticed, looked as crisp and perfect as ever in his linen blazer.

"You said to hurry."

"I'm not used to people understanding what that means. You forget, I spend my day with university students. They have a different view of time."

He opened the front door and gestured for her to step outside. "Shall we?"

Like many of Paris's art galleries, the Galerie Gaspard Theroux was in the Marais, the historic district, near the Place des Vosges. Piper stepped into the sunshine with a silent sigh of relief.

"I have to admit," Piper said as she stepped out of the cab, "I like this section of the city much better." The business district was beautiful but modern. But here… This was the Paris she dreamed about. "The statues in the middle of the street and the cobblestones…it's all so…"

"Romantic?"

His drily spoken answer made her blush. "I know, typical American, right?"

"Yes, but also no. This is my favorite part of the

city, too. As impressive as skyscrapers are, you cannot top classic French design. Did you know this square is one of the first examples of urban planning? Henri IV was ahead of his time." He swept his arm wide in an animated arc. "It was also one of the few times all the building fronts were designed the same way. See the arcades lining the perimeter?"

He went on, talking about the different sections of the building, architectural and historical details Piper wished she could appreciate. She was far more entertained by the expression on his face. His enthusiasm was obvious, despite the sunglasses masking his eyes. The way he spoke was reverent. So much lighter than his usual tone, which was so serious it bordered on short, she could have listened to him go on forever. Good thing Chef Despelteau didn't have such a voice. She'd be so distracted by the way the words dripped off his tongue she'd never get any recipe right.

"For an art history expert, you sure know a lot about architecture," she teased.

There was no mistaking the pink spots peering out beneath the rims of his aviators. "In my opinion, architecture is its own form of art," he told her. "The gargoyles of Notre Dame, for example. Or Louis the thirteenth's statue in the park. I appreciate the effort that goes into creating beauty. When I think of this section of the city, especially, and the disasters and wars it has survived, I cannot help but be impressed.

"Come," he said, taking her elbow, "Bernard's gallery is on the western side." Taking her by the elbow, he led her toward the shaded walkway on the far end of the plaza.

Art galleries and antiques stores lined the sidewalk beneath the arch. As they walked, Piper tried to appreciate the various pieces in the windows, but she was too distracted by the lingering sensation on her elbow. Twice she needed to check, even though Frederic released her seconds after touching her.

"Bernard's gallery is number thirty-three," Frederic said. "He often keeps the door locked. We might have to ring the bell."

"A locked store and visits by appointment. You're right, he is selective about his customers."

"He can afford to be."

"Must be nice. Hopefully I make the cut."

"You will," Frederic said with a smile. "You are with me."

Piper spotted the gallery before he did. A quick tug showed the door to be unlocked. As Frederic opened it wide, a bell tinkled overhead.

"Bonjour!" Bernard Theroux appeared from the back of the gallery. He was a tall, slender man with a wispy gray mustache and thinning gray hair that he wore combed back. The moment he saw Frederic, his porcelain features broke into a grin and he began speaking in rapid French, far too fast for Piper to keep up.

"I'm sorry," he said, switching to perfect English. "I was lecturing someone about being a stranger."

"And I was explaining how busy work has been."

"I can vouch for that," Piper remarked. "He's hardly ever home." The comment made her sound like a disgruntled wife. "I mean, he works a lot." That didn't sound much better.

Thankfully, the gallery owner was more interested in dragging Frederic toward one of the paintings. "Like I told you on the phone, you are going to love this piece. He's a new artist out of Prague—I discovered him on my last trip. Wait until you see what he does with shadow."

"I'm sure it's spectacular," Frederic said. "But before I look at anything, Piper had some questions she wanted to ask. About a friend of your father's."

Although his sigh said he'd rather talk about the painter from Prague, Bernard turned to Piper. "Of course. Although like I told Frederic, my father had a lot of painter friends over the years. If it was before I was born, I doubt I can help you."

"He wasn't only a friend—he was possibly a client," Piper replied. "His sister thinks your father sold one or two of his paintings."

She reached into her purse for her cell phone. Patience had emailed her a snapshot that featured one of the paintings. "I'm hoping that a record of the sale still exists. The artist's name was Nigel Rougeau. The painting would have looked like this one."

She held out her phone so he could see the image. Instantly, Bernard's eyes became saucers.

"Dear God, I don't believe it. This is the painting you're looking for? This nude?"

"Yes?" Although she suddenly wasn't sure she should say so. The gleam in Bernard's eyes made her nervous. "Why?"

"I grew up looking at that woman."

"You—you did?"

"Yes, she hung in our dining room."

No way. Piper couldn't believe her good luck. She'd been prepared to strike out, and here the man was saying he'd seen the painting. "Does your father still have the painting?"

Bernard shook his head. "I'm afraid not. I sold most of the collection when we closed down his house. To pay his expenses. The nude was sold with the others."

She should have known the search wouldn't end easily. Still, there was hope. "You wouldn't know the name of the man who bought it, would you?" she asked.

"I keep records for every painting," Bernard replied with a sniff.

"Could we get the name?" Frederic asked. Piper started. She had assumed he was studying the painting, and so his deep voice caught her off guard.

"Yes, but it will take me a few minutes to pull up the record on the computer."

"Thank you," Piper said, speaking as much to Frederic as to Bernard. "I truly appreciate the help."

"I'll be back with the information as soon as I can. In the meantime, you now have plenty of time to study the Biskup. It's called *Zoufalstvi.*" His smile was smug as he gestured toward the painting. "I know you're going to be as impressed with his style as I am."

Piper walked up to the painting. It was contemporary art, a mash-up of black, white and red, which she assumed had some kind of meaning. She understood the price well enough. She paid less for the entire year of culinary school.

"What do you think?" she asked, looking over her shoulder.

Frederic stood where she left him, taking in the painting from a distance. "Interesting," was all he said.

"Your friend isn't really expecting you to buy it today, is he?"

"Oh, he is. Bernard never jokes when it comes to artwork. If he says the painting is a good investment, then I'm sure it is."

"And you would what? Just write a check if you liked it?"

"If I liked it."

She shook her head. The idea of writing a check for an amount that took her months upon months to save—and that was with pinching every single penny—boggled her mind. Here Frederic talked about dropping that amount like he was buying a new shirt. "Do you like it?" she had to ask.

"Do you?" he asked back.

"Honest opinion?" He nodded. "I'm not sure what I'm looking at. It all looks like a bunch of colors to me."

She squinted, trying to make sense of the image. In a way, it was similar to the other paintings in Frederic's house. They too were modern, but warmer and with brighter colors. This painting was definitely not warm. It did conjure up emotion, a weirdly familiar feeling in the pit of her stomach, but she wouldn't call the sensation pleasant. Nor would she want to feel it every day.

"It's a very sad-looking painting," she said.

"I should hope so." Footsteps sounded on the

wood floor, and suddenly Frederic was at her elbow. "*Zoufalstvi* is Czech for *desperation*."

No wonder it left her feeling empty. "I don't see why anyone would want to buy such a depressing picture. But then, I'm not much of an artist."

"Really? I thought chefs considered cooking an art form."

"Great cooking, sure. All the best chefs are artists." As Chef Despelteau reminded them so often. "But I was talking about *art* art. You know, paintings and stuff." She turned her attention to a different piece. "Growing up, the fanciest thing on our walls was a framed poster of Monet's *Water Lilies*. I'm going to go out on a limb and say Bernard doesn't sell posters."

"No, he does not."

"Too bad." They stood quietly in front of the painting. This second one had prettier colors, but the image wasn't nearly as powerful to look at.

That was it, Piper realized suddenly. Why the Biskup painting seemed so familiar. The image reminded her of Frederic. He, too, was forceful and compelling. Where did the sadness come in, though? Her boss could hardly be described as sad.

He was solitary, though. For all his activity, the man was alone much of the time. If there were family and friends in his life, they certainly didn't visit the house.

"I hope you don't buy the painting," she said aloud.

He turned at that moment and looked into her face, his eyes grayer than usual. "Why not?"

"Because I—" What was she supposed to say? Because it made her think sad thoughts about him? Like she told herself yesterday, she was pushing her thoughts onto him. Solitary didn't mean lonely. For all she knew, Frederic was simply a man who liked his privacy.

Her answer didn't matter anyway, because the moment she met his eyes, any explanation she might have come up with disappeared. All this time, she'd thought his eyes were gray, but they were really far softer. Like feathers or a fluffy cloud of smoke. She could almost feel the haze in the air, surrounding her like a warm plume.

A shock of hair had fallen over one eyebrow, knocked loose when he took his sunglasses off. The dark strands begged to be brushed aside.

"Piper?" she heard him ask.

Oh, good Lord, she was staring at him with her jaw half open like an idiot.

"What I meant," she said, tucking imaginary hair behind her ear, "was that I don't like the idea you might have to buy something on my account."

"You're afraid I won't know how to say no?"

"Of—of course you can. Say no, that is. I just don't want…"

"Don't worry," he said, saving her from making a bigger fool of herself than she already had. "I stopped acquiring pieces a while ago. Bernard forgets I no longer have the eye for detail I once had."

Piper's heart gave a little twist at the wistful shadow that flickered over his features. Bernard wasn't the only one who'd forgotten. The man was so capable and self-assured. *Who wouldn't forget?*

"I'll take that as a compliment," Frederic said with a chuckle.

Meaning she'd spoken her thoughts aloud. The floor could swallow her up any time now.

"So, what do you think? Do you not love the expressive way he plays light on shadow?" Bernard came around the corner, saving her. "I am predicting this artist will be very popular. Already, several serious collectors have put him on their watch lists. This would be your chance to acquire a piece before his popularity drives the price up."

"Don't you mean while you still have him on a string?" Frederic replied. The teasing retort caught Piper by surprise. "Bernard only pushes this hard when he's personally involved," he explained to her. "Isn't that right, Bernard?"

The gallery owner's cheeks turned crimson. "I do predict big things for him. You know I only push if they have talent."

"Yes, I know. Did you find the address?"

"I did." He turned to Piper. "The painting is called *Ana Reclining*. I'm ashamed that I didn't remember. It was purchased by a man named John Allen. Whether or not he still owns the piece, I do not know."

Piper took the slip of paper. This was fantastic. They had a real live name. Wait until she told Patience. "Gloucestershire," she read. "England?"

"Northwest of London," Frederic replied.

There was no way of knowing if the address and phone were current, either. Still, it was a start. A very good start.

"Two days ago, we didn't know if a painting even existed," she remarked when she and Frederic stepped outside. "And now here I am with a name. I feel like Piper Rush, art detective."

"It's always exciting when a lost work is discovered. Did you know they once discovered a seventeenth-century Le Brun hanging in a suite at the Ritz-Carlton?"

"I wouldn't put this painting on the same level. But Ana's nephew will be excited." She had no idea who Le Brun was, but seventeenth-century sounded important. "Lucky for him that Bernard's father decided to keep one of the paintings for himself."

"Indeed." Although they were standing in the shade, he lowered his sunglasses in place anyway. As the dark lenses slid over his features, Piper felt a flutter in her stomach. Relief that she'd been saved from whatever that strange sensation was when she looked into his eyes before. As it was, the moment had left her with this restless, jumbly sensation, as if her insides drank too much caffeine.

"So what is your next move, Madame Detective?" he asked her.

"Give the information to Patience so they can track John Allen down, I suppose."

"You don't sound very excited about the prospect."

In a strange way, she wasn't. "I'll miss playing detective," she said. "The past couple days have been a nice break in my routine." That included the unexpected time she spent with him. Having finished her favor for Patience, life would go back to normal. Normal and lonely.

"You don't have to stop."

She laughed. "You know another piece of art that needs to be tracked down?"

"No, but the search for this one is not complete."

True. Bernard's information could be woefully out of date. "Guess I should make a phone call or two to make sure my lead pans out." She added the detective lingo on purpose, just because it was fun to use.

"And if need be, travel to England to inspect the canvas."

"Now that might be going a little too far." Piper could see herself now, knocking on John Allen's door and asking if she could inspect his nude portrait.

"Why? Do you not want a chance to see the painting up close?"

"Sure, but… Would you?"

"For a chance to discover a lost painting, I'd go anywhere. I've traveled farther for far less."

"Well, if you don't mind, I'll start with a few phone calls," Piper replied.

Just then, the car arrived, pulling to the curb with the soft *beep* of the horn. "Sorry to keep you waiting," Michel said as he hurried to open the passenger door.

The switch from bright sunlight to the car's interior temporary plunged Piper into darkness, making her blink several times before she could properly see her surroundings. Today was the first time she'd ever ridden in a limousine, and while she told herself the experience was no different from riding in a cab, it was. For one thing, cabs didn't have supple seats that molded to your body. And they definitely didn't smell like leather and spicy aftershave. Yesterday's decision to ride the Métro had definitely been the right one. In fact, she inhaled deeply, she wondered if she shouldn't have made the same decision this afternoon.

The car itself was not nearly as fancy as she expected. On TV, the limousines always had skylights and crystal decanters. Frederic went for a sleek simplicity. All the more impressive, really. Reminded her of how quality food didn't need a lot of trimmings to taste impressive. Frederic didn't need trimmings, either.

If only she didn't feel so jittery. She'd love to blame the feeling on being out of her element, but that wouldn't explain why the sensation didn't fully grip her until she lost herself in Frederic's gray eyes. Or why the quiet determination in his voice just now turned her insides upside down.

Frederic slipped into the seat beside her and the driver shut the door, sealing them together in the dimness. If only he weren't so tall and broad-shouldered. A smaller man would take up less space. His body heat wouldn't cross the distance to buffet her body. It turned the air thick.

Piper smoothed her skirt. The yellow was suddenly way too bright for the space. "Thank you again for arranging the meeting with Bernard," she said.

"You already thanked me twice on the trip here. There's no need to do it again."

"I'm excited the trip was successful, is all." Not to mention talking eased her tension and thank you was the only thing she could think of. "I feel like I owe you something. After all, you did give up part of your afternoon to help me. You could have let me deal with Bernard on my own."

He laughed, teeth white in the shadows. "If I had, you would still be leaving messages on his machine."

True enough. Bernard was a character. "We have a name for guys like him back home."

"There are names for guys like him everywhere," Frederic replied. "And again, I was glad to help. I'm as intrigued by this painting as you are. It's been a while since I've played art detective myself. If this painting is as good as Bernard believes, it will be quite the discovery."

Piper thought of his comment from earlier, about traveling farther for less. "Do you miss it? Tracking down art?"

"Yes, but what can you do?" He shrugged. "Life is what it is. It's not as though I can change anything, is it?"

"I guess not." Remembering his wistful expression at the gallery, Piper couldn't help wondering if he was as Zen about his circumstances as he sounded. If she were losing her sight, she would be railing against the universe. She certainly wouldn't talk about it as matter-of-factly as he did.

She turned to steal a look at him, only to find he was looking back at her with that unnaturally intense gaze of his.

"I'm glad helping me didn't keep you from anything important," she said, jumping back to the original conversation. Her attention returned to her lap and the imaginary wrinkles she needed to smooth away.

Leather crinkled as Frederic shifted, too.

"Definitely not," he replied. "The only thing on my schedule is tonight's meeting of the Société pour la Conservation Artistique. We have a speaker coming to discuss new methods of varnish repair."

"Really." Piper didn't have a clue what that meant. "Sounds..."

"Tedious? Sleep-inducing?" He chuckled, cutting off any chance of her arguing otherwise. "I understand. I'm sure I would feel the same way about a lecture on flaky pastry. What about you? What are your plans for the evening?"

"You mean other than looking up John Allen on the internet? Nothing unusual. Do the cleaning I missed today, stream a little American television on my computer..."

"You should go out."

Piper shook her head. Clearly he was only saying that to be polite. They both knew she had no social life. The suggestion was as silly as her suggesting he stick around the house more. "I don't think so."

"Why not? Surely your culinary school friends..."

It was instinctive. As soon as he mentioned the word *friends*, she stiffened. "Culinary school isn't the kind of place where you make friends," she said. No sense hiding the reaction. "It's too competitive."

"You're surprised?"

"No. And yes." She struggled to explain. If the never-ending competition was the only problem, school wouldn't be so bad. "I guess I hoped that even with the competition, people would be friendlier. Supportive.

"Naive, I know," she added before he could say it. "I should have realized, school is school. Some things don't change."

"I don't understand. What does being at school have to do with anything?"

Of course he wouldn't understand. How could he?

"Were you popular in school?" she asked.

She watched as he contemplated the question. That he had to stop and think was almost an answer in itself. "I never paid attention to whether I was or not."

Bet he was, then. People who were well-liked never paid attention.

"And you were not popular?"

"I was chubby, poor and being raised by my sister." *Who stripped for a living*, she added silently. "Plus I caught lice in fifth grade. You can guess where that put me on the popularity scale."

"Where were your parents?"

"My mom died when I was little."

"I'm sorry."

"Happens."

Piper hated the sympathy in his voice. Pity parties were one thing, but to have others feeling pity for her... that only made her pathetic. "Needless to say, I was always a bit of an outsider."

Frederic nodded, attention on the space in front of him. "Personally, I always found being on my own to be the easier path," he said. "Being involved only means more drama."

"Oh, there was drama anyway." She didn't mean to say anything aloud, the words just came out, so when he frowned, she did her best to play the comment off. "I mean, you know how kids can get."

She should have known he wouldn't let her get away with it. "What did they do?" he asked.

"Do? Nothing really. They mostly said stuff." *Hey,*

Piper, I got twenty bucks. Think your sister will give me a lap dance? She winced at the memory. "That's how school works. Once you get a reputation, you're stuck with it. I learned to suck it up over time."

"Suck it up?"

"Cope," she said, translating the slang.

"Ah. I know what that is like."

Of course he would. He had his own issues, and they were far more serious than being teased in school. In a way it was funny, how they were both more alone than not. Piper wasn't sure why, but that made her like him all the more.

A very dangerous feeling.

"I'm making it sound worse than it was," she told him, hoping to break the spell. "To be honest, I don't know why I brought high school up in the first place. We were talking about culinary school, which is supposed to be competitive, right? People are fighting for their livelihoods.

"Besides…" She went back to examining imaginary wrinkles. "It's not like I came to Paris to make friends."

Frederic leaned forward and knocked on the glass that divided them from the driver. "Michel," he said. "Would you pull over at the next stoplight?"

"Are you getting out?" They must have arrived at his meeting. That she knew he had a prior engagement didn't stop her stomach from dropping with insecurity.

"No," Frederic replied, *"we* are."

CHAPTER FOUR

THAT WAS POSSIBLY one of the weakest lies Frederic had ever heard, and Frederic had heard a lot of them. *Did not come here to make friends, indeed.*

He slid his hand along the door panel until his fingers curved around the handle. Blasted poor lighting made seeing details difficult. "We are going to see Paris," he said, letting daylight in.

"What are you talking about?"

"This is the second time you've mentioned Paris disappointing you. I refuse to let you think my city is cold and unfriendly."

Stepping onto the sidewalk, he motioned for her to do the same before scanning his surroundings to determine his location. Took only a moment before he managed to spy the Louvre's familiar Pyramide to his left. Perfect.

"We're going to walk a bit," he told Michel. "I will call you when we're ready to go home."

"What about your meeting?" Piper had joined him on the sidewalk. Her dress was ridiculously bright, much like the sun-filled sidewalk. The color filled his view every time he looked in her direction. He liked it. It was like looking into sunlight. It was not a color that should be lonely.

He stepped back so he could see more of her face. "The society will live without me. Defending our city's honor is far more important."

"You really don't have to do this."

"Don't I?" He started down the sidewalk, forcing her to catch up.

"But I thought you said Americans have unrealistic expectations about Paris."

"Yes, but that was before."

"Before what?"

Before he heard her trying so hard to sound casual about her loneliness. Perhaps it was the resignation in her voice, as though she didn't expect to have better. A tone that sounded suspiciously like the voices from his childhood. *Don't complain. Don't need.* The lessons he'd learned hurt when he heard them applied to someone else.

Or perhaps it was simply because he himself had only so long to appreciate his surroundings. Either way, he was suddenly gripped with the urge to show her more.

"Before I realized you spent your evenings inside streaming American television," he told her.

"I watch French shows, too."

He shot her a look. "Paris is a city meant to be experienced, not watched from the sidelines like a spectator. No wonder you have been disappointed. I bet you took one of those double-decker tour buses as well."

"What's wrong with that? You get to see all the important landmarks in one trip."

"Would you enjoy a gourmet meal in one bite?"

Her resulting silence told him she didn't have a counterargument. Smiling to himself, Frederic continued walking, his focus on the sidewalk unfolding in front of him. The *click-clack* of Piper's heels on the concrete made a pleasant rhythm for counting out steps.

"If we're going to the Louvre, I've already been," she said when they passed a street sign. "The bus stopped there. I even went in and waited in line to see the *Mona Lisa*."

It was amusing, the way she insisted on defending her tour. "I'm glad. I hope you saw some of the other great works as well. We are not going to the Louvre, however."

"Where are we going, then?"

"You will see."

Based on her exasperated sigh, Frederic could only imagine her expression. She probably rolled her eyes dramatically the way one of his students might.

"Don't you like surprises?" he asked.

"Only when I know what they are."

"Well, this time you'll simply have to trust me."

Having reached a cross street, he turned his head. They stood too close for him to see her entire face, but in scanning, he saw that she was worrying her bottom lip. The pink flesh was pinched tight beneath her teeth.

"It's nothing bad, I promise," he told her. Then, because he could not stand to see that lip gnawed red, he reached out and cupped her cheek. Instantly, her lips parted with a tiny gasp of surprise. He lifted his eyes to meet hers. "Trust me."

"I—I do."

Frederic could feel curve of her earlobe teasing his fingertips. Without thinking, he brushed his little finger along the patch behind her ear. The skin beneath his hand was still cool from the car's air-conditioning and smooth as satin.

Her jaw muscle pulsed against his palm, making him realize what he was doing. "Good," he said, pulling his hand back. "Because we're almost there."

Resisting a suddenly inexplicable urge to grab her hand, he started across the street.

There turned out to be the Musée de l'Orangerie in the Jardin des Tuileries, a smaller museum a block away from the Louvre. Piper gasped as she stepped through the vestibule. The room she entered was all white, with soft light that turned the color smooth as cream. A beautiful canvas of a room created specifically for one purpose. To display the panels that covered its walls.

"Monet's *Nymphéas*," Frederic said. "As it was meant to be displayed."

The water lilies. Piper stepped toward the center of the room. A sea of color surrounded her. Blues, greens, purples. She was swimming in them.

"This is way better than a poster," she whispered. The room called for sounds no louder.

"I had a feeling you would like it."

"Like it? It's amazing."

"I'm glad you think so."

His breath tickled her ear, causing Piper to brush at the sensation. In doing so, her fingers accidently traced the same spot Frederic had touched when he cupped her cheek. Goose bumps danced across her skin. She rubbed her arms, chasing them away.

"I read about this museum when I was planning my trip." She forgot about it, though, once she realized visiting museums on her own wasn't much fun.

"It's one of my favorite places," Frederic told her.

Piper went back to studying the panels filling the room. They were larger than the painting she'd seen in Boston. These paintings loomed over her, dwarfing their surroundings with their magnitude.

"That's because they are murals," Frederic replied when she said as much. "This building was built specifically to house them."

"They're immense. I wonder how long it took to paint each panel?"

"I am guessing a very long time."

"Is that your expert opinion?"

"It is indeed." His grin was warm and endearing. If they were different people, Piper might think he was flirting.

Being late afternoon, most of the tourists had already filed through, leaving the two of them with the room to themselves. Frederic took a seat on the benches in the center of the room. "Monet has always been my favorite of the Impressionists," he said. "Did you know he painted over two hundred and fifty versions of his lily pond? Many of them he painted while he had cataracts. You can tell which ones because they have red in them."

"Is that why you like him?"

"You mean, do I feel some sort of affinity for him

because we both have bad eyes?" He shrugged. "Never thought much about it. But now that you ask, I suppose I do have a unique appreciation for what he accomplished."

Piper joined him on the bench, her legs stretched in the opposite direction from his. "Did you ever think of becoming an artist?" All the art talk the past couple days had made her curious. His interest in art history had to start somewhere. Was it the backup for a different goal? It would be nice to know if someone else stumbled while chasing a dream.

It was hard to picture Frederic failing at anything, though...

"I dabbled a little when I was younger. I'm not sure you'd call the results art."

"Worse than the painting Bernard tried to sell you?"

God, she liked his laugh. It sounded so rich and throaty, even when soft. "Don't let Bernard hear you say that," he said. "And yes, it was worse. For the record, the Biskup was not a bad painting."

"No, just depressing."

"Some people like depressing art. As for my abilities... I'm afraid the artistic gene stopped with my mother."

"So your mother was an artist. Do you have any of her paintings?" The floral one in the salon, she bet.

"Unfortunately, no. She had to give up her work."

"Why?"

His gaze dropped to the floor. "She just did."

Not by choice, either, she'd say, based on the sorrow in his voice. What happened? She wanted to ask, but it was obvious Frederic didn't want to share and who was she to push? After all, there were things in her life she wasn't ready to share either. She settled for giving his shoulder a nudge to draw him back to the moment. "So your lack of an art gene… Is that why you became a teacher? Because those who can't, teach?"

If ever a comment didn't fit a person. Fortunately, Frederic got the joke and nudged her shoulder in return. "Professor, thank you very much. There's a second set of panels in the next room. Then I want to take you upstairs to see another favorite of mine. If you're a good girl, we can stop at the gift shop and buy you a new poster as well."

"Don't let Bernard hear you say that," Piper shot back with a smirk. She was holding him to that promise, though.

Piper assumed that once they finished at L'Orangerie, Frederic would call for the car so they could return to the house, but he did not. Instead, he asked her for the time.

"Almost half past six," Piper replied.

"Good. We have plenty of time."

"Plenty of time for what?"

"To walk along the river, of course. We'll walk until we get hungry, and then we'll find a place to eat."

"You don't have to take me to dinner," she told him.

"Why not? You can tell me if the food holds up to your culinary school standards."

"Because…" Because she hadn't forgotten that she was talking about her sad, friendless state just before he stopped the car, which made her fear this adventure was nothing more than a very romantic pity trip. "I've already taken up too much of your day as it is." Along with half of yesterday too. "I'm sure you've got other things you'd rather do."

"I already told you, I do not. What I do want is to enjoy this beautiful summer night."

Taking her by the elbow, he stepped off the curb only to jump back when a car horn blared loudly.

"Perhaps we should wait until the light changes." He spoke with a smile, but Piper saw a pair of pink spots peering out beneath the rims of his aviators nonetheless. "I'm usually quite good about checking traffic, but sometimes I get distracted."

"I didn't look, either," she pointed out. "We both deserved the horn in this case."

Even so, the incident must have bothered Frederic more than he let on, because once they were across the street, he fell quiet.

Once again, Piper didn't push. People needed to work out their embarrassment their own way, even people like Frederic, who didn't get embarrassed all that often. As they walked in silence, she contented herself with studying the riverbank. The bag carrying her posters from L'Orangerie slapped against her thigh, and she imagined the sound was the water lapping the river's edge.

The view was a familiar one. Over the past eight months, Piper had walked the river dozens of times. After school. On errands. In all four seasons. Yesterday, if someone had asked her, she would have said the

path didn't live up to the billing… Today, though…
Today, it was as though she was seeing the riverbanks
for the first time. Probably because she wasn't walking alone.

More than that. For the first time in months, she
didn't *feel* alone.

Looking over at Frederic, she wondered how many
of the people passing them envied her his company.
A man who so obviously could have his pick of any
woman in Paris. Her insides toppled end over end that
she was the one he picked. So what if today was a pity
date? Tomorrow's routine would return soon enough.
Today she would take his pity, and enjoy the break.

"My mother."

Frederic's voice was soft and unexpected. Yanked
from her thoughts, Piper nearly stumbled.

"You asked me why I studied art history," he said.
"My mother was the one who taught me to appreciate art."

Strange that he would choose now to address a remark made at the museum. Here she thought he'd been
dwelling on their near miss with the car. Unless the two
were related.

"Sounds like you got part of the art gene after all,"
she said.

"More likely she wanted to make sure I was exposed
to as many beautiful things as possible."

There, Piper realized sadly, was the link. She had this
image of Frederic's mother exposing him to sight after
sight. How young had he been when his eyes started to
fail? "It's funny," she heard herself saying, "but some-

times I forget you have trouble seeing. You certainly wouldn't know it at home."

"That is because I work hard to make sure I function without assistance. I made up my mind very early in life that blindness wouldn't leave me helpless."

"You're not blind, though."

"Yet."

Her stomach sank. In the back of her mind, she'd known what his response would be, but she'd hoped otherwise. "I'm sorry."

"Don't be," he said cutting her off. "I accepted my fate a long time ago. Someday, I will wake up and my eyesight will be gone. Perhaps not so drastically, but it will happen."

"What will you do then?" Piper wasn't sure she wanted to know. There was a resignation to his voice that made her sad.

Frederic stopped so he could turn to face her. The sunglasses masked his eyes, but the rest of his face was resolute. "I will deal."

A fair enough answer. Why then did it make her want to throw her arms around him and hold on tight?

"If my sister were here, she'd add, 'then figure out a way to fix the situation'."

His mouth curved into a smile. "Somehow I doubt she was referring to degenerative eye disease."

"No, although she definitely got us out of some dark times."

"Dark?"

Probably not the best word to use. Giving a shrug, she started to do what she always did and play off the comment, but then changed her mind. "Things weren't always great when I was growing up. Patience always did her best to make them better. I owe her everything." A small wedge of guilt worked its way into her throat, the way it always did when talking about her sister.

"Sounds like your sister is a special woman."

"I always thought so," she said.

"Must run in the family."

Was he talking about her? Piper shook her head. "I don't think…"

He pressed a finger to her lips. "Never turn down a compliment, Piper."

What was it with Frederic touching her and walking away? Twice now his fingers had stroked her face. She traced the spot on her lips, convinced his fingers left a part of himself behind. Why else would they continue to tingle?

"Piper?" Ahead a few feet, Frederic had stopped and was looking for her.

"Sorry, I was think— Do I hear music?"

She did. The soft sound of violins and accordians could be heard in the distance.

"It's coming from around the bend," Frederic said.

"A concert?" It sounded like too many instruments to be a regular sidewalk performance. A dinner cruise maybe. She tried to remember if there was a dock ahead.

Meanwhile, Frederic was trying very hard to hide a smile. "You know what it is, don't you?"

"Perhaps," he replied.

Oh, he definitely knew. He was holding out on her, just like he did with the Monet exhibit. Question was, what was he hiding? A thrill of anticipation passed through her, strengthened by her still-tingling lips. They rounded the corner, and she spied a large crowd surrounding the amphitheaters. "It *is* a concert."

"Is it? You might want to look closer." He flashed another one of those mysterious smiles, making Piper think her insides might melt.

Drawing closer, she saw that the crowd was watching a swirl of movement. "Oh my God, are they dancing?"

"Ballroom dancing at dusk," Frederic murmured in her ear. "A summer tradition."

It was a beautiful sight to see. Dozens of couples twirling to the music.

Piper pointed to a graceful blonde woman moving between the dance groups. "The woman in the red shirt. Is she a judge or something?"

"Instructor, more likely. Here to help the less-skilled dancers learn the steps."

Didn't look as if anyone needed lessons. The pairs moved in graceful synchronicity to the slow, pulsing beat. "Do you know what dance they are performing?"

"Based on the music, I would say the tango."

She should have known. The air was ripe with sensuality. You could literally feel the passion as the more experienced dancers stalked the dance floor. Piper felt her breath quickening in response. Behind her, Frederic breathed quickly as well, his chest brushing against her back with each rise and fall of his lungs. A dinner boat passed, its bow lights creating a fairy-tale background just as the music peaked.

"Wow," she whispered when the song had ended. She

looked over her shoulder. "I've never really seen ballroom dancing up close before. It's beautiful to watch."

A new song began to play. Piper recognized the strands of "La Vie en Rose."

"The dancing is open to everyone," Frederic said. "Would you like to join them?"

"Out there? I'm no ballroom dancer."

"You don't have to be. The only requirement is to enjoy moving to the music."

More couples were making their way to the dance floor, made brave by the familiar music. Piper couldn't help noticing that several of the pairings barely moved. They were content to simply hold each other and sway to the beat.

She imagined Frederic's arms holding her and grew warm all over. Before she could say a word, a hand molded to the small of her back and she was propelled forward.

"Stay by the edge, where there isn't too much of a crowd," he said. Piper really wished his breath wouldn't tease her skin the way it did.

He led her to an open space near where they were standing. "I hope you can do this without stepping on anyone's toes, because I can't," she said.

His arm slipped around her waist and pulled her tight. "Moving to the music is the easy part," he told her. "It's the crowds that are the problem."

The crowds, she repeated to herself. The crowds were why he was holding her so close. Another inch or so, and her cheek would be flush with his shoulder. The music's familiar three-beat rhythm echoed in her ear. Head bobbing in time, Piper counted her steps. "Relax," he said. His chest rumbled against her cheek as he spoke. "Let the music guide your feet."

"I think my feet might be tone-deaf."

"Nonsense. You're in Paris. Everyone is graceful in Paris." He tightened his grip, his cheek pressing against her temple. "Let yourself go and enjoy."

Why not? When would she ever have this opportunity again? The sun was setting, the breeze was warm and the spires of Notre Dame were keeping watch. What could be more magical? Piper closed her eyes and let the music take control. It couldn't have been more perfect.

"See?" Frederic said. "I told you that you could dance."

Truthfully, they weren't so much dancing as swaying in time, but Frederic didn't mind. The crowd made more complex moves difficult for him. Holding Piper's hand against his chest, he contented himself with inhaling the scent drifting off her skin. How was it a woman could smell so good without perfume?

Piper had her head nestled against his shoulder, the crown of her head tucked near his chin. He wondered if she realized how much like an embrace their dance had become. Not that he was averse to the position. It had been a while since he held a beautiful woman so close. And he couldn't remember the last time he actually danced with a woman.

"Hold me close and hold me fast," Piper was singing under her breath. "The magic spell you cast."

"This is *la vie en rose*," he finished.

She lifted her head and they were close enough that he could see the dreamy expression in her eyes. The soft glow brought his awareness to life.

"I always loved this song," she told him. "Before I came here, I used to imagine the city with accordion players on all the streets playing this song, just so people could walk around to it."

She really did have a romantic's view of his city. Shame on those other students for destroying that dream. "I'm sorry we let you down."

"It's okay," she said, putting her head back on his shoulder. "This works, too."

They walked the rest of the way home. He would probably regret using his eyes so much, but at the moment, listening to Piper hum "La Vie en Rose" under her breath, he thought it worth the sacrifice.

Ahead, the Eiffel Tower blinked in all its lit-up glory. Frederic couldn't help but stop. "Beautiful, isn't it?" he said.

"Yeah, it is," she said, craning her neck to get a better view. "No matter how cranky I get about life in Paris, I can never hate the tower."

Neither could he. He didn't know why, but he found himself feeling very open and poetic tonight. Wasn't like him. As a rule, he preferred to keep the world at arm's length. He never wanted to get to a point where someone felt obligated to him because they shared a closeness. He knew only too well what obligation led to. Far easier—and safer—to stay charming and superficial. Tonight, though, it seemed he was destined to break that rule.

"I told myself a long time ago that I would never take

the tower for granted," he told Piper. "Ever since then, I've made a point of looking at her every day."

Because you never know when you'll have the chance to see it again.

He heard a soft cough. Turning his head, he saw Piper smiling at him. "Thank you," she said. "For this afternoon. For showing me the Paris I've always dreamed of. I'll never forget it."

Frederic didn't know what to say. He still wasn't 100 percent sure why she compelled him to be so whimsical. Inexplicable as his decision was, however, he had to admit that she wasn't the only one who'd enjoyed the day. "I'm glad," he said. "I had a good time, too."

She was smiling, and he could make out a sparkle shimmering in her eyes. Their sheen was luminescent. So was her skin, he thought, letting his eyes take in as much as they were able. The smell of vanilla and spices wafted toward him, like a siren's call. Then suddenly, she was closer, and her lips brushed his cheek in a shy kiss.

The feel of her lips on him stayed long after Piper disappeared into her rooms. Not yet ready to head upstairs, Frederic sat in the dark and studied his tower. Today was not what he expected. Piper wasn't what he expected.

Whether or not that was a good thing, he didn't know.

CHAPTER FIVE

IT WAS OFFICIAL. Piper hated Chef Despelteau as much as he hated her. There was no way her culinary skills were that far below the rest of the class. Honestly, she was beginning to think the man would have a problem with Julia Child's French cooking.

Wonder what Chef Despelteau would think if he knew she didn't like half the foods they were preparing? They were all so froufrou.

Feeling rebellious, she stopped at the grocery on her way home and bought a roast and potatoes. She'd like to see Chef Despelteau make a Yankee pot roast as well as she could.

Might as well face it, babe, you're a common food girl at heart. A common girl, period.

Maybe so, but she was also a girl who had waltzed under the Paris moon. How many people back home could say that? No sooner did the thought enter her head than the memory washed over her. Piper smiled. If she concentrated, she could remember every detail, right down to the smell of Frederic's skin.

So many of the guys she knew used slow dancing as

an excuse to cop a feel. They'd rest their hands on your rear or plaster their bodies so tightly against yours that the two of you might as well be sleeping together. Frederic held a woman like a man who had nothing to prove. Of course, it didn't matter how he held her. It wasn't as if last night was like some magic spell that changed them from boss and employee into something else.

Still, he'd given her a great memory. Now if anyone asked, she wouldn't have to lie about having spent time with a handsome Frenchman.

She arrived at the house to find her handsome Frenchman stretched out in his chair again. Amazing how he could make something as simple as sprawling in a chair look elegant. He had one arm flung over his eyes while the other rested gently on his stomach. Piper's gaze fell to the long fingers that were curled ever so slightly against his shirt. As though it remembered their touch, her skin began to tingle.

"I know you're standing there," he said, stirring.

Piper winced at getting caught. Thank goodness she was behind the chair so he couldn't see how red her cheeks were.

"I thought I might have to wake you up again," she said. "You looked dead to the world."

"Only resting. My meeting for tonight had been canceled, so I decided to rest my eyes for a moment. They tend to get tired this time of day."

"Sorry I disturbed you then." It never occurred to her, what with his limited field of vision, how much energy it must take for him to focus. Making yesterday's adventure all the more special.

"No worries. Are you carrying something?" She held up the brightly colored bag she used for errands. "Ahh, I thought I saw a pink handle."

"Groceries. I decided to make a pot roast." Piper paused. If his meeting was canceled, did that mean he would be home for dinner?

"Will that be a problem?" Frederic asked when she checked.

Before today, she would have said no. While Frederic's schedule kept him out of the house most nights, there were times when he stayed home and expected her to cook. All those nights happened before they'd danced together, however. Those few minutes in his arms had colored their relationship. An ordinary activity such as cooking now had a more intimate flavor.

But the inability to separate last night and today was her problem, wasn't it? When push came to shove, Frederic was still her boss and she still his housekeeper.

Offering a smile, she replied in as casual a voice as she could muster. "Why would it be a problem? Cooking is part of my job, isn't it? I mean, the title is house-keeper-slash-cook."

"Yes, but when I mentioned staying in, your voice sounded a little…off. Made me concerned."

"I was calculating cooking times in my head is all. To make sure I don't serve you too late." *Please don't ask what time I consider late because I'm totally making things up.*

"You don't have to worry about the time. I'll eat whenever the meal is ready."

"Well, I better go change uniforms and get started.

Oh, by the way," she said, remembering. "I called the carpet cleaning company. They're closed for vacation. I made a note to call them next week."

"That's not necessary, you know."

"It is if you want to get rid of the coffee stain."

"No, I mean, changing. You don't have to switch uniforms on my account."

"You might change your mind when you realize how badly this jacket smells like today's seafood lesson."

"I meant you don't have to wear a uniform. Put on your regular clothes."

But she always wore a uniform. The employment agency insisted. *To maintain a barrier between staff and the house* or something like that.

"I've been thinking about it for a couple days. There is no reason you should have to keep changing from one uniform to another and back every day. You should be comfortable."

Comfortable while cooking for him. Yeah, that wouldn't feel domestic at all. "Thanks," she told him. "I'll do that."

A short while later, the kitchen smelled like beef and onions. Piper breathed in the familiar scents to calm her nerves. *Get a grip*, she told herself. It's no different from any other night. In fact, this was a good reminder to keep her head on straight. As her little stare-fest in the living room proved, she was crossing the line from attractive boss to being attracted to her boss—something neither of them needed.

Her attention shifted to the phone on the counter.

Odd. She had two missed calls. She must have been so engrossed in chopping vegetables she didn't notice the phone vibrating. Both were from Patience. Wanting to know how the painting search was going, no doubt. Piper wasn't going to have much to tell her. John Allen hadn't returned her phone call yet.

Only, Patience's voice mail wasn't about the painting. It was about her and Stuart Duchenko. She replayed the message twice to make sure she heard her sister correctly. Difficult, since Patience was sniffling throughout.

Oh, Patience. Sick to her stomach, she dropped into one of the kitchen chairs and stared at the call screen. You'd think after everything else, her sister would catch a break.

"I can smell dinner from up in my office. It smells delicious."

"Thanks," she replied, attention stuck on the phone. She didn't even bother to look up when Frederic joined her.

"Something has upset you." His arm reached across the table and brushed the top of her wrist, drawing her attention. "Is it about the painting? Did Monsieur Allen have bad news?"

"No, I'm still waiting to hear from him. My sister left her job." Her thumb wavered between texting and calling direct. Video chatting would be best, but she didn't know if Patience had her laptop.

Frederic drew up a chair and sat down. "She is no longer working for Ana Duchenko? Why not? I was under the impression she cared about the woman."

"She does. Problem is she cares about Stuart Duch-enko more."

"The nephew who is searching for the painting. I didn't realize they were...friends."

Piper had to smile at his use of euphemisms. "According to her voice mail, they aren't 'friends' any longer. They had a fight about something in her past. She was crying, so I couldn't understand the whole message. I'll find out more when I call her back."

Piper's eyes dropped back to her phone screen. "And here I thought after everything she'd been through, she'd finally found happiness."

"Everything she'd been through? I don't understand. Yesterday you said you both suffered through tough times."

"We did. But Patience suffered more, or at least I think so."

"What do you mean?"

Piper exhaled. She hadn't planned on sharing the story with him, but now that she opened the door, she might as well walk all the way through. After all, Frederic opened up about his eyesight, right?

"Do you remember when I told you that no matter how tough life got for us, Patience found a way to make it better?"

"Yes."

"Well, life got real tough. Like the two of us living in a car tough."

She tried not to cringe at his sudden sharp breath. "You—you were homeless?"

"Only for a week or so." Yesterday's sympathy had

returned to his voice. Hearing it left a sour taste in her mouth and so she rushed to erase it as quickly as possible. "It was right after my mom died. Soon as we could afford to, we found a cheap motel room and then later an apartment."

"Must have been terrifying."

"I was more scared someone would find out and take me away. Patience promised we would stay together."

"She kept her promise."

"Yes, she did. She took the only job she could find to pay the bills."

"Working for Ana Duchenko as a housekeeper."

"The job with Ana came later, after I moved here. When I was a kid, she was a dancer in a club. A club where women were paid to dance."

There was a pause as the full meaning of her answer sank in. "I see," he said finally.

"She didn't have a choice." The defense came automatically, before he could say anything judgmental. "I told you, it was the first job she could find."

Twirling her phone end over end, she thought about those dark days. Remembering how she sat shivering in a blanket in the backseat, crying because the only thing she'd eaten that day were the free saltines they swiped from the local convenience store. "For most of my life it's been just me and Patience. Couldn't have been easy being stuck raising a kid right out of high school."

"I would think it was hard for both of you."

He spoke frankly, exactly the way Piper preferred. Bluntness was so much better than pity or sarcasm.

"When she first got the job I was too young to understand what she was doing," she told him. "Then when I was old enough…" Hopefully, her shrug filled in the blanks. When she was old enough, she sucked it up, for Patience's sake.

"The argument your sister and the Duchenko nephew had? This is the information he discovered?"

"I think he learned a few of the more sordid details. From the sound of it, there were things I didn't even know about."

It made her wonder how many more difficulties her sister bore alone for Piper's sake. The guilt she carried on her shoulders pressed heavier.

Meanwhile, Frederic sat stiffly in his chair, drawing patterns on the table with his index finger. "Sounds as if both of you were very brave. I've known people who weren't half as brave when life kicked them."

Who? Certainly not him.

"If your sister is as strong as she sounds," he continued, "then I am sure she will weather this storm as well. Did you not just say she always found a way to fix a bad situation?"

"You're right. She did." Patience was a survivor. A fact Piper needed to remember. "Being over five thousand miles away has got me on edge. I'm sure that once I have a chance to talk with her, I'll feel better."

In fact, her spirits were already beginning to lift, in large part because of the man across from her. "Who knows? Maybe once he's had a chance to get over the shock, Stuart will realize Patience's past is no big deal."

After all, life has a way of doing a one-eighty on you. Last week she would have been sitting here dealing with Patience's message on her own.

"Thank you," she said.

"For what?"

"Listening. It was nice having a shoulder for a change." Reaching across the table, she covered his hand with hers. It was a simple gesture, meant to be an expression of gratitude, but it sent warmth coiling through Piper in unexpected ways. She looked up, wondering if Frederic noticed her reaction, and saw that his eyes were dark with an unreadable emotion. Her pulse skipped.

"I should go call her back," she said, standing. Her hand didn't seem to want to separate from his; she had to force the command down her arm to make it move. "I'll try to be quick."

"Take as much time as you'd like," Frederic told her. His attention was on the hand she had just released, his voice distracted.

Piper didn't want to think about it. Pushing the moment from her thoughts, she headed toward her suite, her finger hitting redial before she reached it. Patience's phone went straight to voice mail. "You can't call me crying, then not answer your phone," she said. "Call me back ASAP. Everything will be okay," she added in a gentle voice.

Barely two seconds went by before a message appeared on her screen.

Doing better. Checking into a motel. Will call u later.

Soon, OK? Piper typed back. Love you.

Her sister would bounce back, Piper reminded herself as she tucked the phone in her back pocket. Frederic was right about her being a survivor. It still sucked though that Patience couldn't seem to catch any happiness.

Maybe it wasn't in the Rush girl DNA. What with them being common girls and all that, maybe they weren't meant to be anything more. She tapped the phone against her lips. At least Piper was here making sure some of her sister's sacrifices were worthwhile.

A thought came to her. There was one more thing she could do. She could talk to Stuart herself. Piper opened her email.

Frederic was moving about the kitchen when she returned a short time later. Whatever the thickness was that had been in the atmosphere before she left had eased. "Did you talk to your sister?" he asked.

"No, but she texted me. Said she's feeling better."

"You seem to be, as well."

Yeah, she was. "That's because after I heard from Patience, I decided to take a page from her playbook and do something to fix the situation. I decided to contact Stuart to see if I could make him see how backed in a corner Patience was back then."

"Good thinking."

"Unnecessary too. When I logged on, I found an email from him asking how he could make things right."

Might not be perfect, but it was a start.

"There you go. He's already over whatever news he learned. I'm sure that means they will talk things out."

"I really hope so."

All of sudden she saw that Frederic was setting the kitchen table. With two place settings.

"I thought we'd be more comfortable in here," he said when he noticed her staring.

"We're eating together?" All the other times she'd served him, he'd eaten in the dining room.

"Foolish for us to eat in separate rooms, is it not? Especially now that we are friends."

Friends. Apparently, he forgot that he used the same term to describe Patience's and Stuart's relationship.

She watched as he moved from cupboard to table. She never noticed before, but he looked at the space in sections, presumably until the object he was seeking came into view. Methodical, but subtle and graceful at the same time. To the unknowing eye, he was simply a man in supreme control. Heck, he looked that way to her *knowing* eye. She couldn't imagine him being anything but in control.

What was it she was supposed to remember about finding him attractive and being attracted?

"...going?"

He was looking in her direction waiting for an answer. "Should I assume from your lack of response that class did not go well again today?"

Right, he was talking about school. Piper shook her head. "No, but school never does go well, so it's no big deal."

"I am sorry." His voice lifted at the end, as if he wasn't sure he should offer condolences or not.

"Hey, like I said yesterday, great cooking is an art. Don't all artists suffer?"

"Some do."

"Well, so do some chefs. I'm telling myself that in the end, the hassle is making me a better chef.

"In the meantime," she said, reaching for the corn-starch, "I'm learning a whole bunch of new ways to insult a person's dinner. Today's word was *mundane*. My sauce was mundane. I like to think it's a step up from earlier this week when my food was uninspired."

"I see your teacher is one of those instructors."

"What do you mean, 'one of those'?" she asked as she mixed thickener for the gravy.

"I mean the type who believes insulting their students makes for good motivation."

"Assuming he is trying to motivate and not simply telling the truth."

"The aromas in this kitchen suggest otherwise."

It felt so good to have someone compliment her cooking, Piper decided to not worry about whether he was being polite and smiled instead. "Pot roast is one of my specialties. I've always been wicked good when it comes to New England cooking. Your country..." She waved her hand back and forth. "Not so much. I should have realized after I tried to make vichyssoise." Good Lord, she hadn't thought about that in ages. The memory made her laugh. "I think I was seven."

"And attempting French cooking?"

"What can I say? I was a prodigy." She left out the

part about how if she didn't cook, she didn't eat. "Anyway, someone mentioned cold potato soup on TV. I figured it couldn't be that hard to make, so I tried it. Ended up serving Patience a can of condensed potato soup straight out of the cupboard. No water or anything." She could imagine what Chef Despelteau would say.

"I'm glad your skills improved."

"Me, too. And for the record, I know how to make a kick-ass vichyssoise now. Patience refuses to eat it, though. Can't really blame her. Too many canned soup dinners burned her out."

Piper stared at the cloudy liquid in front of her. "She's the reason I'm here, you know. In Paris. She never stopped encouraging me. Telling me I could do anything I wanted."

"Like a good parent should."

"She'd laugh if she heard you say that, but yeah, exactly like a parent. I remember when I got my acceptance letter. She was more excited than I was." There was no way Piper couldn't fulfill their dream after that.

Distracted by memories, Piper forgot she was supposed to be stirring the thickener. The bowl slipped from her hands, bounced off the counter edge and landed on the floor.

Shoot. Cornstarch splattered the cabinets. That's what she got for not paying attention. She reached for the paper towels only to collide with Frederic as he did the same. Their fingers linked together.

Just like that, the thickness returned to the atmosphere. Piper felt it pressing around them, like energy waiting to hum. She looked at their interlocked fingers and wondered why neither of them had pulled away.

"Guess this is the week for spills," she joked.

"This is the week for a lot of broken rules," he said, a strangely serious response to what was meant as a tension breaker. She'd been looking for something to distract from the pull of attraction gathering strength in her belly. Piper didn't have to look up to know Frederic felt similarly. They were both breathing faster. Out of the corner of her eye, she saw his head dip closer, intentions clear. If she said no, he would stop.

She met him halfway.

Their mouths slid together as easily as their hands. Piper sighed at how well they fit. Frederic kissed like he moved, each caress of his lips deliberate and sure. His hand still gripping hers, he wrapped his other arm around her waist and pulled her close. *Just like dancing,* she thought as her eyes fluttered shut.

A moment later, Frederic broke away. Shaking and out of breath, Piper leaned her forehead against his. Holy cow! Never in a million years did she think a kiss could feel like that.

Frederic looked shell-shocked himself. She took pleasure in seeing his hand shake as he swiped a thumb across her lower lip. "Your phone is ringing," he said in a tight voice.

Phone? Piper blinked. Sure enough, she heard the sound of computerized jazz coming from her pocket. "Th-that's probably Patience."

"You should answer."

Yes, she should. Balling the hand Frederic had been

holding into a fist, she reached for the phone with her other.

Not Patience. The number on her call screen was unfamiliar. She didn't know if they had telemarketers in France, but if this was one, she was not going to hang up politely.

"Hello!" a cheery voice replied. "Am I speaking with Piper Rush? This is John Allen. I understand you're interested in a painting of mine."

While Piper spoke to John Allen, Frederic moved across the room. He needed to put some space between them before he took his housekeeper on the kitchen floor. It wasn't that he was against making love in the kitchen; he simply wasn't sure he should make love to Piper. As she was quickly proving, Piper was no ordinary housekeeper. She was soft and sweet in ways he wasn't used to. There was an essence about her that demanded connection, compelling him to reach out to her. She made him want to comfort her.

She... God, she tasted like vanilla. She made him want to taste her again. But was that a good idea?

Just then, Piper laughed, a sweet sound that reminded him of tinkling crystal, and he thought, perhaps it was a very good idea.

"Are you sure?" he heard her ask. "That would be great. Miss Duchenko would be thrilled."

Thrilled at what? Curiosity overrode his desire. Did this mean Allen had the painting? That they had tracked down the work so easily was almost comical. Experts searched lifetimes for paintings and sculptures and here his houskeeper locates one in three days? Amazing.

He was surprised at his investment in the search. Naturally, he would have a passing interest in tracking down a lost painting of any kind, even a scandalous portrait by a no-name artist like this one. The fact that his interest ran deeper he attributed to his frighteningly intriguing housekeeper.

"Looks like I'm going to England on an art hunt after all," Piper announced when she hung up. "Mr. Allen has invited me to see *Ana Reclining* in person."

"Congratulations." Her smile was contagious. "Does his invitation mean he is willing to part with the painting?"

"He said he would have to think about whether he was willing to sell. The painting is one of his favorite pieces."

But of course it was. As anyone hoping to net a good price would say.

"However, he did offer to let me inspect the painting's condition and to take a photograph of the work for Ana. If he doesn't sell, she will at least have proof one of her portraits survived."

Explaining why Miss Duchenko would be thrilled.

"I thought I would go this weekend. Mr. Allen's leaving on a business trip next week and wasn't sure how long he'd be gone. I figured I could take the train out tomorrow. That is, if you can spare me for a few days."

"I can," he replied. But did he want to? It was clear from the excited energy in her voice that the rest of tonight would be absorbed by itineraries and trip planning. To then have to wait an entire weekend before having the chance to kiss her again?

The words were out of his mouth before he had a chance to think them through. "Actually, I thought I would go with you."

"You did?"

"Why not? I've been part of your search for the last two days. Surely you didn't expect me to stay home when you got to the best part?"

"Do you really want to?" he heard her ask. "Go to England?"

"Yes, Piper, I do."

He could see her fidgeting as she tried to decide. After the kiss they just shared, there could be no doubt as to what traveling together to England might lead to. Frederic stayed quiet; he wouldn't push her one way or the other. No matter how tempting the thought of kissing her into agreement.

From her spot across the room, Piper nodded. "What time do you want to leave?"

CHAPTER SIX

PIPER WASN'T AN IDIOT. She knew perfectly well what could happen if Frederic accompanied her to England. Especially after the kiss they shared.

What she hadn't known was that kissing Frederic would leave her with some kind of ultra-hyper responsiveness that would fade. Every move, every sound Frederic made—right down to the crinkle of his shirt when he bent his elbow—sent a rush of awareness running through her. You'd think it was her first kiss. In a way, it was. It was certainly the first kiss that made her insides feel as though they were being kissed, too. If one short kiss could make her feel this way, she hated to think what would happen if he kissed without interruption.

The only thing that kept her from throwing herself at him to find out was, ironically enough, arranging their trip.

They caught the first train the next morning.

Piper took out the map of England she'd bought at the station and located the town where John Allen lived. "Have you been to this place before?" she asked Frederic.

"The town? No. I've been to the Cotswolds several times, though."

As he answered, he shifted in his seat, causing his jeans leg to brush hers. Impossibly the contact managed to reach through the layers to leave goose bumps.

The hyperawareness was as strong as ever.

Piper shifted in her seat as well, hoping she could add a little space between their legs. Otherwise, it would be a very long tunnel ride. "I read about the Cotswolds online last night." Mainly because she needed to do something to calm the hyperawareness. Turned out reading up on the trip you were taking with the man who kissed you senseless wasn't a relaxing solution. "It looked gorgeous in the pictures." Not to mention romantic. Another reason she had trouble sleeping.

She suddenly wondered what kind of visits Frederic's other trips to the Cotswolds were. "Did you go there on vacation?"

"There's an abbey not far from Chipping Campden that has the most unique ninth-century mural of Saint Michael. I wrote a journal paper on it." There was nostalgia in his smile. "I heard they restored it a few years ago. I wonder how it turned out."

"Why don't we go see it while we're in the area?" As far as she was concerned, anything that put such a smile on his face had to be worth a visit.

"I was already planning to," he replied. "Did you know that for centuries, no one knew this mural was there? At some point, it was covered by a second layer of stone. It was discovered when a lightning strike knocked a piece of the outer wall loose."

"Do they know why it was covered up?"

"No one knows for sure. My personal theory is that it was hidden during the Reformation so as not to anger Henry VIII." He launched into an explanation about the monks and allegiance to the king only to stop suddenly with a blush. "Sorry. I'm afraid I get carried away."

"It's okay—I don't mind," Piper replied. She'd been only half listening anyway. Too busy enjoying the sparkle in his eyes. "I have to be honest," she told him. "It's hard to imagine you poring over books in a research library." Today, for example, in his jeans and silk T-shirt, he looked more like a vacationing playboy or professional soccer player.

"Sit in one of my classes sometime. My students will say I must spend all my time there. That is why my lectures are so boring."

"They are not." She could listen to him talk all day.

"You are in a rarefied group then. Sometimes I think it's a good thing my lecture hall has low lighting. Keeps me from seeing how many of my students have fallen asleep. It's difficult enough when I call on them and they can't repeat what I mentioned five minutes earlier."

He was exaggerating. Piper honestly couldn't see him as boring, no matter how dry the topic. Distracting, however, was a far different story. If she were a college student, she could see herself spending class time fantasizing about the professor. "Your classes wouldn't be mostly female, would they?"

"About a seventy to thirty percent ratio. Why?"

"Trust me, those girls aren't sleeping."

The blush creeping over his cheeks was as captivating as the rest of him. "Is that your way of suggesting they're captivated by my looks?"

Piper joined him in blushing. "Is that your way of fishing for a compliment?"

"Perhaps." He traced a pattern across the map with his index finger. Piper followed with her eyes, and wondered if he was drawing a route or tracing aimless lines.

"I could say the same for you as well," he murmured without looking up.

"That I'm fishing for compliments?"

"That it's easy to be distracted by your good looks."

"Says the man who can't see." Realizing what she said, Piper started to cringe, only to stop when Frederic let out a laugh.

"Even through a pinhole, a man can see a diamond."

"Now I know you're exaggerating."

"Only a little." He moved his tracing from the map to her arm, his finger following the same lazy, loopy path across her skin. "You are a beautiful woman."

Piper pushed back a shiver. "I bet you say that to all your housekeepers."

"Only the American ones."

"Let me guess, you only hire Americans."

"No. You are the first." His finger took one last trip down her arm and disappeared. "I don't make a habit of kissing the help."

"Then why…?" What made her so different? She wasn't used to being singled out as special.

"I don't know," Frederic replied. He looked past her for a moment as if trying to figure out the answer himself before smiling at her again. "Why don't we enjoy it for what it is?"

"What is it?"

"Today? It is a road trip."

"And tomorrow?"

"Why don't we take things as they come? Stay in the present."

In other words, no strings attached.

"When I was a little kid, living in the present meant we were sure we'd have enough rent money." It was meant to be a joke, but the catch in her voice killed the effect.

Frederic shifted so they were face-to-face and took her hand. "I don't believe in giving false expectations," he told her. "Especially when it comes to relationships. It wouldn't be fair."

For whom? The other day he said being involved only meant more drama. Was that what he feared? That she might grow too attached? If so, maybe he should work on being a little less charming and attractive.

"Maybe I'm old-fashioned, but I like to know what I'm getting into," she said, only to realize that he had told her in very clear terms. No strings.

"You're thinking too much. Let us take one moment at a time, all right? Whatever happens, happens. There is no pressure."

Piper nodded. No pressure she could do.

Hopefully.

There was a car and driver waiting for them when they arrived at Saint Pancras station. A girl could get pretty spoiled by this kind of travel, Piper decided as she slid into the backseat. Definitely beat struggling to drive on the wrong side of the road with a rented stick shift. Which is what she'd be doing if Frederic weren't with her.

Best not to get too spoiled, though. At some point this whole Cinderella experience was going to end. There would be no limousines driving her around Boston. No guarantee she would have limousines driving her around Paris much, either. Taking things moment to moment could mean going back to being a housekeeper on Monday.

One good thing did come out of Frederic's "no pressure" comment, though. She managed to put the lid back on her over-boiling senses, meaning she could actually sit in the backseat without too much awareness. The only time she had real problems was when Frederic leaned into her space, sending a hint of his spicy wood aftershave in her direction. Then she would get a most unwelcome flutter below the waist. Fortunately, he didn't lean toward her too often.

"How long a drive is it to the Cotswolds?" she asked the driver.

"Ninety minutes or so. Little less maybe depending on traffic."

She reached into her bag to see if she missed any calls while underground. Nothing. "Patience still hasn't checked in."

"Perhaps she's been too busy."

"That's what I'm hoping." Too busy working out her problems with Stuart. "Do you know I still haven't told her about John Allen?"

"That could be for the best, since you haven't seen the painting yet. After you have met with Monsieur Allen, you will be able to give her much more information."

Like whether the collector would be willing to sell. "Do you think his position will change once he hears the painting's history?"

"It could. Or it could sway him the other way. Knowing the painting is attached to a world-renowned silver dynasty makes it—"

"Worth more, I know."

"Notoriety often does. Regardless, I'm sure no matter what the outcome of our meeting, Stuart Duchenko will spare no effort in trying to get his aunt's portrait returned."

"You are?"

"I know if it was something I wanted badly, I'd be relentless," he replied. The promise in his voice turned her insides upside down.

The English countryside was even more beautiful than the photos she saw online. Piper couldn't stop snapping pictures of the rolling green landscape.

"We have beautiful countryside in France as well," Frederic said, when she commented on a passing sheep farm.

"Yes, but that's French countryside. This is England," Piper countered. Spying a flock of grazing sheep, she took another photo.

"So?"

He almost sounded pouty. "You make it sound like it's a competition."

"It's always a competition when England is concerned."

"Well, at least it's easier to read the roadside signs here," she replied. Competition indeed. Both countries were better than any place she'd been before.

"Is there a place you can pull over so I can get a really good shot?" she asked the driver.

"The dozen or so you have already taken are not enough?" Frederic asked.

"I've got one more I want to take." And a moving car wouldn't do the subject justice.

"Will the shoulder ahead do?" He pointed to a particularly beautiful piece of scenery. A large checkerboard field in shades of green sprawled from the road to the horizon.

"Perfect."

The car slowed to a stop. "You have to get out, too," Piper told Frederic when he opened the door.

"Why?"

"Because I want you in the picture, that's why."

"A photograph of me standing on the side of the road."

"Actually, standing in front of that tree," she replied, pointing to a shrub-like tree a football field away.

From behind his sunglasses, Frederic was focusing in on her in his concentrated way. She tried to figure out his thoughts based on the rest of his expression, but it was impossible.

"Please?" she said, "I didn't think to take photos yesterday." Leaving her with zero visual evidence the magic day even happened. "I don't want to forget again this weekend." And be left with nothing.

"Only for you would I do this," he said.

"Thank you. Go stand by the tree and I'll be as quick as possible. Watch your step!" she added when he stepped down into a gulley.

"You're supposed to warn a person before they stumble," he said. Piper grinned. Hard to take the admonition seriously when he was grinning, too.

Not wanting to push her luck too much, she snapped three pictures in rapid succession. Her only regret was in forgetting to ask him to take off his sunglasses. She would have liked a picture with his eyes showing.

Maybe another time. "All done," she called to him. "You can get back into the car."

"Not yet. Gregory," he called to the driver, "Will you take mademoiselle's phone?"

"Yes, sir."

"You made us stop to take these photos. It is only fair you pose as well."

"Oh, no." Piper shook her head. "I hate having my picture taken."

"Gregory…"

The driver held out his hand expectantly.

"Watch out for the dip," Frederic said.

"Fine." Would be nice to have a photograph of her and Frederic for a memory. Giving her hair a quick fluff with her fingers, she stepped into the field.

Frederic met her under the tree. "Stand right here," he told her. Piper did as she was told, figuring they would pose side by side. Therefore she was caught off guard when Frederic moved behind her and wrapped his arms around her waist. "Smile for the camera," he murmured before pressing his cheek to Piper's temple.

"Got it," Gregory called.

Piper went to step forward, only to find herself held tight against Frederic's torso.

"Hold on," he said.

Keeping one arm around her waist, he caught her chin with the other, turned her head sideways and kissed her. Hard and thorough. "Now we can go."

Piper nearly forgot how to breathe. "What happened to no pressure?"

"No pressure, yes. I never said I wouldn't try to convince you, though, did I?" He held out a hand. "Shall we? Gregory is waiting."

"This is the inn John Allen recommended," Frederic said.

"It certainly is something," Piper replied.

It was a quintessential romantic country inn. A crooked building made of stone and quirky angles that sat at the top of the main street, while the rest of the village spread below. The whole thing was a postcard come to life. Thatched-roof buildings surrounded by rolling green hills and woodland. A local farmer driving his sheep down the road was all it needed to complete the picture.

It looked like the kind of place lovers went to hide. Precisely the kind of place a man would take a woman like Piper.

Why that thought left Frederic antsy, he wasn't sure.

The proprietress, a Mrs. Lester, met them at the

front door. "You must be the people who called last night." She smiled widely. "You are lucky. We don't usually have rooms this time of year, but we had a family cancel at the last minute, leaving us with two rooms open."

He almost chuckled at Piper's relieved breath.

While Piper went in search of a Wi-Fi signal so she could contact her sister, Frederic made arrangements with Gregory for the next day, then went upstairs to lie down. His head ached. He was not used to traveling outside Paris anymore. Navigating unfamiliar locations and crowds took extra concentration. Especially Saint Pancras station, where he had the additional strain of translating signage.

He'd been pushing himself harder than usual the past couple days. Piper was having such a good time; he wasn't about to spoil her happiness by asking that they slow down. Besides, the truth was, he didn't want to slow down, either. He was having a good time, too. No knowing how many more days like these he would have.

He was breaking his own rule about taking things day by day. Something about Piper made him reflective.

As his head sank against the pillows, he turned his focus to a more pleasant thought: the kiss he stole earlier. He'd been craving a second kiss since their first one ended, and after three hours of forced proximity —where her vanilla scent surrounded him like a cloud—he could no longer wait. She tasted as sweet as he remembered. There was a delicious innocence to her kisses. Then, there was an innocence to her, too.

As rocky as her childhood was, she still saw beauty in the world. She was the type of woman for whom fairy tales could exist. Look at how she was with her sister, going so far as to email Stuart Duchenko to salvage the sister's romance. She no doubt thought this portrait she was chasing represented a wonderfully tragic grand passion. It was infectious, this spirit of hers. Why else would he stand stupidly under a tree on the side of an English highway?

It was also why he made sure she understood from the start that whatever was between them would be a very finite fairy tale that would end when she returned to America.

Until then, though, he would show her a romantic time. And while he would not pressure her into his bed—he would never pressure any woman—he would do his best to convince her that his bed was where she wanted to be.

He must have fallen asleep, because the next thing he knew there was a soft knock on the door.

"I'm sorry," Piper said when he opened it. "Were you sleeping?"

"Dozing. Happens when I rest my eyes." He ran a finger through his hair, tugging the roots to clear the cobwebs. "Did you reach your sister?"

"I did. We had a good talk. I'm actually very hopeful for her and Stuart."

"That's good." He stepped aside to let her come in, only for her to start and stop. The way she toyed with the neckline of her jersey suggested she wasn't entirely sure what she wanted to do. Her hesitancy fit with all the other innocent facets of her personality.

It was utterly charming.

"I thought I'd take a walk through the village. See if any of those eight buildings was a gift shop. I was going to ask if you wanted to join me, but if you're not feeling well…"

"My eyes are tired is all," he replied.

"Do you want to rest?"

Hardly. "If I stayed behind every time my eyes weren't one hundred percent, I would never leave my house." And he would not be that person in a million years. "I would love to walk the village with you."

"You believe in pushing yourself, don't you?" she asked when they were downstairs. "I mean, you're on the go all the time."

"I don't believe in holding others back." An understatement if ever he made one. "And I believe in making the most of every moment."

"We've certainly crammed a lot of stuff into the past couple days, that's for certain."

He leaned close and said in a voice only she could hear, "The weekend is still young. Who knows what interesting activities we will discover." He didn't need peripheral vision to know he'd made her blush. So adorable.

Based on the village center, Frederic guessed this was not one of the Cotswold villages that catered to weekend travelers. They found a wine shop, a real estate business and a law firm. The only shop was an apothecary, where Piper bought a handful of postcards and two bottles of English lavender bath salts.

"What do you think?" she asked as she held the bottle under his nose. "Will it make a nice souvenir?"

"Very nice." Although her own scent was much nicer.

They contented themselves with walking the sidewalks after that. Piper was enchanted with the houses and hidden walkways. "I feel we walked onto a Hollywood set," she said, stopping to smell a hedge of blackberries. "If I were going to make a movie about an English country village, this is what it would look like."

Frederic had to admit, the gardens and brambles were beautiful. He liked the quiet. Moreover, he liked the comfortable silence the two of them shared. He noticed the other day that there wasn't a pressure to fill the space with noise the way there was with some of the women he spent time with. He was able to focus on navigating the uneven sidewalks without distraction. Well, almost without distraction, he thought, as his companion stopped to admire another garden. While he had been resting earlier, she pulled her hair into a ponytail. He liked when she wore her hair back; he could see her features better.

Because he could, he curled a stray hair behind her ear. She immediately ducked her head. "I don't know about you, but I'm getting hungry. I haven't eaten since the train," she said. Did she know her fingers were retracing the path he just made? "The man at the store told me there's a pub about a half mile to the north. The Hen & Chick or something like that. Should we try it out?"

"I don't think we have much choice. There seems to be an equal number of inns and restaurants."

"True," she said, smiling. "Considering how nice the rest of the town is, I don't see how the pub could be bad. And you did say to take things as they come..."

The subtext of her comment sent a thrill through him. "Good to see you're getting into the spirit."

"As far as dinner is concerned, anyway." She ducked her head again, but he caught the tiny smile she was trying to hide nonetheless.

"Dinner's always a good start," he told her.

They started walking again. "I wonder what the chances are that this place has a traditional pub menu. I've always wanted to try steak and kidney pie. And steamed pudding. Like spotted dick or treacle."

Frederic had to laugh at her enthusiasm over her potential menu. "I'm beginning to understand why you became a chef. You clearly love food."

"Good food," she corrected. "I'll try anything once, but to be honest, some of the froufrou stuff I can do without."

"Froufrou?" He didn't understand.

"Overly fancy. I'm not a fan of when chefs try too hard with food. I mean, don't get me wrong. I'm all for mixing things up, but sometimes a steak is best when you leave it a plain old steak." She let out a soft laugh. "Guess that explains why Chef Despelteau hates me. He's the king of froufrou."

"I'm sure you're exaggerating, and he doesn't *hate* you."

"Don't be so sure. I know you think he's pushing me

to be better, but I think he just doesn't groove on the way I cook. Hasn't since day one."

They were passing under an oak tree. She reached up and plucked one of the leaves. "You know, the other day when you found me crying in the kitchen, I was thinking of quitting," she told him.

"Really?" He knew she was upset, but thought she simply had a bad day. If she had quit, they wouldn't be walking this sidewalk. "What made you change your mind?"

"We worked too hard to get me to Paris. It'd be wrong not to see things through."

We. Meaning her sister and her. Frederic wasn't sure why, but talk of her sister and culinary school together unsettled him. There was an element of obligation to the way she talked about the combination that he didn't like.

"Surely if you are unhappy, your sister would not want you to continue." At least not the sister she'd described to him. "She'd want you to be happy."

"Oh, she does," Piper replied. "She would tell me to come home in a second, but like I said, quitting doesn't feel right.

"Besides," she added, "I'm not unhappy. Not right now, anyway."

"I'll take that as a compliment." His satisfaction almost outweighed the uneasiness he was feeling on her behalf. "So you finish your coursework. What then? What will you do when you go back to Boston?"

"Get a job at one of the local restaurants and work my way up the chain," she said. "Isn't that what one does with a culinary certificate?"

Yes, but one usually sounded more enthusiastic about the prospect. Then again, most students enjoyed school as well. This was one of those times when he wished he could walk and focus on his companion at the same time. To be able to see what she was thinking.

"You could open your own restaurant. Café du Piper."

She laughed. "Someday, maybe. A little bistro where I could design my own menu. Patience and I used to talk about my doing that."

Again, Patience. The woman was beginning to bother him, she was so ubiquitous. "Are all your dreams tied to your sister?" he asked, sharply.

"No." But her voice was too defensive to be convincing. "I have plenty of my own dreams."

"Like what?" Suddenly, very interested in hearing what she wanted, Frederic stopped walking and positioned himself so he could look her in the eye. "If you could do anything you wanted, what would it be?"

"Cooking, of course."

"Is that all? Just cooking? Tell me, what is Piper's passion?"

He was glad he stopped if for no other reason than he was gifted with the sight of her lashes sweeping downward like a thick black curtain. "You'll think it's silly."

"No, I won't." There was nothing about her he'd ever find silly. "I'd truly like to know."

"All right, but I'll warn you, it's not all that fancy."

"No one said it had to be."

She took a deep breath. "If I could do anything in the world, I would spend my time cooking wonderful meals for the people who matter to me. Food was there for me when I needed a friend. I would like to give people the same gift.

"Told you it was silly," she said, turning her head.

"Not silly at all. It's a lovely sentiment." One that fit her perfectly. How lucky those people would be.

Leaning close, he kissed her cheek. "I hope you get your dream," he whispered.

Don't let it die for your sister's sake, he added silently.

The pub was called the Hen & Rooster, and while the plaque next to the front door said it was established in 1666, Piper was pretty sure it had been modernized many times. The blast of comfortable, clean-smelling air that greeted them upon entering was her clue.

Aesthetically, the inside looked exactly like a seventeenth-century tavern. So much so, in fact, that Piper almost expected the bartender to be wearing period clothing and a leather apron. The floors were slanted. The walls were uneven. As they were walking into the dining room, Frederic clipped the top of his head.

"Must not have had too many people taller than six foot," she teased.

"More like five. There should be a sign warning people. Or padding on the cross beams."

"Poor baby. Does this help?" She massaged the top of his head, where he had tapped the beam.

"Much better," he replied. She couldn't see his eyes for the sunglasses, but she could feel their stare on her skin nonetheless. Felt as if he was concentrating all his attention on her face. Her mouth, to be precise. Taking her hand in his, he brought it to his lips. "Thank you."

She slipped her hand free and fought the urge to run it nervously across the back of her neck. Amazing how the air between them shifted so quickly, easy one moment, humming with awareness the next.

Of course, the fact that he'd kissed her twice in ten minutes probably helped that cause along.

Other than a pair of men at the bar, the restaurant was empty. That didn't stop the hostess from placing them at a table in the corner near an unused fireplace. Intimate and romantic. What a surprise. Maybe there was a competition between France and England, after all. To see which one could make her fall under Frederic's spell the fastest.

She could have told them they needn't work so hard. Frederic was doing fine without their help. Desperate for a distraction, she studied the single-sheet menu the hostess handed her.

"Do they have your pie?" Frederic asked.

"Afraid not. Looks like the chef prefers more continental than traditional British. Unless quinoa is an English staple I didn't know about."

"I'm sorry."

"Me too," she said, giving an exaggerated sigh. More to best him in the dramatics department than anything. "I'll simply have to make do with roasted guinea fowl."

"Poor baby." Just like that, the mood went back to being easy. If only they'd struck up a friendship earlier in her employment. The year could have been so much nicer. In the back of her mind, she sent up a silent thank-you to Ana. Without her portrait, they would still be virtual strangers.

"Good evening. Can I take your order?" The bartender appeared at their table with a pad in his hand. Piper gave her order.

"The same, along with a bottle of sauvignon blanc," Frederic said when she was finished.

"Did you even look at the menu?" She saw him fingering the paper, but the sheet never actually left his plate.

"I trust your judgment. Plus, I left my magnifying glass in my overnight bag."

"Ahh, the truth comes out. Now it's my turn to hope you aren't disappointed."

"I haven't been so far."

A flutter danced through her. *Better be careful.* She already liked him more than she should.

Now that they were seated, he'd removed his sunglasses, giving her the chance to study him straight-on. What she saw left her feeling guilty. There were lines around his eyes and mouth. The kind that came with fatigue. He was rubbing his thumb and middle finger across his eyebrows, massaging the skin underneath.

She waited while the bartender served the wine, then asked him, "Eyes still tired?"

"A little."

She had a feeling the two of them had different definitions of the term. "You didn't have to come with me, you know. I could have gone sightseeing on my own."

Wouldn't have been as enjoyable, but she would have endured.

"Absolutely not. I told you before, I am not going to sit in my room acting like an invalid because of a little eyestrain." The fierceness with which he spoke startled her. Way more than you'd expect for a simple suggestion.

He must have realized how sharp he sounded, too, because when he spoke again, his voice was softer and more in control. "I thought we settled this back at the inn."

"We did. But then I started thinking about how tired you looked. I feel bad that I didn't think about your needs."

Apparently, she said something wrong, because he immediate stiffened. "My need is for you not to accommodate me," he said, glaring over his wineglass.

"I only meant…"

"I know what you meant." Again, he corrected his voice, clearly trying to cover whatever nerve she'd touched with her comment. "I'm sorry," he said. "I don't mean to be sharp. Let us say I have done my share of accommodating people's needs in the past and it wasn't pleasant."

Clearly. "Would it help if I told you I won't be one of those women?" It was the only thing she could imagine had happened. That a former girlfriend had been overly demanding.

"It wasn't a woman."

Who, then? Piper watched as he rolled the stem of his glass back and forth between his fingers. His eyes were focused on the contents, but she had a feeling he wasn't really looking at the wine. Rather he was debating what kind of answer to give.

She wasn't sure why, but she expected some kind of clever deflection. Thus it surprised her when he said, "The problem with accommodating is that it is very easy for a person to turn someone else into their servant."

A harsh way of thinking. Whoever this person was must have really been demanding. "All I said was I could have gone to the drugstore alone. It's not like I offered to cut your meat or anything. Although technically you could order me to do that since I am your servant."

That should have earned a laugh, but it didn't. Frederic simply went back to rotating his wineglass. His features had grown stormy; in the dim light, his eyes were like thunderclouds.

"My mother did everything for my father," he said.

"Some women are traditional that way." Even as she spoke, however, the words sounded flat.

"This had nothing to do with traditional. My father was incapable of doing anything without help. He needed my mother constantly. She had no life of her own. Everything revolved around him."

"You don't have to explain." She hoped he would—there was so much she wanted to know about him—but from his sudden hoarseness she could tell the subject was a painful one.

"What about all the things she did with you? You said the other day she exposed you to art…"

"I said she made sure I was exposed. The nanny would take me, and when I came home, she and I would talk about what I saw." He looked down at his wine again. "To be fair, if she had a choice she would have taken me herself."

Piper knew all about not having choices. "Why was he so…" She wanted to say *selfish*, but it didn't seem her place.

"He was blind."

Piper blinked. "How?" It explained a lot.

"Retinitis pigmentosa is hereditary."

And Frederic, as the lucky heir, was doing his best to handle the disease differently than his father, was that it? Was that why he flew off the handle at what was a minor gesture of kindness? "I'm—" With a shake of her head, she cut the apology off. No way Frederic would want to hear her tell him she was sorry. Not now. So she said nothing.

"Let's talk about something else," Frederic said, breaking her thoughts. "I don't want to spoil the evening being maudlin. Tell me what you think about the wine."

Not wanting to spoil the evening either, Piper complied.

CHAPTER SEVEN

FREDERIC LISTENED AS Piper talked about how she could never tell the difference between an oak sauvignon blanc and a dry sauvignon blanc. "You'd think I could, being a cook and all, but wine is a whole different science," she said.

For the second time this week, he appreciated how she knew when not to push. Perhaps because of her own touchy childhood subjects, she understood when a conversation stepped too close to a nerve. Whatever the reason, he was grateful she decided to let the news about his father's blindness go by without comment.

Why he brought up the subject in the first place was beyond him. He certainly didn't intend to. His childhood was something he *never* discussed. Sharing the past—sharing anything personal—implied intimacy, which could lead a person to believe the relationship had a future. The last thing he wanted to do was mislead someone like Piper.

But then, he thought about all the secrets she'd shared about her childhood, and he started to feel as if he owed her some measure of equality. A secret for a secret. And so he shared his.

Now he wished he hadn't, because the memory was alive in his head. His father's voice, broken and slurred, the ice in his tumbler rattling. *I need you. I can't do it on my own.* "It" being so many things. Generations of being waited on by servants left their mark. His father had been left incapable of doing for himself. As a result, his neediness knew no bounds.

Frederic, on the other hand... He might have inherited his father's fortune, but his life taught him how not to need. And so he forced the conversation back to superficial, happy conversation, and Piper, bless her heart, played along.

It helped that dinner turned out to be delicious. "See?" he said, setting his fork down. "I was right to trust your judgment. I enjoyed my fowl."

"It wasn't bad," she replied. "Though I would have cut back on the thyme."

"Would that make the dish thyme-less?"

The tinkle of her laugh left him wanting to hear more. It was disturbing how easy he found her company. She was fun, she was smart. And, her kisses aroused him in a way he hadn't felt since his teenage years.

A hollow feeling started to spread behind his breastbone, causing him to squeeze his hand into a fist. Ninety-nine days out of one hundred, he accepted his future without complaint. Every so often, however, he would feel the ache for what he would miss. Unless he decided to be as selfish as his father...

I need you, Patrice. His father's constant mantra.

Frederic would not need. Would never need.

He could, however, *want*, and at the moment, he wanted the woman seated across from him very much.

Piper gave a soft cough. She knew he was studying her. "I was cursing the poor lighting," he said. "I want to be able to see you better." Her cheeks were no doubt turning as crimson as the roses they passed on their walk. Would the color spread to other parts of her body?

He reached across the table for her hand, feeling a victorious thrill when she met him halfway. "Do you still want your pudding?" he asked, playing with her fingers.

"I didn't see it listed on the menu."

"What a shame. I would hate for you to miss out on dessert."

"I'm sure I'll find something that will tempt me." She leaned closer and added, "On the menu."

The little minx. Two could play that game. "You should know," he said, leaning as well, "that when we're finished here, I plan to kiss you senseless. Then I'm going to kiss you again."

He might not be able to see her face clearly in the shadows, but he definitely heard her breathing quicken.

"Now that I think about it," she said, "I don't have to have the cheesecake."

"Good." Not bothering to signal for the bill, he took out his wallet and tossed down a stack of notes thick enough to cover ten dinners and grabbed her hand. "Let's go."

Amazingly, he made it the entire walk back without pulling her into his arms. Safety first, he reasoned. Kissing her would obliterate his concentration.

He also took masochistic pleasure in pushing the anticipation to its peak. He tortured himself by holding only her hand on the walk, and when they climbed the stairs to their rooms, he walked a step behind so that her that her vanilla scent filled his nostrils.

When they reached the top of the staircase, he finally broke and put his hands on her waist. From the trembling beneath his fingers, he knew he was not the only one who had been tortured. "I believe I promised you something," he said, turning her around.

Cupping her cheeks, Frederic focused all his attention on her lips. Last night was but an appetizer. Tonight, he would take his time. Savor. He kissed one corner of her mouth, then the other. Her quickened breath was his reward. When he finally lowered his mouth to hers, she let out a whimper. Relief.

"My room or yours?" he whispered when they broke to breathe.

"Doesn't matter."

She was right. It didn't. He reached for a door.

"There you are. I've been knocking on your door for ten minutes."

Piper looked up from the French press she'd been timing. Frederic stood barefoot in the dining room doorway, his shirt untucked and buttoned incorrectly. He looked the picture of a man who had just rolled out of bed. Which, of course, he had. Piper knew because up until an hour ago, she'd been in bed with him.

Thinking about what they did there made her flush.

"Mrs. Lester and I were talking about breakfast recipes," she replied, her voice overly bright. Could she sound any more like she was trying to be in control? "I gave her the recipe for huevos rancheros and she's going to give me hers for bangers and mash."

"The least I can do after all your help," Mrs. Lester replied. The innkeeper swiped back an errant red curl. "Guests aren't supposed to be allowed in the kitchen, but hard to say no to a real chef."

"I might have done a little of the prep work while we were talking," Piper added, sheepishly. She needed something to burn off her nervous energy. Speaking of...she checked to see if the grounds had brewed long enough. "Would you like some coffee?"

"I'm surprised you're awake so early," Frederic said. Leaning forward, he added in a voice only she could hear, "I wasn't expecting to find your side of the bed empty."

Piper shivered as his voice tickled her ear. "You were asleep," she told him. "I didn't want to wake you."

And okay, maybe she might have wanted to avoid any potential morning-after awkwardness. Last night had been amazing, with a capital *A*, but she knew as well as anyone that night and morning were two vastly different times of day, and what seemed like a good idea after a couple glasses of wine might look like a disaster in the daylight. She was afraid to face the regret in Frederic's eyes.

It wasn't regret she was seeing right now, however. The expression looking down on her was as predatory

as ever. "My ego is hurt," he said. "Usually when I am
with a woman, it's the other way around. I must be losing my touch."

No, he definitely wasn't losing that. Piper's insides
melted from simply thinking about the things his hands
could do. She looked over her shoulder to see if Mrs.
Lester had heard. The innkeeper had her head in the
oven, checking on pans of bread dough.

"I'm sorry. I started thinking about this morning's
meeting and couldn't fall back asleep." It wasn't a complete lie. She did think about the meeting in passing.
"I decided to come down here for a cup of coffee, and
that's when I ran into Mrs. Lester."

"Who put you to work making your huevos ranchos.
Come back to bed."

"Huevos *rancheros*," she corrected automatically,
"and I wasn't just giving her the recipe. I was making
breakfast potatoes."

"Come back to bed." His lips moved to her ear again
despite Mrs. Lester being a room away. "I want to show
you what you missed by leaving early."

Piper's knees buckled. "Is—is it all right if we take
the coffee upstairs?" she asked Mrs. Lester.

"Sure thing," Mrs. Lester replied. "Leave the press in
your room, and I'll have the cleaning girl bring it down.
Thank you, too, for your help this morning. First time
I ever have had a guest who made breakfast potatoes
better than me."

"That's sweet of you to say. We'll be back down—"
Frederic was pushing her toward the stairwell. "You
didn't let me finish," she said to him.

"I don't care," he replied. "Do you have any idea how many downstairs rooms I looked in before I found you?"

"There are only three."

"Three too many. Now, back to our room with you, young lady. The door is unlocked."

Our room. The words gave Piper as big a thrill as Frederic's intentions. With his hands holding her waist, Piper climbed the stairs.

A couple hours later, they were back in the dining room, showered and ready for the day.

Mrs. Lester greeted them with a knowing smile that had Piper blushing again. "Sit anywhere you'd like. You're the last ones for the day.

"By the way," she added, "Your driver arrived while you were upstairs." Gregory sat at a corner table reading the paper. He too gave them a smile and a nod.

"The whole room knows what we were doing," she whispered to Frederic.

"You mean Gregory, and I don't think he's surprised. If anything, he is jealous. I know I would be in his shoes."

All it took was a trace of his finger running down her forearm and Piper melted again.

"Do you do this often?" she asked him.

"Steal away to England with a beautiful woman?" When she didn't take the bait, he grew more serious. "My bedpost doesn't have too many notches, if that is what you're asking."

That was exactly what she was asking. Now that he had answered, Piper realized that he rarely stayed away all night. He had guests in his house even less. Off the top of her head, she remembered one, possibly two, and they had both gone home before breakfast.

"I'm glad." Based on the way his eyes widened, her honesty surprised him. "No woman wants to think she is one in a long line." Knowing there were but a few women made her less mundane, to steal one of Chef Despelteau's words. More in keeping with what Frederic meant to her.

Mrs. Lester appeared, pot of coffee in hand, to end the conversation. "Piper tells me you're meetin' with John Allen this morning. About a painting."

"We are," Frederic replied. "Do you know him?"

"A bit. Comes in here for tea now and again. A queer little fella, he is—I don't mean that in the politically insensitive way or nothing. He's just quirky."

"Quirky, how?" Piper asked. They were heading to the man's house. If he was a crazy person, she'd like to know.

"Little things really. Like he always insists on bringing his own pastries when he comes here. Richest man in town and he won't pay for a bloody scone, but then leaves a one hundred and fifty percent tip."

"Sounds like he's very particular," Frederic said over his coffee cup.

"*Particular* is a good word for it. I've got one last basket of breads. Do you folks want it?"

"Yes, please," Piper replied. Once Mrs. Lester was out of earshot, she looked back in Frederic's direction. "Is *particular* good or bad, do you think?" It sounded suspiciously like Bernard's selectivity, if you asked her.

The Frenchman shrugged. "Hard to say. Art collectors are a bit like snowflakes. No two are the same."

"Maybe I'll get lucky, and Ana's story will break his heart to the point he wants her to have the painting."

"Or your friend Stuart will write enough zeroes that he can't refuse."

"He's not my friend—he's Ana's great-nephew. And hopefully Patience's—"

"Friend?" he finished with a smirk to rival Mrs. Lester's. He dragged the word out, long and with plenty of subtext.

"When you say it that way, Stuart is definitely not my friend." Piper reached for her coffee. She wasn't forgetting that *friend* was also how he described their relationship.

His lips were wet with coffee as he smiled from across the table. "I'm glad. I don't like sharing."

He didn't like to share and he didn't like to think about tomorrow. Kind of put her in limbo, didn't it?

John Allen's house was at the end of a long road tucked between two giant lavender fields. With nothing marking the turn, they drove past the place twice before locating the winding dirt road. Considering Allen was supposed to be a wealthy patron of the arts, Piper had been expecting someplace more upscale and artsy, or at the very least, someplace large, not this crooked cottage with a thatched roof. But then, maybe this was what passed for artsy and upscale out here. They were in the middle of nowhere. She looked for a car, but the only item with wheels was a bicycle propped by the garden shed.

"Are you sure we have the right address?" she asked Gregory.

"GPS says we do."

"Perhaps he is trying to discourage thieves," Frederic said.

That was one theory. Stepping out of the car, she was greeted by the smell of flowers and freshly tilled dirt.

"It appears Monsieur Allen does not believe in landscaping," Frederic remarked as he joined her. He had a point. Time and rain had cut deep ruts into the dirt driveway, turning the already-rough surface into a bumpy hazard. There were primroses that lined the walk leading to the door, and a container of annuals, but other than that, the outside of the cottage was bare. "Maybe he figures the lavender fields were enough."

"Perhaps." Frederic took a deep breath. "The aroma certainly is pervasive."

"The better to hide bodies. A joke," she said when he turned with a frown. She slipped her hand into his, stealing comfort from his grip. "I'm glad you are here."

Something she couldn't read flickered across his face. "Thank you," he said, squeezing her fingers. He looked about to say more when the cottage door flew open.

"Helloo!" the newcomer greeted. "You must be Piper. It's good to see you. I was worried you'd gone and got yourself lost." With his thick accent, the last word sounded more like "loost." "And you brought a friend. Hullo." He smiled widely in Frederic's direction.

Mrs. Lester's description suddenly made sense. Dressed from head to toe in white linen, John Allen looked like a miniature version of a 1920s English gentleman. The crown of his silver head barely reached Piper's nose. How on earth could Bernard not remember meeting him?

Piper introduced them, and he shook Frederic's hand enthusiastically. "Call me John, please. Both of you."

"Thank you for meeting with us," Piper said.

"Well, I must admit you have me curious. I had no idea my impulse purchase had such notoriety."

Frederic caught her attention and pointed a finger upward, letting her know where the price would be heading.

Unlike the outside, which looked ignored, the inside was a modern showplace. John had knocked down several walls to open one large room with vaulted ceilings. There was a kitchen that could rival Frederic's. Piper was half tempted to chuck looking at art so she could explore the appliances. Out of the corner of her eye, she saw Frederic doing his best to take in details.

Their host noticed as well. "Bought the place on the cheap at auction a few years ago, I did," he replied when Frederic complimented him. "Had to completely gut the place, though. Didn't hold up in the wet and got a bad case of rot. Place is climate-controlled now. Wouldn't hang the canvases until it was installed."

"Sound thinking," said Frederic.

"I thought so. Seemed daft to spend a fortune and not see to it properly. The main collection is on the back wall."

"How many pieces do you have?" Piper asked.

"Right now? Fifteen. A couple of the larger works are on loan in New York. Haven't got the space here."

She could see why. The large back wall had half a dozen paintings already. Frederic was squinting at a watercolor of a woman tilling a garden. "Bergdahl?" he asked.

"Good eye, Professor. Bought it from a gallery in New York around twenty years ago."

"His pieces seldom come on the market now."

"I heard a rumor one of his seascapes might be going up for sale next month. I've already let my man know I'm interested. Ana's back here, in my dining room. Help yourself to tea and scones, by the way. I baked them myself."

Piper tugged on Frederic's sleeve. "I hate to sound tacky, but how much would you pay for that painting? It was barely the size of a piece of copy paper."

"Trust me, you do not want to know."

John was waiting in the dining room doorway. "And here she is. *Ana Reclining*."

"Wow" was all Piper could say. Hard to believe the woman reclining on the settee was the same little old woman who popped in to say hello during one of their video chats.

"Beautiful, isn't she?" John said.

"Breathtaking."

"I fell in love the moment I saw her. I love how he made her skin so luminous-looking. And her lips. The way he caught them in mid sigh? Doesn't she look like a woman who'd just been—"

"Right," Piper said. This was her sister's elderly boss

they were talking about. Some images were best left to the imagination.

Unfortunately, John was right. The painting dripped with sensuality. It wasn't the sexiness that caught your attention, though. At least not as far as Piper was concerned. It was Ana's expression. She was looking at the artist with nothing short of adoration. They weren't looking at a seventeen-year-old girl draped naked across a sofa. They were looking at a woman in love. Piper wondered if that wasn't the reason Theodore Duchenko wanted all the paintings destroyed.

She tried to imagine how it would feel, to be that deeply in love and have it ripped away from you.

"Are you all right?" John asked.

"Fine. I was thinking about poor Ana Duchenko is all. She's going to be so happy to know this painting survived." She reached into her bag for her cell phone. "You said I could take a few photographs?"

"Yes, yes. Be my guest. Just make sure the flash is off, if you don't mind. I don't want the colors to fade."

"Thank you." Whether he sold Stuart the painting or not, Ana needed to see proof her love for Nigel still existed on canvas.

While she clicked away, John maneuvered his way around the dining room table to pour tea. Frederic, meanwhile, had moved to the opposite of the room to study the painting. Piper caught the telltale movement of his head that said he was looking at it in sections.

"You said on the phone, you were trying to locate the painting for the real Ana?" John handed her a teacup, then offered one to Frederic.

"Ana Duchenko," Piper replied. She proceeded to tell him the story. As the details poured out, she realized she was destroying any chance Stuart had at buying the painting cheaply, but that didn't matter. It was more important John Allen understand that the painting was more than "notorious."

"Fascinating," John said. "So as far as you know, this is the only painting left that Nigel Rougeau painted."

"Unless someone has one hidden in their basement, yes." Frederic gave a soft cough, a warning that she ignored. "Nigel died shortly after Ana went back to the States."

John gave an odd sigh. "Such a tragic story. I knew that painting had to be a work of love the first time I saw it. You can see the emotion in her eyes."

So he did understand. "You know, Ana never married."

"She didn't?"

Piper shook her head. She felt as if she were gossiping about some old Hollywood romance the way her host was hanging on every word. "She lives in Boston with her cat, Nigel."

"The cat is named Nigel?" John clutched his chest. "I think I might cry."

"So you can see why her nephew wants to buy the painting. He wants to return the portrait to her while she's still alive."

"That's such an amazing story," John said. "To think, poor Nigel, robbed of his potential greatness. Can you imagine what he could have achieved if Theodore Duchenko hadn't destroyed his work?" He looked to Frederic, as if waiting for confirmation.

"A genuine loss," Frederic replied.

"Not to mention a great inspiration," Piper added. She snapped a few more pictures to be safe. She'd already made a mental note to send Nigel's sister a copy as well. "I think Ana really was his muse."

"I think so, too. I see why her nephew wanted to track the work down."

"The question is…" For the first time since they'd sat down, Frederic addressed the elephant in the room. "Would you be willing to sell her?"

"Well…" John drew out the word for several beats. Never a good sign. "I'll be glad to talk with Mr. Duchenko, of course, but like I said, she is one of my favorite pieces. I love looking at her while I eat."

That was an image Piper could do without.

They spent another hour or so looking at the rest of the collection, the older man thrilled to show his paintings to someone who "appreciated them." When they were finished, Piper once again urged him to consider selling *Ana Reclining*.

"I promise I'll think about it," he said. "I do have a soft spot for star-crossed lovers."

"Thank you." Looking at Ana's portrait one last time, she crossed her fingers that the painting would be heading to Boston soon.

"Mrs. Lester was right," she said when they were on the way to the car. "He is quirky."

"Quirky but savvy. His collection is amazing. The Bergdahl alone was worth the trip.

"Congratulations, by the way." With his arm around her shoulders, Frederic kissed her temple. "Your treasure hunt was a success."

Yeah, it was. Still, Piper frowned.

"Is something wrong?"

"I don't know. I thought I'd be more excited, but..."

"You're sad because your hunt is over. That is not unusual."

It was more than the end of the hunt. She was reminded all of a sudden that looking for Ana's painting was what kept Frederic in her orbit. Now that the search was over, would she be enough to make him stay around? Or would their affair be over when they returned to Paris?

She really stank at this taking-things-as-they-come stuff.

"These last couple days of adventure have spoiled me." In more ways than one.

"The day is not over. We can still have adventures."

"Like what?" she asked, as if she couldn't guess already.

Frederic stopped walking and stared at her with a focus Piper had never seen before. Part desire, part... confusion? Whatever the emotions behind his eyes, it set off a slow burn in the pit of her stomach.

"May I show you something?" he asked, running his thumb across her lower lip.

"Of course," she replied. When he looked at her like that, he could show her anything.

CHAPTER EIGHT

IT HAD TO be the ugliest painting Piper had ever seen. Not depressing ugly like the painting in Bernard's gallery, but ugly-ugly. From what she could tell, the mural had been a group effort. Different sections reflected different styles. In the center of the mess, Saint Michael wrestled a fire-breathing dragon. At least the description said it was a dragon. Piper thought it looked more like a winged cow. The army of angels behind him was one giant block of white and gold, on which black lines had been painted to represent limbs while the villagers on the ground…she wasn't quite sure what the artist was thinking when he painted them. As for poor Saint Michael, he was rewarded with a protruding nose and lips so large he looked as if the dragon had slammed his face into a rock.

To her right, Frederic beamed at the work like a man looking at his child. "Saint Michael vanquishing evil," he said, reverence in his voice. "What do you think?"

"Umm, it's different."

"Have you ever seen anything so ugly? It's even worse than I remembered."

Oh, good. She was afraid she was going to have to pretend something way beyond her acting skills.

They were in the chamber by themselves, the abbey ruins not being one of the area's more popular attractions. Piper could see why. Ugly mural aside, there wasn't much else to see. Much of the monastery had fallen into ruin. Only the room they were in survived.

She turned back to the painting. "You wrote a paper on this piece?" After all the beautiful things he'd shown her the past couple of days, it was a bit of a letdown.

And yet Frederic seemed thoroughly enchanted. "Yes, I did."

"Why?" She had to be missing something. Maybe there was some historical connection she didn't understand.

Taking her hand, he led her closer. "Because I don't think this painting was ever about being good. The men who painted it had to know they didn't have talent. Or perhaps they thought they did. It doesn't matter. This painting is perfect because of its flaws. You see ugly, I see joy. Passion."

The passion was Frederic's. You could feel it radiating off him as he spoke. Like the day in the Place des Vosges, only ten times stronger.

"Of all the paintings I have seen in my life, this is one of my favorites. Because it is pure."

"When you put it that way." Piper's heart was suddenly too big for her chest. She felt so amazingly honored that he would share the piece with her. Wanting to thank him for the gift, but afraid he'd hear the emotion in her voice, she settled for a smile. "To think, all the other tourists will look and see a saint with swollen lips."

"Poor Saint Michael. He does look like he's had one too many collagen treatments, doesn't he?"

"I'm glad you got to see him again."

"I am, too."

They studied the mural in silence. Or rather, Frederic studied the painting while Piper studied him. From the moment this affair began, back in the kitchen in Paris really, she'd been haunted by a sense of surrealism, unable to believe they were together in the first place. Now this. She could feel herself starting to fall. If she hadn't already fallen, that is.

"Can I show you something else?" he asked.

"Here? At the abbey?" Frederic nodded before catching her hand in his again.

"It is outside," he told her.

Behind the monastery, the land spilled into a large grassy field dissected by boulders and a few errant black-eyed Susans. Still holding hands, they picked their way across the uneven ground until they reached the top of a large swell. From there they could look out over the entire abbey grounds. They were high enough that Piper could make out the shape of the old building in the ruined rock.

Frederic sat down, then tugged on her wrist so she would join him. They sat back on their elbows, legs stretched out in front of them.

"When I was studying the mural, I would take my lunch in this spot," he told her.

"It's beautiful." Taking out her phone, she snapped

a picture. She was going to want to remember this day when she returned to Boston in a couple months.

She was going to want to remember a lot of things.

Off to their left, she spotted a roped-off section where the ground appeared dotted with markers. "Wonder what is going on other there?" she said, pointing.

"Archaeological research, no doubt. Before the abbey, this was a pagan ritual site."

"No way."

"It's the reason the abbey was built here in the first place. They would have painted Saint Michael as a way of discouraging rituals and protecting the land from evil."

"He does look scary. Wonder if it worked."

"You'll have to ask the pagans. From what I understand, there are some who come every solstice."

Kicking off her sandals, Piper wiggled her bare toes, enjoying the feel of the sun on her skin. The air was quiet but for the birds and buzzing bugs. Now that she thought about it, there was a kind of mystical feel to the air. Although she was certain it had more to do with her companion.

She turned and snapped a photo of him. His attention on the view, Frederic didn't notice.

When he was studying something very closely, his focus would grow intense, with all his energy directed at his target. It was more than simply trying to see; it was as if he was trying to see into whatever it was he was looking at. Piper had felt that intensity directed at her more than once. Each time, she'd melted under its strength.

This time she saw a sadness to his stare. She brushed the hair from his face to bring him back. "Trying to find a pagan?" she teased. Seeing the enthusiasm fading from his face had made her heart ache. "You're a million miles away."

"Sorry," he said, giving her a half a smile. "I don't know when I will be back here, so I was trying to memorize the view."

Piper was about to tell him that wasn't necessary because she'd taken pictures when she realized what he was really saying.

"I wasn't thinking," she said softly.

"I have read theories that if you stare at something long enough, the image will become ingrained in your memory. I don't know if blind people can see their memories or not, but in case they can..."

"Is that why you are always looking at the Eiffel Tower?" And at her?

"One of the reasons."

The full force of what lay in his future hit her. It was easy to forget with his matter-of-factness, but there would come a day when he couldn't see the sun or the grass. Not even his own hand. She couldn't imagine. A man who loved visual beauty as much as he did. Who saw beauty in ugly art.

"What are you going to do?" she asked him. "I mean, when..." A sob threatened, and she pushed it back along with the rest of her question.

"Carry on, of course. What else can I do?"

"Nothing, I suppose."

She watched as he plucked at the grass between

them. Tugging blade after blade, only to discard each one atop a small pile of clippings. "Tell you what I won't do," he said. "I won't turn myself into a victim, making the whole world bow to my disability."

Like his father? That was what he meant, wasn't it? He did call his father needy last night.

"I asked him once," Frederic said, switching gears, "when I first learned I might have the disease, what it was like to be blind."

"What did he say?"

"He told me it was awful, and that I would find out for myself soon enough."

"That's it?" No reassurance, no advice? Surely the man wouldn't be so self-involved as to leave his son to face the unknown without some kind of support?

But then parents could be selfish. Hadn't her mother been more interested in everything other than Piper?

"Saying more would require him dealing with his own blindness. My father was more interested in wallowing. And in his cocktails," he added, swiping at the grass clippings. "Did you know I could make the perfect *soixante-quinze* when I was eight years old? That is gin and champagne, if you were wondering."

Piper wasn't. The little boy forced to make them was far more interesting. She wished she could tell him she understood what that was like, that she'd been in his shoes. Oddly enough, however, alcohol abuse wasn't one of her mother's many crimes.

"I can still picture him. Proving you can memorize an image," he added with a toneless laugh. "He had this giant easy chair where he would sit and listen to the stereo. All day long. Every day. He only left the house if my mother took him. I was so relieved when they decided to send me to boarding school, because it meant I wouldn't have to see him in that chair anymore."

Relieved, but guilty, too. Piper could hear the regret in his voice. He'd escaped to school, but his mother had stayed behind.

"I'm sorry," she said. "He must have been in a lot of pain."

"What he was, was a selfish bastard who never should have married my mother in the first place. He knew he was going blind. A real man wouldn't have asked her to stay."

No, he would have lived in the present and made no promises for tomorrow. A chill swept through Piper. "How do you know your mother didn't want to stay?" She already knew his answer from last night; Frederic believed his mother stayed out of guilt.

"How would she know that life would stop the moment my father lost his sight. If you're trying to defend him, you're wasting your time. I lived it. I watched day in and day out while she took care of him. Waited on him, walked with him. She cut his meat, for God's sake, while I..."

Stayed out of the way and made cocktails. No wonder his mother sent him away finally. Just imagining what it had been like for him made Piper's heart ache.

Frederic looked up. "Sometimes I wonder why they ever had a child."

Because once upon a time, they were in love and believed in the future. At least his mother had. Piper longed to tell him that it was okay. That it was okay for him to want more than a moment in the present.

You mean to want you. Tears burning the back of her throat, she rolled onto her side. "I'm glad your father was selfish," she told him. "Because if he hadn't been, we never would have met."

"Then he did something good after all."

The back of his hand caressed her cheekbone. Piper grabbed it and kissed his knuckles. It was her time to memorize for the future. "Thank you for showing me your ugly mural," she said.

"It's not my ugly mural. It belongs to Great Britain."

As far as she was concerned, the painting belonged to him, and she would be forever grateful that he chose her to share it with. Frederic would never know how special being here made her feel. She was beginning to understand the joy the monks must have felt when creating their art. Her heart was suddenly so full she feared it would burst.

She wanted to tell him. But how could she explain without sounding like a lovesick idiot that his sharing this part of himself—that these past few moments of vulnerability—meant everything to her?

There were words, three very huge words that summed up everything in her heart, but she wasn't ready to say them out loud. The feelings were too new, too fresh; now wasn't the time to say them. Piper wasn't sure there would ever be a time.

"I don't care who owns this place," she said. "There's still no place in England I would rather be."

Damn his sunglasses for blocking his eyes. She

couldn't tell if he was happy or frightened by her admission. Halfway committed, there was nothing to do but keep going. "Or anyone else I'd rather be with."

"Piper, you know that I can't give you…I won't be selfish like my father."

"I know." But it broke her heart, too. He was telling her that he planned to live out his blindness alone because his father was a self-absorbed drunk, and he couldn't be more wrong. He could—should—have more. Arguing the point, though, would only break the moment. And in the end, he'd still believe the same way.

Better she go along. At least for now. "Hey…" Reaching for his sunglasses, she pulled them away so she could finally look him in the eye. "You're not blind yet. And I'm right here."

She watched as slowly the gray grew black with desire. "Here, and beautiful."

His palms were warm as they brushed the hair from her eyes. "I never want this picture to fade."

His kiss was slow and possessive. It wrapped around her soul, binding them together. Piper gladly gave herself over. Their surroundings disappeared. It was just them, the birds and the grass. When his hands grew bold, she clutched at his back. When they slipped beneath her shirt, she whimpered. And when the moment was over, and he lay heavy, his breath sounding in her ear, she had to bite back the emotions fighting to get out. Her heart belonged to him. Taking one day at a time had just become impossible.

And she was sunk.

* * *

Later that night, Frederic lay in bed staring at the ceiling. In the pitch-black bedroom, he couldn't see beyond shapes, but that did not matter. His mind was at the abbey. He was reliving the afternoon frame by frame so as to not forget a moment. *Thank you for showing me your ugly mural.*

What an amazing five days. To think, all these months there'd been a treasure living under his roof and he'd had no idea. Piper wasn't like other lovers he'd shared a bed with, and not simply because she was American and from a world different from his. The difference had nothing to do with sophistication or worldliness, although her guilelessness was amazingly erotic.

No, what made her different was the way everything felt magnified when he was with her. Bigger, brighter, stronger. *More.*

If only he'd discovered her gifts sooner. So much time wasted.

Well, he would not waste further. Between now and when Piper returned to Boston, he would show her a time she'd never forget.

When Piper returned to Boston… The thought left a chill. He'd miss her. More than he thought possible. Somehow, over the past five days, she'd slipped under his skin to become someone special.

What was he supposed to do, though? Ask her to stay indefinitely? How fair was that?

No, better to give her a magical few weeks and then set her free. She would move on. Find a man who appreciated her, and he would have a wonderful memory to hold on to when the world grew dark.

Beside him, there was the rustle of sheets as Piper curled her body closer. Sliding one arm across his chest, she rested her head on his shoulder. Automatically, he began stroking her skin, seeking the contact that he could never seem to get enough of. "I thought you were asleep."

"Couldn't. Someone is thinking too loudly. Is everything all right?"

The gentle concern in her voice made his heart seize. For a brief moment, he let himself be wrapped up in her compassion. *If only*, he caught himself thinking.

"That wasn't thinking, that was my stomach," he said. "We missed dinner, you know."

"Whose fault is that?"

"Yours. For being irresistible." He kissed the teasing out of her voice, smiling at the tiny moan she made deep in her throat. "But now I am hungry."

"I can fix that," she whispered against his lips.

"Can you now?" In the back of his mind, he wondered if the hunger he felt for her could ever be completely satisfied. Like everything else, it was greater than he thought possible.

He reached for her, but to his disappointment, she slipped from his grasp. There was more rustling. Clothes. She was getting dressed.

"What are you doing?" he asked when she opened the door. Light from the hallway spilled through the crack into the room.

"Told you," she said. "I'm taking care of your hunger. Be right back."

"I know a better way," he called to her. But she'd already closed the door.

Alone, he went back to contemplating the dark ceiling. His eyes were unusually scratchy and tired tonight. Too much time in the sunlight. He had been overdoing things the past few days. Perhaps he should slow down. Or perhaps not. There would be plenty of time to slow down when he was alone.

He must have lost track of time, because before he realized, the door swung open.

"Voilà!" Piper announced. "Food."

Squinting, Frederic tried to see what Piper held in her hands. With the light behind her, however, all he could see was a hazy silhouette. "We have apples, candy bars and a package of something called McVitie's, which I think are cookies."

"How on earth did you find all this?"

"Mrs. Lester keeps a stash of snacks in the front room in case guests get hungry when the kitchen is closed. I found it when she asked me to restock the cabinet this morning."

"She asked you to restock *and* cook?" Even though she couldn't see him, Frederic grinned. "Should I be worried that Mrs. Lester hired you while I wasn't looking?"

A cellophane-wrapped package landed on the pillow near his head. "Shut up—I was doing her a favor. Can you switch on the nightstand lamp? My hands are full."

"Do you mind if we leave the lights off?" he asked her.

"Why? Are your eyes bothering you?"

Again, the concern in her voice gripped him with a warmth that made him want to hold her tight. "No," he said. "My eyes are fine." A small lie, not that it mattered. His eyes weren't the reason. There was an intimacy to the darkness he wasn't ready to give up.

Sliding out from beneath the covers, he crossed to the window and pulled back the wooden shutters. A beam of soft silver lit the floor by his feet.

"A picnic in the moonlight," Piper remarked as she joined him on the bed. "Romantic."

"I blame the company," he teased. "You inspire the romantic in me."

"You'd be the first." Her voice was soft, barely a whisper. Had there been street traffic or some other kind of outside noise, Frederic would have missed the comment altogether. Realizing he heard her, she quickly added a louder, "Sorry."

"Don't be." If it was up to him, she'd have romance every day. He cursed those idiots at school who were too blind to see her gifts. "Anyone who isn't inspired by you is a fool."

"Eat your snacks," she murmured. Frederic could practically hear the blush darkening her cheeks.

A comfortable silence settled over the room, punctuated only by the occasional sound of cellophane crinkling. This was nice, he thought. Comfortable. A man could become very attached to feeling this way if he wasn't careful. So attached he might not want to let go. Longing sprang to his chest, its strength catching him off guard. *You're going to be very hard to give up, aren't you, Piper?*

Piper's voice drifted from across the bed. "Penny for your thoughts?"

"I was thinking we should make the most out of the next couple months," he replied. "Make them unforgettable."

"I'd like that."

"Good. Why don't we start right now?" Rolling to his side, he kissed her into the pillow.

He woke to his face buried in a pillow and an empty bed. Vaguely, he remembered Piper saying something about cooking with Mrs. Lester. The older woman was definitely taking advantage of having another chef in the house. Looked as if he was going to have to go pry Piper away again. Yawning, he lifted his head.

No...

Something was wrong. While he could see, everything he looked at was hazy and faded, as though someone had wrapped the world with a thin gray film.

Frederic held up his hand. His trembling fingers were five muted shapes. Not even squinting could bring back the sharpness.

He willed himself to take a deep breath. No need to panic yet. His eyes could simply be overtired. God knows, he'd pushed himself very hard the last couple days. Give his eyes a little more rest; that is what he should do. Sleep a little longer. He closed his eyes and focused on his breathing.

An hour later, however, nothing had changed. He was still staring into a haze.

Frederic's heart started to race. He wiped a hand over his face. *Do not jump to conclusions*, he reminded himself.

Making his way to the bathroom, he grabbed his shaving kit and dumped the contents on the vanity. He must have packed eye drops in case his eyes got tired. Slowly, he scanned the items on the counter. Which one was the eye drops? In his new blurry world, all the small bottles looked suspiciously alike. For all he knew, he could squirt his eyes with alcohol. Perhaps Piper…

No. He wasn't going to run to Piper, no matter how appealing the thought might be. The situation wasn't anything he hadn't struggled with before. Inhaling deeply, he looked again. The bottles were color-coordinated. Eye drops were in the green bottle. Where was the green bottle?

On the edge of his bathroom sink at home. He had used them right before they departed. Distracted by thoughts of Piper, he forgot to repack them.

No problem. He would simply go into the village and buy more.

Took some stumbling around the room—the room was foreign and he hadn't exactly been thinking of maintaining order when taking Piper to bed last night—but he finally got dressed. Then, with one hand on the wall, he made his way down the stairs.

His foot was barely on the landing when he nearly collided with a warm, familiar body.

"Whoops! You almost ended up wearing your coffee.

Sorry about that." Piper's voice greeted him, warm and sweet. His first thought was to lean into her until the knot in his stomach went away. "I was going to leave the pot on the nightstand for when you woke up. Guess I was down here longer than I thought."

Her fingers touched his cheek. "I don't think I've ever seen you without a shave. I like the look. Very sexy." She stepped back. "Is everything all right?"

No, he wanted to say. *Your features have been blurred by a film.* The words were on his tongue, and he swallowed them. Piper's voice was still rough with the remnants of last night; he couldn't kill the spell by complaining.

Instead, he focused on her face with all his might, hoping that by sheer will, he could bring it into focus. "I'm fine," he said. "I'm still waking up."

"Well, then go into the dining room and I'll get us some coffee. I told Joan—I mean, Mrs. Lester—I'd make more breakfast potatoes, but I'm sure she won't mind if I back out to eat with you. After all, I am a gues—"

"No, don't." Frederic wasn't ready to navigate breakfast yet. "That is, I need to get something at the apothecary first."

"Do you want me to come with you?"

Yes. Please. "Why don't you help Mrs. Lester? I will be back as soon as I can, and we'll have breakfast then."

"Okay."

He couldn't help himself. He needed contact, to reassure himself everything would be all right. Cupping her face, he kissed her, tasting her as though it were his last taste. *Which is could very well be.*

"Whoa, cowboy," Piper said with a laugh. "You're going to spill the coffee. Go run your errand. We can finish what you started when you get back."

The sun was already bright when Frederic stepped outside. He'd hoped the light would improve things, but no. If anything, the colors were more muted.

He wished he had thought to count the steps yesterday. He remembered turning right and crossing the street at the corner, but after that...

A car horn blared, forcing him back on the curb.

Frederic, you arrogant idiot. This wasn't Paris, where he knew every street with perfect familiarity. This was a strange village in a foreign country. A town made up of identical stone facades that, thanks to the film, blurred into one giant building. He scanned the storefronts looking for a sign that would tell him his location.

"Pardon," he murmured as he bumped a woman's shoulder. "Excuse me," he said when he bumped into another. He couldn't look where he was heading and read the store signs. If he had Piper come with him she could have...

...helped.

Disgusted with himself, he stopped in his tracks.

"Your butter is browning."

Shoot. Piper snatched the frying pan off the burner, but it was too late. The butter was already dark. "Sorry. I lost track of what I was doing."

"You do seem a little out of sorts," the innkeeper replied. She reached over and took the frying pan from

Piper's grip, before gently pushing her backward away from the stove. "I'll tell you what," she said. "You're not in a cooking mood today, so how about I do the potatoes and you finish your coffee and wake up."

Piper didn't really have much choice but to agree. Mrs. Lester was right; her head wasn't into cooking.

"You know..." the innkeeper was saying, "I don't know how they do things at that fancy cooking school of yours, but here in England, we get a good night's rest if we're cooking in the morning." Her lecture came with a twinkling smile. "You new lovers always think you can burn the candle at both ends, don't you?"

"Since I'm not an employee, I'm technically only burning one end," Piper shot back. She pointedly ignored the lovers comment. Was that what she and Frederic were? Lovers? The word sounded so sex-based, and what they shared last night was so much more. It had been for Piper, anyway. Her feelings had shifted while standing on that hill behind the abbey. Just how much, she was still too afraid to say.

It wasn't her late-night activities that were destroying her concentration, however. It was her morning conversation. She couldn't put her finger on why, but something about Frederic was different. He wasn't the same man who reached for her in the middle of the night. Since he stepped outside, Piper had been racking her brain trying to think whether she'd crossed a line and said too much. Maybe her emotions weren't as hidden as she thought. Maybe she was too obvious, and he was worried she wouldn't be able to handle this no-strings relationship they had going on.

That would certainly explain why his kiss felt strangely like goodbye.

On the other hand, maybe she was being a paranoid loon. Frederic was going to a drugstore, for goodness' sake. He probably had a headache.

Meanwhile, Mrs. Lester had taken over cooking duties, giving Piper a silent lesson in bed-and-breakfast cooking.

"Would you like me to sit in the dining room out of your way?" she asked.

"Goodness, no. I like your company. I don't let just anyone in my kitchen, you know." Picking up a nearby cutting board, the woman scraped a pile of diced onions into a heated fry pan. The vegetables crackled, filling the room with aroma. "What were we talking about, anyway?"

"You were giving me your recipe for Cornish pasties."

"Right. Although I'm surprised that someone studying haute cuisine would be interested in making something like hand pies."

"For your information, I happen to like hand pies," Piper shot back.

"I can cook them a lot better than haute cuisine, that's for sure," she added, speaking to the inside of her cup.

"What did you say?"

"Nothing." Now wasn't the time or place to go into her problems with Chef Despelteau. "I'm in a comfort food phase, is all."

"Can't blame you there. I've been in one my whole

life. The mister took me to eat in London on my birthday last year. A couple medallions of beef drowned in
sauce and an itty-bitty dollop of risotto. Seems to me, if
you're going to charge fifty pounds for dinner, a person
shouldn't need a snack when she gets home."

"I totally agree," Piper said. One of her pet peeves
about Chef Despelteau was his emphasis on presenta-
tion instead of serving size. "I was telling Frederic the
other night that sauces are great, but sometimes a steak
should be left a steak." She paused to take a sip of coffee. "Good comfort food isn't all that easy to make, either. Half the time the restaurants try to trendy it up,
and end up getting it all wrong."

"Like up at the Hen & Rooster. That's why I prefer
the old-fashioned pubs. Give me fish and chips any day."

"Same here," Piper said. "Same here."

"Then why are you in that class?" Mrs. Lester asked.

"I beg your pardon?"

The woman shrugged one of her shoulders. "Seems
to me if you don't like fancy foods, you shouldn't be in
some fancy French school. So why are you?"

Why did everyone ask her the same question?

She had only herself to blame this time. She had
opened the door by talking about comfort food.

"Because I want to become a chef, and where better
to learn than in Paris?" Her answer sounded flat even
to her this time. She was tired. Frederic kept her up
half the night. Plus, she was tired of justifying herself.

Justifying yourself or justifying to yourself?

"Well, I suppose if you want the prestige…"

At Mrs. Lester's comment, she shook off the strange

thought. "Of course English cooking is pretty awesome, too." She didn't mean to hurt the woman's feelings. "That's why I want to make Cornish pasties."

"Mine do get a lot of compliments," Mrs. Lester said, smiling. "But so you know, Cornish pasties are Welsh, not English. You don't want to be messing up the two."

"Yes, ma'am."

Just then, the front doorbell rang, signaling an arrival. "I'll get that," she told Mrs. Lester. "It's probably Frederic back from his walk." At least she hoped so. His odd goodbye continued to plague her. "Would you mind writing down your recipe so I can take it back with me?"

"Of course I can," Mrs. Lester replied. "Soon as I finish breakfast, I'll do it. Oh, and if that is a guest, let them know the rooms don't turn over until after twelve. They can leave their luggage in the tea room."

"Will do." Piper had to laugh. Apparently, over the weekend she'd become an employee, only no one told her.

It was Frederic, all right. He stood at the base of the stairs, staring down at his shoes. As lost and distant as she had ever seen him.

Don't overreact. There could be lots of reasons why he didn't go to the kitchen himself.

"Did you get what you needed from the store?" she asked him.

"No. I didn't go."

He didn't? Where had he been, then? As she stepped closer, Piper saw his hand had the banister in a vise grip. His was squeezing the wood so hard his knuckles were white.

"I've got a headache," he said. "I'm going to lie down."

"I'll go with you." She hurried to catch up with him, her fingers brushing his elbow as she reached the bottom step.

Frederic stiffened at her touch. "No," he told her. "I don't need anyone keeping me company." With one hand on the wall and one hand on the rail, he walked slowly upstairs.

Her stomach felt as if it had been kicked.

Pushing her fear aside, she headed upstairs to find out what happened.

She found Frederic sitting on the edge of the unmade bed, staring into space. His head didn't so much as turn when she closed the door. "I thought you were going to lie down."

"I changed my mind."

"Would you like me to see if Mrs. Lester has any aspirin?"

"No, thank you. I will be fine."

The change in his voice frightened her. Last night's warmth had disappeared in favor of a tone so polite and distant it hurt her ears. She hadn't heard him use that voice since the days when she first started work. Back when they'd been strangers.

Where was the man who was whispering sweet nothings in the dark a few hours ago? She raced through everything they said and did yesterday, wondering what could have happened to make him disappear so abruptly.

Oh, no... Not that. It hadn't even been twenty-four hours...

"It's your eyes, isn't it?"

Frederic stood up, only to stand stock-still, as if he wasn't sure where to go. "Yes."

"Oh, Frederic." It wasn't fair. She hugged him from behind, holding him as tightly as possible. Letting him know best she could that he wasn't alone, and that he could lean on her in any way he needed to. Frederic's body was rigid. Even with their bodies pressed together, it felt as if he were a million miles away. He was in shock. Who could blame him? Even the most prepared man would need time to adjust.

"Everything will be all right," she told him. Ignoring the hairs rising on the back of her neck, she kissed his shoulder blade. "I'm here, and I'll do whatever you need me to do."

For a moment, she felt Frederic's body relax as he leaned against her. Before the moment could take hold, however, he stepped away, leaving her standing alone at the foot of the bed.

"I have to pack," he said. "Can you let Mrs. Lester know we're checking out?"

It couldn't have sounded more like she was being dismissed if he had tried.

CHAPTER NINE

IT WAS LATE when they returned to Paris. Frederic called ahead to his doctor, and the man met them at the hospital. To run tests, he said. Personally Frederic thought it a waste of time. What would a battery of tests show that his eyes couldn't tell him already?

Now that the shock had time to wear off, he was coming to terms with his new reality: his vision had deteriorated again, and while he wasn't completely blind, he was much, much closer. The translucent film draping his view wasn't going away. He would never see sharply again. Only a matter of time before he woke up and his sight was gone forever.

He always knew this day would come—the day he moved another step closer to blindness. His eyes getting worse had always been a matter of when, not if. He only hoped to have more time. With Piper, that is.

Frederic closed his eyes. After the catastrophe in the village, he had managed to rally fairly well. Until Saint Pancras station with its crowds and low lighting. The confusion made his head pound. If not for Piper playing guide dog... *Watch your step. Turn left. Wait here.*

Her voice echoed in his ear, steady and soft. Like the woman herself. A calm in his storm.

It was so easy to hand over control. Terrifyingly so. More terrifying was the security he felt when she linked her arm with his. He followed her lead with complete trust, knowing that if something went wrong, she would be by his side.

Finally, after all these years, he understood how his father had become so needy. Surrendering control—the peace that came from surrendering control, that is—was addictive. Why not let someone else carry the burden, especially when they offered things like goodness and light in return?

He couldn't do that to Piper. Life had dragged her down enough.

At least he would always have yesterday at the abbey.

The sound of sandals flapping caused his pulse to speed up. He already knew the sound of her walk, he thought dejectedly. So much for his goal of a quick, unencumbered affair.

The curtain drew back. "You've got to love Paris. The hospital cafeteria has better pastries than most American bakeries. I brought you a croissant. Do you want it in front of you or…?"

"Leave it on the side table."

"Are you sure? You haven't eaten all day."

"I think I would know if I was hungry." The words came out far sharper than he meant. She had no idea her kindness made things worse. "I'm sorry," he said. "I didn't mean…"

"You've had a long day."

"So have you."

"I'll live."

"It's late. You should go back to the house."

"Not so late," she said, pulling one of the plastic chairs closer to the bed. The metal legs scraped against the floor with a loud *squeak*. "At some point, Dr. Doucette will release you, and we'll go home together."

The idea of the two of them as a team left Frederic warm all over. Another warning bell. "I'd rather you left now. I'll have Michel drive me home later."

"Don't be silly. I'm sure Dr. Doucette will be here very soon."

"Piper, I want you to go." This time, he didn't mince words.

There was no mistaking Piper's confusion. "You don't want me here?"

Exactly the opposite. Frederic wanted her by his side so badly it hurt. "I think it would be a good idea if you left," he told her.

"I see."

For several minutes, she stared at the floor. Frederic assumed she was angry, and after she'd taken a couple long, clearing breaths, she would leave. Thus, when her hand settled over his, he started. "You're not alone," she said. "You know that, right?"

That was the whole point. He wasn't, but if he was any kind of decent human being, he would be. He should have never pursued her in the first place. But no, he'd been selfish, thinking with his desire, not with his head. Warmth spread up Frederic's arm, mocking his already-aching heart. If he let her stay, he would lean on her. And lean, and lean and lean.

He would never let her go.

"Please go, Piper. You are not obligated to stay here." Painful as it was, he tried to pull his fingers free of her grip. She surprised him by holding on with ferocity, as though she was the person leaning on him.

"Yes, I am," she said. "I know we haven't been together very long, but I…"

"Don't." He didn't want her to say something that couldn't be forgotten. A sentiment that would make the inevitable that much harder.

Forcing his voice to stay as even as possible, he said the words that really needed to be said. "We had a good time together, but we both knew from the start that this was a short-term relationship. No promises."

"No strings. Thanks for reminding me." At last, she yanked her hand free, the loss of contact traveling straight to his chest. "Funny how you decided tonight is the perfect night to cut me loose. Here I thought that after last night… What happened to having an unforgettable couple of months?"

Frederic dropped his gaze to the sheet. Ironic that even with his deteriorated vision, he couldn't look her in the eye. He knew that even the gauzy haze couldn't obliterate the hurt he would see there. "Last night we were both carried away. Now that I have had a chance to think clearly, I've come to realize that the longer we continue this affair, the harder goodbye will be. We should make things easy by ending it while we both have happy memories."

"Easy on who? Me or you?"

"Both of us."

She let out a derisive snort. "Right."

The chair legs scraped across the linoleum as she stood up. Her sandals made angry slaps as she paced the floor. "Tell me something, Frederic. Would you have come to this decision if you hadn't woken up this morning with your eye problem?"

Denying the truth would only insult her. "No."

"I didn't think so. Honestly, do you think I care that your eyes got worse?"

"I care." And while she might not now, she would come to resent it, and by extension, him. "I would rather you remember me fondly."

"No problem. Dumping me is the perfect way to do that."

"Better I dump you than drag you down."

"Drag me…? Is that what you think would happen?"

It was what he *knew* would happen. Last night he had promised her romance. "It's not very romantic if your lover can't see."

"Except as you've pointed out many times, you can."

"But at some point I won't. Today was a reminder of that fact. That is why we would be smart to end things now. Before either of us gets too attached." He refused to listen to the voice telling him it was too late.

"What if I don't want to? End it, that is."

Frederic sighed. *Stubborn woman.* He accepted that this was the way it was supposed to be; why couldn't she?

His eyes searched the room until he found her standing near the foot of his bed. Staring straight at her, he spoke with great deliberation, to make sure she understood. "You don't have a choice. This is for the best."

"Says you."

She didn't move. She stood at the foot of the bed, with her eyes bearing down on him. Frederic could feel their wounded glare. "You're wrong, you know. You wouldn't drag me down."

You say that now... "I have no doubt my mother said the same thing to my father." And look how well that turned out. A woman so broken from taking care of the man, she wasn't able to live a life for herself. A son who grew up never respecting the man who fathered him. "I'm not going to be selfish enough to make the same mistake." Not with Piper or anyone else.

"Even though you can see, and I'm scheduled to go back to Boston in a couple months."

They both knew if their affair continued, he wouldn't be able to let her return to Boston. The feelings between them were already deeper than a mere affair. "Even though," he replied.

Through his haze, he saw that Piper was trembling; she was fighting to keep herself from crying. Keeping her pride. Admiration swelled in his chest, along with deeper, unmentionable emotions. Someday she would thank him.

"You deserve nothing but the best, Piper." He meant every blessed word.

"Go to hell."

Frederic listened to the slap of her sandals until he couldn't hear them anymore before giving in to the frustration gnawing at his insides and punching at the bed as hard as he could. As moments went, this was not his finest.

I did the right thing. What would prolonging the affair do other than make the pain of saying goodbye worse? At least this way, her heart wasn't so damaged it wouldn't heal. She would meet someone else, a man who wouldn't grow to need her quite so much.

Dammit! His chest felt as if someone had torn it open. Who knew you could fall so hard so fast?

He should have. He should have realized it the other night in his kitchen when his body was on fire and his head was warning him that Piper wasn't like other women. All he could do was dream of making love to her. This... He punched the bed again, this time hitting the side rail so hard it rattled. This was his punishment for being selfish.

At least he would have a lifetime of solitude to get over his mistake.

"Is everything all right?" A nurse suddenly appeared in the doorway from which Piper just left. "Monsieur, do you need anything?"

Frederic stared blankly at the space across the room. "No," he replied. "I don't need anything."

Better to break things off before either of us becomes too attached, Frederic had said.

Too late. Piper made it as far as the taxi before giving in to her tears. The driver stared at her through his rearview mirror as tears streamed down her face.

"Mademoiselle?" he asked in a soft voice. "Are you all right?"

"Fine," she replied, sniffling.

A moment later, the safety glass slid back and he handed her a tissue through the opening. Seeing it reminded her of how Frederic offered her a paper towel, and she burst into a fresh batch. "Thank you," she managed to choke out between sniffs.

Damn Frederic Lafontaine. Why couldn't he have left her alone and miserable? Why did he have to decide to get involved in her art search and make her fall for him? Now instead of lonely and miserable, she was brokenhearted and miserable.

Here she thought living in Paris couldn't feel worse.

She blew her nose. Frederic was wrong, too. Two days, eight weeks—the length of their affair didn't matter because she had already fallen in deep. What she felt for him went way beyond lust or romantic fantasy. She loved him. With all her soul. Blind, sighted, purple, green, two-headed...none of that mattered. The part she loved was inside. The tender, intelligent man who loved art and history, and who made her feel as though she could do anything.

Stupid her, she thought Frederic felt the same. Really stupid her, she still thought it.

Surely she didn't imagine the feelings between them last night. Frederic said himself that they would still be together had his eyes not gotten worse this morning.

All because of his parents. Why was it that parents always screwed things up for their kids? Her mom's leaving Patience and her to survive on their own. Frederic's parents' making him think his disease was better suffered alone. If Frederic's parents were alive, she'd kill them for turning their son into a self-sacrificing idiot. Why couldn't he see that he wasn't like his father? The Frederic she knew was far too strong to let blindness beat him, if and when he finally lost his sight.

So what now? Suck it up and soldier on as she always did? How was she supposed to go back to being Frederic's housekeeper after the last two days? Simply being in the same room as him made her pulse race. No way could she live in the same house.

She'd have to move out, she realized, letting out a sigh. Move out and find some place cheap to finish out the term. Great. Twenty-four hours ago she was wrapped in Frederic's arms, listening to him sleep and dreaming of the days ahead. Now she was on the brink of homelessness with nothing to look forward to but days filled with being lectured by Chef Despelteau.

She wished she'd never come to Paris.

Who was she kidding? If she hadn't come to Paris, she wouldn't have met Frederic, and lousy as she felt, she wouldn't have traded the past five days for anything.

Then fight for them. Patience's voice was loud in her head. *Figure out a way to fix the situation.*

Her sister was right. Wasn't the whole point of coming to Paris so that she could achieve her dreams? Frederic was part of those dreams now.

She wasn't walking away without a fight.

CHAPTER TEN

SHE WAS IN the kitchen waiting on a pan of brownies when Frederic finally returned home. "What are you doing?" he asked.

The day had been hard on him. His face was pale and drawn, with dark circles under his eyes. She moved to take him in her arms, then stopped. Any compassion she offered would only get rejected.

She returned to the sink and the bowl she was washing out. "Making brownies. They'll be ready in a few minutes if you want to wait."

"I wasn't expecting you to be here."

"Where else would I be? This is my job. Unless I'm fired, too," she added, turning the bowl upside down.

From behind her, she heard him let out a long sigh. "Why would you want to stay?"

For you. "Because I've already done homeless once in my life. I don't feel like doing it again."

"I wouldn't let that happen. I'll pay for you to stay at a hotel or find a new apartment."

"Would you find me a new job, too?"

"We would find some kind of arrangement."

"Wonderful. In other words, you'll pay me to stay away." The oven timer rang. "If it's all the same to you, I'll finish out my contract here," she said, reaching for the oven mitt.

"I know what you're doing," he said. "Staying won't make me change my mind."

"Then it shouldn't be a problem for you." Dropping the pan of brownies on the cooling rack, she waited for him to mount a new argument. Dared him to.

"It won't work," he said. "I'm going to bed. Dr. Doucette wants to meet with me before I go to the university."

"What for?" Did something show up in the tests they ran today?

"To fit me for a white cane, I presume. He mentioned something about transition lessons. I won't need breakfast."

The last part meant to remind her she was back to being a housekeeper. Very well, she'd let him have his way tonight. She sighed. "Yes, sir."

As it turned out, Frederic found a reason to not need breakfast or dinner the next two days. For all she saw of him, he might have been the one who took a room at a hotel. Not that he ignored her. No, he talked to her when their paths crossed. Politely worded requests about laundry and other household business. In other words, they'd turned back the clock to when she was simply his housekeeper.

On the third morning, she found him asleep in his chair.

He must have come home very late. She'd waited until well after midnight before going to her rooms.

For a few minutes, Piper contented herself with simply watching him sleep. Kind of on the obsessive side, she knew, but she couldn't help herself. She hadn't had a good look at his face in two days, and she needed to see how he was doing.

In England, she had noticed how Frederic's features would relax while sleeping. His lips would part in a smile as if he was dreaming happy thoughts. There was no smile today. His face was drawn tight. "You foolish man," she whispered. "We could be sleeping together."

A lock of his hair hung over his eye. She brushed it aside, letting her fingers linger on his face. Felt so wonderful to touch him again. It might have been only two days, but it seemed like an eternity.

Frederic stirred. "Mmm, nice," he said in a drowsy voice.

This was the Frederic she knew in England. Stuck between sleep and consciousness, he hadn't raised his defenses yet. Piper's heart ached for his reappearance. "You fell asleep in the chair again."

"I was watching the tower."

With his eyes still closed, he curved into her touch, catching her hand in his and pressing a kiss to the palm. Piper gave a soft sigh. *I missed you.*

His eyes fluttered open. The defenses returned. "Piper…"

She lifted her hand away, but it didn't matter. The moment was there, between them. Frederic could protest all he wanted, but it was clear that the feelings they discovered in England weren't about to go away.

"Nothing's changed," he said, pushing to his feet.

"I can tell," Piper replied.

"That's not what I meant, and you know it." She watched as he stalked his way to his favorite window. He stood with his hands pressed against the molding, the muscles in his shoulders playing beneath his jacket as he attempted to push the wooden frame apart. "This isn't going to work," he said. "You staying here. Let me…"

"Find a hotel? No, thanks."

"For God's sake," he said, spinning around to face her again. "Why are you being so stubborn?"

"Why are you?"

When he didn't answer, Piper stepped closer. "Tell you what." She kept her eyes locked with his, so he would be sure to see the determination on her face. "I will leave if you can honestly tell me you don't care about me as much as I care about you."

Frederic looked away. "You know I can't." Piper's heart skipped a beat.

"But," he said, raising his eyes again, "that doesn't mean we have a future. Not even a short-term one. I can't."

Good Lord, but she was tired of hearing the word *can't*. He most definitely could, if he let himself. "What are you so scared of?"

"I'm not scared of anything."

"Liar. I think you're terrified. You're afraid of the day you wake up and can't see anymore."

"That's where you're wrong. I've been expecting to go blind since I was fifteen years old. I know exactly how my life will play out."

"And how is that?" she challenged.

"Alone."

He said the word with such finality, it ripped her insides in two. Did he really believe that he was meant to be by himself for the rest of his days? How could one man be so incredibly wrong?

"It doesn't have to be that way," she said.

"Yes, it does. I've known that since I was fifteen years old, too. I will never turn the life of the person I... I care about upside down the way my father did ours."

"Even if the person is willing to take the risk?" She touched his wrist, offering.

"It's always easy to be willing at the beginning. It becomes obligation."

"Not necessarily."

"Says the woman who is attending a school she hates because she owes her sister."

Piper stepped back. "That's not true."

"Isn't it?" Frederic asked. "Then tell me when the last time was that you enjoyed cooking?"

When she made him pot roast.

"Do you even like French food?"

"What does that matter?" she countered. "People cook things they don't like all the time." Why were they talking about school all of a sudden, anyway? This wasn't about her.

Narrowing his eyes, Frederic stared down at her with so much intensity it made her insides squirm. "The other night you asked me 'what if' to prove your point, remember? Now it is my turn. What if Patience hadn't been so excited about you going to Paris? What if she hadn't sacrificed so much? Would you still be here?"

"I..." She couldn't say the answer aloud.

"That's what I thought. You're so determined to give back to your sister. Have you ever asked if she cared what you did for a living?"

"She sacrificed for me to be here."

"No, she sacrificed for you to have a *good life*. You were the one who decided that meant being a French chef."

"Not true." France was both their dreams. Hers and Patience's. Frederic was using this as an excuse.

"You can keep telling yourself that all you want, but I will not be another person to whom you feel obligated."

"For crying out loud, Frederic, *I'm not your mother. Don't treat me like I am.*" It was the only argument she had left.

Like all her other arguments, it fell on deaf ears. "Finish your school and go home, Piper," he said as he brushed past her.

Piper gnawed the inside of her cheek as she watched him make his way to the staircase. How dare he twist her argument against her? Cooking school was an entirely different situation. For starters, she and Patience dreamed this dream together, meaning it was 50 percent her sister's. Maybe 60 percent. Or 70.

Stupid "what-if" games. Sinking into the chair, she threw her head back to stare at the ceiling. Maybe she was sticking it out because of Patience. If she hadn't, though, she never would have started her affair with Frederic. And wanting to be with him was 100 percent her idea. There wasn't a drop of obligation involved.

Of course, she could see how that might be hard to believe. Why would he think she was sticking with him by choice if her Paris track record said otherwise?

What should she do now? Maybe Patience…

She stopped halfway to her pocket. No. The solution had to be her own. Besides, there was nothing Patience could say that Piper hadn't heard a hundred times before. *Go for your dreams. You can do anything. I just want you to be happy.*

Happy.

That had always been her sister's dream: for Piper to be happy. *So long as you're happy, then it's all worthwhile*, she used to say whenever Piper felt guilty.

She wasn't happy in culinary school. *Face it, Piper, you'd rather be cooking mac and cheese instead of foie gras.*

Was it any wonder her assignments were uninspired? She didn't love making them the way she loved making good old-fashioned comfort food. If she wanted to be brutally honest, she'd been going through the motions the past couple months. Frederic was right; she might have come to Paris on her own, but she'd stayed out of obligation to her sister. Patience would smack her if she knew.

Suddenly Piper was very disgusted with herself.

But it wasn't the same when it came to Frederic. Being with him, being needed by him, could never be an obligation. She didn't fall in love with his ability to see. She fell in love with the man who accepted his blindness and survived anyway.

How could she make him see that they weren't doomed to repeat his parents' mistakes?

The first step would be to get her own life in order.

"Leave?" Chef Despelteau said. "There are only eight weeks left in the program."

"I know," Piper replied. "Trust me, this wasn't an easy decision."

That wasn't true. Actually, the decision had been very easy, once she thought everything through.

The best way to thank Patience wasn't struggling to become something she wasn't simply because she was afraid she would let down Patience. In fact, just the opposite. She was letting Patience down by being so unhappy. If she wanted to truly thank her sister, she should create a life she loved. Cooking would be part of that dream. Just not French cooking.

"I've decided to take my cooking in a different direction," she told Chef Despelteau.

"I am very sorry to hear that. You had the potential to be a great French chef."

Piper smiled. His attempt at sincerity was uninspired.

She left his office feeling a hundred pounds lighter. Now if she could only get through to Frederic, then she would be truly happy.

Frederic was there when she returned home. He was standing by his window as usual. Something about it felt off, though. It didn't take long for her to realize what. Propped against the wall was a white-and-red cane. "Dr. Doucette wants me to use it when I'm walking around the city to avoid accidents," he said when she asked about it. He didn't say anything further.

Leaving the floor open for her announcement. "I quit culinary school."

Frederic turned away from the window to look at her. "You what?"

"You were right," she told him. "The only reason I was staying was because I thought I owed Patience. I realized that was wrong. She would never want me to do something that made me miserable out of obligation. She would want me to choose what made me happy."

"Oh."

That was it? She thought he would show a little more reaction. Maybe not jump up and down, but something more than a flat monosyllable.

"I assume that means you'll be leaving for home soon, then," he said. There was a strange note to his voice that Piper couldn't decide was disappointment or relief.

She certainly knew the emotion deadening her stomach. "No, I'm not leaving," she said. "Don't you understand? I quit because I know the difference between doing something for obligation and choosing something I want to do. *I know the difference.*

"I also know what makes me happy." What she wanted to say next was important. She cupped his face in her hands, so he had no choice but to look her in the eye. "You make me happy, Frederic. For months I was miserable. I hated Paris—I hated school. Then you shoved a paper towel in front of my face and everything changed. I wasn't miserable anymore."

"Piper—"

"Let me finish. Do you know what made me so happy? It wasn't dancing by the river or a whirlwind trip to the English countryside. It wasn't just physical, either. It was sitting next to you on the train and listening to you complain that England had terrible coffee. It was hearing you explain why you loved that God-awful mural. It was being with you. You were all I needed to make Paris worthwhile."

She could see his defenses crumbling. The cracks showed in his eyes. "Everyone feels that way at the start of a new romance," he said. "You'll get over it."

"I don't want to get over it. I don't want to get over you. I'm falling in love with you."

She kissed him, letting her lips do the rest of the talking for her, and for a moment, as he kissed her back, everything slid back into place. *Say you don't love me back, Frederic. I dare you.*

His hands reached up to cover hers and gently pulled them away. "Then walk away," he whispered. "Don't let me drain you dry."

"Damn you!" Damn him *and* his parents. She shoved at his chest, then shoved again. "I am so sick of your dumbass self-sacrificing. For what? Because your parents had a bad marriage? Because your dad was a needy jerk? Did you ever stop to think that maybe it wasn't helping your father that burned your mother out, it was his constantly feeling sorry for himself? News flash Frederic. You're acting as badly as he ever did."

"I am not my father."

"Oh, that's right. You're not going to drag anyone down with you. No, you'll just shove aside anyone who cares about you. To hell with what they want."

Frederic didn't answer. He looked past her, to the tower, his expression more distant than ever. They were back where they began. Two people, separate and alone.

Piper was done. What fight she had left disappeared as soon as she saw his expression. Some situations couldn't be fixed, no matter how hard you tried.

"I'm going to Gloucestershire," she told him. The backup plan she hoped to never use. "Mrs. Lester said I was welcome to come and cook any time I wanted— I'm going to take her up on the offer. I'll be packed and out of here by the end of the day."

Halfway across the room, she paused, unable to help one parting shot.

"There's a difference between needing help and self-pity, you know. Too bad you're too blind to see it. But then, maybe you're too blind to see a lot of things."

Leaving him to his solitude, she went to her room and packed. Frederic never came to say goodbye. She didn't expect him to.

The Eiffel Tower greeted her as she stepped onto the sidewalk. Tall and gray, it would forever be her symbol of Paris. A reminder of both the best and worst of her time in this city. Taking out her cell phone, she took one last picture.

And said goodbye.

* * *

Time, Frederic decided, was playing tricks on him. When he was with Piper, time whipped by. Their few days together were over before he realized. So how was it the forty-eight hours since Piper moved out had stretched endlessly?

Oh, he was busy enough. He had his classes to teach, and classes to take. The life transition classes Dr. Doucette suggested. There were the social and professional obligations that kept him out until late at night. His eyesight might have dropped another notch, but his lifestyle hadn't missed a beat. There was only one problem: he missed Piper.

At night, he would lie in bed and remember the afternoon at the abbey. The way her eyes had looked so blue as he hovered above her. Frederic cherished the memory. It had been his last day of clear sight, and life had blessed him with a wonderful view. Funny, he always thought the visual memory he'd long for most would be some piece of art. Or the tower, perhaps. His trusty friend, whose lights twinkled invitingly, albeit a little hazier now.

No. It was the memory of Piper's eyes that he prayed he'd never forget. He wouldn't trade the memory of her eyes for a thousand Eiffel Towers.

God, he missed her. Breathing hurt without her. The air was too thin, and his shirt collars were always strangling him. He missed her voice. He missed her smell. He missed her touch. And who did he have to blame? No one but himself.

Thanks to him, she was in a completely different

country, charming the locals with her bright smile. He bet she was making plans for her return to America right now, too. All because he was afraid she would bail when things got hard.

You fool. He could have had Piper in his life for as long as she'd have him. Instead, he didn't have her at all.

There's a difference between needing help and self-pity, Piper told him. His father had needed *so* much. He remembered when he was a kid, wanting to go to the tower, but his father had refused because of the crowds. *I can't handle all those people*, he'd said. And so Frederic had gone with the nanny while his mother stayed home, because his father didn't want to be alone. The man couldn't handle being by himself any more than he could handle being with people.

Was there ever a day when his father didn't remind them he couldn't see? How many family events did they miss? How many holidays had to be rearranged? His father wore his blindness like a shield and demanded that it—no, *he*—be acknowledged at every turn.

Had Frederic done the same? Was his insistence on bearing the burden alone a different version of the same self-absorption?

Exhaling long and slow, he closed his eyes. His brain still believed breaking up with Piper was the right thing to do. His heart, on the other hand, needed her. He'd tried listening to his brain, and as a result, he was sitting in a giant house by himself while his heart threatened to break in half.

It didn't have to be this way. He could go to England.

Then what? Beg her to come back, and risk her falling out of love with him?

Better to risk than to live as he had the last forty-eight hours. Piper made the days worthwhile. Without her, they were simply days.

It was time he listened to his heart.

"So I said to myself, why are you playing hardball? There is no reason why you should be hangin' on to that gorgeous painting when Ana Duchenko is in Boston, heartbroken and alone. You can tell her nephew I am more than willing to sell."

Digging into the paper bag he set on the table earlier, John Allen pulled out a blueberry scone. Immediately, Mrs. Lester scoffed. "I'll have you know, there's a perfectly good scone right here."

"I'm sure you make a wonderful scone, but these are gluten-free. I make them with my own flour mix. Try one."

The innkeeper pinched a bite from the pastry on his plate. "Not bad," she said, chewing slowly. "Not as good as mine, but not bad. Do you want to try some, Piper? Piper?"

"Huh?" Piper looked up from her coffee to find John and Mrs. Lester staring at her.

"Sorry," Piper said. "I'm trying to concentrate, but my head doesn't want to cooperate." It was too busy thinking about a stubborn idiot who didn't—no who *couldn't*—love her.

"Still out of sorts, are ya?"

"Afraid so." She was beginning to think she would

be out of sorts forever. "Maybe I should have stayed in Paris."

"And do what?" the older woman asked. "Finish at that snooty cooking school?"

"No. Chef Despelteau and I parted ways for good." Quitting school was the one decision Piper didn't regret. Frederic was right; Patience didn't care whether she stayed enrolled or not. On her way out of Paris, Piper had texted her sister and asked that very question.

All I've ever cared about is you being happy, whatever you decide to do, her sister had texted back. *Is everything okay?*

Piper gave her one last lie and said everything was fine. This time it wasn't to appease her sister, but to avoid feeling worse. Her sister and Stuart had repaired their relationship and were in a serious honeymoon phase. Piper was afraid hearing the happiness in her sister's voice would cause her to break down.

"I don't think it's the school she's missing," John said.

"I keep thinking if I stayed in Paris, I might have been able to convince Frederic he was being a stubborn idiot." She couldn't believe how much she loved him after such a short time.

"People gotta work out their demons for themselves," Mrs. Lester said. "You stickin' around waiting on him won't make the process go any faster."

"True." In a way, staying where she wasn't wanted would be as bad as staying out of obligation.

Staying with Mrs. Lester might have been a mistake as well. Everywhere she looked she saw some kind of reminder of the weekend she spent with Frederic. Even the damn kitchen wasn't safe. Nights were worse. She lay in bed reliving the ones they had shared.

"Why don't you come stay with me?" John said when Mrs. Lester went to answer the front doorbell. "We could experiment with grain-free recipes."

Piper smiled. "You are a very sweet man, Mr. Allen, but I think I'm better off staying here." Perverse as it was.

"For the last time, call me John, and if you change your mind, the offer will always be there. It's the least I can do for a fellow Ana lover."

Just then, Mrs. Lester called from the front hallway. "Piper? Could you come here a minute, dear? I need you for something."

"Coming, Mrs. Lester."

She found the innkeeper standing at the base of the stairs waiting for her. The older woman had the oddest expression on her face. "Is something wrong?" she asked.

"You tell me," Mrs. Lester replied, nodding her head toward the entryway.

Piper gasped. "Frederic?"

She couldn't believe her eyes. Was he really standing in Mrs. Lester's doorway?

At the sound of her voice, he took off his sunglasses. Piper saw that his hand was trembling. He looked as bad as she felt, with circles turning his eyes dark and gloomy.

"What are you doing here?" she asked.

"You were right," he said. "I *was* blind."

"You were?" She had to ask to make sure she wasn't dreaming. When she walked out of his house, she was certain she would never see Frederic again. Now he was here, and echoing the words she left behind... It was all too unreal.

Frederic stepped closer, stopping just short of her arms. "I thought the only way I could avoid being like my father was to shut myself off. If I didn't need anyone, then I couldn't drive them away. I didn't see that..." He let out a breath. "I thought I was protecting you. Instead I was doing exactly what I swore I would never do. And that was drive the woman I love away."

"Do you mean that?" Out of the corner of her eye, she saw Mrs. Lester disappearing into the kitchen to give them privacy. It was just her, Frederic and the declaration he made.

"That I love you? More than I thought possible. And I was an idiot for pushing you away. You are the best thing that has ever happened to me, Piper. I never should have let you walk out the door. Can you ever forgive me?"

"I..." She wanted to laugh and cry at the same time. Could she forgive him? "You put me through hell," she reminded him.

"I know, love. And I understand if you can't forgive me. I took too long to come to my senses." He lowered his head. "Perhaps if I hadn't been so stubborn..."

"I can't believe you came to England," Piper said. She wasn't quite ready to forgive him, but she also didn't want him to leave.

"I would have gone twice as far. I had to come. I had to let you know that while I don't deserve your forgiveness—not for one second—I...I need you."

That was all she needed to hear. Before he could say another word, Piper was in his arms, lost to the warmth of his embrace.

"I missed you so much," he whispered against her cheek. "My world was dark without you. Please, please tell me you forgive me."

"I forgive you," she whispered back. She had to squeeze her eyes shut to keep the tears back.

Frederic's eyes were as wet as hers. "There's a lot we have to work out. Being with a blind man isn't going to be easy."

"I know."

"There might be days when the frustration gets to me, and I become a selfish boor."

It wasn't funny, but Piper had to laugh. "You mean more so than these past few days?"

"I only want to make you happy."

"Then..." She took his hand. "Then be strong enough to let me help you. Don't push me away."

"Never again," he said. "But you have to promise that if you are ever unhappy..."

"I will let you know, and we'll work on a solution together."

"I love you, Piper Rush, and I want...no, I *need* you by my side." Cradling her face, he kissed her, a kiss so much like the one they shared at the abbey, and Piper gave up battling the tears.

"Please don't cry, love," he said, wiping at the dampness. "This is a happy time. Besides, I don't have a handkerchief."

"Maybe we can steal a paper towel from Mrs. Lester," she said with a laugh. It felt good to feel light again after all these days. She sniffed back as many tears as she could. "And I am happy. More than you can imagine."

Frederic looked wonderful in his tuxedo. He balked at renting one at first, but Piper insisted. *If I'm wearing a gown, then you're wearing a tuxedo*, she told him. After all, the man was born to wear black tie. Especially for his wedding.

It wasn't a real wedding ceremony. Two weeks was way too soon for any kind of official ceremony, especially when neither of them knew what the future held. Frederic had a lot of adjustment ahead of him. Preparing for a sightless future. And Piper needed to figure out what she wanted to do with her life now that she'd parted ways with French cooking. She and Mrs. Lester had talked about maybe opening a small bistro in Paris specializing in classic comfort food. There would be plenty of expatriates looking for a home-cooked meal.

One thing she was certain of, though, was that Frederic owned her heart and that, when the time came, she would be thrilled to make their commitment legal. In the meantime, she was more than happy with being his makeshift bride.

They "married" themselves in the field behind the abbey. Frederic's idea. "I want to watch you walk down the aisle," he said. "In case…" He didn't need to finish his reason why.

Frederic held her hands in his. "I promise to never push you away again," he said. "I will accept your help, and I will never let you lose yourself."

"And I promise to never act out of obligation," Piper replied. "Whatever happens in the future, we will face it together."

She smiled a watery smile at the man she planned on loving forever. Funny how things worked out. She came to Paris with one dream and found another. One that was far better. As for the future…they would simply have to figure it out as they went along. Time was theirs to make what they wanted. So long as she and Frederic stood together, they would be fine. More than fine. She'd be happier than she'd ever imagined.

And to think it all started with Ana's missing portrait.

"Oh, no!" The exclamation burst from her mouth, disrupting the moment and turning Frederic pale.

"What's wrong, love?"

"I never called Patience. With everything going on between the two of us… It's been almost two weeks since I've talked to her." Her sister hadn't called her, either, a point she would make if Patience complained. "She has no idea what's going on." She held out her hand. "Can I borrow your cell phone?"

"Married for two minutes, and already you are pushing me aside for your sister? I have not even kissed the bride."

Piper kissed him long and slow, a promise of what was to come. When they finally broke apart, she rested her forehead against his. "That better?"

"Perfect."

"Good. Give me your phone." She was grinning from ear to ear. "Patience! Did I wake you? I've got good news and I've got more good news. The good news is we found Ana's portrait and the owner's willing to talk to Stuart about selling." Legs bouncing, she waited impatiently for her sister to relay the news. Frederic laughed and kissed her forehead.

Finally, Patience's voice came back on the line. "You said there's more good news. What is it?"

"I got married!" she exclaimed.

And, holding her husband's hand, she filled her sister in on her happy ending.

Christmas Day

Ana knew something was up from all the looks Patience and her nephew exchanged during Christmas dinner. Of course, she assumed they planned to announce their engagement, so when Stuart asked her to close her eyes, she was confused.

"Why do I have to close my eyes?" she asked him. "We've already opened the gifts."

Stuart gave her one of his annoying smirks, the one he reserved for when he had a secret. "Maybe not. Maybe there's a surprise present."

Goodness, how could there be more gifts? You could barely move around the room as it was, what with the tree and all the presents.

A slender arm wrapped around her shoulders. It was Patience, her nephew's partner in crime. "Please, Ana. I promise you won't be disappointed."

"Oh, all right." She couldn't say no to that girl if she tried.

Although she should have pointed out that no matter what the surprise, she couldn't possibly be disappointed. Certainly not after such a wonderful Christmas celebration. In addition to Patience and Stuart, Patience's sister was visiting from France along with her boyfriend. *Boyfriend,* Ana chuckled. Frederic was no boy. Her Nigel would have said *sa grande passion,* the way the two of them lit up whenever the other entered the room. But then, he would use the same phrase for Stuart and Patience as well.

How wonderful it had been to spend the day surrounded by love. To see the people she loved in love. It thrilled her to know that while she had lost her chance, others had not. She ran her hand over the cat nestled in her lap. Sweet Nigel. He'd be thrilled, too. He used to say it was love that gave his art life. For a man who claimed to be a rebel, he was a hopeless romantic.

"Okay, *babushka.* Open your eyes."

No… It couldn't… Ana's heart leaped to her throat. "How…?" Her legs were shaking so hard, she was afraid they wouldn't hold her.

Patience was at her elbow, supporting her. "Piper and Frederic tracked her down in England," she said.

"Turns out a man named Gaspard Theroux held out on Grandpa Theodore," Stuart told her. "He never told him that he owned one of Nigel's works."

"Dear sweet Gaspard. He believed in Nigel's talent before anyone else." She ran her trembling fingers across her younger self, along the brushstrokes she remembered so well. Nigel painted with such vitality, such passion. "He was so proud of this work."

Time turned backward, and she was in Paris, stretched across the velvet settee. "Don't move, *mon amour*. The light on your skin is perfect. I want the whole world to see you the way I do."

She would have lain in place forever if that's what he needed.

A tear ran down her cheek. "Please don't cry," Patience said.

The dear girl didn't understand. These were happy tears. Nigel's work survived. In spite of all Theodore's efforts to erase it, proof of their love lived on.

Leaving the tears to fall, she turned to Piper and Frederic. "Thank you."

"No," Piper said. "Thank you. If not for your painting, Frederic and I would still be..."

"The two loneliest people in Paris," Frederic supplied, pressing a kiss to her forehead. "Your Nigel brought us together."

He would have been so glad to know that. Ana turned back to the portrait. The years hadn't diminished its strength. She could still feel the emotion in every stroke. *I miss you so much, my darling.*

"We'll be together soon enough, mon amour."

In the meantime, she would celebrate. She would bask in the love shared by the young people around her, and give thanks for the happy endings she knew would be theirs.

With Nigel close by. "This moment calls for a celebration," she said. "*Lapushka*, go get some champagne

from the wine cellar. And you, my furry rascal..."
Reaching down, she scooped up the cat she'd uncer-
emoniously dumped when she stood up. "Let us toast
to your namesake. And to happy endings."

It was exactly what Nigel would have wanted.

* * * * *

He was gorgeous.

Even standing in his kitchen whisking eggs, Marco couldn't have looked sexier.

"You're a nurturer."

She didn't realize she'd said that aloud until he looked up at her. "What are you talking about?"

"It's in your nature to take care of people," she explained. "You anticipate their needs, try to fulfill them."

"You got that from watching me make French toast?"

She smiled. "I've seen you with your nieces, heard you with your siblings."

"Sounds like you've been keeping a pretty close eye on me." He nudged her. "Sounds like you might even like me a little."

"I might. A little."

"And why does that worry you?"

She didn't deny it. "Because you're looking for a committed, long-term relationship. And I don't know that I can give you anything more than this one day."

"That's okay—because I do." He gave her a confident look and went back to stirring.

She felt a stirring of her own. She'd been alone for a long time, and numb for most of that time. But now, with Marco, she was feeling things she didn't think she'd ever feel again. And wanting things...

Dangerous things...

* * *

Those Engaging Garretts!
The Carolina Cousins!

THE BACHELOR
TAKES A BRIDE

BY
BRENDA HARLEN

Published in Great Britain 2015
by Mills & Boon, an imprint of Harlequin (UK) Limited,
Eton House, 18-24 Paradise Road, Richmond, Surrey, TW9 1SR

© 2015 Brenda Harlen

ISBN: 978-0-263-25166-1

23-0915

Harlequin (UK) Limited's policy is to use papers that are natural, renewable and recyclable products and made from wood grown in sustainable forests. The logging and manufacturing processes conform to the legal environmental regulations of the country of origin.

Printed and bound in Spain
by CPI, Barcelona

Brenda Harlen is a former attorney who once had the privilege of appearing before the Supreme Court of Canada. The practice of law taught her a lot about the world and reinforced her determination to become a writer—because in fiction, she could promise a happy ending! Now she is an award-winning, national bestselling author of more than thirty titles for Mills & Boon. You can keep up-to-date with Brenda on Facebook and Twitter or through her website, www.brendaharlen.com.

For me, writing is truly a labor of love.
Every day that I sit down at my computer, I feel fortunate
to be doing a job that gives me so much pleasure and
satisfaction—and I want to dedicate this book
(my thirty-fifth project for Harlequin) to some of the
people who have helped make that possible:

To Gail Chasan, who long ago decided that she wanted
Once and Again for Special Edition—and who has
since found a home for many more stories.

To Susan Litman, who discovered *McIver's Mission* as a
contest judge in 2002 and has been with me for every single
book I've published since then. I realize I am incredibly
lucky to work with an editor who supports me and my
writing and always finds ways to make my stories better.

To Carly Silver, who may be the newest member of the
Harlequin Special Edition editorial team but has already
provided invaluable assistance as a title guru—thank you!

To everyone in the art and marketing departments for
helping to ensure that the books have polish and appeal.

While all of these people have played a part in transforming
my stories from manuscript to bookstore, even then, the
journey is not complete. A book is only a collection of pages
(or coded words in a file) until a reader opens it up. For that
reason, I would like to extend my sincere appreciation to all
of the readers who have taken my characters and stories into
their homes and hearts—I am truly humbled and grateful.

The last dozen years have been an exciting adventure in my
publishing career and I look forward to sharing many
more with all of you!

I'd also like to acknowledge and thank Maria Rosati and
Mike Boccalon for their assistance with the Italian
dialogue in this story. Any errors are my own.

Chapter One

As Marco Palermo squinted through the windshield of his small SUV—as if squinting might somehow improve visibility—he realized that he might as well have been blindfolded.

Though it was early May and not yet eight o'clock, the sky was black and the rain was pouring down so hard the windshield wipers couldn't clear it away fast enough for him to see more than three feet beyond his vehicle's headlights. Why anyone would choose to be out in such weather was a mystery to him, and yet here he was, at the behest of his sister—because he never could refuse her anything.

"I have an insatiable craving for tiramisu," Renata had said, explaining the reason for her call. "I'd come to the restaurant myself, but Anna and Bella are in their pj's and ready for bed."

The restaurant was Valentino's—an establishment in Charisma's downtown core that had been started by their grandparents nearly half a century earlier; Adrianna and Isabella were Renata's daughters, ages five and three years respectively, and Marco loved them both to bits. A definite benefit of doing this favor for his sister was getting to spend some time with his adorable nieces.

"Tiramisu, huh?"

"It's not me—it's the baby," she said, referring to the third child she was carrying.

He figured pregnancy cravings were the responsibility of the baby's father, and he knew that his brother-in-law wouldn't hesitate to drive through a torrential downpour to get his wife anything she wanted or needed. The fact that Renata had called Marco suggested that her firefighter husband was at work and unable to cater to her every whim, as Craig was usually happy to do.

"Well, the baby's going to have to wait at least half an hour," Marco told her. "Because I'm not at the restaurant right now."

"Oh. I'm sorry, I just assumed…"

"That I spend twenty-four hours a day at Valentino's?"

"Something like that," she admitted.

"It's Saturday night," he said, reminding her of the one night a week he forced himself to take away from work to ensure that it didn't become all consuming. He could— and often did—take more days and nights, because a well-established restaurant pretty much ran itself even without one of his siblings or cousins on-site to oversee every little detail.

"Ohmygod—I didn't think…you have a date. I'm interrupting a date. I'm *so* sorry."

"Relax, Nata. I'm just working at home tonight—you're not interrupting anything."

"It's Saturday night," she repeated his words back to him. "*Why* don't you have a date?"

He shook his head. The abrupt change of topic and the demanding yet concerned tone in her voice were so typical of his sister, he didn't know whether to chuckle or sigh.

"I'll be there with your tiramisu in half an hour," he said. "You can grill me in person then."

"And I will," she assured him.

He had no doubt, but all he said was, "Don't let the girls go to bed before I get there," then he disconnected the call.

And so he'd abandoned the blueprints on his desk, picked up his keys, dashed through the rain to his car and headed to Valentino's.

Why don't you have a date?

He considered various responses to Renata's question as he drove the familiar route, hoping to come up with something that was believable and reassuring. The truth—that he was tired of dating the wrong women—wouldn't satisfy his sister. She would insist that he not give up, because the right woman was out there, waiting for him as much as he was waiting for her. But he was getting tired of waiting.

All of his siblings were in settled relationships. Nata and Craig had been married for almost eight years. His oldest brother, Tony, had been married to his high school sweetheart, Gemma, for nine. And Gabe, his other brother, had recently—finally—gotten engaged to Francesca, the woman he'd started to fall in love with more than two years earlier but for whom he'd only recently acknowledged his feelings. His sister and brothers had each found the right people to share their lives with and were happy and settled. Marco yearned for the same thing.

When you find her, you'll know. Nonna's words—spoken to him at Gabe and Francesca's engagement celebration—echoed in the back of his mind.

Caterina loved to tell the story of her first meeting with Salvatore, which happened to be on their wedding day. "It was like lightning—a surge that tingled through my veins. I had worried about what marriage to a stranger would bring, but I knew then that I would love him forever."

Marco figured sixty-one years was pretty close to forever. And from what he could see, his grandparents were still very much in love with each other. Sure, they argued—sometimes loudly and passionately—and they often made up the same way. The key to a long and happy marriage, Nonna told him, was to never go to bed alone or angry.

So he didn't question the conviction in her words, because that was how it happened in his family—starting with his grandparents, then his parents, and his sister and both of his brothers. No, he didn't doubt it would happen

that way, but he was starting to worry about the *when*—
or even *if*—it would happen for him.

He'd dated a lot of perfectly nice and undeniably attractive women, but none of them had been the right woman.
He'd wanted them to be; each time he'd embarked on a
new relationship, he'd had high hopes that *this* woman
would turn out to be *the* woman who would make him
fall head over heels in love forever after. But it had never
happened. Not yet.

So he was waiting, albeit a little less patiently with each
year that passed. He wasn't ready to give up, but he wasn't
holding his breath, either. And if he didn't actually experience a lightning moment of recognition, he would settle for
a tingle of attraction—or even a spark of static electricity.

He backed into his usual parking spot behind the restaurant and turned off the engine. As he did, thunder crashed
and the skies opened up again, the strong and steady
thrumming of the rain on his windshield washed away by
an absolute deluge. He unhooked his belt but didn't reach
for the door handle—he wasn't leaving the shelter of his
vehicle until the downpour eased up.

After a couple more minutes, when the rain finally
began to slow, he saw the take-out door of Valentino's
open and a woman step out. She exited from under the red-
and-white-striped awning with her pizza box in hand and
hurried across the parking lot. Despite the ongoing storm,
something about her snagged his attention and wouldn't
let go.

Her hair was short, dark and wet from the rain. She
didn't wear a coat, and her dress showcased some nice
curves as she moved surprisingly fast in the heels she
wore on her feet. Lightning flashed, illuminating the sky
for what might have been a heartbeat if not for the fact that
his heart literally skipped a beat.

His eyes continued to track the mystery woman's path to

her vehicle. She opened the driver's side of a light-colored compact car and ducked inside, setting the pizza box on the empty passenger seat before closing the door, extinguishing the interior light.

He'd barely caught a glimpse of her, yet he felt an ache beneath his breastbone, a yearning that suggested she might be the one. Finally.

The initial sense of jubilant relief was supplanted by frustration as he watched her taillights disappear in the night.

He might have finally found her—but he didn't have the first clue as to who she was or when and where he might see her again.

When Marco entered the restaurant through the same take-out door a few minutes later, he found his sister-in-law, Gemma, behind the counter.

Usually a hostess in the dining rooms, Gemma was happy to fill in wherever she was needed. And since their cousin Maria was currently on an extended holiday/honeymoon with her new husband—because it wasn't just his siblings but also his cousins who were happily pairing up—they were short-staffed at the take-out counter.

Gemma glanced up when she heard the bell over the door and smiled at him. "What are you doing in here on a Saturday night?"

"Renata says the baby wants tiramisu," he told her.

"She couldn't even stand the scent of coffee when she was pregnant with Adrianna and Isabella," Gemma noted. "Makes me think Nonna is correct in her prediction that this one's a boy."

"Well, she does have a fifty percent chance of being right."

"She predicted that both Adrianna and Isabella would

be girls," Gemma reminded him. "And that Christian and Dominic would be boys."

"She also predicted that you and Tony would have half a dozen babies."

His sister-in-law laughed. "Well, I can promise you that's *not* happening."

"But speaking of Nonna's predictions," Marco said, "did you notice the woman who walked out that door?"

"Lots of women walk out that door. And sometimes they come in. Sometimes men, too."

He rolled his eyes. "I was referring to the last customer who left with a pizza box in her hands."

"You mean Jordyn Garrett?"

"You know her?"

"Yeah—she's Rachel's husband's cousin."

Rachel Ellis—now Garrett—had been a friend of Gemma's since high school, and Rachel and her husband, Andrew, were regular customers at Valentino's, along with Maura, Andrew's daughter from his first marriage. The previous November, they'd added another daughter, Lily, to their family.

"What else do you know about her?" he asked.

"I know that she left her phone on the counter," Gemma said, glancing at the slim case on the ledge in front of the cash register.

"How do you know it's hers?"

"Because I saw her set it down when she got out her wallet to pay for the pizza."

The device hummed quietly, a light in the corner blinking.

"Maybe you should answer that," she suggested.

"Why me?"

"Because I'm going to the kitchen to get the tiramisu for Nata."

"Throw in a couple of cannoli for the girls," he suggested.

"Of course," she agreed, already moving past the pizza ovens and slipping through the door to the main kitchen.

Leaving him alone with Jordyn's phone and its blinking light.

He touched the screen, expecting to see a password request, which would, of course, prevent him from accessing anything on her phone. But there was no password protection—the screen immediately illuminated to reveal the recent communication to the phone's owner—assumed to be Jordyn—from someone identified at the top of the screen as Tristyn.

12 med wings would go good with the pizza and wine ☺

He stepped behind the counter and peeked through the window into the take-out kitchen.

"Hey, Rafe—how long would it take for a dozen wings?"

"Ten minutes," his cousin said, already with tongs in hand to count them out and toss them into the fryer basket. "You want 'em extra hot?"

"Medium," he said. He figured it wouldn't take Jordyn long to realize she'd left her phone behind, and when she came back for it, hopefully the wings would be ready for her.

"Your taste buds getting soft in your old age?" Rafe teased, dropping the basket into the hot oil.

"They're not for me."

He returned his attention to her phone—feeling a little like the prince left at the ball with no clue to Cinderella's identity except a single glass slipper. The phone wasn't nearly as sexy as a shoe, but at least it was something.

The bell over the door rang and he glanced up to greet the new customer, but the words died in his throat when she walked in. Obviously it had taken less time than he'd anticipated for Jordyn to realize she'd left her phone—the phone that was currently in his hand.

In the bright light of the take-out area, he could see her clearly now: smooth, creamy skin; a delicate heart-shaped face; and short, dark hair dripping with rain. Her eyes were dark green and framed by thick, long lashes.

He'd thought the dress she wore was black, but he could see now that it was a deep shade of purple. But he'd been right about her curves—the sleeveless sheath style hugged her feminine shape in all the right places. The wedge heels on her feet made it difficult to accurately estimate her height, but he guessed that she was about five feet five inches tall.

Her fingernails were neatly trimmed and unpolished, her makeup subtle. Earrings dangled from her ears, colorful purple and silver beads on different lengths of chain jingled as she moved, suggesting a playful side that contrasted with the simple dress and no-fuss hairstyle.

She was simply and spectacularly beautiful, and in that moment, the possibility that had been teasing the back of his mind—and nudging at his heart—since that first quick glimpse through the rain became a certainty.

"Nonna's going to love hearing that she was right."

Neatly arched brows drew together. "I beg your pardon?"

He shook his head. "Sorry. My mind was wandering."

"A wandering mind and sticky fingers," she noted.

"Huh?"

She gestured to the phone in his hand. "That's mine."

"Oh. You left it on the counter."

"Apparently."

He held it out to her.

When she reached for it, her fingertips brushed against his—and he felt it again, an arrow of heat straight through his heart. She snatched her hand away quickly, making him suspect that she'd felt the same thing—or at least something.

"That's it?" she said. "No explanation for reading my text messages? No apology?"

"You left the phone on the counter—I was only trying to figure out who it belonged it to."

"Me," she said again.

"And you are?"

"Hoping to get home before my pizza's cold." And with that, she turned away.

"Wings up," Rafe said, setting the take-out container on the ledge.

"Wait," Marco called out to her.

She paused at the door.

"You forgot your wings."

"I didn't order any wings."

"There was a message on your phone—from Tristyn. A dozen medium."

She scrolled through the text conversation on her phone, frowned. He offered her the foam container.

"I didn't pay for those."

"Consider them an apology for reading your message."

"You wouldn't have to apologize if you hadn't read my message," she pointed out.

"And you'd be going home without the wings," he countered.

She took the container from him, making sure that there was no contact between them in the transfer. "Thank you."

"Marco," he told her. "Marco Palermo."

"Thank you, Marco."

He smiled. "You're welcome…"

"Jordyn," she finally said, confirming the identification his sister-in-law had made as she moved toward the door.

He reached the handle before she did, pushed it open for her. "Enjoy your pizza and wings, Jordyn."

"We always do," she assured him.

He stood at the door and watched as she made her way back to her vehicle.

"Jordyn came back for her phone," he told Gemma, when he turned and saw her standing at the counter with a take-out bag in hand.

"I caught the end of your conversation," she admitted. "Actually, most of your conversation."

His heart was so filled with happiness it was overflowing, and he couldn't hold back the smile that curved his lips. "She's the one—I've finally found her."

His sister-in-law sighed. "*Caro*, why do you do this to yourself?"

"Maybe because I see how happy you and Tony are, and I want to know the same thing."

"You will fall in love with the right woman at the right time, but if you keep throwing yourself headfirst over cliffs looking for it to happen, you're only going to get hurt again."

"There was a spark," he insisted.

"It wasn't a spark—it was a flame," Gemma said. "You just crashed and burned, and you don't even know it."

He was disappointed by her response. He knew that she cared about him—she'd been part of his family for so many years he'd thought of her as a second sister even before she became his sister-in-law—so he didn't understand why she was determined to burst his happiness bubble.

Or maybe he did. And maybe there was some foundation to her concern that he'd been trying too hard to find the right woman. Certainly, his recent relationship experience would substantiate her point.

But the alternative—to passively sit back and wait for his soul mate to land in his lap—was inconceivable to him. Sometimes destiny needed a helping hand, and he was more than willing to give it.

But first he had tiramisu to deliver.

Chapter Two

The rain had lessened to a drizzle by the time Jordyn got home to the Northbrook town house that she shared with her sister. Tristyn met her at the door, offering a towel in exchange for the food boxes so that Jordyn could dry off.

"Maybe the weather was an omen," Jordyn said, kicking off her shoes. "As soon as I saw the forecast, I should have canceled the date and stayed home."

"Or at least taken a jacket or umbrella," her sister teased.

"Neither would have made this evening any less of a disaster."

"Was it really that bad?" Tristyn asked, setting the food on the table.

Jordyn draped the towel over the back of her chair and picked up the glass of wine her sister had poured for her. "I don't think there are words to adequately describe it."

"What did he do?"

"Well, he opened the conversation by asking if I'd ever thought about changing my name."

Tristyn frowned as she lifted a slice of pizza from the box. "Why would you want to change your name?"

"Because it's misleading. Apparently when Carrie offered to set him up with me, Cody initially refused because he thought I was a guy." And, he promised her in a mock deep voice accompanied by a leering grin, he was strictly and exclusively heterosexual. She shuddered at the memory.

"I get that sometimes, too, but never on a date."

"Well, the criticism of my name wasn't the worst of it—after that, even before I'd had a chance to peruse the wine list, Cody asked me what kind of birth control I used."

"You're kidding."

"I wish I was." She peeled a slice of pepperoni off of her pizza slice, popped it into her mouth.

"How did you respond to that?"

"I think my jaw hit the table, because he actually apologized for the bluntness of the question—not the question itself, just the delivery of it."

Tristyn shook her head.

"Apparently he's got a six-year-old son from a short-term relationship with a woman who lied to him about being on the Pill. Now half of his paycheck goes to child support and he's saddled with the kid every other weekend."

Tristyn choked on her wine, obviously shocked by the statement.

Jordyn held up her hands. "His words—not mine."

"I should have realized," her sister acknowledged.

"And the whole time he's talking, he's looking at my breasts instead of my face."

"Well, you do have exceptional breasts."

"I'm flattered you think so," she said drily.

"And that dress really does emphasize your curves." Her sister looked down at her own chest, sighed. "Even with Victoria's very best secret giving me a boost, I can't fake cleavage like yours."

"Does that make it okay for him to stare at my chest all through dinner?"

"Of course not," Tristyn immediately denied.

"Not that I actually stayed through dinner," she admitted, helping herself to a wing. "When I waved my hand in front of his face—for the third time—to draw his attention upward, he didn't even apologize. He just said, 'You've probably realized by now that I'm a breast man—and I'm *so* glad Carrie hooked us up tonight.'"

"He didn't."

"Oh, yes, he did." She licked pizza sauce off of her thumb. "And when I assured him that we weren't hooking up, he promised that he would change my mind before dessert."

Tristyn grimaced.

"I'm just glad I met him at the restaurant, so that when I walked out, I didn't have to wait for a cab."

"I'm so sorry," her sister said sincerely. "Carrie told me he was a terrific guy."

"Obviously Carrie needs to raise her standards."

"I just wanted you to go out and have a good time. You've been a recluse since—"

"I work with the public," she interjected, because she knew what her sister was going to say and didn't want to hear it. "I think that's pretty much the opposite of a recluse."

Tristyn's gaze was sympathetic. "But you don't date."

"After tonight, do you really need to ask why?"

"There are a lot of really great guys out there," her sister insisted.

"Probably," she acknowledged. "But you've dated most of them, and that's a whole other category of awkward."

"I haven't dated that many men," Tristyn protested.

Jordyn's only response was to pick up the bottle of wine and top up their glasses.

"And why should I feel pressured to go out and meet guys who don't interest me when I'm perfectly content with my life?"

She reached down to rub Gryffindor, who had followed the scent of food into the kitchen and rubbed himself against her leg in a silent bid for attention—or scraps. Not that she ever fed him from the table, but the battle-scarred cat she'd rescued from the streets seven years earlier was eternally optimistic.

"You should not be content hanging out with your sister on a Saturday night," Tristyn said.

"Which begs the question of what you're doing home on a Saturday night."

Her sister shrugged. "I didn't feel like going out."

"Are you ill?"

"I've just got a lot on my mind."

"Like what?"

"I had lunch with Daniel yesterday."

"He's trying to lure you over to GSR," she guessed, referring to Garrett/Slater Racing—the company their cousin had founded in partnership with his friend Josh Slater.

Tristyn nodded.

"And?" she prompted.

"I'm tempted," her sister admitted.

"But?"

"I love working at Garrett Furniture, being part of the business that Granddad founded."

Gryff, finally giving up on the possibility that he would get anything more than affectionate but inedible scratches, wandered off again.

"Then tell him no."

"But it would be really exciting to be part of the business that he's building, too."

Jordyn sipped her wine. "You're not usually so indecisive. What aren't you telling me?"

"I'm not sure I could work with him," Tristyn confided.

"Daniel?"

Her sister shook her head. "Josh."

"Well, well, well," Jordyn mused, as her sibling pushed away from the table and carried their plates to the dishwasher.

"Not for the reason you're thinking."

"Not because the man looks likes sex on a stick?"

Tristyn choked on a laugh. "Sex on a stick?"

She shrugged. "Just because I'm not interested in taking anything home from the market doesn't mean I don't enjoy browsing."

Her sister finished loading the dishwasher, then wrapped the leftover pizza.

"You were saying that your objection to potentially working with Josh has nothing to do with the fact that you want to rip his clothes off and have your way with him," she prompted.

"I do *not* want to rip his clothes off."

"It's been a while since I've had sex," Jordyn admitted. "But I seem to recall it's easier if you're naked."

Tristyn huffed out a breath. "He's arrogant and obnoxious and thinks he knows everything."

Since those were uncharacteristically strong words for her sister, Jordyn let it go. For now.

"So you're not going to take the job?"

"I haven't decided." She returned to the table and picked up her wine. "Maybe Daniel could set you up with Josh."

Jordyn's brows lifted. "You want me to go out with a guy you just described as arrogant and obnoxious?"

"You could tame him. You don't take any crap from anyone."

"And then you'd have an excuse to ignore your attraction to him," she guessed, seeing right through her sister's plan. "Because it would be too weird to go out with a guy who'd gone out with your sister."

"We're not talking about me—we're talking about you."

"But your life is so much more interesting than mine."

"Because I get out and meet new people."

"I met someone tonight," Jordyn said.

"Your date from hell doesn't count."

She should have nodded her agreement and let the topic slide—but she wasn't thinking of Cody. She was thinking of Marco. In fact, she hadn't stopped thinking about

Marco since she'd seen him standing behind the counter at Valentino's with her phone in hand.

She should have been outraged by his audacity—instead, she'd found herself intrigued by the man. And because her sister had a lot more experience with the opposite sex than she did, she wanted her assessment of the brief interaction.

"Actually, I met someone after," she said now. "When I was at Valentino's."

"Really?" Tristyn somehow managed to sound both skeptical and intrigued. "Who did you meet at Valentino's?"

"Marco."

Her sister's lips curved. "Ahh—the sweet and sexy bartender with the melted-chocolate eyes and the dimple at the corner of his mouth?"

Now it was Jordyn's turn to be surprised. "You know him?"

"I've seen him at Valentino's," Tristyn admitted. "Shared some conversation."

"Along with lingering glances and fleeting touches?"

"I might have flirted with him a little," her sister acknowledged, because flirting was as natural to her as breathing. "But it never went any further than that."

"Why not?"

Tristyn shrugged. "No chemistry. Although I'm guessing you had a different experience, or you wouldn't have mentioned his name."

"I've always thought chemistry was overrated," she hedged.

"As a woman with much more dating experience than you, I have to disagree," Tristyn said. "I don't think a relationship can work without at least some degree of chemistry."

Jordyn wasn't sure what she believed when it came to

matters of the heart, since her own had been shattered more than three years earlier.

"So—what did you feel?" Tristyn prompted. "Butterflies? Tingles? Heat?"

"Just...curiosity."

"Considering that's probably more than you've felt in a long time, I'd say it's a good start."

She rolled her eyes. "I don't see how a three-minute conversation with a guy is the start of anything."

"That depends on what you plan to do next."

"My only plan right now is to take my glass of wine into the living room to watch the *Ryder to the Rescue* episode that I missed last night."

"Sounds like a good plan to me," her sister agreed.

Marco rapped his knuckles against the wood before he turned the knob and opened the door of his sister's two-story colonial in western South Meadows, only a few blocks from where they'd grown up and where their parents still lived.

His mother always chided her kids for knocking before they walked into the house that she insisted was still their home, despite the fact that none of them lived there anymore. Renata didn't subscribe to quite the same open-door policy, but she usually made sure the front entrance was unlocked when she was expecting company. With two busy kids, it was hard to predict what she might be in the middle of when the doorbell rang—or how long it would take her to answer the summons.

Five-year-old Anna's face lit up when she saw him in the doorway. "Uncle Marco!"

"Unca Mahco!" Bella, her three-year-old sister, echoed the greeting.

He set the paper bag containing the desserts on the seat of the deacon's bench inside the door so that he could catch the two little girls who flung themselves at him. As Renata had said, they were both in their pajamas—coordinating outfits with ruffled cuffs and hems: Anna in purple and Bella in pink.

"We haven't seen you in *forever*," Anna lamented.

"Fo'eva," Bella agreed.

He squeezed them both tight. "Has it really been that long?"

"Uh-huh," Anna said solemnly, and her sibling nodded.

He usually stopped by to see his sister and her family at least once a week, but he'd been so busy working on plans for the new restaurant that he'd been unaware more than three weeks had passed since his last visit. Until now. And he felt a sharp tug of guilt to realize his nieces had noted the absence.

"What's in the bag?" Anna asked. "Did you bring us a surprise?"

"A 'pwise?" Bella echoed, looking at him hopefully.

"It's tiramisu for your mom," he told them.

His nieces wrinkled their noses in identical expressions of displeasure.

"And a cannoli for each of you—if you go sit up at the table."

They raced to the kitchen to comply with his request.

Nata took two small plates out of the cupboard, setting one in front of each of her daughters so that Marco could distribute the pastry.

"I wike cannowi," Bella told him.

"I knew that about you," Marco agreed, kissing the top of her head.

"Your uncle Marco spoils both of you," Renata said.

He lifted his brows as he handed her the bowl of tiramisu.

"Uncle Marco spoils all of us," she amended.

"Sit," he told her, nudging her toward a chair.

"I was going to get you a cup of coffee."

"I can get it," he said, moving over to the counter. He selected a pod, inserted it into the machine, then pressed the button to start it brewing.

"Can we have milk?" Anna asked her mother.

"Of course." Renata started to rise from the table.

"I've got it," Marco told her, easily locating the girls' favorite plastic cups and filling them with milk, then pouring a glass of the same for their mother.

"Thank you," they chorused, when he set the drinks in front of them.

Marco carried his mug of coffee to the table and sat down beside his sister.

"So how are you feeling these days?" he asked her.

"Hungry." She dipped her spoon back into the bowl.

He chuckled. "I guess that means the morning sickness has passed."

She nodded.

"Mommy's got a baby in her belly," Anna said, in case he'd somehow forgotten that fact. "And it's gonna grow *really big* and she's gonna get *really fat*."

"Wike dis," Bella said, stretching her arms out in front of her as far as they could reach to demonstrate.

"Well, hopefully not quite that big," Renata said drily.

"But Daddy says that just means there'll be more of her to love," Anna added.

Marco had to give his brother-in-law points for that response, because he knew his sister was already self-conscious about the weight she'd gained and she was only four months into her pregnancy.

"And soon, you'll have another sister or a brother to love," he said, hoping to shift their attention away from their mother's belly and to the baby she carried.

"I wanna sisda," Bella said. "I don' wanna be da widda sisda anymo."

"I wanna brother," Anna countered, rolling her eyes in the direction of her younger sibling. "Sometimes one sister is one too many."

"I want both of you to go wash the powdered sugar off of your faces and hands, and then brush your teeth," Renata said.

"We aweady bwush our teef," Bella sad. "Befo Unca Mahco comed."

"Which was also before you ate the cannoli he brought for you," her mother pointed out with patient firmness.

"Oh." Bella sighed as she slid off the chair to follow her sister upstairs to the bathroom they shared.

Nata pushed her mostly empty bowl aside and rubbed her tummy. "Hopefully that will settle him down for a while."

"Him?"

She shrugged. "Nonna hasn't been wrong yet."

"Are you hoping for a boy?"

"I know I should say that I just want a healthy baby—and I do. But if I had a choice, yeah, I'd like a boy this time."

"Well, you and Craig make beautiful babies, so if it's not a boy this time, there's no reason you can't keep trying."

"Even if this one is a boy, we're probably going to go for one more."

"You're a brave—or maybe crazy—woman."

His sister laughed. "Probably both."

He heard the water running in the bathroom upstairs, proof that the girls were brushing their teeth again.

"Can I tuck them in when they're ready?" he asked.

"They made you feel guilty about not visiting for so long, didn't they?"

"It hasn't been that long," he protested.

"More than three weeks."

"But who's counting?"

"We missed you," she told him.

"Rebecca—the new waitress—asked for a couple of weeks off in July to go home to Minnesota because she hasn't seen her parents since Christmas."

"Because they live in Minnesota," she said, stating the obvious.

"Maybe I should move."

His sister chuckled. "As if. When you moved out, Mama cried for three days, and you felt so guilty, you almost moved back home again."

"No one knows how to guilt a man like his mother," Marco agreed.

"We done bwushed our teef," Bella called down.

"Uncle Marco's on his way up to tuck you in," Renata told her daughters. Then, to him, "They're going to want a bedtime story."

"I haven't forgotten the routine in three weeks," he assured her, already heading for the stairs.

He sat on Anna's bed, between both of the girls tucked under the covers, and read them a bedtime story. They giggled at the different voices he gave to the characters and responded with gasps and sighs in appropriate places. When the story was finished, they were both fighting to keep their eyes open. He slid off the bed, returned the book to its shelf, kissed Anna's forehead, then scooped Bella up and carried her across the room to tuck her into her own bed.

He loved sharing the nighttime routine with his nieces—and with his nephews, when he was at Tony and Gemma's house. But it was always a little sad to go home to his too-quiet apartment afterward and crawl into an empty bed.

It wouldn't be much of a hardship to find a woman to share his bed for one night or even a few. The harder part was finding the woman he wanted there for the long term. He wasn't one of those commitment-shy guys who was only looking for a good time—he wanted to fall in love and get married and read bedtime stories to his own kids at night. But until that happened, he had be content spending time with his nieces and nephews.

When he returned to the main level, Renata was in the living room folding a load of laundry with the news on TV.

"Are they asleep?"

"You know they won't fall asleep until their mom kisses them good-night."

She pushed herself up from the sofa. "Then I'd better go do so."

While she was upstairs, he busied himself washing up the plates and cups the girls had used.

"You're going to be a great father someday," Renata said when she came back downstairs. "And a great husband to some lucky woman."

"You're only saying that because I'm tidying up your kitchen."

"And because you brought me tiramisu."

"At least you're honest."

"The right woman is out there," his sister said.

He nodded. "I know."

"I just don't want you to get discouraged—wondering when you're finally going to meet her."

"I already did."

She considered that as she picked up a towel to dry the dishes he'd washed. "So when are the rest of us going to meet her?"

"Not for a while."

"Why not?"

"Because I want some time and space to get to know her better before the family scares her away."

"We're not scary," she protested.

"Are you kidding? I was born into this family and I'm terrified by major holiday events with the whole clan."

"If she's going to be the mother of your future children, she's got to meet us someday."

"Someday," he agreed.

Nata sighed. "Are you at least going to tell me her name?"

"No."

"Does she really exist?"

"Of course she exists."

"That's what you said about Tessa Wheeler, your make-believe girlfriend in high school."

He glanced away. "She was real."

"A real person," his sister acknowledged. "But she wasn't really your girlfriend—she didn't even know you existed."

"I was a sophomore," he pointed out in his defense.

"And while I would certainly hope you'd outgrown manufacturing fantasy girlfriends, you should appreciate how your refusal to give me a name is cause for concern."

"If I'd made her up, don't you think I would have made up a name for her?"

"And what name would that be?" she challenged.

Renata was nothing if not relentless, and he knew she wouldn't quit badgering until he gave her something. He decided her name was harmless enough.

"Jordyn," he finally said.

Her brows lifted. "Jordyn Garrett?"

He frowned. "Where did that come from?"

"Ohmygod—I'm right. It *is* Jordyn Garrett."

"I never said it was Jordyn Garrett."

"But you didn't say it wasn't."

"How do you know her?" he finally asked.

"Duh. She's a bartender at O'Reilly's and Craig plays on the Brew Crew, the team they sponsor."

He'd forgotten that his brother-in-law played recreational baseball—but he should have remembered that his sister knew almost everyone in Charisma.

And the way she was worrying her bottom lip right now made him suspect that she knew something that she wasn't telling him.

"What's your objection to my interest in Jordyn?"

"I like her," Renata assured him, though her tone was cautious.

"But?" he prompted.

"But she's always seemed a little…guarded," she decided. "And I don't want you to get your heart broken."

Again.

Although she didn't say the word, they both knew she was thinking it. As he was, too. But this time, he was confident there wouldn't be a sad ending but a happy beginning, because Jordyn Garrett was the woman he'd been waiting his whole life for.

Now he just had to help her see that she'd been waiting for him, too.

Chapter Three

Jordyn dreamed of him—and woke up feeling restless and out of sorts because of it.

She didn't remember the details of the dream, except that her heart had been pounding with anticipation and her body aching to feel things that she hadn't felt in a very long time. And she'd awakened thinking of Marco. The sweet and sexy bartender with the melted-chocolate eyes and the dimple at the corner of his mouth. It might have been her sister's description, but she couldn't deny that it was an accurate one.

She hadn't dreamed of anyone but Brian in a lot of years. More significantly, she hadn't even dreamed about her former fiancé in more than a year, which she figured was a sign that her heart was finally healing. But his disappearance from her dreams worried her, too, because she didn't want to forget about him. She didn't want to forget how completely in love they'd been or how her heart had been decimated by his death. And she especially didn't want to be attracted to another man, to even consider moving on with her life with someone else or hope for the future that she'd once believed she would have with Brian.

She'd told Tristyn that her date with Cody the night before had been a disaster—but the fact that it had been such a disaster was also a relief to Jordyn. Her experience with Cody reassured her that she wasn't missing out on anything by not dating and reinforced her belief that she'd rather spend her free time alone than with a man who obviously wasn't right for her. Because no man who wasn't Brian was right for her.

Then she'd walked into Valentino's and come face-to-face with Marco Palermo. And she'd felt...something.

She wasn't sure what it was—maybe a spark of awareness or possibly a tingle of desire—she only knew that it was more than she'd expected or wanted to feel.

She'd pushed it aside, refusing to delve too deeply inside herself. So she'd met a guy and she'd felt a tug of something—so what? It didn't have to mean anything, because she wasn't ever going to see him again.

Except that she instinctively knew that wasn't true. Whatever she'd felt, she was certain that he'd felt it, too, and she didn't doubt that their paths would cross again—probably sooner rather than later. And when they did, she'd be ready to let him down easy. There was no other option.

Tristyn was drinking coffee and reading the news on her tablet when Jordyn finally ventured into the kitchen after her shower. She brewed herself a cup of French vanilla, added two teaspoons of sugar and a generous dollop of cream, then took a seat across from her sister.

"How much wine did I drink last night?"

Tristyn looked up from her tablet. "No more than I did. Why?"

"I feel like crap this morning, and I had some weird dreams."

"Any special guests in those dreams?" her sister teased.

Jordyn scowled at her over the rim of her coffee mug.

"I'll take that as a 'yes.'"

She sipped her coffee and willed the caffeine to jumpstart her system—or at least her brain.

"It's a good sign," Tristyn said gently.

"What's a good sign?"

"That you're thinking about him."

She swallowed another mouthful of java.

"Brian's been gone for more than three years."

Three years, two months and sixteen days. But of course

she didn't say that aloud, because she knew that Tristyn would get that familiar little line that appeared between her brows whenever she was worried about something. And her family had worried about her enough already.

Instead she only nodded.

"It's time for you to put yourself out there again."

"Isn't that what I was doing with Cody last night?"

Tristyn shook her head. "Cody was a setup that was never going to work, because you had it in your mind before you even sat down at the restaurant that you weren't going to let it go any further than dinner."

It was both a curse and a blessing to have a sister who knew her so well.

"Maybe that's why meeting Marco made more of a lasting impression on you," Tristyn continued.

"Or maybe I made it into a bigger deal than it was," Jordyn said, considering that he'd never asked for anything more than her name.

"Maybe you did," Tristyn allowed. "But you won't know for sure until you see him again."

It was almost two weeks later before she did.

Ten days to be precise. And not a single one of those days passed without her thinking about him at least once. After the first week, she considered stopping by Valentino's—just to see if he was working—but she'd ignored the impulse.

Because if he *was* working—what then?

It was her inability to answer that question that kept her away from his family's restaurant. But it didn't stop her from thinking about him.

On Tuesday night, just a couple hours before closing, he walked into O'Reilly's.

She was wiping down the bar when she looked up and saw him come through the door.

Even from across the room, she felt the hum of something between them—or maybe, nearing the end of a double shift, she was just overtired.

He nodded to her as he took a seat farther down the bar.

"Hey, Jordyn," Bobby Galley called out, snagging her attention. "What's your number?"

For the first six months that she'd worked at the bar, every night that Bobby came in, he would ask for her number. And every night, she would refuse.

The familiar banter grew tiresome after a while, until one night, when he asked for her number, she said, "One hundred and forty-six." He'd blinked, wary of this unexpected response, and she'd told him it was the number of times he'd asked her out and she'd turned him down. Not that she'd actually counted, but her recital of the random number sounded credible.

After that, it had become something of a game. Although he hadn't stopped asking, he had given up hope that she would ever answer him with her actual phone number.

She took a moment to consider the request. "Thirty-eight," she finally told him.

"I know that's not your age," he said. "I'm hoping… maybe…it's your bra size?"

She shook her head. "Wrong again—it's the number of months that I've been serving you from behind this bar."

"Which only proves that we both need a change of scenery," Bobby said. "Let me take you away from here."

"If by 'away' you mean 'Hawaii'—keep talking, Bobby. If you meant something else, then I've got other customers to serve," she said, and moved toward Marco.

"What can I get for you?"

"A draft beer."

"You're going to have to be more specific than that," she said, indicating the array of faucets bearing the labels of a dozen different brands.

"I'll try a Smithwick's," he decided.

She picked up a pint glass and angled it beneath the tap.

As he waited for his beer, Marco glanced around, noting that despite the lateness of the hour, about half a dozen tables were filled and there were few empty stools around the bar. He suspected that the popularity of the seating in that area had more to do with the pretty woman working the taps than the two small screens showing sports highlights, especially when the Bar Down—a popular choice for die-hard sports fans—wasn't too far down the road.

"How were your wings the other night?"

"They were great—thanks."

"How are the wings here?"

"You checking out the competition?"

He shook his head. "I'm sure there's some crossover between our customers, but I wouldn't consider O'Reilly's and Valentino's to be in competition."

"Our sweet-and-spicy honey barbecue are my favorite," she said, setting a menu beside him. "But the dry-rub salt and black pepper are popular, too."

"If I order the honey barbecue, will you share them with me?"

"No." She smiled. "But thanks."

"You're good at that."

She selected a clean glass and began pouring a Harp for another customer. "What am I good at?"

"The brush-off."

"I work in a bar." She lifted a shoulder. "It's a necessary job skill."

"So I shouldn't take it personally?"

"I didn't say that." But the words were softened by another smile that made his heart do a slow roll inside his chest as she carried the draft to the end of the bar.

"Did you want those wings?" she asked when she returned.

"Do they come with your phone number?"

"No."

"Not even the first digit?"

"No."

"The last digit?"

One side of her mouth quirked at the corner. "No."

"So the only thing I get if I order the wings is the pleasure of sitting here and making conversation with you for a little while longer?"

"That's not true," she denied. "You also get the wings."

He smiled. "Sold."

"Honey barbecue?"

"Sure," he agreed.

She keyed his order into the computer that linked to the kitchen. "Anything else?"

"Not right now."

She nodded and moved away to check on her other patrons, exchanging a few words here and there, smiling or laughing on occasion.

"What brings you in to O'Reilly's?" she asked.

"I was looking for you."

"Well, now you've found me."

His smile was quick. "Can I keep you?"

"You wouldn't want to," she told him. "I'm very high maintenance."

"In my experience, most high-maintenance women don't realize they're high maintenance."

"See—I'm challenging your perceptions already."

"About more than you probably realize," he acknowledged.

"How did you find out where I worked?"

"You don't believe it's a coincidence that I decided to stop in here for a beer?"

"No."

He grinned at the blunt response. "My sister, Renata, told me I'd probably find you here."

"Renata and Craig," she realized. "He's the firefighter who plays third base for the Brew Crew."

He nodded.

"Small world."

"And strange that our paths never crossed until recently."

"Or maybe not so strange considering that we probably work similarly unusual hours," she countered.

The blonde waitress who was taking care of the tables sidled up to the bar. "I need two pints of Guinness, a glass of white and a G&T, extra lime."

"Excuse me," Jordyn said to Marco, and busied herself filling the order.

"It's hard to have a conversation when you keep moving away or we keep getting interrupted," he commented when the waitress had gone.

"I'm working," she reminded him.

"I know," he acknowledged. "And if you give me your number, I'll gladly relinquish this stool to another customer."

"I can't do that."

"I won't tell Bobby," he promised.

"I'm not worried about Bobby."

"Then what are you worried about?"

"I'm not worried. It's just that…" Her explanation trailed off and she shook her head. "I don't know."

He feigned surprise. "You don't know your number?"

The hint of another smile tugged at the corners of her mouth. "I don't want *you* to know my number."

"Why not?"

"Because then you'll call and ask me to go out with you,

and I'll either feel really bad for saying no or I'll say yes and afterward wish that I'd said no."

"There is a third option," he told her. "You could say yes, have a fabulous time, fall head over heels in love with me, and want to spend the rest of your life as my wife and the mother of my babies."

She shook her head. "I don't think so."

"Why not?"

"Because I work fifty hours a week serving beer to mostly male customers in a pub. Trust me, there isn't a pickup line I haven't heard."

"That's probably true," he acknowledged. "But I would hope you'd learned to distinguish between the guys who just want a quick roll between the sheets and the ones who are sincerely interested in getting to know you better."

"And then I'd recognize you as one of the sincere ones?" she asked doubtfully.

"You would," he confirmed.

"I'm flattered by your interest," she told him. "But I'm not going to go out with you."

"You don't believe I'm sincere," he realized.

"Even if you are, I'm not looking to fall head over heels in love, get married and have babies."

"My grandmother says that love often sneaks up when we least expect it."

"I'm sure she's a wise woman," Jordyn said. "But she doesn't know me."

"Not yet."

She huffed out a breath. "You're relentless—I'll give you that."

"Persistent," he decided.

"I really don't date customers."

"Is that your boss's rule or a personal philosophy?"

"A personal philosophy," she admitted. "Although the

statement would be equally true without the 'customers' part."

"You don't date?"

"Aside from one recent and ill-advised setup, no," she confirmed.

"Why not?"

"Because it's more hassle than it's worth."

"Maybe you just haven't been dating the right guy," he suggested.

She looked away, but not quickly enough that he could miss the pain that moved in those beautiful green eyes.

She nodded to a man seated at the end of the bar and poured him another beer. She delivered his glass, taking a few minutes to chat and smile as they exchanged beverage for money, then took a few more orders before she returned.

She picked up the plate of wings from the pass-through window and delivered them to Marco, along with a refill of his beer.

"So what's with you and Bobby?" he asked.

"Nothing. He's just a regular customer."

"And the number you gave him?"

"It's a game we play," she admitted. "Random numbers that he tries to guess the significance of."

"Since you've made your phone number off-limits, what number would you give me?"

She held his gaze for a minute, considering. "Three," she decided.

"Three," he echoed, as he selected a wing from his plate. "Is that the number of dates we'll have before you let me see you naked?"

She rolled her eyes, but the color that rose in her cheeks suggested she wasn't as unaffected by the idea as she was pretending to be. "The number of times you'll come in here to hit on me before deciding to turn your attention in another direction."

"That response shortchanges both of us," he told her. "You, because you're worth a lot more effort than that. And me, because it suggests I'm fickle and/or shallow."

She lifted a shoulder—a dismissive half shrug. "I guess time will tell."

Of course, Marco wasn't the type to turn down a challenge.

He went back to O'Reilly's on Wednesday and again on Thursday, but he stayed away over the weekend. His absence was for both strategic and practical reasons. Strategically, he wanted her to have some time to think about him and, hopefully, to look forward to seeing him again. Practically, he had his own responsibilities at Valentino's and he knew that the pub would be too busy for them to talk.

Monday night, he left his family's restaurant after the dinner rush, arriving at the pub just before nine o'clock. Jordyn looked up when he walked in, and her eyes met his from across the room. When she smiled, he knew that she was happy to see him—even if she wasn't willing to admit it aloud.

"Smithwick's?" she asked as he settled onto a stool at the bar.

"Sure."

He watched her pour his beer, admiring the dark green vest with the O'Reilly's logo above her left breast worn over a simple white T-shirt tucked into slim-fitting jeans. He wasn't sure if it was a uniform, but it was her standard attire for working behind the bar.

"If you want food tonight, you should let me get your order in before the Brew Crew shows up."

He'd forgotten that the baseball team played on Monday nights, after which the players would head to O'Reilly's for food and drinks.

"It gets pretty busy then?" he guessed.

"It gets crazy," she admitted.

Half an hour later, he saw that she wasn't kidding.

There were two waitresses working the floor tonight, and they pushed together several tables to accommodate the group that arrived. It wasn't just the ballplayers—some of the men had their wives or girlfriends with them, and a few had even brought their kids. The ones who were single flirted with the waitresses—or stopped by the bar to order their drinks directly from Jordyn and flirt with her instead.

Since it was a little crowded around the bar, he took his beer and joined his sister and brother-in-law at their table, listening to their recap of the game—an exciting, come-from-behind victory over the Badge(r)s, a team primarily made up of local law enforcement.

For the better part of two hours, they ate and drank and chatted. Pitchers of beer were emptied, platters of finger foods devoured. He was pleased to see Renata out with her husband, enjoying a break while their mother watched over her granddaughters. When they finally left, he made his way back to the bar.

Jordyn was shelving a tray of clean glasses when he returned to the stool he'd vacated earlier.

"I thought you left when Craig and Renata did."

"No, but I did switch from beer to coffee about an hour ago," he said, putting his empty mug on the bar.

She picked up the carafe from the heating element and refilled his cup. "Four."

"The fourth time I've stopped in here to see you," he noted.

"It is that," she agreed. "It's also one of the digits of my phone number."

He grinned. "Progress."

"I guess that's a matter of interpretation."

"Which digit?" he wondered. "The first? The last?"

She shook her head. "One of the five in between."

"It's a start," he said.

And possibly, Jordyn realized as she moved away, a mistake.

What was she doing? Why had she given him the number? Was she actually flirting with him? Encouraging his attention?

Apparently she was. Even more surprising was that she actually looked forward to seeing him. He didn't come into the bar every night—and she didn't work every night. But every night that she did, she found herself wondering if he would walk through the doors, and just the possibility caused butterflies to flutter around in her tummy.

Saturday afternoon—twelve days and four more visits to the pub later—she'd given Marco five random numbers of the seven that comprised her phone number.

"After two more nights, I'll have your complete phone number," he noted, keying the eight into the memo pad on his smartphone.

"*If* you can figure out the order of the digits," she agreed.

"You're having fun toying with me, aren't you?"

"I told you I wasn't going to go out with you," she reminded him. "But if you can figure out my telephone number from the random single digits I've been giving you, I might change my mind."

"That's probably the most encouraging thing you've ever said to me," he told her.

She shrugged, uneasy with the truth of his statement, because she knew that she shouldn't be encouraging him at all. No good could come of continuing to play this game with him, and yet she couldn't seem to stop herself.

"As for figuring out your number, it won't be too hard," he told her. "From seven digits, assuming no duplicate numbers, there are five thousand and forty possibilities."

She narrowed her gaze. "Did you just pull that number out of thin air?"

He shook his head. "No, it's a simple matter of permutations and combinations—"

She held up a hand. "I always hated math."

"Then you'll have to trust that my calculations are accurate."

"If they are, that's a lot of dialing," she warned.

"As you pointed out a few weeks back—I'm persistent."

"That was your word," she reminded him. "I said relentless."

"I can be—when I want something badly enough."

And for some reason, he'd decided that he wanted her, and she was finally beginning to accept that she wanted him, too. Or at least wanted to satisfy the yearning that stirred inside her whenever he was near.

"You might want to consider," he continued, "that you've finally met your match."

Shivers of excited anticipation danced along her spine as she acknowledged his words might possibly be true.

Chapter Four

Twenty years earlier, the Northbrook area had been considered one of the more "undesirable" parts of Charisma, but over the past decade, concentrated efforts to renew the neighborhood had been enormously successful. The storefronts that had long been dormant and boarded up now housed an appealing assortment of offices, shops and cafés, so that almost everything they wanted or needed was now within walking distance of the neighborhood residents.

"What do you think?" Marco asked his grandparents, his deliberately casual tone in contradiction to the nerves that were tangled up inside him.

They'd said very little as they toured the empty space that had previously housed Mykonos. The Mediterranean restaurant had done a brisk business serving quality food until the owner's wife was arrested for selling other services in the upstairs apartment six months earlier. Since then, the restaurant space had been vacant.

Salvatore Valentino looked around the kitchen—barely recognizable as such since the ovens, fryers, sinks and refrigerators had been taken out and sold by the landlord.

"It's better than what we started with on Queen Street," he acknowledged. "But it needs a lot of work to turn it into something worthy of the Valentino name."

"But you can see the potential," Caterina said, her tone slightly more encouraging.

"I'd like to make an offer on the property," Marco told them.

"So make an offer," his grandfather said.

Caterina elbowed her husband sharply in the ribs and

muttered some unflattering words about her spouse in Italian. Then she reverted back to English to say, "Our grandson is asking for our approval."

"Our grandson should know we trust him to do what is right for the business."

"I appreciate that," he told them. "But I want to make sure you're aware of the risks."

"Such as the fact that sixty percent of new businesses fail within the first three years?" Salvatore asked.

"That statistic is exaggerated," Caterina said.

"How do you know?" her husband challenged.

She lifted her chin. "I watch CNN."

"Statistics aside," Marco interjected, eager to diffuse the argument he sensed was brewing, "we should have an advantage in that we're not opening a new restaurant—we're expanding an established business to a second location."

"What's your timeline?"

"At this point, it's a guess—but I'm hoping no more than four to six months, if we enlist the family to do most of the renovations."

"With you working regular hours at Valentino's and overtime here?" Caterina guessed.

"I'm going to pull everyone in for this project," he assured her. "Including Nonno."

His grandfather's face brightened perceptibly; his grandmother's gaze narrowed. "His heart—"

Marco touched a hand to her arm, silently reassuring her that he understood her concerns. But he also understood that it was important for his grandfather to keep busy and feel useful. "We'll keep a close eye on him," he promised.

"Mi tratta come se fossi un bambino," Salvatore grumbled.

"A toddler has more sense than you do sometimes," his wife shot back.

Then she turned to Marco. "What are you smiling about?"

"Just thinking how lucky I am to have both of you in my life."

"Don't you forget it," Caterina said.

At the same time, Salvatore said, "Suck-up."

His grandmother moved to the window, looking at the boutiques and shops across the street. "It's a more upscale neighborhood than downtown."

"It is," he confirmed. "Which translates into the local residents having deeper pockets and eating out more often."

"Will you change the prices?" Salvatore asked worriedly.

"Not on our traditional pasta dishes," Marco promised. "But we'll offer some higher-priced special entrées and a higher-end wine selection. Nonna and Rafe will create the menu, if I can convince him to run the kitchen here."

"You should hire Lana as a hostess."

Marco frowned. "Who?"

"Elena Luchetta's granddaughter."

"We've got a lot of work to do before we can start thinking about hiring anyone," he said with more patience than he felt.

"But she'd be perfect," Nonna insisted.

"Because she's Italian?"

"*Sì.* And single."

He sighed. "You've got to stop dangling all of your friends' granddaughters under my nose like they're bait."

"I will when you finally snap one of them up," she said unapologetically.

"There's no need for the boy to rush into marriage," Salvatore defended.

"I want great-grandbabies," Caterina said.

"You have six," Marco reminded her.

"No thanks to you," she retorted.

"What are your plans for the upper level?" Salvatore asked.

Marco turned to him, grateful for the abrupt change of topic. "There are two bedrooms, a bathroom, small living area and kitchenette."

"Private entrance?"

He nodded.

"Could generate some rental income," his grandfather noted.

Marco had considered that possibility. "Or we could renovate it to offer private event rooms."

"We already do that."

He shook his head. "We host group events—bridal and baby showers, engagement and birthday parties. I was thinking of promoting the space for more intimate gatherings and private celebrations."

"Intimate and private sounds like what got this place shut down," Salvatore warned.

Marco choked on a laugh. "I was thinking of something like dinner for two—to celebrate wedding anniversaries or set the stage for marriage proposals."

Caterina sniffed. "What do you know about proposals?"

"I know that if and when I finally meet the right woman, it would be nice to have a romantic—and private—setting in which to pop the question."

"Or to celebrate a sixty-fifth anniversary," Salvatore said, lifting his wife's hand to brush his lips over the back of it.

"If we make it to sixty-five years," she told him, a teasing glint in her eyes, "I don't want a private dinner. I want a big party—*una grande festa.*"

"And I want whatever you want," her husband assured her.

"Now who's the suck-up?" Marco said.

His grandfather just grinned.

"So we're going to put in an offer?"

"If you're really sure you want to do this," Caterina said.

"We've been planning it for two years," he reminded her.

"I know. I just wish…"

"What do you wish?" he prompted gently.

"That you didn't have so much time to devote to this endeavor."

"I don't understand," he admitted. "Are you saying that you don't want to expand?"

"No—I'm saying that you need *equilibrio* in your life. Not just work, work, work all the time. You need *romanticismo*."

"Right now, I need to get in touch with the real estate agent," he said.

"And we need to get over to the restaurant," Salvatore reminded his wife.

Caterina nodded. "We'll see you tomorrow."

He bent down to kiss both of her cheeks, gave his grandfather a quick hug, then walked them to the door.

Looking around the empty, dusty room, there was no denying that it needed a lot of work, but most of it was cosmetic. The wide storefront windows definitely needed a good cleaning, but he could already envision the gold-leaf lettering that would announce Valentino's II.

It was also easy to picture the concrete pad between the door and the sidewalk as a summer patio, with wrought iron tables and chairs, and he made a mental note to look into whatever permits would be required.

Then she stepped into view, and everything else was forgotten.

Jordyn loved living in Northbrook. Almost everything that she wanted or needed was within walking distance, including Sweet Serenity Boutique & Spa, which is where she was heading for a mani/pedi appointment with her sisters. She enjoyed the monthly ritual they shared, not just for the pampering of her body but the time that it afforded them together.

Because in addition to being her sisters, Tristyn and Lauryn were her best friends. They might not always agree on everything, but they always had one another's backs. When Lauryn got married, Jordyn was her maid of honor; when Jordyn was planning her wedding, she'd asked Tristyn to be hers; and whenever Tristyn was ready to exchange vows, it was understood that Lauryn would fulfill the role for her. In the meantime, they each had their own lives and responsibilities but they made a point of spending time together as much as possible—which was easier for Jordyn and Tristyn, considering that they lived together, and why they planned a girls' day with Lauryn at least once a month.

Today they had planned to meet for brunch at the Morning Glory Café followed by manicures, pedicures and hot stone massages at Sweet Serenity. Because Jordyn had worked until closing at O'Reilly's the night before, she'd opted to sleep in rather than join her sisters for brunch, promising to meet them at the spa at two o'clock.

The window display of Zahara's caught her eye and halted her steps. Though her wardrobe was usually simple and functional, she was a sucker for fun jewelry, and the dangling cherry earrings were calling to her. A quick glance at her watch assured her that she didn't need to rush.

Five minutes later, she walked out of the boutique with her silver hoops tucked into the zippered change compartment of her wallet and the red-and-green crystals sparkling at her ears. She might have resisted them if not for the fact that they went so perfectly with the cherry-red capris and simple white T-shirt she was wearing.

"Hey, Jordyn."

She was just starting up the flagstone path to the entrance of the spa when she heard his voice behind her, and her heart started to race. Chastising herself for the frustrating and inexplicable reaction to his presence, she turned to face him.

"Hi, Marco. What brings you to the neighborhood? Or is this your usual destination for manscaping?"

He looked at her blankly. "What?"

She pointed to the sign in the window offering manicures, pedicures, facials, hair removal and body treatments.

To his credit, he recovered quickly, holding his hands out for her inspection. "Now that you mention it, I'm hoping to get something done about these ragged cuticles."

Except that there was nothing wrong with his hands. They were broad and tanned, his fingers long and lean, his nails clean and neatly trimmed.

"Ask for Lori," she suggested.

"I'll do that," he promised, and his smile—quick and easy—made her knees feel weak. "Actually, I was just in the neighborhood on business."

She glanced across the street. "Business by any chance linked to the rumor about a new Italian restaurant opening up where Mykonos used to be?"

"You don't strike me as the type of person who would pay much attention to gossip."

"Which isn't a denial but a deflection," she noted.

"And proves that you're as smart as you are beautiful," he said.

Out of the corner of her eye, Jordyn saw that Tristyn and Lauryn had arrived. "And that's another deflection."

"A fact," he assured her.

"What's a fact?" Tristyn wanted to know.

"It's a fact," Marco said, encompassing both of the new

arrivals with a smile, "that all of the Garrett women are smart and beautiful."

"And you're as handsome and charming as always," Tristyn assured him.

He looked at Jordyn again. "See? Some women think I'm handsome and charming."

"Some women are easily impressed," she replied. "And we're going to be late for our appointments."

"Full-body massage," Tristyn said, winking at Marco. "They give us a discount if we rub the oil all over one another."

Marco's eyes went wide—and then glazed over.

Lauryn laughed even as she smacked Tristyn in the arm.

"She's kidding," Jordyn assured him.

He blinked and refocused. "Oh. Right. Of course." He took a step back. "Have a good day, ladies."

Sweet Serenity Spa was located in a renovated three-story colonial revival home with different services offered on different floors. The lower level had eight pedicure stations in a circle around the outside of the room, usually separated by movable folding screens. Two of the screens had been removed so that the sisters could chat while they were pampered.

"So tell me about the hunky guy outside," Lauryn said after they'd picked their polish and had their feet soaking in individual baths of warm, bubbling water.

"You mean Jordyn's new boyfriend?" Tristyn asked.

Jordyn sighed. "He isn't—"

"I'm *so* glad you're dating again," Lauryn said.

"I'm not dating Marco," she said firmly.

Lauryn's brow furrowed as she turned to their other sister.

"Well, he *wants* to be her new boyfriend," Tristyn said.

"And I'm not looking for a boyfriend," she told both of them.

"It's been more than three years," Lauryn reminded her gently.

"I'm well aware of how long it's been."

"Brian wouldn't want you to grieve forever."

"I'm not still grieving," she denied.

"Then why won't you go out with Marco?" Tristyn demanded.

"I'm just not interested in dating anyone right now."

"I understand that in theory," Lauryn said. "But the man knocking on your door is a mouthwateringly tempting reality."

"And she's the married one," Tristyn pointed out.

Jordyn couldn't deny that Marco was mouthwatering. And tempting. But she was more scared than she was tempted. Because in the few short weeks that she'd known him, she'd realized that she liked him. And if she spent more time with him, if she actually went out on a date with him, she might find that she *really* liked him. Then that liking might lead to her wanting more, and she wasn't willing to risk anything more.

"How's Kylie?" she asked, referring to Lauryn's fourteen-month-old daughter in a not-so-subtle attempt to change the topic of conversation.

"She's getting so big," Lauryn said. "And so independent. Since she started to walk, she doesn't like being carried anymore."

"Which probably isn't a bad thing, considering that you're going to be carrying another baby in a few months."

"Not for another eight months," she reminded her sisters. "Which is why Rob and I agreed not to tell anyone about the pregnancy yet."

"We're not anyone," Tristyn protested. "We're your sisters."

Lauryn picked up the glass of spring water infused with cucumber and lime, and sipped. "He's a little worried about having another child so soon," she admitted. "Since Kylie was born, I've only been working part-time hours at the Gallery, and business isn't great at the Locker Room."

The Gallery was Garrett Furniture's showroom where Lauryn had been a sales supervisor prior to her maternity leave, and the Locker Room was her husband's sporting goods store downtown.

"How are the renovations on the house coming along?" Jordyn asked, hoping the shift in topic might ease the furrow in her sister's brow.

But Lauryn only sighed. "They've stalled," she admitted. "Rob's been spending so many hours at the store, it doesn't seem fair to expect him to tackle another job when he gets home."

What wasn't fair—at least in Jordyn's opinion—was that her sister was living in a dump. Tom and Susan Garrett had given their daughter and her husband a generous cash gift for their wedding, with the understanding that the money would be used for a down payment on a house.

Lauryn had found what she wanted in Ridgemount— a simple craftsman-style house with pretty gardens and a modest backyard. Rob had agreed that the house was perfect, but he'd been reluctant to tie up all of their money in real estate when he was trying to make a go of his business. Instead, he'd convinced her that they could buy a fixer-upper for much less money and use the additional funds to purchase inventory for his fledgling business.

It was a solid plan—except that the fledgling business was now apparently a struggling business, and he'd done almost nothing to fix up the fixer-upper. In fact, the only reason the nursery had been fixed up before Kylie was born was that Jordyn had enlisted the help of Andrew and Nathan—two of their cousins—to get it done.

"I like that color." Lauryn gestured to the polish that was being applied to her sister's toenails in an obvious attempt to steer the conversation away from another uncomfortable topic. "What's it called?"

"Cherried Away." Jordyn pushed her hair behind her ear to show off her new purchase. "It matches my earrings."

"I wish I was brave enough to wear color like that," Lauryn said, her gaze shifting to her own toes.

"French pedicures are classic," Tristyn assured her.

"Says the woman sporting Buxom Bronze on her feet and a quaternary Celtic knot tattoo on her ass."

Tristyn grinned. "I get a lot of compliments on that tattoo."

"We don't want to know," Jordyn told her.

"Maybe *I* do," Lauryn said. "I'm an old married woman who needs to get her thrills vicariously through her single sisters—and since you won't share anything about Marco—"

"Because there's nothing to share," Jordyn insisted.

"At least, not yet," Tristyn said.

Thankfully, they were called upstairs for their massages, saving Jordyn from having to deny what she really wanted.

An hour later, the sisters walked out into the late-afternoon sunshine, and Jordyn's gaze shifted to the empty property across the street.

"Did either of you hear anything about a new restaurant opening in place of Mykonos?"

"There have been rumors floating around for a couple of months," Tristyn confirmed. "Is that why Marco was in the neighborhood?"

"He didn't say, but that's my guess."

"You didn't ask him?" Lauryn wondered.

"I did. He was evasive."

"We could use a good Italian place nearby," Tristyn said. "We've got three cafés, two diners, a deli, bakery, vegetarian bistro, pizza place, Asian fusion cuisine, Southern barbecue and Indian buffet, but nowhere to get a good plate of pasta."

"The Spaghetti House isn't very far," Jordyn reminded her.

"I said '*good* plate of pasta.'"

"All this talk of food is making me hungry," Lauryn said.

"Me, too," Jordyn agreed. "Let's head over to Marg & Rita's before it gets too busy and we have to wait for a table."

But Tristyn shook her head. "It's my turn to pick where we're going for dinner," she reminded her sisters.

Which was technically true. Their monthly "girls' day" that usually involved the spa and/or shopping was always followed by dinner and drinks, and they alternated who got to choose the restaurant. Except that they'd become addicted to the signature drinks at Marg & Rita's and hadn't gone anywhere else in the past five months.

"We always go to Marg & Rita's," Lauryn said.

"Not always," Tristyn denied.

Jordyn sighed. "Let me guess—you're in the mood for Italian food tonight?"

"My mouth is watering for Valentino's seven-layer lasagna."

"I thought you were trying to cut down on carbs."

Tristyn waved a hand dismissively. "That plan went out the window with the banana-pecan waffles I had this morning."

"Now that you mention it, Italian sounds really good," Lauryn agreed.

"I want fajitas," Jordyn insisted, because she did. And because she wanted no part of whatever plan she suspected her sisters were concocting to throw her into Marco Palermo's path.

"Sorry," Tristyn said, not sounding sorry at all. "We can do Marg & Rita's next month, when it's your turn to pick. Although maybe by then, you'll be craving Italian, too."

Jordyn ignored the innuendo and crossed her fingers that Marco wouldn't be working tonight.

Chapter Five

"You're late," Gemma said when Marco walked into the kitchen at Valentino's just after four o'clock Saturday afternoon.

"And I might feel guilty about that if not for the fact that it's supposed to be my night off."

"You have a night off?" This came from Rocco, a fifteen-year-old neighborhood kid who was the grandson of one of Nonna's oldest friends and one of their weekend dishwashers.

Marco cuffed him playfully in the back of the head. "It's interesting how everyone likes to harp on the fact that I have no life outside of the restaurant but then, when I'm not supposed to be here, I get called in anyway."

"You're right," Gemma agreed. "I'm sorry. But Rebecca's roommate called to say that she was sick, and I could hear her retching in the background."

Marco grimaced. "And what are the specials tonight?"

"The pasta is gnocchi with tomato-cream sauce and fresh basil, the pizza is grilled vegetable on a whole-wheat crust. Sydney is working the front of the dining room. You get the back."

"Lucky me."

"You only need to stay through the dinner rush," Gemma promised. "After that you can get back to… whatever."

"I'm going to hold you to that," he told her, pretending that "whatever" was something other than a Yankees–Red Sox game on television.

He understood why she'd called. Within half an hour, both he and Sydney were beating a steady path from the kitchen to the dining room and back again. He'd forgotten how much he'd once enjoyed this interaction with the customers, hearing their rave reviews of the food, answering their inquiries about his grandparents and other family members. There was one screwup: the sous chef put fusilli instead of rotini with Mrs. DiCenzo's chicken Parm, but the error was quickly rectified and the customer's displeasure alleviated by a complimentary serving of tiramisu.

He was delivering two large pizzas to a family of six—regular Saturday-night customers—when he saw them walk in. Jordyn and her sisters. And, as usual when he saw the stunningly beautiful middle Garrett sister, his heart skipped a beat.

He held his breath as Gemma guided them through the dining room. She paused beside a booth near the front, then shook her head and continued along, gesturing to an identical booth at the back of the restaurant.

In his section.

In that instant, any annoyance that had lingered over being called in to work immediately and completely vanished.

Luck was not on Jordyn's side.

Not only was Marco working, but he showed up at their table to take their order after they'd been seated by Gemma and given a few minutes to browse the menu.

"I thought you were a bartender, not a waiter," Jordyn commented when he set the basket of warm bread sticks on the table.

"Obviously he's a man of many talents," Tristyn said, winking at him.

He winked back. "A prerequisite of working in a family business," he confirmed, then proceeded to tell them about the daily specials. He gave them a few more minutes to decide while he went to fill their drink orders.

Tristyn folded her menu and set it aside. "I'm having the lasagna."

"I'm having serious doubts about Jordyn's sanity," Lauryn said, turning to her middle sister. "Because if I were single and any man looked at me the way he looked at you, I'd snap him up—no questions asked."

"Which part of 'not interested' don't you understand?" Jordyn asked her sister.

"We understand it, we just don't believe it," Tristyn said.

Jordyn couldn't blame her sisters for their skepticism. Because the truth was, she felt a tug of something whenever Marco was near; she'd just decided to ignore it. After Brian died, it had taken a long time for her heart to heal, and she wasn't ready to risk it again. Not even for a sweet and sexy bartender with a dimple in his cheek and a twinkle in his eye that warmed the deepest parts of her.

"What's on the vegetarian pizza?" Lauryn asked when Marco returned with their drinks.

"It has a thin whole-wheat crust topped with homemade pesto sauce, grated mozzarella cheese, thin slices of Roma tomatoes, green peppers and cremini mushrooms."

"Is it good?"

"Of course," he said, then lowered his voice to add, "but a better vegetarian option—in my opinion—is the classic Margherita pizza with tomato sauce, buffalo mozzarella and fresh basil."

"I'm not a vegetarian," Lauryn said. "I'm just not a fan of meat on pizza."

Jordyn knew that wasn't true. On more than one occasion, she'd seen her sister enjoy pizza with pepperoni, hot sausage and bacon, so she suspected the truth was that the baby was protesting the idea of meat on pizza.

"I'll try a small Margherita pizza," Lauryn decided.

"Good choice," he said, turning to Tristyn.

"I'll have the seven-layer lasagna," she told him.

He nodded before turning his attention—and bone-melting smile—to Jordyn. "And what can I get for you?"

She told herself that she wasn't affected, but the annoying flutters in her belly suggested otherwise.

"The gnocchi," she decided, handing him the menu.

"One of my favorites," he said, and smiled at her in a way that made her recently painted toes curl.

"Maybe we don't need an Italian restaurant in our neighborhood," Tristyn said when she pushed her mostly empty plate aside. "If I ate like that on a regular basis, I'd have to spend a lot more time at the gym."

Jordyn raised her brows. "You go to the gym?"

"Not if I can help it," Tristyn admitted.

"So what are you doing with the rest of your night?" Lauryn asked her sisters.

Tristyn shrugged. "No specific plans."

"Mom and Dad are keeping Kylie overnight, so I thought maybe we could catch a movie. There's a new Bradley Cooper flick playing at the multiplex that I heard was fabulous."

"You had me at 'Bradley Cooper,'" Tristyn told her.

"Great—how about you, Jordyn?"

"I'm the one who told you it was a fabulous movie," she reminded her sister. "I saw it a couple of weeks ago."

"Oh." Lauryn sighed, obviously disappointed. "Well, maybe there's something else playing that we all want to see."

"No—you guys should go," Jordyn said. "I've got a ton of laundry to do, anyway."

Tristyn shook her head. "You're going to spend a Saturday night doing laundry?"

"My dirty socks don't know or care what day of the week it is."

"And I thought *I* didn't get out much," Lauryn mumbled.

"You forget that I'm out almost every night."

"Work doesn't count."

"Well, tonight I want to relax at home, so you can drop me off there on your way to the theater."

Lauryn shrugged. "Your call. And speaking of calls—I left my phone charging in the car. Can I borrow yours to text Rob to let him know our plans?"

"Sure." Jordyn found it easily in the front pocket of her purse and passed it across the table.

Lauryn quickly texted the message; Rob's response came back almost immediately. "He says no problem. He's working late tonight, anyway."

"What are you guys doing tomorrow?" Tristyn asked. "Any big plans for your anniversary?"

Lauryn shook her head. "I don't think so."

Jordyn frowned at that. "I'm sure Rob has something planned—he probably just wants it to be a surprise."

"I'm pretty sure he plans to work," Lauryn said, trailing her finger through the condensation on the outside of her water glass.

Jordyn and Tristyn exchanged a worried look. They'd both had some concerns when their sister accepted Rob Schulte's proposal six and a half years earlier, but Lauryn had been head over heels in love, so they'd kept those concerns to themselves. And although Lauryn never said or did anything to indicate that she was unhappy with the choices she'd made, her sisters both knew that she wasn't as happy as she pretended to be.

"You're not doing *anything*?" Tristyn prompted.

"Like I said, Rob has to work all day, so I was planning to make his favorite buttermilk fried chicken and potato salad and pack it into a picnic basket to take to him at the store."

"That sounds lovely," Jordyn said.

It also sounded like her sister was making all of the effort for their anniversary—as she'd done throughout most of their relationship, but she kept that comment to herself.

"Have you decided on dessert?" Marco asked, returning to their table.

"Since I can't watch a movie without popcorn, I think I'm going to have to pass on dessert tonight," Lauryn said.

"Popcorn has nothing on cannoli," Tristyn said. "But you're right—if I have both, I'll end up feeling sick and won't enjoy the movie."

Jordyn sighed. "I guess that means I don't get any cannoli. It's no fun eating dessert alone."

"Any coffee or tea?" Marco offered.

"Just the bill," Lauryn said.

He nodded and moved away from the table.

"I'm going to hit the bathroom to wash up before we head out," Tristyn said.

"I'll come with you," Lauryn said. "Since I had Kylie, my bladder capacity isn't what it used to be."

Jordyn sat at the table, waiting for the bill.

After several minutes had gone by, she realized that Marco seemed to have disappeared, and the waitress who had been working the front of the restaurant had taken over the whole dining room. After she delivered appetizers to a nearby table, Jordyn flagged her down.

"Can I get you something else?" the woman, whose name tag identified her as Sydney, asked.

"I'm just waiting for the bill."

"It's been taken care of. Your friends paid on their way out."

"They *left*?"

"I think so," Sydney said, though she looked a little uncertain now. "I saw them settling up with Marco at the bar, then they headed toward the door."

"Thank you," Jordyn said, reaching into her purse for her phone as the waitress returned to her duties.

But of course, her phone wasn't in her purse, because Lauryn hadn't given it back to her after she'd texted Rob.

She waved the waitress over again. "Sorry to bother you again, but is there a phone that I could use?"

Sydney nodded. "At the bar."

Jordyn forced a smile. "Great. Thanks."

She picked up her purse and made her way to the bar. Marco was now behind the glossy expanse of mahogany, chatting with a young couple who were sipping wine and nibbling on antipasti.

She slipped between two high-backed chairs and folded her arms on the bar. He glanced over, his easy smile widening when he saw her. "I didn't realize you were still here."

"Not by choice," she assured him.

He looked at her quizzically.

"You didn't have anything to do with this?"

"With what?" he asked.

She sighed and shook her head. "Never mind."

"Can I get you something?" he asked, setting a cocktail napkin on the bar in front of her.

"A phone?"

"Not a usual request," he admitted, lifting a handset from the charger beneath the counter and setting it on the napkin.

"Thanks." She dialed Tristyn's number.

The call went directly to voice mail.

"I'm going to kill her," she muttered.

"Who?"

"My sister. Actually, both of them," she decided. "If you hear about a double homicide on the eleven-o'clock news, it will be them."

"Any particular reason?" he asked.

"I could give you a thousand, but the most recent is that they stole my phone." She dialed her own number next, and although it rang several times, the call wasn't picked up at the other end. "And now they're not even answering it."

She dialed again, still got no answer.

"Do you have the number of Gold Hub Taxi?" she asked him.

"Sure," he said. "But why are you calling a cab?"

"Because not only did my sisters steal my phone, they abandoned me here."

His brows lifted. "What did you do to them?"

"Nothing."

He set the phone back down, out of her reach, obviously waiting for more of an explanation.

She huffed out a breath. "It's a setup."

"What's a setup?"

"They abandoned me here to make me a damsel in distress and give you the opportunity to ride to my rescue, to prove that you're some kind of Prince Charming. Now can I please have the phone?"

One side of his mouth turned up in a half smile. "So that you can call a cab to take you home and deprive me of the opportunity to play my part?"

"Exactly," she confirmed.

"I think your sisters would be disappointed if I let that happen."

"You don't need to worry about disappointing them."

"All the same, I'd feel better if I saw you safely home."

She was about to tell him that she wasn't concerned with his feelings, but his words were followed by another one of those slow smiles that made her toes curl and her heart pound. Which was probably another reason she should insist on taking a cab. He waved over the hostess, said something to her that Jordyn couldn't hear.

Gemma nodded and disappeared into the kitchen.

"I appreciate the offer, but you can't just take off in the middle of a shift," Jordyn protested.

"I only got called in tonight because the restaurant was short staffed," he told her. "Now that the dinner rush is over, they don't need me here."

"You really shouldn't let my sisters draw you into their game."

He winked at her. "Why would I object when it gives me a chance to play with you?"

She rolled her eyes at the innuendo, refusing to acknowledge the quick spurt of her pulse that suggested that she might want to be played with. "It will save us both a lot of grief if you just let me call a cab."

"Would you really rather take a cab?"

"No," she admitted. "But I really don't like being manipulated."

He took a bakery box from Gemma when she returned. "Sydney has the dining room under control and Rafe is going to cover the bar."

"Where are you going?" she demanded.

"I'm giving Jordyn a ride home."

The hostess looked at her suspiciously. "Car trouble?"

She sighed. "Sister trouble."

Some of the suspicion faded from Gemma's eyes, and one side of her mouth turned up in a half smile.

"That I can relate to," she acknowledged. "Have a good night."

Jordyn had agreed to let him take her home, but it was obvious to Marco that she wasn't too pleased with the arrangement.

He'd probably be pissed, too, if his siblings had pulled that kind of stunt on him. But while he understood her feelings, he couldn't share them—he was too grateful to Tristyn and Lauryn for giving him this excuse to spend more time with Jordyn.

"I hope I'm not taking you too far out of your way," she said now.

"A drive with a beautiful woman is never out of the way," he assured her.

"You're every bit as charming as Tristyn warned me."

"I'm confused," he said. "Are they pushing us together or warning you away?"

"Okay, the comment about your charm was probably a commendation rather than a warning," she allowed. "But I don't trust charming men."

"Then I'll do my best to be—what's the opposite of charming?"

"Now you're making fun of me."

"Maybe a little," he acknowledged.

"At least you're honest."

"Do you trust honest men?"

"There it is again," she said.

"What?"

"The effortless charm."

"Sorry," he apologized, trying not to smile.

"No, you're not. You look at a woman with those dreamy eyes and easy smile and that damn dimple, and you know it's just a matter of time before she succumbs."

"Is it?" he asked. "Just a matter of time before you succumb, I mean."

She huffed out a breath. "We weren't talking about me."

"I'm only interested in you."

"Really? Because you had both of my sisters swooning."

He shook his head. "Tristyn is hardly the swooning type and Lauryn seems happily married."

Her brows lifted; he shrugged.

"I saw the ring."

"Is that a guy thing—checking the left hand every time you meet a woman?"

"Not every woman—just the really hot ones."

"I'm sure Lauryn would be flattered to know you put her in that category."

"Both of your sisters are stunning," he told her. "But you're the only one who makes my heart skip a beat every time I see you."

"Since it's dark and you're watching the road, you probably didn't see me roll my eyes at that."

"You don't believe it's true?"

"No," she said bluntly. Then, "Turn right here."

"I'll let that pass because you don't know me very well yet," he said, flicking on his indicator to make the turn.

"Yet?"

His lips curved. "The night is still young."

"The third street on the right," she said.

He made the next turn.

"And the second driveway on the left."

He pulled into the brick driveway and parked behind the silver-colored Prius that he recognized as her vehicle. The two-story town house was stone and brick, with a covered porch and lots of windows. The flower beds that flanked the steps leading up to the front door were a riot of red and purple and yellow blooms.

"Nice place," he said.

"We like it."

"We?"

"Me and Tristyn."

"How long have you lived here?"

"Almost four years." She dug her keys out of her purse. "Well, thanks for the ride."

"If you're really grateful, you could invite me in for a drink," he suggested.

"Or I could pretend you're Gold Hub Taxi and leave ten dollars on your dash."

"There's no need to take your anger on your sisters out on me," he pointed out reasonably.

She sighed. "You're right—I'm sorry. Would you like to come in for a drink?"

"I wouldn't say no to a cup of coffee."

"I've got coffee" she admitted.

"I've got cannoli," he told her.

"If you intended to share that cannoli with me, you might have mentioned that in the first place."

"I was hoping you'd be more interested in my company than my mother's pastry."

"Come on, Charm Boy."

He turned off the engine. "Charm Boy?"

She laughed at his indignant tone. "Would you prefer it if I called you Pastry Purveyor?"

"As long as you call me," he said with a grin.

Chapter Six

The front foyer was wide and inviting—the floor covered in sand-colored ceramic tiles, the walls painted a pale gold color and set off with glossy white trim. It was tasteful and elegant and probably professionally decorated, which shouldn't have surprised him, considering that she was a Garrett.

His own family was hardly poor—except in comparison to one of Charisma's oldest and wealthiest families. Which made him wonder why Jordyn would choose to work erratic hours behind the bar in an Irish pub instead of holding down a nine-to-five job in one of the offices of Garrett Furniture.

Jordyn stepped out of her sandals, drawing his attention to her feet—and her sexy toenails. "Nice color," he said.

She glanced down and smiled. "Thanks."

"Did you have a good day with your sisters?"

"Until they ditched me—yeah." She led the way down a narrow hallway, past a cozy-looking living area with plush pillow-back sofas and dark mission-style tables, skirting past a curving staircase leading to a second level.

"What's upstairs?"

"Three bedrooms and another bathroom."

"You're not going to give me a tour?"

"No, but I will give you the coffee you said you wanted."

He decided to be grateful for that much and try not to think about the fact that her bedroom was somewhere at the top of those stairs.

"What kind of coffee do you like?"

"Regular."

A wide arched doorway led into the kitchen. Jordyn hit a switch on the wall, flooding the room with light.

"Almond biscotti, caramel drizzle, half caff, bold extra, Italian roast, Irish cream, French vanilla or breakfast in bed."

He smiled. "I didn't know breakfast in bed was an option."

"It's a flavor of coffee."

"Oh." He glanced over her shoulder at the coffee carousel. "Italian roast."

She pulled a mug out of the cupboard, set it on the drip tray, popped the flavor cup into the machine, then set it brewing. She turned around, her lips curving as she looked past him to the doorway. "There you are, sweetie."

Sweetie?

Marco felt as if the bottom had fallen out of his stomach, then he turned and saw the object of her affection: a mass of white, black and rust-colored fur that was emitting a sound that was a cross between a wheeze and a rumble from deep in its belly.

"What is that?" he asked cautiously.

"Gryffindor."

"But *what* is it?" he asked again.

"He's my cat."

A cat.

Marco narrowed his gaze, finally nodded. Although it didn't look like any cat he'd ever seen, he could acknowledge that it fit the general description, except—

"Where's its tail?"

Jordyn laughed. "He's missing an eye and half of one ear, and you notice his tail."

"If he had a tail and it was twitching from side to side, I'd be less convinced that he was planning to attack me."

"He's a Manx," she said. "They don't have tails."

"Are the eye and ear also characteristic of the breed?"

She shook her head. "No. He's been through a lot more than I want to imagine."

"How long have you had him?"

"It would probably be more accurate to say that he has me," she said. "And it's been almost seven years."

"Did he come with the name?"

"No. He was a stray—battered and bruised and about three years old when I finally managed to convince him to give up his life on the streets."

"A stray with the heart of a lion," he guessed.

She nodded, surprised that he immediately recognized the origin of the name. "He's loyal and affectionate. And very protective of me," she added, when Marco squatted down to get closer to the feline.

But he didn't reach out to the cat—which would likely have earned him a swat or a hiss. He just kept talking to Jordyn and let Gryffindor approach him.

Except that Jordyn knew he wouldn't. There was a very short list of people that Gryff tolerated being near, and none that he'd known for less than three years.

Marco held perfectly still while the cat moved closer, his one gold eye narrowed suspiciously as he sniffed the stranger's trousers. Jordyn took the bakery box from him, certain the scent of the sweet pastries was the reason for the cat's interest, and set it on the counter.

But Gryff's attention didn't shift away from Marco. "Do you have catnip in your pockets?"

"Excuse me?"

"Gryff hates strangers." She frowned at the cat. "Usually."

"Maybe he senses that I'm not going to be a stranger for long."

"Or maybe he's being kind because he senses that you're delusional," Jordyn suggested.

The cat rubbed its cheek back and forth against Marco's

thigh, leaving a few white and orange hairs on the dark fabric. He didn't complain; he didn't even attempt to brush them away.

She removed his cup from the drip tray. "Cream? Sugar?"

He shook his head. "Black."

She made a face as she handed him the cup, then set another in its place and popped in a French vanilla pod. Gryff wound between Marco's feet, emitting some kind of noise that sounded suspiciously like purring.

"When I was a kid, my grandmother on my father's side had a cat—a fluffy white thing that was spoiled and mean."

"Gryff can be plenty mean," she told him. "And there's no doubt he's spoiled."

"And loved."

She shrugged. "I'm a sucker for a sad story."

"Should I tell you about the time my grandmother's cat clawed my arm when I was twelve?"

"Did it leave a scar?"

"Actually, it did," he said, unfastening the cuff of his shirt to roll it back.

His forearm was muscular, the skin tanned and dusted with dark hair. But she could see the trio of barely visible lines, all that remained of what had once been nasty five-inch gashes. As if of its own volition, her fingertip touched the top edge of one line, slowly traced the length of the scar. His muscle tightened beneath her touch, and her blood pulsed, hot and heavy, in her veins.

She pulled her hand away, swallowed. "Looks like it was a nasty scratch."

"Bled like crazy," he told her, unapologetically milking the incident for every ounce of sympathy he could get. "And I had to get a tetanus shot."

"What did you do to the cat to make him scratch you?"

"Her—the cat was female." He rolled his sleeve back

down, refastened the button at the cuff. "And I didn't do anything—she was just mean. Nonna P.—that's what we called her, to distinguish her from Nonna V.—told me it was an important life lesson to learn that all females had claws."

"That's a pretty harsh lesson for a twelve-year-old."

He shrugged. "Nonna P. wasn't really the warm and fuzzy type."

"You're close to your family?"

"Too close sometimes, but that's probably to be expected when I work with half of them and live within spitting distance of the other half."

"I can relate," she said. "I worked at Garrett Furniture for several years, and I still live with my sister."

She went to the fridge to get the cream, added a generous splash to her cup, then stirred in two teaspoons of sugar.

"How can you even call that coffee?"

"It's the only way I like it." She gestured for him to sit at the table, then she got plates and napkins and the box of cannoli.

"Why bother to drink it at all if you have to disguise the true flavor?"

She shrugged as she sat down across from him. "I started drinking coffee in college—now it's an addiction."

"Probably the sugar more than the caffeine."

"Probably."

"So what did you study in college?"

"Mostly marketing." She opened the box, lifted out the cream-filled pastries and set them on the plates.

"And leastly?" he prompted.

She smiled. "This and that. How about you?"

"Restaurant and hotel management."

"A good choice, especially considering the family business." She lifted her pastry to her mouth, bit into it. Flaky crumbs and powdered sugar rained down on her plate, but she didn't notice. She was too busy humming with pleasure as the rich flavor exploded on her tongue. "Oh. My. God. This is...unbelievable."

"You've never had cannoli before?"

"Not from Valentino's," she admitted.

"From where?"

"The Spaghetti House."

"Seriously?"

"Valentino's is downtown," she explained. "The Spaghetti House is two blocks away."

"The Spaghetti House uses dry noodles and canned sauce."

"When I make pasta at home, I use dry noodles and canned sauce," she admitted.

"Why don't you save yourself the trouble and just get the noodles already mixed with the sauce in a can?"

"Are you a hater of boxed macaroni and cheese, too?"

He muttered something in Italian that she was pretty sure she was glad she didn't understand.

"You should spend a few hours in the kitchen at Valentino's someday," he suggested. "To see and appreciate how real Italian food is made."

"I may not be a connoisseur of fine cuisine, but I'm not a food snob, either."

"I'm not a food snob," he denied.

"Do you ever eat at a restaurant not called Valentino's?" she challenged.

"Not if I want Italian food."

"Exactly my point."

"Do you have any furniture in this house that doesn't have the 'GF' logo stamped on it?"

She frowned at the question. "Of course not."

He lifted his brows.

"Okay—I get your point." She licked powdered sugar

off her fingers. "If I accepted your invitation to hang out in the kitchen at Valentino's, would I see how the cannoli are made?"

"Sorry—my mother does the baking in her kitchen at home. But if you wanted to go home with me for a family dinner, she might be enticed to share her secret."

"Thanks, but it's probably easier just to stop at Valentino's to pick one up if I have a craving."

"Easier," he agreed. "But not nearly as much fun."

"I guess that depends on your interpretation of fun."

"Speaking of—why didn't you want to go to the movie with your sisters tonight?"

"I've seen it," she said. "And I had laundry to do."

"I think I understand now why they felt that you needed to be rescued."

"From laundry?"

"From your belief that a washing machine is suitable company on a Saturday night."

"Well, Charm Boy, you are a better conversationalist than my Maytag," she acknowledged.

"And hopefully less agitating."

She smiled at that. "Much less, so thank you for rescuing me."

"I'd say we rescued each other." He finished his coffee, then pushed away from the table. "But now I should let you get started on that laundry."

She carried her empty plate and cup to the sink, set them beside his. She'd enjoyed his company, but she didn't know how to say that without giving him the impression that she was open to anything more. So she said nothing, silently following him to the door.

"Thanks again for the ride home," she said. "And the cannoli."

"Thanks for the coffee." He lifted a hand to touch the

crystal cherries dangling from her ear, then tipped her chin up. "And the kiss."

The—

Before her brain fully grasped the implication, his mouth was on hers.

Marco half expected Jordyn to slap him. Or at the very least, push him away. She'd given him no reason to believe that she would be receptive to a romantic overture, but he'd been unable to resist sampling the flavor and texture of her lips.

She didn't slap him.

And she didn't push him away.

After a brief moment of surprise and indecision, her eyelids fluttered closed and her mouth yielded to his.

He was nearly as stunned as he was aroused to realize she was kissing him back. Tentatively at first, as if she wasn't quite sure this was a good idea. But after a few seconds—brief and yet somehow endless seconds during which he held his breath and fervently prayed that she wouldn't suddenly decide to slap him or push him away— a soft sigh sounded deep in her throat, then she lifted her arms to his shoulders and melted into him.

He settled his hands lightly on her hips, holding her close but not too tight. He wanted her to know that this was her choice while leaving her in no doubt about what he wanted. She pressed closer to him, and the sensation of her soft curves against his body made him ache.

He parted her lips with his tongue, and she opened willingly. She tasted warm and sweet—with a hint of vanilla from the coffee she'd drunk—and the exquisite flavor of her spread through his blood, through his body, like an addictive drug.

He felt something bump against his shin. Once. Twice.

The cat, he realized, in the same moment he decided he didn't dare ignore its warning.

Not that he was afraid of Gryffindor, but he was afraid of scaring off Jordyn. Beneath her passionate response, he sensed a lingering wariness and uncertainty.

Slowly, reluctantly, he eased his lips from hers.

She drew in an unsteady breath, confusion swirling in her deep green eyes when she looked at him. "What…what just happened here?"

"I think we just confirmed that there's some serious chemistry between us."

She shook her head. "I'm not going to go out with you, Marco."

There was a note of something—almost like panic— in her voice that urged him to proceed cautiously. "I don't mind staying in," he said lightly.

She choked on a laugh. "I'm not going to have sex with you, either."

"Not tonight," he agreed. "I'm not *that* easy."

This time, she didn't quite manage to hold back the laugh, though sadness lingered in her eyes.

"You have a great laugh," he told her.

Her gaze dropped and her smile faded. "I haven't had much to laugh about in a while."

"Are you ever going to tell me about it?"

He braced himself for one of her flippant replies, a deliberate brush-off, and was surprised by her response.

"Maybe," she finally said. "But not tonight."

It was an acknowledgment that she would see him again, and that was enough for now.

Though Jordyn and Tristyn lived together, their different work schedules meant that the sisters were often going in opposite directions. As a result, Jordyn spent a lot of time alone, and she was usually content with only the cat for company. But after Marco had gone, the house seemed oddly quiet and empty.

She carted her laundry down to the basement and began sorting it into piles. Brian had planned to move the washer and dryer to the main floor, but he'd died before he had the chance to do so.

They'd bought the house on the basis of their combined incomes, and Jordyn had trouble making the mortgage payments on her own after the accident. A financial hole that got even deeper when she decided to walk away from her job at Garrett Furniture.

Her family had been surprised and worried when she'd handed in her notice, but she knew it was what she had to do. She'd met Brian in her office at the company; she'd fallen in love with him there, too. And when he'd proposed—he'd gotten down on one knee beside her desk, where he claimed to have lost his heart the day they met. When he was gone, it was just too hard for her to go into the office every day and not see him there.

She'd struggled for a few months after that—not just financially but emotionally. She worried about losing the town house, but she wasn't entirely certain she wanted to keep it. The reality of living alone in the place they'd chosen together wasn't just lonely but painful.

She'd been surprised—and hesitant—when Tristyn offered to rent one of the spare bedrooms until Jordyn decided whether she wanted to stay in the house or sell it. Three years later, they were both still there.

Jordyn was folding the last load of laundry and watching *Ryder to the Rescue* on television when her sister came home.

"How was the movie?" she asked as Tristyn kicked off her shoes and dropped onto the other end of the sofa.

Gryff, sleeping on the middle cushion, opened his one

eye—an acknowledgment of the disruption—then he stood up, turned his back on Tristyn, and settled into sleep again.

"Every bit as good as you said it was."

"So why do you sound so melancholy?"

"I guess it just made me realize how much I wish I could meet a man like Bradley Cooper in real life."

Jordyn carefully placed the folded laundry back in the basket to take upstairs. "There are no men like Bradley Cooper in real life."

"That's a depressing thought."

"On the other hand," Jordyn couldn't resist teasing her sister, "there is Josh Slater."

Tristyn ignored her comment. "How was *your* evening?" she asked instead, reaching for her sister's glass to steal a drink of her sweet tea.

"I got three loads of laundry done, made the grocery list and gave serious consideration to letting Marco get to second base."

Tristyn choked on the drink. "Excuse me?"

"Wasn't that part of your plan—the reason you abandoned me at Valentino's?"

"I was hoping you'd spend some time talking to the guy. I didn't expect...are you saying that you let him get to *first* base?"

"He made it to first and turned toward second."

"Way to go, Marco," Tristyn said approvingly. Then, to her sister, "How was it?"

She considered lying, because she knew that telling her sister the truth would only open her up to more questions. But she was genuinely confused about the unexpected attraction and she needed some honest advice, which she could hardly ask for without being honest herself.

"It was...spectacular," she admitted.

"Heart pounding? Knee quivering? Toe curling?"

"Yes."

"Wow." Her sister leaned back into the cushions again, considering the response. "Damn."

Jordyn's brows lifted. "Damn?"

"I saw him first," Tristyn reminded her.

"Are you calling dibs?"

Her sister sighed. "No. There really was no chemistry between us. But why was there no chemistry between us?"

"Don't ask me," Jordyn told her. "I'm not sure I buy into the whole chemistry thing."

"Says the woman who shared the heart-pounding, knee-quivering, toe-curling kiss," Tristyn noted drily. "Of course, that might explain why there was no chemistry between me and Marco—because he was always meant to be with you."

"I don't buy into the destiny thing, either."

"Heart pounding, knee quivering, toe curling," her sister said again.

"It was just a kiss."

Tristyn smirked. "You keep telling yourself that."

Chapter Seven

It wasn't yet ten o'clock when Marco got back to his own place.

It was a Saturday night and there were plenty of other places he could have gone, but he'd never been the type to hang out at bars—at least not on the customer side and not until he met Jordyn. He didn't feel like going to the gym, he wasn't in the mood for a movie, and he had no interest in going back to Valentino's and facing a barrage of questions from his sister-in-law, who had witnessed his leaving the restaurant with Jordyn.

He parked in his usual spot and walked up the metal staircase to his one-bedroom apartment. On Hawthorne Street, most of the shops and offices occupied the street level of buildings, with apartments on the upper level. For the past two years, Marco had lived above Buy the Book—owned by Phoebe Lamontagne, who happened to be one of his grandmother's oldest and dearest friends.

There was a front door, located beside the entrance to the bookstore, and a buzzer used by guests, but Marco most often used the back door. He kept a spare key beneath a flowerpot on his balcony, and as he sifted through the keys on his ring he noticed that the flowerpot had been moved and there were lights on inside the apartment.

He glanced down at the parking lot again—only now noticing the black BMW parked in one of the designated visitor's spots as belonging to his brother Gabe. He turned the knob, knowing that his brother wouldn't have bothered locking the door again once he was inside. Gabe was on the sofa, his feet up on the coffee table, the baseball game on the television and a glass of pinot noir and bowl of Cheezies at his elbow.

His sister and sister-in-law had helped him decorate his apartment, insisting that female guests would feel more comfortable if it looked a little less like a bachelor pad and a little more like a home. Unfortunately, most of the female guests who visited were related to him in some way. And his male guests—most of them related to him, too—usually sneered at the feminine touches. As Gabe had likely done when he tossed the colorful cushions from the sofa onto the floor.

"Hey, I paid good money for those pillows," Marco protested, picking them up off the ground and piling them on a chair.

"You shouldn't have," Gabe told him. "They make it look like a chick lives here."

"Says the guy who used the box from his television as a coffee table for almost two years," Marco noted.

"It served the purpose. Tell me what purpose those things—" he gestured to the discarded cushions "—serve?"

"I don't know," he admitted. "Nata picked them out."

"You let our sister help you decorate?"

"She didn't really give me a choice."

"Is she responsible for the decorative bottles of oil on the counter in the kitchen, too?"

"They're not decorative, they're real," Marco told him. "I do cook on occasion."

"What occasion?" Gabe teased.

Marco just shook his head. "What are you doing here, anyway? And where is your lovely fiancée tonight?"

"She went to Denver for the weekend."

"And you didn't go with her?"

"She flew out Thursday and I was tied up in a settlement conference until late yesterday."

"And you didn't know what to do with yourself without her?" Marco guessed.

"I thought—who do I know that would be home on a Saturday night? And I came here."

"But I wasn't home, was I?"

Gabe shrugged. "I figured you got called in to help at the restaurant and would find your way home eventually."

He had, of course, which his brother probably knew already. "For your information, I left Valentino's before eight and went for coffee with a stunningly hot brunette."

"Oh, yeah?" Gabe sounded intrigued. "Anyone I know?"

"You have your own stunningly hot brunette," he reminded his brother. "And I don't kiss and tell."

"Just tell me if there was kissing."

Marco kept his lips sealed as he went to the kitchen to get himself a glass of the wine his brother was drinking.

"Okay, so tell me if it was the 'merigan Gemma said you've been making a fool of yourself over."

"I have not been making a fool of myself," he denied.

"It happens to all of us eventually," Gabe warned. "One minute, you're flirting with a pretty girl and the next, you're shopping for an engagement ring."

"Speaking of," Marco said, eager to shift the conversation away from his lack of a love life. "Have you and Francesca set a date for the wedding?"

"Actually we have," Gabe confirmed. "November seventh."

"That's pretty fast," Marco noted, lifting his brows in silent question.

His brother shook his head. "She's not pregnant—we just didn't see any point in dragging the planning out for a year or more when we're ready to start our life together now."

"I remember when Nata was planning her wedding—

I think it took her at least six months to pick out a dress, and another six for it to be made."

"Francesca's going to wear her grandmother's wedding dress. We're going to have the ceremony at St. Mark's and a small reception at the Briarwood Alumni Club."

"Sounds like you've got everything figured out," Marco noted, although he knew his future sister-in-law deserved most of the credit for that.

Gabe nodded. "All I need now is a best man."

"Have you decided—oh, you mean me?"

"Yeah, I mean you."

He felt humbled and honored to be chosen. But of course, he didn't admit that to his brother. "I think I can clear my calendar for that day."

"Good." Gabe reached for a handful of Cheezies—because what went better with a thirty-five-dollar bottle of wine than a three-dollar snack? "You going to bring a date to the wedding?"

"I'll let you know."

"Come on, Marco—give me something to report back."

"Who are you supposed to be reporting back to—Francesca? Nata? Mom?"

"Nonna."

He shook his head. "Nonna's too busy to worry about my dating status."

"You'd think, but she said to me, 'Gabriel, you go talk to your brother and see if you can't find out what's going on with him and this girl who has him all tied up in knots,'" he said, in a fair imitation of their grandmother's voice.

Marco fought back a smile. "Do I look like I'm all tied up in knots?"

"Not yet," his brother said. "But not all women are comfortable with bondage on a first date."

He decided to turn the tables. "Which camp is your fiancée in?"

Gabe scowled. "Don't drag Francesca into this."

"You were the one you brought it up."

"Nonna's worried about you."

"Well, you can tell Nonna there's nothing to worry about."

"As if that's going to stop her," his brother noted.

While the Palermo brothers were griping over a double play that ended the inning with the bases loaded, the Garrett sisters were cheering the same play that got the Yankees out of a tight spot with their two-run lead intact.

As the broadcast went to commercial, Tristyn went to the kitchen and poured a glass of sweet tea for herself.

"Rob wasn't home when I dropped Lauryn off," she said, returning to the living room.

"He said he was working late," Jordyn reminded her.

"The store closes at eight on Saturdays."

"He probably stopped at the Bar Down for a beer."

"Maybe," her sister allowed.

"Was Lauryn upset that he wasn't home?"

"Not that she let on. In fact, she didn't even seem surprised."

"I don't think she's been happy for a long time," Jordyn admitted.

"Then why does she stay with him?"

"Because he's her husband and the father of her child—soon to be children."

"He's a crappy husband and a crappier father."

Jordyn didn't disagree. "And because she doesn't like to fail at anything. Walking out on Rob—or kicking him out—would require her to admit that the marriage isn't working. And she isn't ready to admit that—not even to herself."

"How do you know?"

"You heard her talking about their anniversary—her

plans to make his favorite foods and pack them in a picnic basket to take to him at the store. Even if she's not happy, she's pretending to be."

"I'd rather be alone than feel stuck with someone," Tristyn decided.

"As you've made clear to numerous suitors over the years."

Her sister frowned. "I wouldn't say numerous."

"Sam, Brendan, Liam, Kevin, Carter, Alex—and those are just since you've been living here."

Tristyn reached over for the remote, disrupting Gryffindor, who turned and growled at her. She growled back and he crawled into Jordyn's lap.

"What did attack cat do while you were locking lips with the sexy bartender?"

"He's not an attack cat," Jordyn said, stroking his back so that he began to purr like a rusty motor. But she frowned, remembering that Gryff—usually as possessive of her as he was wary of strangers—had exhibited little resistance to Marco's presence. "And he liked Marco."

Tristyn's brows lifted. "That beast doesn't even like me—and I've lived here for three years."

"Maybe because you call him a beast."

"Maybe," she acknowledged, unapologetic. "So when are you seeing Marco again?"

"I'm not."

Her sister scowled at that. "He had his tongue in your mouth but didn't ask you out?"

"I never said he had his tongue in my mouth."

"You said he was heading toward second."

"And then he put on the brakes."

"*He* did?"

Jordyn nodded.

"Interesting," her sister mused.

"It might have been more interesting if he hadn't stopped."

"Obviously he doesn't want to push for more than you're ready for."

Except that she'd been ready and willing and eager. But when she'd gotten over her disappointment, she'd realized that she would have regretted letting things progress any further.

"I haven't had sex in more than three years," she reminded her sister. "I'm not even sure I remember how it's done."

"You could always ask Marco to tutor you."

She shook her head, almost regretfully. "He doesn't seem like the kind of guy who has casual sex."

"Are you sure that's what *you* want?"

"I'm not sure about anything," she admitted.

Then she thought about Marco's kiss, the feelings that had churned inside her, the ache that still throbbed in her secret places, and she realized that she was sure about one thing: she wanted to feel again the way she'd felt in his arms.

Jordyn wished she could give Rob Schulte the benefit of the doubt.

She wanted to trust that the man her sister had fallen head over heels in love with would not forget the anniversary of the day they married. But when Tristyn stopped by Lauryn and Rob's house Sunday morning to drop off the sweater Lauryn had left in her car the night before, Rob was already gone and there was no evidence of a card or flowers or anything.

When Tristyn got home, she and Jordyn debated over what—if anything—to do. While they both agreed that Lauryn could have done a lot better than the man she'd married, she had married Rob. If he'd forgotten his wedding anniversary, it wouldn't change that fact, it would only hurt Lauryn's feelings. And neither of them could bear to see their sister hurt, especially if they were able to prevent it.

And that was why Jordyn was walking through the door of the Locker Room at noon on Sunday instead of lounging around the house in her pajamas. The bell jangled over the door when she entered. There weren't, as far as she could tell, any other customers in the store, and she headed toward the back, looking for her brother-in-law. She was halfway down the aisle, between golf bags and tennis rackets, when she was intercepted by a perky blonde with a big smile and a bobbing ponytail.

"Hi," she said. "I'm Roxi. Can I help you find something?"

"I'm looking for Rob," she said.

The blonde's smile never wavered. "Mr. Schulte's not available right now."

"Mr. Schulte is my brother-in-law."

"Oh." Confusion flickered in Roxi's big blue eyes.

"He's married to my sister," Jordyn clarified.

"Oh," Roxi said again, her smile faltering for just a second before she firmed it up again. "I've only worked here for a couple of weeks—there's obviously a lot I don't know."

"Mr. Schulte?" she prompted.

"He's in his office."

"Thank you."

She found her brother-in-law precisely where Roxi told her he would be—in the small room at the back of the store. He was relaxing in his chair with his feet up on the desk, watching prerace coverage from Pocono. He glanced up at her perfunctory knock on the door, a dark flush creeping up his neck as he hastily dropped his feet and pushed his chair back.

"I heard D'Alesio got the pole for today's race—I just wanted to catch the start."

Ren D'Alesio was the driver of the green-and-gold number seven twenty-two car, owned by Garrett/Slater Racing—the company that was currently attempting to lure Tristyn away from Garrett Furniture to take over its PR department.

Jordyn propped a shoulder against the doorjamb. "I met your new employee out front."

"Oh, yeah. Roxi. She's great."

"I thought you couldn't afford to hire any extra help."

He shuffled some papers on his desk. "Gordon quit."

"Really? Because his mother told me that he was let go because there was nothing for him to do."

Rob's gaze shifted away. "That was true. But then after Memorial Day weekend, business picked up again, so I hired Roxi."

Jordyn wondered what the woman's qualifications were—aside from her perky smile and perkier boobs. "Does she have any retail experience?"

"She's learning," he said defensively. "She also teaches yoga upstairs."

"I thought upstairs was your storage room."

"It was, but it's been mostly empty for a while now. I can't afford to keep tens of thousands of dollars of inventory on hand, so I'm renting the space to Roxi. The money helps pay the bills and her students get a twenty percent discount if they shop here."

Which would explain the surprising selection of yoga mats and apparel she'd noticed in the front window.

"Maybe you could turn your house into a yoga studio—then you might actually put some effort into making it livable."

"Has Lauryn been complaining to you about the house again?"

"No, Rob. Lauryn doesn't complain. Ever. But I've been to the house… Don't you want something better for your wife and child?"

"I'm doing the best that I can."

"I'd suggest you figure out a way to make your best better."

"Did you come in here to buy something or just to bust my balls?"

"I came in to see if you knew what day it is today."

"Sunday."

She waited for him to expand on his answer, but he didn't seem to have anything to add.

"Any particular Sunday?" she prompted.

He glanced at the calendar pinned up on the wall behind his desk, then closed his eyes and swore under his breath.

She shook her head. "You really did forget."

"Okay—yeah, I forgot," he admitted. "I've been a little preoccupied lately trying to figure out how to keep the store going when all my potential customers are shopping at that damn superstore in Raleigh."

"Well, I'm here so that you can forget about the store for a few hours and celebrate your anniversary with your wife."

"Lauryn understands that I have to be here."

"Except that now you don't," she told him. "Now you can go to Buds & Blooms, pick up some flowers and take them home to your wife."

"Are you sure you can handle things here?"

"If I get stuck, Roxi can help me out."

"Okay," he finally relented. "Thanks."

The words were right but the sentiment was spoiled by the fact that he sounded more annoyed than appreciative.

"One more thing," Jordyn said as he made his way to the door.

"What's that?"

"Put your wedding ring back on your left hand before you go home."

Marco genuinely loved spending time with his nieces and nephews. He wasn't nearly as fond of shopping.

But when he stopped by his sister's house to pick up Anna and Bella for lunch at Nonna's—a weekly tradition that Renata had excused herself from because of a head-ache, which everyone in the family knew was code for her husband being home after finishing a four-day shift at the fire hall—she somehow convinced him to take Anna for new soccer shoes after lunch.

His eldest niece had a practice the following night and apparently her feet had grown since the start of the sea-son so that she could barely squeeze them into her shoes. She hadn't told her mother when the shoes started to feel small because she loved the bright pink color and didn't want a new pair. Now, however, they pinched her toes so badly that she couldn't wear them without crying.

He'd been to the Locker Room a few times, but not at all in the last year. Generally he found the selection to be limited and the prices high. But his sister, a firm believer in supporting local businesses, had bought the now-too-small soccer cleats there, so he figured it was worth checking to see if they had the same shoes in a bigger size. Fingers crossed, it would be their first and last stop.

The bell over the door jingled when he pushed it open and the woman behind the counter glanced over.

Jordyn seemed as surprised to see him walk through the door as he was to find her there. Then her gaze shifted from him to the little girls by his side, and her eyes grew even wider.

"My nieces," he said quickly, before she could con-sider any other possibility. "This is Adrianna—" he put a hand on her shoulder, then her sister's "—and Isabella. Also known as Anna and Bella." Then to the girls, he said, "This is Miss Garrett."

"Jordyn," she said, smiling at them. "It's nice to meet both of you."

"How long have you worked here?" Marco asked her.

"I don't. It's my brother-in-law's store—I'm just helping out for a few hours today because it's his anniversary."

"Then you have to realize that our paths crossing here is a complete coincidence and I'm not stalking you?"

She laughed. "Yeah. I had a moment—when I first saw you—but then I realized you couldn't possibly have known I was going to be here today because, up until a few hours ago, I didn't even know I was going to be here." She came out from behind the counter. "Is there something I can help you find?"

"I hope so," he said.

"I need new shoes for soccer," Anna piped up.

"I'm not sure what we've got," Jordyn admitted. "But I know footwear is at the back."

"I want pink ones."

Jordyn held out her hand. "Let's take a look."

Chapter Eight

"The shoes she has now are a ten and a half," Marco said. "Renata figured she needs at least an eleven but maybe even a twelve."

"There should be one of those foot-measuring things around here," Jordyn said, looking on the shelves and between the boxes, but to no avail.

"Or we could just check the inventory and see if you've got anything that might work," Marco suggested, when she came up empty-handed.

"Or we could do that," she agreed.

"What about this one?" Marco picked up a display shoe to show it to his niece. It was black with silver flower decorations on the heel.

Anna immediately wrinkled her nose. "They're not pink."

"But they have pink laces," he pointed out.

She folded her arms over her chest and shook her head.

Jordyn skimmed the boxes on the shelf. "We don't have her size in that one, anyway."

"What other colors do you like?" she asked Anna.

The little girl pursed her lips, considering. "Yellow and orange."

"Okay—" she pulled a display shoe down for Anna to examine "—what do you think of this one?"

The shoe was bright yellow at the toe, the color fading toward the middle, shifting to a light orange that was neon at the heel. He had never seen a shoe so bright—or so ugly. But Marco bit his tongue as his niece turned the shoe around in her hands, checking it out from all sides and angles, even peering inside.

"I'll try them on," she finally said.

Jordyn pulled the size-twelve box off the shelf while Marco settled Anna on the padded bench seat and helped her remove her own shoes.

Her foot slid easily into the soccer cleat, with a little bit of room at the toe when it was laced up. Anna took a few tentative steps, testing the feel. Then she walked to the mirror to see how they looked.

Jordyn suggested she try running up the aisle to be sure, but she cautioned her to stay on the carpet so the cleats didn't slip on the floor. Of course Bella wanted to run, too, and the girls raced up and down between the rows for several minutes.

"Those are some really ugly shoes," Marco noted.

"That might be why Rob still has them in stock," she acknowledged. "But at least Anna seems to like them."

He surveyed the assortment of shoes, noted the empty display shelves, the meager inventory. Walking through the store, he'd noticed the same issue with other areas: empty shelves and hangers and bins.

"How long has your brother-in-law owned this place?" he asked Jordyn.

"As long as he and Lauryn have been married, so five years."

"Your family has a phenomenally successful retail business," he noted. "You'd think someone could help him figure out why this place is struggling and how to fix it."

"He's had offers," Jordyn told him. "Truthfully, I'm not sure he wants to fix it. He likes to blame the sporting-goods superstore in Raleigh for his lack of customers, but I've always suspected it has more to do with his complete lack of business acumen combined with an unwillingness to actually work hard."

"I'm getting the impression you're not a big fan of your sister's husband."

She shrugged. "I don't need to be a fan—I'm not married to him."

But the casual response was belied by the shadows in her eyes that made him suspect there was something she wasn't telling him. Not that she should confide in him, but he found himself wishing he could...if not alleviate, at least take her mind off, her concerns.

Before he could say anything else, though, Anna and Bella were back.

"I like these ones," Anna announced. "Can we get them, Uncle Marco? Please?"

He could never refuse her anything, especially when she looked at him with those big brown eyes pleading. And if he bought the shoes, his shopping was done. "Yes, we can get them."

"Thank you." She threw her arms around him and hugged him tight.

"Me, too," Bella demanded.

He put his arm around her and hugged her, too.

"No." She stamped her foot. "Me want soes, too."

"But you don't play soccer," he reminded her, as he helped Anna onto the bench to change back into her regular shoes.

Bella ran off again and returned with a pair of sandals with a fat orange flower on the front. "Dese," she said.

She usually loved pink as much as her sister, but he suspected that she'd been drawn to the orange sandals because they were the same color as Anna's new shoes.

"Okay, let's see if we can find a pair that fit."

Luckily they did, and both girls were smiling as they carried their purchases to the cash register.

"Two pairs of shoes sold in my first hour on the job," Jordyn mused. "I think I should ask for a raise."

"I don't doubt there would be a lot more customers in the store if you were here every day," Marco told her.

"I prefer my real job. Besides, Rob already has a new employee." She put each pair of shoes in its own bag so that Anna and Bella could each carry one. "A yoga instructor."

He took out his credit card to pay for his purchase. "You don't like yoga?"

She lifted a shoulder. "It's not my thing. And it's not Roxi's fault that she's gorgeous and about twenty years old."

Before he could respond to that, he heard a voice call out.

"Marco Palermo?"

He turned around in time to see a slender ponytailed blonde in stretchy capri pants and a sports bra beelining toward him.

"Apparently you're acquainted with my brother-in-law's new employee," Jordyn remarked to Marco after Roxi had gone upstairs to teach a class. "Ex-girlfriend?"

"No," he said quickly, firmly, adding a shake of his head for emphasis. "Just someone I knew, vaguely, in high school."

She seemed to absorb that for a minute. "Roxi went to high school with you? She barely looks twenty-one."

"I'd guess she's twenty-three or twenty-four," he said. "Because she was a couple of years behind me."

"So you're...twenty-six?"

"Almost."

She frowned.

"Is my age a problem?"

"Not at all," she said. "Why would it be?"

"I don't know," he admitted, though he was starting to have his suspicions. "How old are you?"

"Older than you."

He nodded, finally understanding the reason for her

tone. "You're not comfortable with the idea of dating a younger man."

"Which isn't an issue, because we're not dating," she pointed out.

He glanced over at Anna and Bella, to ensure they were still occupied with the basketballs they were attempting to dribble. "Okay, you're not comfortable with the idea of kissing a younger man."

Jordyn's cheeks flushed. "It was one kiss."

"A first kiss," he clarified.

"First *and* last," she insisted.

He just smiled. "So how old are you?"

"Don't you know you're not supposed to ask a woman that question?"

"And I wouldn't have except that it seems to be a matter of some concern to you."

"I turned thirty in April," she admitted.

"Oh, wow, you are old," he teased.

She glared at him.

"And unmarried? Does that make you a spinster?"

"It might—if that term weren't even more archaic than me."

He chuckled. "We'll have to continue this conversation at a later date—when I don't have two little girls tugging on me."

"You'll find me at the nursing home."

"I'll find you," he said, holding her gaze for a long moment. "You can count on that."

It bothered her that she did count on it.

She'd become accustomed to seeing Marco show up at O'Reilly's at least a couple of times a week. He wasn't always there on the same day or at the same time, but it was rare for three days to pass without him making an appearance.

So when she left for home after work Thursday night, Jordyn was suddenly aware that she hadn't seen him since Sunday afternoon—and annoyed with herself for being aware of that fact. And even more annoyed to realize that she missed him.

She dreamed of him that night, as she'd dreamed of him every night since that single kiss they'd shared. And every morning, she woke up aching for something she wasn't sure she wanted and knew she couldn't have.

Tristyn was humming along with the radio when Jordyn shuffled into the kitchen in search of a much-needed cup of coffee the following morning.

"Didn't you close last night? Why are you up already?"

Jordyn shrugged as she stirred sugar into her cup. "Couldn't sleep."

"Something on your mind?"

Jordyn lifted her cup to her lips, drank deeply. "Nope."

"Marco show up at O'Reilly's last night?"

"Nope."

"Ahh." Tristyn set her empty mug in the dishwasher and picked up her bag. "That would explain it."

She scowled. "Explain what?"

"Your mood this morning."

"There's nothing wrong with my mood," Jordyn snapped.

Her sister just raised a brow.

Jordyn swallowed another mouthful of coffee.

"You know—you could go see him."

"Who?"

Tristyn snorted.

"If you're not interested, tell him you're not interested—don't string him along."

"I'm not stringing anyone along," she denied. "And I have told him I'm not interested."

"And then you kissed him," Tristyn reminded her.

"*He* kissed *me*."

"Because the man is seriously smitten with you," her sister warned.

"He is not."

If he was smitten with her, he wouldn't have stayed away from O'Reilly's for five nights. Not that she was counting. And certainly not that she would ever admit to her sister.

"He is," Tristyn insisted. "And if you're not careful, you're going to break his heart."

"He asked me out, I said no, and I haven't seen him in five days—I don't think his heart was broken."

"He hasn't given up." Tristyn paused on her way to the door. "Five days?"

Jordyn clenched her jaw shut. Obviously she'd already said too much.

"Maybe he's not the only one who's smitten," her sister mused.

Before Jordyn could formulate a reply, the door closed behind Tristyn's back.

He came into the bar that night—just when Jordyn had convinced herself that he wasn't going to show up. And when she looked up and saw him, her heart started to race.

Maybe he's not the only one who's smitten.

She shook her head, refusing to consider the possibility. She didn't get smitten. In the more than three years that had passed since the death of her fiancé, she hadn't even had a second date. More importantly, she hadn't been on a single date with Marco. How could she possibly be smitten with a guy she hadn't gone out with even once?

The simple and obvious answer was that she wasn't. Okay, yes, she was attracted to him. The way her heart was bouncing around inside her chest made it impossible to deny that fact, but her head—the protector of her heart—refused to let that attraction lead to anything else.

His usual seat at the bar was vacant, but before he made his way to it, he stopped to exchange a few words with some of the regular customers. He asked Ed about his job, then chuckled over something Bobby said. He was good with people—all kinds of people. She might have nick-named him "Charm Boy" because of his flirtatious man-ner, but the truth was, he made friends with everyone. Even Carl, who preferred hanging out at the bar to being home with his wife and didn't make conversation with anyone, had exchanged half a dozen words with Marco the previ-ous weekend.

She knew he worked a lot of hours at Valentino's—not just behind the bar but wherever he was needed. And yet somehow he'd found the time to stop by O'Reilly's to see her. And why would he do that unless he was, as Tristyn suggested, smitten with her?

And while she was flattered—because what woman wouldn't be flattered to have a man like Marco interested in her?—she knew that she couldn't continue to encourage his flirtations. Her sister was right: she owed it to Marco to be honest about what she wanted—or didn't want.

"I haven't seen you in a while," she said, when he set-tled himself at the bar.

He winked at her. "Did you miss me?"

She had. She wasn't willing to admit it, but it was true. "Carl did," she told him. "He could barely pick his chin up off of the bar to drink his beer Wednesday night."

"I wanted to be here, but I had business to take care of."

"You don't owe me any explanations."

"But you owe me a number—six of seven."

She busied herself cutting a lime into wedges. "I thought you'd given up on that."

"It hasn't been that long since I've been in here," he said. "And I don't give up that easily."

"I'm afraid our little game may have given you the wrong impression."

"What impression is that?"

"That if you managed to put the numbers together in the right order and called to ask me out, I might say yes."

"And you wouldn't?"

She shook her head. "No, I wouldn't."

"That's too bad," he said.

She frowned as she tipped another glass beneath the tap and poured a Kilkenny for Ed.

"'That's too bad'?" she echoed. "That's all you have to say."

He shrugged. "I'm not really surprised. I kind of figured that kiss would have you running scared."

"I'm not running scared," she told him. "I just don't want to get involved."

He held her gaze for a long minute before he nodded. "Your call."

"Thank you."

He lifted his head up to sniff the air as Melody walked by with a bowl of Guinness stew. "Mmm…I'm starving and that smells really good."

"You didn't eat at Valentino's?"

"Not tonight." He sipped his beer. "Can I get some of that?"

"Sure." She put the order through to the kitchen, then moved down the bar to serve other customers.

When his dinner came, he continued to sit at the bar, eating his stew and drinking his beer and chatting with Bobby. When he was finished, he paid his bill, wished her good-night and walked out.

The next night, he came back again, taking a seat at the bar and chatting and flirting with her as if nothing had changed. He returned two days later, and again, three days after that.

"I'm a little confused," she admitted, setting a refill of his draft in front of him.

"About what?"

"Why you're still hanging around here."

"I like being around you."

"But I said I wasn't going to go out with you, and you said you were okay with that."

"I never said I was okay with it," he corrected. "I said it was your call."

"Which still doesn't explain what you're doing here," she pointed out.

"There are some people—a very select few—who make the world a better place just by being in it. For me, you're one of those people. Yeah, I'm disappointed that you don't want to explore this attraction between us," he said. "But I'm happy just to share your company."

"That's probably the nicest thing I've ever heard from a guy who wasn't trying to get me naked."

"Is naked an option?"

She laughed. "No."

He shrugged. "Can't blame a guy for trying."

She delivered a couple of drinks to the end of the bar. "For what it's worth," she said, when she returned, "I like when you hang around here."

"You know that mixed-signal thing you were worried about?"

"Yeah."

"You're doing it again."

Her cheeks colored. "You're right. I'm sorry."

"Sorry you said no when I asked you to go out with me?"

"Sorry I'm not ready to say yes."

"Then maybe we could just go out for dinner some-time," he suggested.

"What?"

"Dinner," he said again, as if it was a perfectly reason-able suggestion.

She stared at him, sincerely baffled. "Have you listened to a single word I've said?"

"I've listened to every word," he assured her. "You aren't ready to start dating—so we won't call it a date, we'll call it dinner."

"And the difference?"

"Expectations."

She noted Ed's drink was empty and put a fresh glass under the tap. "Maybe you could elaborate on that."

"When a man and woman go on a date, there are cer-tain expectations. Where is this going? Will she let me kiss her good-night? Will she invite me in for coffee? And when she says 'coffee,' does she mean something else?"

"Those are some heavy expectations," she acknowl-edged.

"Which is why I understand and sympathize with your desire to avoid the 'date' label."

"It's not just the label, but the whole scenario."

"I get that," he assured her. "But when you go out for dinner—your expectations are much more limited, are they not?"

"I guess so."

"Because dinner might be a date, but it could also just be a meal shared with someone else—a sister or a coworker or a friend. Do you agree?"

"I can see myself being backed into a corner, but I can't disagree," she said.

"So you'll have dinner with me?"

"I didn't say that."

"You didn't say you wouldn't," he pointed out.

"If I say yes—isn't that another mixed signal?"

"No, it's only a signal that you'd like to enjoy a meal, and considering that we both need to eat, I don't think it requires any further interpretation."

She wiped a condensation ring off the bar. "So you're asking me to have dinner with you—just the sharing of a meal with no expectations?"

"No expectations," he confirmed.

"Then I guess—" she set out new drink coasters "—that's a yes."

He was surprised by her easy capitulation.

Of course, it was only easy if he overlooked the fact that he'd been putting himself in her path for more than four weeks, watched her chat and flirt with other men, and tortured himself every night throughout the past week with the memories of the one kiss they'd shared.

"When?" he prompted.

She laughed. "I don't know."

"How's tomorrow?"

"I'm working."

"When aren't you working?"

"Next Tuesday."

He frowned. "Tuesday?"

"What's wrong with Tuesday?"

"Nothing except for the fact that I have an early meeting on Wednesday."

"It's just dinner," she reminded him.

"Right," he agreed. "I'll pick you up at seven o'clock on Tuesday, then."

Chapter Nine

Jordyn rolled her shoulders. "I have to get back to the gym—my muscles are already burning."

"Mine, too," Lauryn admitted. "I knew this would be a messy job, but I had no idea it would be this difficult."

Jordyn renewed her attack on the wall with the scraper. "It's as if whoever put this paper up actually used superglue."

"Such a lack of common sense would correspond with their obvious absence of good taste." Lauryn swiped at the perspiration on her brow. "I mean—who puts rooster wallpaper in a bedroom?"

"Who puts rooster wallpaper anywhere?"

"Good point."

"We should have waited until the weekend when we could have enlisted Tristyn's help," Jordyn grumbled, thinking of her sister in her tidy little suit behind her desk at Garrett Furniture while she and Lauryn were covered in sweat and glue and tiny bits of ugly wallpaper.

"She did offer," Lauryn said. "But I really didn't think it would be this hard. The paper in the dining room downstairs came off without any difficulty."

Since griping about the job wasn't making it any easier, Jordyn decided to look beyond the process to the end result. This room, across the hall from the nursery, would be Kylie's new bedroom before the new baby came along. "So what color are you thinking for this room?"

"Pink," Lauryn said. "Because it's Kylie's favorite color. But a really pale pink, maybe even more of a blush. And I'm going to go to that auction house off the highway toward Raleigh and see if I can pick up some decent secondhand furniture that can be revived with a coat of white paint."

"You know, Mom and Dad have three bedrooms filled with furniture they're not using," Jordyn pointed out. "Including your old bedroom."

"I never thought of that," Lauryn admitted. "Kylie would love that canopy bed."

"And the little dressing table and chair."

Her sister soaked another patch of wallpaper with the sponge. "You really think Mom and Dad wouldn't mind if I asked for it for Kylie?"

For herself, she wouldn't ask. But there wasn't anything she wouldn't do for her daughter.

"I think they'd be thrilled."

Lauryn looked around the room, as if mentally setting up the bedroom. "It would work perfectly in here," she decided.

"With white organza curtains on the windows?" Jordyn guessed.

Her sister smiled. "Yeah."

"She'll love it."

"I'll ask Mom when she gets back from story time at the library with Kylie." She looked around the room again and sighed. "Of course, there's a lot of work to be done before this room will be ready for furniture. If we ever get this wallpaper off, I've got to patch the holes and replace the broken trim."

"You don't have to do everything on your own," Jordyn reminded her. "There are any number of people who would help if you just asked."

"I know—I got you here, didn't I?"

"Only for another couple of hours—then I need to go home to shower and get ready for work."

"Are you seeing Marco tonight?"

Because just the mention of his name—and the possibility—made her pulse skip, she attacked the wall with renewed vigor.

"I'm working tonight," she said again.

"Yeah, but Tristyn told me that Marco's been hanging out at O'Reilly's and flirting with a certain bartender."

"He's been in a few times when I've been working."

"Any more toe-curling kisses?"

"Tristyn has a big mouth."

"We're sisters," Lauryn reminded her. "There aren't supposed to be any secrets between sisters. And we both think he could be very good for you."

"Oh, well, if you both think so, then why should my opinion matter?"

Lauryn ignored her sarcasm. "Your opinion would matter if it wasn't obvious that you're so twisted up over him you're not thinking straight."

"I'm not twisted up," she denied.

"Tell that to your forehead."

She turned away, because that was easier than smoothing the scowl she could feel etched in her brow.

"You deserve to be happy," Lauryn said. "And Marco makes you happy."

"When he's not making me crazy," she admitted.

Her sister smiled. "As long as it's a feel-good kind of crazy, there's nothing wrong with that."

"I thought I had my chance," Jordyn said. "And when Brian died, I didn't think I'd ever be able to put my heart back together enough to care about anyone again."

"Everyone deserves a second chance," Lauryn told her. "Very few people ever get love right the first time around."

Jordyn smiled. "My first love was Jimmy Chelminski."

"Second grade doesn't count."

"It should—he was perfect."

"Because he always gave you his red gummy bears."

"I still love red gummy bears."

"And Jimmy Chelminski?"

"Living happily ever after with Debbie Turlington, their two kids and two dogs in Charlotte. And speaking of happily ever after," she said, grateful for the opportunity to shift the topic of conversation away from her conflicted feelings about Marco, "I was thinking about your idea of a princess-slash-fairy-tale theme for Kylie and came up with a sketch."

"Already? I just mentioned the idea to you yesterday."

"It's just a rough sketch," she said.

Lauryn dropped her sponge back into the bucket of water and wiped her hands down the front of her shorts. "I want to see it."

Jordyn rolled her shoulders again, grateful for the excuse to take a short break. "Okay."

They went downstairs and Lauryn poured them each a glass of sweet tea while Jordyn retrieved the sketch from the side pocket of her purse.

"The wall would be painted to look like it was made of stone, as if she was sleeping inside a castle, with three arched 'windows' providing a view of the fairy-tale kingdom."

Lauryn scrutinized the drawing. There were mountains in the background, with a waterfall spilling down into a lake at the bottom and a castle in the distance—a fanciful design with turrets and towers and a gate guarded by a knight with sword and shield on one side and a dragon on the other. On the long, winding road leading to the castle was an exquisite glass carriage drawn by a pair of white horses.

"This is...wow." Lauryn traced the outline of the castle. "Even in my mind, I didn't imagine anything like this."

"If it's not what you want—"

"No," her sister interrupted. "It's perfect." She studied the sketch for another minute, noting the bunches of wildflowers in the grass and the fairies peeking out behind the trees. "I know Kylie would love it, but it looks like a lot of work."

"It will be fun," Jordyn said.

"Which makes me wonder why you never pursued a career in art."

"What kind of career? Giving tours of the local art gallery or teaching watercolor to a group of high school students?"

"With your talent, you could do anything you wanted to," Lauryn said.

"And this—" she gestured to the sketch "—is what I want to do for my niece."

Marco stayed away from O'Reilly's over the weekend. Not just because he was busy at Valentino's and helping with the renovations they'd started at the new location, but because he was pretty sure that Jordyn had talked herself out of going to dinner with him and if he showed up, she'd make up some kind of excuse as to why she'd changed her mind. He wasn't going to give her a chance to change her mind.

He still didn't have her phone number, and she didn't have his, which meant that she couldn't call or text to cancel their plans. She could have tracked him down through Valentino's, but he didn't think she would.

Tuesday afternoon, his sister had a prenatal checkup so she asked him to watch the girls while she was out. He was happy to help, happy to have something to do to stop obsessing about his evening plans. In fact, the girls kept him so busy, he barely had a chance to think about his nondate with Jordyn.

"Everything good?" he asked Renata when she got home.

"Everything's great," she assured him. "Baby is measuring right where he should be, his heart rate is good, he's got ten fingers, ten toes and is very active."

"He?"

She shook her head. "Unconfirmed. I'm just assuming that Nonna is right."

"And you're feeling good?" he prompted.

"Just tired—which probably has as much to do with chasing Anna and Bella around as the extra twenty pounds I'm carrying."

"I'd say that Anna and Bella are the primary reason—I've only been here an hour and a half, and I'm exhausted."

"You've definitely earned dinner," Nata said. "I'm making roasted chicken with peppers and red-skin potatoes, if you want to stay."

"Thanks, but I've got plans for dinner tonight."

His sister turned back to him. "A date?"

"Yeah."

"With a woman?"

He scowled at the disbelief in her tone. "Is that really so hard to believe?"

"No." She pulled a bag of potatoes from the pantry, dumped half a dozen into the sink. "It's just that, considering all of your recent commentary about how you're too busy focusing on the restaurant expansion to even think about anything else, it's a little surprising."

"Aren't you the one who always says we make time for the things that matter?"

"Jordyn Garrett," she guessed, programming the oven to preheat.

He nodded.

"She finally agreed to go out with you?"

"Yes, but it's not a date."

Nata frowned as she scrubbed potatoes. "You just said it was."

"Well, it is, of course—but Jordyn insists that she isn't ready to start dating again, so we're just going for dinner."

"Clever," she acknowledged.

"I thought so."

She pulled a knife from the block on the counter and pointed it at him. "Be careful."

"You think she's going to break my heart?"

"I'm not suggesting she'd do it on purpose—" she began cutting the potatoes into bite-size chunks "—but I'm worried because I think she's the first woman in a long time who would be able to."

"Let me worry about my heart," he suggested.

"I would—except that you don't." Nata continued to chop, setting the pieces on a baking tray. "Where are you going to take her for dinner?"

"Not Valentino's."

She gasped. "Blasphemy."

"It's the best place for Italian food in Charisma," he said loyally. "But not a good choice if I want a second date."

"If Mom and Dad or—God forbid—Nonna finds out that you took her somewhere else to eat, you won't be allowed to walk through the door of Valentino's ever again."

"Which is why we're going to Raleigh," he told her. "There's a new steak place there that's been getting a lot of buzz."

"The Idle Plough?" She melted a chunk of butter in the microwave.

"You've heard of it?"

"I've been there," she admitted. "Craig and I went last weekend—it was definitely worth the trip."

"Romantic?"

"I'd say it's more rustic," she admitted, drizzling the butter over the potatoes. "But you don't want over-the-top romantic."

"Why not?"

"Because it's not a date," she reminded him, sprinkling the vegetables with seasoning and Parmesan. "And if you take her someplace casual, someplace where she doesn't have to worry that maybe it *is* a date, she'll relax and enjoy herself and be more open to seeing you again." She looked at her brother, who was shaking his head. "What?"

"All this time… I had no idea there was such a devious mind behind that pretty face."

"You'd be wise not to forget it." She slid the tray of potatoes into the oven. "And make sure you take her to Valentino's for the second date."

"Let me get through the first before worrying about a second."

Jordyn hadn't decided what to tell her sister about her plans with Marco for Tuesday night, so she was relieved when Tristyn texted to say that she was working late. Because she knew that, no matter how she explained it, Tristyn would never believe it wasn't a date. And judging by the butterflies winging around in her belly, Jordyn wasn't entirely convinced, either.

Several times throughout the day, she'd decided she couldn't do it, that she was going to have to call him to cancel. Except she didn't have his number. She could have called Valentino's and left a message for him there, but that would require explaining the situation to someone else, and she wasn't willing to do that.

Even as she got ready, she wasn't sure she would answer the door when he showed up. But still, she tried on several different outfits, trying to decide which set the right tone for "dinner" without suggesting "date." A dress was too dressy; jeans were too casual. The capris with the tailored shirt made her look like she was on her way to a business meeting; the deep V-neck top showed too much cleavage. In the end, she opted for a short skirt with a ruffled hem and a scoop-neck T-shirt with lace overlay. Then she put on her favorite wedge sandals with the laces that wrapped around her calves.

Gryff strolled into the room while she was slipping a trio of chunky silver bangles on her wrist to go with the hoops in her ears. He hopped up on the bed and stretched out in the middle of her comforter.

"What do you think?" she said.

The cat yawned.

She shifted her attention back to her reflection in the mirror. "I'm aiming for feminine without being overtly sexy and casually dressy without trying too hard."

The cat turned his head to the chair in the corner— where she'd piled the rejected outfits.

"Okay, but *he* doesn't have to know how hard I tried to get this look."

Gryff rolled onto his back and closed his eye, signaling that the conversation was over.

"Is it too much to ask for you to show a little support?" she muttered. "I'm nervous enough without you judging me." She shook her head. "And now I'm talking to my cat. Which wouldn't be so bad if he would respond, but he's not even listening to me."

And she was nervous. As much as she tried to convince herself that it was no different than going for dinner with one of her sisters or a friend, this was Marco—the man who had turned her inside out with a single kiss.

She opened the top drawer of her dresser and pulled out the photo that she'd finally tucked away on the third anniversary of Brian's death. She felt a pang in her heart as she looked at her fiancé's smiling face, and a second when she saw the smile on her own. They'd been so in love, so happy, full of hopes and dreams for their future together. Only a few weeks after that engagement photo was taken, she'd lost him.

She'd grieved for a long time—feeling as if her heart had not just been shattered, but the pieces ripped right out of her chest, leaving only a gaping emptiness. But eventually, over time, she'd started to heal; she'd learned to look forward to each new day again. In the past year, she'd even been on a few dates—though more to appease her sisters than because she was interested in any of the men she'd gone out with. But while she'd been preparing for those other dates, she'd never felt the kind of giddy anticipation that danced through her veins now. And she'd certainly never thought about kissing any of those other men, but she couldn't stop thinking about kissing Marco.

Was she ready for this?

Her heart jolted inside her chest as the doorbell sounded.

She honestly didn't know, but it was too late to back out now.

As Jordyn made her way down the stairs, her heart was pounding so hard inside her chest she was certain Marco could hear it through the closed door. Then she opened it, and her already-racing heart went into overdrive.

"Hi," she said, feeling unaccustomedly shy.

"Hi." He stepped into the foyer and smiled at her. "You look fabulous."

It wasn't the words so much as the sincere appreciation in his gaze that made her skin tingle and the blood in her veins heat.

"So do you," she told him, noting the khaki chinos paired with a pale blue shirt and darker blue jacket. She also noted that they were standing in almost the same spot as when he'd kissed her that night. And the way he was looking at her, she knew he was remembering that kiss, too.

So she was almost as disappointed as she was relieved when he said, "We should be on our way."

"Where are we going?" she asked as he guided her to his vehicle.

"That depends—do you like steak?"

"Mmm," she agreed. "My mouth is watering already."

He opened the passenger side door, helped her in. "There's a new steak house in Raleigh that I've heard good things about."

"There are steak restaurants in Charisma, too," she said when he was settled in his seat.

"There are," he confirmed. "I just thought there would be less talk about us having dinner together if no one saw us having dinner together."

"I guess that makes sense, in a convoluted kind of way."

"And maybe, during the drive to Raleigh, you'll start to relax a little," he suggested.

"Sorry—I guess I am a little nervous."

"No expectations," he reminded her.

"Right." But his reassurance didn't magically disperse those damn butterflies still fluttering around in her tummy. "So tell me about the new Valentino's."

"Why are you so convinced there's going to be a new Valentino's?"

"Because there's a sign in the window of what used to be Mykonos that says 'Future Home of Valentino's II.'"

"I guess that's a pretty good reason," he acknowledged.

"Are you going to duplicate the original restaurant?"

"No—even if the space lent itself to a similar design, we want customers to have a unique dining experience at each location."

"Most successful eating establishments in the current economy are recognizable chain restaurants," she pointed out.

"Two restaurants hardly gives us the status of a chain," he countered. "Besides, if people want Valentino's—they'll go to Valentino's. The purpose of the new restaurant isn't just a second location but to broaden our appeal to a wider clientele—a wealthier clientele."

"No pasta special on Tuesday?"

He smiled. "We'll have the same specials and the menu will include most of our customer favorites, but we'll offer some new dishes, too—entrées that are a little more daring and innovative."

Listening to him talk, she realized there was a lot more to him than she'd originally thought. "And all this time, I believed you were just a bartender."

"I am a bartender."

"And, I'm beginning to realize, you're also the mastermind of this expansion."

He shook his head. "It wouldn't be happening if not for my grandparents."

"But whose idea was it?" she pressed.

"It's been the subject of discussion among numerous parties for a while now," he said, hedging a bit.

"And I'll bet you were involved in every single one of those discussions."

"I had some input," he confirmed.

"Why are you so reluctant to take credit?"

"Maybe I don't want to take the blame if the project fails."

"It won't," she said confidently.

"While I appreciate your faith, you can't possibly know that."

"But I do—because I know you won't let it fail. You don't give up or give in and you'll stick with the new restaurant until it succeeds."

"You think you have me all figured out, don't you?"

"Well, you got me to go out with you—even if it isn't a date." She looked out the window. "So the original Valentino's was started by your grandparents?"

"Forty-seven years ago," he confirmed.

"Are they still involved?"

"Sometimes I think too involved. Almost every morning, my grandmother is in the kitchen making pasta or sauce—or both."

"She must really love to cook."

"She loves to be in control, and she doesn't trust anyone else to do things the way that she does. And of course, her way is the only right way."

"So the pasta really is made fresh every day?"

"Absolutely."

"How is that going to work with Valentino's II?"

"Nonna's going to train and supervise the new kitchen staff—when we have a new kitchen staff—and then she'll probably split her time between the two restaurants for a while."

"What does your grandfather do while she's in the kitchen?"

"He's the quality-control supervisor."

She smiled at that. "Meaning he eats what she cooks?"

He nodded. "And samples any new additions to the wine list."

"They sound like an interesting couple."

"They're wonderful," he said sincerely. "They drive me insane at times, but I couldn't imagine my life without them."

Chapter Ten

The Idle Plough was a little more rustic than Marco had anticipated, but Jordyn seemed genuinely charmed by it.

The restaurant was actually a converted barn with exposed rafters and beams and a wooden staircase—thankfully not a ladder—leading to additional seating in the former hayloft. Wagon-wheel chandeliers hung on heavy chains from the ceiling while more intimate lighting was provided by old-fashioned lanterns on each table.

Their server—dressed in a Western-style shirt with blue jeans and cowboy boots—asked if they wanted drinks while perusing the menu. Jordyn asked for a glass of wine, and Marco decided to have the same. For dinner they, of course, ordered steaks. She opted for the strip loin, he chose the T-bone, and they both went for loaded baked potatoes and green salads.

While they ate, they talked. Even after several weeks of chatting, there was so much he wanted to know about her. She read science fiction novels, liked old movies—and not just vintage romances but classic mysteries such as *Rear Window* and *Sorry, Wrong Number.* She had horrible taste in music (new country—really?) and got lost without her GPS, but she knew how to make more than fifty different shooters, was a Durham Bulls fan (and not just because of the Kevin Costner movie—although she admitted to being a fan of that, too) and had lips sweeter than anything else he'd ever tasted.

"How did you end up working at O'Reilly's?" he asked, setting his knife and fork on his now-empty plate.

"I saw the help-wanted sign in the window and applied for the job."

"Okay—maybe I should have asked *why* you're working at O'Reilly's rather than Garrett Furniture."

She shrugged. "There's not a lot of demand for bartenders at Garrett Furniture."

"I'm sensing there's another story there that you're not telling me."

"Actually, it's all part of the same story."

When their server came to clear their plates, they both declined dessert but said yes to coffee. Of course, Jordyn added two creams and two sugars to hers, so he teased her that it was like having dessert and coffee in one.

"Thanks for this—dinner, I mean," she said, wrapping her hands around the mug. "I really enjoyed it."

"You sound surprised."

"I guess I am, a little. I know it wasn't supposed to be a date, but getting ready, I kind of felt like I was getting ready for a date which, of course, made me nervous. But this was...good. Really good."

"I'm glad," he said. "So maybe next time you'll be a little less resistant when I ask you to go out with me?"

She shook her head, perhaps regretfully. "I really don't want to get involved."

"Maybe this is the part where you tell me why."

"Do you really want to hear my sad tale?"

"I want to be with you, Jordyn, and I have a feeling that I'm going to need to hear it to decide if that's ever going to happen."

She took a deep breath. "I was supposed to get married in April—well, April three years ago."

"You were engaged?" Maybe it shouldn't have surprised him, but it did. The knowledge that she'd loved someone else, planned to spend her life with someone else, was more than a little unsettling.

She nodded.

"What happened?"

"He died. It was a car accident." She swallowed. "He was hit head-on by a teenage driver who took a curve too fast and crossed into his lane. Brian was wearing a seat belt, but his airbag didn't deploy. The doctors worked on him for hours at the hospital, but his injuries were too severe."

Her straightforward recital of the facts wasn't unemotional. Though she kept her tone even, he saw the anguish in her eyes, and he ached for her. He didn't know how she felt—how could he? But he could imagine the shock and heartache of the loss, and he wished there was something he could do to ease her pain. He reached across the table and touched her hand. "I'm so sorry," he said.

Early on, he'd figured out that she'd been hurt. Her obvious wariness combined with her determination not to get involved had led inevitably to that conclusion. But he hadn't been prepared for this. It would have been easier to console her if the engagement had ended because her fiancé had walked out or cheated on her. But no—the man she'd planned to marry had probably been a prince of a guy whose death had left a huge hole in her heart. There was no way to ease that kind of pain, no way to expedite the healing process.

But even the deepest wounds healed eventually, and it had been more than three years since her fiancé died. Added to that was the undeniable chemistry between them—another reason he couldn't walk away from her.

"I'm not still grieving," Jordyn said. "I still miss Brian at times, but I've accepted that he's gone. I'm just not ready to get involved in another relationship. I don't know that I ever will be."

"Are you saying that you haven't been on a date in almost three years?"

"No, I've been out on a few," she admitted. "Although mostly just to keep my family off my back."

"Then why won't you go out with me?"

"Because I like you."

"You're going to have to explain that," he told her.

"Usually when I agree to go out with a guy, it's because I know he's going to realize there's no connection and no chance of a second date. As you've already noted, there seems to be some chemistry between us."

"Let me see if I've got this right," he said. "You don't want to go out with me because you're attracted to me?"

"And I'm not ready for a relationship," she confirmed.

The server came by again with the coffeepot, and Marco nudged his cup forward for a refill.

"I thought you said you had an early meeting tomorrow."

"I do," he confirmed. "But if this is truly our first and last time out together, I'm going to make it last."

They left the restaurant after Marco had finished his second cup of coffee. It started to rain on the drive back to Charisma and their conversation lagged a little, but the silence wasn't at all uncomfortable as they listened to the rhythmic *swish* of the wipers on the windshield, pushing away the rain.

In fact, Jordyn felt more comfortable with Marco than she'd felt with anyone outside of her family in a long time. Then he pulled in to her driveway and put the vehicle into Park, and suddenly the silence wasn't so comfortable anymore. Suddenly there was a simmering heat in the air, a sizzling tension between them.

Thunder rolled and rumbled overhead; Jordyn's heart pounded.

"I hate thunderstorms," she admitted.

"Why's that?"

"Because they remind me that we're not as in control of our world as we want to believe."

"I like storms," he admitted.

"Figures."

He grinned. "For the same reason—because they remind me that there are forces in this world stronger than our determination to control them."

The way he was looking at her, she knew he wasn't just talking about the weather.

"I should get in," she said.

"I'll walk you to your door."

"There's no point in both of us getting wet," she protested.

"I'll walk you to your door," he said again.

Since it was obvious that she wasn't going to change his mind, she waited for him to come around and open the door for her. He took his jacket off and put it across her shoulders, to shield her as much as possible from the rain. Thankfully it was only a few steps until they were under the shelter of the porch.

"Thank you for dinner," she said formally.

"You're very welcome."

He waited while she found her key, inserted it into the lock. "Good night, Marco."

"Good night, Jordyn."

And though the door was unlocked, she didn't immediately open it and step inside. Her means of escape was right there, but she didn't take it. Instead, she turned back to him.

"I know this wasn't a date, but…"

That was all she said before she impulsively leaned forward and brushed her mouth to his.

Throughout the entire drive back from the restaurant, Marco had kept reminding himself of his promise to Jordyn that it wasn't a date. And although he wanted, more than anything, to taste her again, he'd held himself back from reaching for her.

Then *she* kissed *him*, and the gentle touch of her lips to his was all it took for the tentative leash on his self-control to snap.

He'd never wanted another woman the way he wanted her, with such passion and intensity, and he knew he wouldn't again. She was it for him—for now and forever.

His arms closed around her, drawing her nearer as he deepened the kiss. He nibbled on the sweet fullness of her mouth and tasted heaven; she pressed herself against him, and he soared through the clouds.

His hands skimmed up her torso, his palms brushing the sides of her breasts through the sexy lace top she wore, and she trembled. Her mouth parted beneath the pressure of his, and her tongue danced with his in a slow, sensual rhythm that had all of his blood rushing south.

Her head fell back against the door; he nibbled on the rapidly beating pulse point below her ear, scraped his teeth down her throat. She gasped and shuddered as her fingers dug into his shoulders. He pressed his lips to her breastbone, just above the vee of her top, and felt the rapid pounding of her heart. He lifted his head to draw in a breath, and the seductive scent of her skin made his head swim.

He tipped her chin up to look into her eyes. They were wide and dark, reflecting the same urgent desire that surged through his blood. He covered her mouth again, his own hot and hungry, and swallowed her low moan of pleasure. His hands moved down her back, over the curve of her bottom, and he found himself wondering what she was wearing under the skirt. Before he could satisfy his curiosity, headlights washed over the porch—a vehicle pulling into her neighbor's driveway. They were deep in the shadows, but the glaring light was a timely reminder to both of them of where they were and the dangers of letting the kiss carry them further away.

She dropped her head back against the door again, her breath escaping between erotically swollen lips in short, shallow pants.

He took a minute to catch his breath, too, then another to ensure that his tone was light when he asked, "Do you think you could give me your number now?"

Her eyes were still dark and clouded with desire, but she managed a soft laugh. "Yeah, I guess I could."

He retrieved his cell phone from his pocket and pulled up his list of contacts. She lifted her brows when she saw that he'd already entered her name, although the other fields remained empty.

"What can I say? I'm an optimist."

She took the phone from him and keyed in her numbers—home and cell—then handed it back to him.

"I'll call you," he said.

She nodded, reaching for the handle of the door. Then she turned back to him again. "I might change my number," she warned, "when my brain isn't so clouded with lust I can't think straight."

"I don't think you will," he said. "Because you're as curious as I am to find out where this is going."

"It might be going nowhere."

He heard the desperation in her tone, but he understood the origin of her fear a little better now. "We'll figure that out together," he promised.

Together.

Jordyn wasn't sure if the word was terrifying or reassuring.

Together implied a connection, a joining of two or more things into a single unit, a relationship. It had been a long time since she'd been anything but alone in her personal life. Three years, four months and two days.

She was unexpectedly struck by the realization that she'd now been without Brian for longer than she'd been with him. They'd known each other for almost a year before they started dating, and he'd proposed exactly six months after their first date, with their wedding date set a year later. They'd been together for two and a half years and she'd been alone for more than three years since then.

Maybe it *was* time for her to take a chance of being *together* with someone again. And there wasn't anyone other than Marco that she wanted to take that chance with.

Tristyn was sitting on the couch in front of the TV with a bowl of popcorn on one side, Gryff on the other and her tablet in hand when Jordyn walked into the house.

"Now that's multitasking," she said.

"It's a new season of *The Bachelorette* and I've got approvals for our major fall ad campaign due tomorrow."

"And somehow you've hypnotized my cat."

"Nah—I just bribed him."

"With popcorn?"

Tristyn shook her head. "I gave him the leftover salmon from my lunch."

"Why?"

"Because I can't understand why he likes Marco more than he likes me."

Jordyn laughed. "He met Marco once—and I'm still not convinced he didn't have catnip in his pockets."

"So where did you go for dinner tonight?"

"The Idle Plough—a new steak house in Raleigh."

"Was it good?"

"It was. Really good."

"And the kiss good-night?" her sister prompted. "And don't try to tell me he didn't kiss you, because your hair is tousled, your lips are swollen and your eyes have that glazed look of a woman who's been kissed senseless."

"Well, for your information, *I* kissed *him* senseless."

Tristyn's brows lifted. "Aren't you full of surprises?"

Jordyn lowered herself onto the edge of the couch. "I'm thinking about sleeping with him."

"Are you asking for my approval?"

"No. Yes. I don't know."

"I like Marco," Tristyn said. "But more importantly, *you* like him. He's a sweet, charming, good-looking guy who turns you on, so if you want my advice, I say go for it."

Jordyn chewed on the side of her thumbnail—a nervous habit left over from her teen years when she used to bite all of her nails. Now it was just the thumb, and only when something was really bothering her.

"I do like him," she admitted.

Tristyn touched her hand gently. "Honey, being with Marco is not cheating on Brian."

"I know." She blew out a breath. "Logically, I know that. And it's not as if I'm thinking about Brian when I'm with Marco. In fact, when I'm with Marco, I almost forget how much I loved Brian…and how devastated I was when I lost him."

"It's okay to be scared—any new relationship is scary."

"Who said anything about a relationship? I thought we were talking about sex."

Tristyn shook her head. "Why are you fighting so hard to deny your feelings for Marco?"

"I'm not denying that I have feelings for him," she said. "But I don't think I need to pretend my heart goes pitter-patter just because he turns me on."

"You don't have to pretend anything," her sister agreed. "Just be careful you're not ignoring that pitter-patter because it's inconvenient."

Marco had a lot on his mind.

He had a meeting with the electrical inspector at the new restaurant at eleven o'clock, another meeting with the tile guy, an appointment at the bank and a liquor order to place. And yet, with everything else that should have been occupying his thoughts, he couldn't stop thinking about Jordyn.

If he'd had any doubts about his conviction that she was the one, the kiss she'd planted on his lips the night before had obliterated them. The memory of that kiss had both fueled and haunted him throughout the day.

He was behind the bar at Valentino's, finalizing the restaurant's monthly liquor order, when Jordyn's sister sat down. It was late afternoon, the lunch crowd had dispersed and the dinner crowd had yet to arrive, so she was the only one at the bar.

"What can I get for you?"

"I'll have a glass of chardonnay," Tristyn said.

"Californian, Italian, Australian or South African?"

She considered the options for a moment. "The one with the house on the label?"

He smiled and selected a bottle from the wine fridge, showed her the label.

"That's it," she confirmed.

"It's Italian," he told her, then dropped his voice to a conspiratorial whisper. "As all the best wines are."

He poured her drink, then set the glass on a cocktail napkin in front of her. "While I'd never want to discourage a customer from coming here, I have to admit I'm curious about why you are here instead of at O'Reilly's."

"Well, for starters, if I asked for a glass of wine there, I'd have only two choices—red or white."

He chuckled. "That's a valid reason."

"Also, I didn't want my brain picked at and prodded."

"As your sister would do," he guessed.

She nodded.

"I won't prod, but I will listen if you want to talk."

"There's nothing to talk about. I'm at a crossroads in my life and I haven't figured out which direction I want to go."

"But you don't want to talk about it?"

"No. I want to know what your intentions are toward my sister."

"My intentions?" He couldn't prevent the smile that curved his lips. "Considering that—prior to last night—your sister refused to even go out with me, don't you think that question is a little premature?"

"Considering that more than five weeks have passed since you first asked and she first said no and you didn't stop asking, I don't think it is."

He nodded in acknowledgment of the fact. "In that case, I will tell you that my intention is to marry her."

"Well," she said. "No one could ever accuse you of dragging your feet."

"She's the one I've been waiting for," he said simply.

She studied him for a long moment, as if to ascertain the sincerity of his words. "What if she doesn't feel the same way?"

"She will."

"Hold on to that confidence," Tristyn said. "You're going to need it. And probably a fair amount of patience, too."

"I've got plenty of both," he assured her. "I've also got a question for you."

"You can ask—I can't guarantee that I'll answer."

He nodded, accepting and appreciating her loyalty to her sister. "Do you think Jordyn's still in love with her former fiancé?"

Apparently he'd surprised her again. "She told you about him?"

He nodded.

She eyed him thoughtfully. "Jordyn doesn't talk about Brian. Ever."

"She thought it would help me to understand why she won't go out with me."

"Obviously her confession didn't have the desired effect."

"I hate knowing that she was hurt, and I understand why she'd be reluctant to open her heart again, but I have to trust that she will, that what's between us is too powerful to be denied."

"You're either an incredible romantic or a complete fool."

"Let's go with romantic," he suggested.

She smiled at that. "I think you could be very good for her, Marco Palermo, *if* you manage to breach the walls she's built around her heart."

"Are you trying to dissuade me?"

"I'd be disappointed if you were dissuaded so easily."

"And I never want to disappoint a pretty lady."

She lifted her glass. "My money's on you, Charm Boy."

He winced. "She told you about that?"

"I'm her sister," she reminded him. "She tells me everything."

"I'll keep that in mind."

"You should also keep in mind that women like flowers."

"Is that a fact?"

She nodded. "Scientifically proven."

"Any particular kind of flowers?"

"Of course."

"And I'm supposed to guess?"

"Consider it a challenge in the game of seduction," she told him. "If you guess right, you move one step closer to the bedroom. If you guess wrong, you go directly to the cold shower."

Chapter Eleven

For as long as she'd worked at O'Reilly's—and probably a lot of years before that, even—Wade Denton had been talking about retirement.

He'd bought the pub from the previous owner, Sean O'Reilly, for little more than a song. It had been the Wexford Arms back then, but because it was the pub owned by O'Reilly, it was more widely known as O'Reilly's Pub. Wade tried to give it a new image and a new name, but he was more successful with the former than the latter. Sean O'Reilly's pub had offered customers the choice of sitting at the U-shaped bar or square tables designed to accommodate four. If groups larger than that came in, he simply shoved two or more tables together.

The lighting was dim, the menu limited, but his customers were loyal. So much so that there had been grumbling and resistance when Wade installed booths around the perimeter of the restaurant, changed the light fixtures, installed a couple of televisions over the bar and expanded the menu to offer more than cottage pie, lamb stew, and fish and chips. And while the shiny new sign on the front might have said Crown & Castle, the locals still insisted on calling it O'Reilly's.

After four years, Wade finally gave up, changing the sign again to officially adopt O'Reilly's as its name. Eighteen years later, little else had changed. And while the customers were still loyal, they were hardly numerous, and from month to month, the pub's books shifted between black and red.

Then Jordyn Garrett saw a help-wanted sign in the window and walked through the door.

She told him to get a satellite dish so customers could follow Premier League soccer, arguing that if they wanted to watch American football or basketball, they were going to drink their beer at the Bar Down. She introduced daily drink specials to bring in new customers and advertised those specials in the campus newspaper. Wade grumbled about spending money on advertising—until the college kids started finding their way to O'Reilly's. He grumbled about sponsoring local recreational sports teams, too— until the players made O'Reilly's their regular postgame stop.

And in October, it would be the twenty-fifth anniversary of Wade's ownership of the pub. He liked to say that a quarter of a century was a good run—a long run. "More than long enough." He planned to have a big party to commemorate the milestone event, and then he would be happy to walk away from the day-to-day responsibilities of pub ownership.

In the past six months, he'd begun talking more and more about his impending retirement and his desire to find someone to take over the business. He'd suggested, on more than one occasion, that Jordyn might be the right person, and she was looking forward to that opportunity.

So when Wade called her into his office, she figured he wanted to talk about either the twenty-fifth anniversary party or his retirement. She didn't expect that their conversation would cause her own plans to begin to unravel.

"Of all the flower shops, in all the towns, in all the world, he walks into mine."

Marco smiled at Rachel's deliberate misquote of the famous movie line. "We could have had a love affair for the ages, but you never gave me a second look."

"My heart always belonged to Andrew," the pretty florist told him.

"He's a lucky man," Marco said.

"A fact I remind him of every day."

He chuckled.

"So what's the occasion?" she asked.

"Does there have to be an occasion?"

"Absolutely not," Rachel said. "Any day that ends in a *y* is reason enough for flowers."

"A good motto for a woman who makes her living selling them," he mused.

She smiled. "Maybe I should have asked—who's the special lady?"

"I'd rather not share that information just yet."

"Now you've really piqued my curiosity," she said.

"We're in the early stages," he confided. "Very early stages."

"Then you want something simple. Something that lets her know you've been thinking about her but doesn't make her worry that you're obsessing over her." Rachel sent him a look.

"I'm not obsessing."

"Okay—does she have a favorite color or favorite flower?"

"Early stages," he reminded her.

"Right." She studied the buckets of flowers in the refrigerated case. "Let's try…some hot pink carnations… bright orange gerberas and…yellow chrysanthemums." She selected a few of each, gathered them together in her hand. "What do you think?"

"I like it."

"I do, too," she said. "But it needs a little something more…maybe some alstroemeria. Pink or orange?"

He studied the flowers she indicated. "Orange."

"Good choice." She added it to the bouquet in her hand. "And some green button poms."

"You are truly an artist."

She smiled. "And you're as charming as ever. Vase or paper?"

"Paper," he decided.

She nodded. "Do you want me to take care of the delivery for you?"

"I don't think so—but nice try." He took a few steps to sniff the white lilies in a decorative brass pot.

She grinned as she finished arranging the blooms. "It was worth a shot." She gestured to the tray of cards beside the cash. "Card?"

"Not necessary."

"You don't want to make sure she knows they're from you?"

"She'll know," he said confidently, picking up the lily and carrying it to the counter. "I'll take this, too."

He passed his credit card across the counter to pay for the flowers.

Rachel completed the transaction, then came around the counter with the completed arrangement.

"I hope she likes the flowers." She kissed his cheek. "And I hope she knows how lucky she is to have you in her life."

She was certain this was it—Wade was finally going to announce a date for his retirement and discuss the terms for Jordyn to take over O'Reilly's. So she wasn't just surprised but disappointed when she walked into her boss's office at the assigned hour and found that he wasn't alone.

"There she is," Wade said to the man seated across from him. Then to Jordyn, "Come in—I want you to meet my nephew, Scott, from Kansas City."

"Las Vegas," Scott interjected. "I was born and raised in Kansas City, but I've been working in Las Vegas for the past few years."

"Your nephew?" Jordyn didn't understand why she'd

been summoned to Wade's office for this introduction, but she offered her hand. "It's nice to meet you, Scott."

"You, too."

He was young, tall and good-looking, and the way he smiled at her, he knew it.

"You're in town visiting?" Jordyn asked.

"No," Scott said. "I recently moved to Charisma."

"Oh."

"It's good to have him here," Wade said. "Especially now."

She wanted to believe that he meant in North Carolina, but she suspected that he meant something different.

"Why especially now?" she asked, a sudden feeling of unease weighing on her shoulders.

"Because I want to get serious about retirement, and having Scott here to take over running the bar will let me do that."

"Six months ago—" She had to pause to draw air into her lungs as the spots in front of her eyes warned that she'd stopped breathing. "Six months ago you said that I was going to take over running the bar."

"What?"

"We talked about it. Not only six months ago but six months before that. In fact, we've been talking about it for almost two years."

"I'm just going to…go…out," Scott said, moving toward the door.

Wade nodded. "I'll catch up with you in a bit."

Jordyn sank into a chair in front of her boss's desk, her legs as hollow as her stomach. "You don't remember those conversations?" she asked Wade when his nephew had gone.

"I remember the conversations," he confirmed. "But come on, Jordyn—you're a Garrett with a business degree from UNC."

"What does that have to do with anything?"

"I always assumed that your decision to work here was more about some kind of rebellion against your family than any desire to take up bartending as a career. To be honest, when you first walked through the front door, I didn't think you'd last three days, never mind three years."

"So for the last three years, you've just been waiting for me to walk out again?"

"And hoping like hell that you wouldn't," he admitted. "You know I couldn't run this place without you."

"But now you're going to turn it over to your nephew?"

"Try to understand—he's my sister's kid and she was worried about him in Vegas."

"I'll try to understand," she said, rising to her feet again and heading to the door. "So long as you understand why I'm not going to hang around tonight to train my future boss."

Jordyn thought about going home when she left O'Reilly's, but she was afraid that if she did, she'd sit around feeling sorry for herself all night. She considered stopping at Zahara's for some retail therapy, but she wasn't in the mood to shop. Instead, she went to Valentino's and took a seat at the bar. She insisted that she wasn't looking for Marco, but she felt let down not to find him there.

"What can I get for you?" the bartender, whose name tag identified him as Rafe, asked her.

"I'll have a glass of the Stonechurch Vineyards pinot noir." She shifted on her chair, trying to peer into the dining room to see if Marco had been enlisted to help out in there tonight.

Rafe poured the wine, set the glass in front of her. "Are you looking for someone?"

"No." She shook her head. "Not really. I just wondered if maybe Marco was working tonight."

The bartender shook his head. "Not tonight."

"Oh." She was surprised at the depth of her disappointment. Or maybe it was the cumulative effect of so many little disappointments, starting from when she got up that morning and discovered there was no French vanilla coffee to finding out that her boss had never seen her as a potential partner but only an employee easily replaced by another.

"Did you want me to give Marco a call for you?" Rafe asked.

"No," she said quickly, because she really wanted to say yes.

"In that case—" the bartender leaned a little closer "—you should know that anything Marco can do, I can do better."

She managed a smile. "I'll keep that in mind."

"Hi, Jordyn," Gemma greeted her as she passed the bar on her way to the kitchen. Then to Rafe, a definite note of warning in her tone, "Stop flirting with the customers."

The bartender backed away, no evidence of his flirtatious smile remaining on his handsome face.

"I'm sorry," he said. "I didn't realize you were Jordyn."

"Did I miss something?" she asked, intrigued by the short but obviously meaningful exchange.

He shook his head. "Just excuse me for a moment while I take my foot out of my mouth."

"I didn't realize you'd put your foot in it."

"Good," he said. "We'll go with that. And if Marco asks—I definitely was *not* hitting on you."

Jordyn sipped her wine and tried to rationalize Wade's actions.

She understood his willingness to help out family, to give the kid a job, but to immediately offer him the keys to the kingdom—not that O'Reilly's was much of a kingdom, but still—seemed not just extreme but unwise. Aside from the fact that Scott was his nephew, what did Wade really know about him? Did he have a head for business? What was his work ethic? On the other hand, at least her boss had been up-front about his intentions. Wouldn't it have been worse, from her perspective, to let her retain her illusions about her future at O'Reilly's, assuming that Wade had just hired his nephew to help out?

She glanced at her watch and decided it was time to go home. But she remembered that Tristyn had a date tonight—some guy she'd met while picking up lunch at the Corner Deli a few weeks back. Jordyn knew her sister had absolutely no interest in him and suspected that she'd accepted his invitation because he was the opposite of Josh Slater. Not that Tristyn would ever admit as much, but she was perverse that way.

Her usually decisive sister still hadn't committed to Daniel's offer to take over PR at GSR, but she'd been helping him out with some things, to give herself a feel for the job while still working at Garrett Furniture. Jordyn swallowed the last of her pinot noir and wondered if her cousin might have a job for her. Traveling with the team—getting out of Charisma for a while—might be just what she needed.

She set her empty glass down and Rafe immediately replaced it with a new one.

"Thanks," she said. "But I should probably be going."

"Hot date tonight?" he teased.

She managed a smile as she shook her head. "No, but I don't want to be one of those pathetic women who hangs out at a bar drinking alone."

"Beautiful women are never pathetic, only appealingly sad," he assured her. "But if you really don't want to drink alone—" He poured another glass of wine and set it on the bar.

In front of Marco, who settled onto the empty chair beside her. "Hey."

"Hey," she said back.

And inexplicably, her eyes filled with tears.

"That bad?" he asked.

She nodded.

He lifted a hand and brushed a strand of hair off her cheek, tucked it behind her ear. "Do you want to talk about it?"

She picked up the glass of wine she'd said she didn't want and sipped. "The road I was traveling on toward my future just had a major roadblock dropped in the middle of it."

Then she told him about the unexpected arrival of her boss's nephew and Wade's intention to groom Scott to take over the bar.

"Maybe it's a sign for you to take a detour," Marco suggested.

"I don't want to take a detour," she said stubbornly. Then, because she didn't want to wallow any longer, "What are you doing in here on your night off?"

"I just thought I'd stop by."

"Rafe called you," she guessed.

"He might have mentioned that there was a really sexy woman sitting at the bar."

"Are you sure he didn't say 'sullen' rather than 'sexy'?"

"I wouldn't have left home for sullen," he assured her.

She managed a smile.

"So why didn't you call me?" he prompted.

"Because I knew I wouldn't be very good company."

"And yet you came here looking for me."

She traced the base of her wineglass with a fingertip. "I'm not claiming my actions were rational."

He covered her hand with his. "I'm sorry you had a

crappy day," he told her. "But I'm glad, when you had a crappy day, you came looking for me."

"Why?"

"Because it shows that you're starting to share parts of your life with me—the good and the bad. And it proves that you trusted me to make you feel better."

She lifted her brows. "Are you going to make me feel better?"

"If you let me take you home, I'll do my best," he promised.

Marco opened the passenger-side door for her.

"I almost forgot—" he picked up the bouquet of flowers from the seat "—these are for you."

"They're beautiful," she said. "But when did you get them?"

"A little earlier today."

"Even before you knew I had a crappy day," she realized.

"Well, I was thinking about you," he said, then smiled wryly. "I do that a lot, you know—think about you."

She put her face close to the colorful blooms and inhaled their subtle fragrance. "And what were you thinking?"

"How much better my life is with you in it."

She kissed him lightly. "You're starting to grow on me, too," she said, and made him laugh.

She buckled herself into her seat while he went around to the driver's side.

"I like your cousin," she said. "He reminds me of you."

"I'm not sure how I feel about that," he admitted.

She touched the smooth petals of a gerbera. "I just meant that he's sweet and kind and charming."

His gaze narrowed suspiciously. "Did he hit on you?"

"Well, he did say that anything you could do, he could do better."

"After I drop you off at home, I'm going back to Valentino's to beat him up."

She laid her hand on his thigh, felt the muscle tense beneath her palm. "I'd rather you stayed with me."

"Okay," he agreed, lifting her hand from his leg and linking their fingers together. "Although I'm having serious second thoughts about offering to let him run the kitchen at Valentino's II."

"If he's busy in the kitchen, he won't be able to flirt with your female customers," she pointed out.

"I don't care about any other female customers—only you." He pulled into her driveway. "Tristyn's not home?"

"She was going out for dinner tonight."

He helped her out of the car. "Speaking of dinner—did you eat?"

She shook her head. "I wasn't hungry."

"Are you hungry now?"

"Not really." Her foot caught and she stumbled a little.

Marco's gaze narrowed as he caught her arm. "How many glasses of wine did you have?"

"Just two."

"On an empty stomach."

She found her key, inserted it into the lock. "I feel fine, Marco. I promise." She turned to lean into him. "But if you don't want to take my word for it, you can feel for yourself."

His Adam's apple bobbed as he swallowed. Then he reached past her to turn the handle of the door and shove it open. "Do you have any food in the house?"

"Probably."

"Probably?" he echoed.

She shrugged as she stepped into the foyer. "Tristyn does most of the grocery shopping."

He followed her into the house, halting inside the door

when Gryffindor stepped in front of him, as if deliberately blocking his path.

"Do you want some wine?" she asked. "You didn't have a chance to finish your glass at Valentino's."

"Maybe."

She interpreted his response as a yes and reached for a bottle of valpolicella from the rack. While she uncorked the bottle, he opened the door of the refrigerator.

"There's a package of chicken breasts, a bottle of white wine and a couple of lemons in here. I could make chicken *piccata*," he said. "Do you have any capers?"

"I don't even know what capers are," she admitted, pouring the wine into two glasses.

He shook his head. "Doesn't matter—I can manage without."

"Marco," she said, with what she thought was infinite patience. "I'm about to start on my third glass of wine and we're all alone in the house—can't you think of something you'd rather do than cook?"

His gaze raked over her, so hot and hungry it made her knees quiver. "I can think of a thousand," he admitted. "But I'm trying to be a gentleman."

She moved closer, her lips curving in a slow smile. "You can be as gentle as you want...as long as you're naked."

He took the glass from her hand, set it aside. She laid her palms on his torso, just above his belt, then slid them slowly upward. He caught her hands in his, pulled them away.

"I want to make love with you," he said, his voice strangled. "I don't think there's anything I want more."

"Then why are we standing around in the kitchen?"

"Because you don't want to make love—you want to have sex."

Her brow furrowed. "I want to get naked with you. Do the semantics really matter?"

"Yes, they do," he insisted. "Although when you say 'naked,' I have trouble remembering why."

She tipped her head back. "Naked-naked-naked-naked-naked—"

He crushed his mouth to hers in a hard, punishing kiss intended to silence her taunting. She didn't balk at the intensity but met it with equal passion. But just as quickly as he'd started, he pulled away.

"I'm going to make dinner for you," he said. "And after dinner, maybe we can go out and catch a movie."

"A movie?"

"Sure."

She sighed. "How long is this chicken *piccata* going to take?"

"About twenty-five minutes."

"Then I guess I'll go upstairs and take a bath…letting my *naked* body soak in warm scented bubbles while you're busy down here."

It was satisfying to hear the *crack* of the foam packaging as his fingers tightened on it. Not as satisfying as various other scenarios she'd considered, but at least she knew he'd be thinking about her.

Chapter Twelve

She did take a bath, letting the warm scented bubbles relax her mind and body. They had more success with her mind, because she believed he meant it when he said he wanted her—he just had some warped sense of propriety and concerns about timing. But her body wasn't nearly as willing to forgive him. Whether it was the result of a crappy day or something more, she desperately wanted to feel good—and she knew Marco could make her feel good.

She considered her options as she toweled off and rubbed lotion on her skin, and decided there was only one course of action: she had to seduce him.

She found candles in the linen closet—a dozen votives in clear glass holders that she set around her bedroom to provide gentle, dancing light. Then she opened the pink bag and lifted out the tissue-wrapped garments she'd purchased on a whim a few days earlier when she'd been thinking about Marco. She looked at the bed and debated with herself for half a minute before she pulled down the covers and fluffed the pillows. She was aiming for seduction rather than subtle.

She carried her shoes down the stairs, to preserve the element of surprise. As she slipped her feet into the skinny four-inch heels, she experienced a brief moment of doubt—a quick flash of uncertainty—that he might still reject her. Then she remembered the heat in his eyes when he looked at her, the hunger in his lips when he kissed her, and—most telling—the press of his arousal against her, and she knew that he wanted her as much as she wanted him. He just needed a little persuasion.

She squared her shoulders, checked the bow between

her breasts, straightened the edge of a stocking and marched into the kitchen to persuade him.

Marco heard the *click* of her shoes on the tile.

"Good timing," he said. "Dinner will be—"

The rest of the words dried up in his mouth when he turned and saw her standing in the doorway.

She looked like a vision out of an erotic fantasy, but he blinked once, twice and she was still there. Dressed in a skimpy baby doll, thigh-high stockings and skyscraper heels. The black lace ensemble was set off with subtle touches of pink in the ribbon straps and the bow between her breasts. The effect was somehow both sexy and sweet, and the fact that Jordyn was wearing it: irresistible.

She was temptation wrapped in seductive fantasy and sinful promise, and he was helpless to resist her.

"I guess we're not going out to see a movie." They were the first words that came to mind, and they spilled out uncensored.

Her slow smile was sexy...and just a little bit smug.

"We're not going out," she confirmed.

She picked up the two glasses of wine she'd poured earlier and offered one to him. He took both from her and set them down again. Then he took her hands and drew her closer. Her fingers were cold and trembled a little, reassuring him that he wasn't the only one who was nervous about the next step.

"I didn't stand a chance," he murmured.

"That was the plan," she admitted, guiding him out of the kitchen.

He followed her to the stairs. In fact, he had one foot on the bottom tread before he remembered the chicken. He raced back to the kitchen to turn off the heat under the pan, then raced back to her again.

"Do I get a copy of this plan?" he asked, following her into her bedroom.

"Not necessary." She closed the door to keep the cat out in the hall, which Gryff protested—loudly. "I think we can improvise from here."

"I can improvise," he agreed. "But I should probably warn you, I took one look at you wearing that, and I was halfway to the finish line already."

She laughed softly as she tugged his shirt out of his pants. "Let's see what we can do to enjoy the rest of the journey."

He slid his hands beneath the ruffled hem of her top to stroke up the silky skin of her torso.

She sighed her appreciation. "That's a good start."

He captured her mouth with his own. Her lips were soft and warm and welcoming. His tongue swept along the seam, and she parted for him, meeting the searching thrusts with teasing parries.

She unfastened the buttons of his shirt and pushed it over his shoulders. Then her hands were on him, her fingers gliding over his skin, her nails scraping lightly. She found the buckle of his belt, unfastened it, then did the same with the button and zipper of his pants.

"You don't believe in slow, do you?"

"I haven't had sex in more than three years," she told him. "I don't need slow—I just need you."

The words wrapped around his heart as silkily as her fingers wrapped around him. He sucked in a breath as his eyes rolled back.

He caught her wrist and pulled her hand away.

She pouted. "Don't you like it when I touch you?"

He nibbled on her lower lip. "You know I do."

"Then let me—"

"No." He kissed her slowly, deeply, as he eased her back onto the bed. "It's been a long time for me, too, and I've waited too long for this—for *you*—to risk it being over before we've really begun."

His lips moved down her throat, over the curve of her breast. His tongue teased her through the delicate fabric. He found her nipple, already beaded into a tight point, pressing against the lace, begging for his attention. He gave it—licking and circling and sucking. She closed her eyes, feeling the tension build in her core and the pooling of moisture between her thighs.

"Marco." She couldn't manage anything more than his name, and even that was more of a sigh than a whisper.

He sat back on his heels and lifted one of her feet off the bed. "These are sexy as hell," he said, as he tugged the shoe off her foot. "They also look dangerous."

His hand slid over her foot, his thumb tracing the arch, his fingers skimming her ankle, slowly trailing up the back of her leg to the top of her stocking. He traced the edge of the lace, all the way around her leg, smiling when he heard her breath catch. He pressed his mouth to the ultrasensitive skin above her stocking, on the inside of her thigh, and the breath shuddered out of her lungs. He slowly peeled the delicate silk hose down her leg, then followed the same routine with her other shoe and stocking.

She blew out a shaky breath. "You know how you said you were halfway to the finish line?"

"Mmm-hmm." He parted the sides of her top to press his lips to the soft skin just above her navel.

"Well, I've caught up."

"Good to know." His teeth caught the end of the satin bow that held the skimpy top together between her breasts and tugged.

The tie slid free easily, and he parted the fabric, exposing her skin to the cool air and his heated gaze. Then his mouth was on her again, wet and hungry, with no barrier between his eager lips and tongue, and her sensitive flesh.

There was a tiny swatch of lace between her thighs, and he quickly dispensed with that, too. His hands slid down her sides, his thumbs hooking into the satin ribbon that held it in place at her hips, and tugged it down her legs.

"You are so beautiful."

She was naked now, totally exposed, but she didn't feel self-conscious at all. The way he looked at her, the way he touched her, made her feel beautiful.

"So are you," she told him sincerely, her eyes glued to him as he stripped away the last of his clothes.

His skin was dusky in the flickering light, his muscles hard and smooth as if sculpted from flawless marble. There was a light dusting of hair on his chest—dark, springy curls. He knelt over her on the bed and she slid her hands up his torso, over the rippling abs to his pectorals, marveling at the contrast between his strength and his tenderness.

He kissed her again, long and slow and deep, then his lips moved down her body, over her tummy, lower.

Her breath caught in her throat.

He parted her thighs, then the slick folds of skin at their apex. Then his mouth was on her, his lips and his tongue stroking and sucking in a way that launched rockets of sensation shooting through every part of her body in a sensual assault that seemed as if it would never end. When it finally did, when her body was trembling with the aftershocks of so much pleasure, she somehow still felt unfulfilled. She wanted—needed—him inside her. "Now, Marco. Please."

He rose up over her, nudging her legs farther apart, then pulled back abruptly.

"Condom," he suddenly remembered.

She blew out a shaky breath. "Under the pillow."

His brows lifted. "You really did think of everything."

"I didn't want any excuses or delays."

"I like a woman who knows what she wants." He opened the package and sheathed himself.

"I do know what I want." She slid her hands up his chest to his shoulders, then pulled him down to her again. "And I want you."

He positioned himself between her thighs and entered her in one long, deep thrust. She gasped as he filled her, tilting her hips to take him even deeper. Sensations battered at her from every direction, tossing her around like an untethered lifeboat on stormy seas. But Marco was there, holding on to her as the climax washed over her, as she shuddered through wave after wave of sensation.

And then, when she was fully and completely spent, when she was certain there was absolutely nothing left inside her, he found more. He stroked deep and sent her flying again. But this time, finally, he soared with her.

They were tangled together in the sheets, sated and satisfied, when the silence was broken by a low, deep growl.

The hand that had been stroking down Jordyn's back stilled. "I thought Gryffindor was in the hall."

"He is," she admitted. "That was my stomach."

"You didn't have dinner," Marco remembered.

"Well, other things took precedence," she said, sounding content.

Then her stomach growled again.

"Come on," he said. "Let's see if there's any hope of salvaging the chicken I left on the stove."

It turned out that there was no hope—and no chicken. Where Marco expected to find dry, shriveled cutlets, there was nothing but some congealed sauce in the pan.

"I think Gryff ate our dinner."

He looked at the twenty-plus-pound cat, sitting on a velvet cushion in the corner of the room, contentedly washing himself. He shook his head, not believing an animal that size could possibly have maneuvered himself onto the counter. "Seriously?"

"He's surprisingly agile when he wants to be," Jordyn said. "And it's probably my fault—I was so preoccupied with getting you naked that I forgot to give him his dinner."

"So much for proving my culinary prowess," he grumbled.

She opened the refrigerator, peered inside. "There's some leftover pizza in here."

He made a face. "You've also got eggs, milk and bread."

"French toast?"

"It's quick and easy and beats leftover pizza."

"Even if it's Valentino's pizza?" she challenged him.

"Yes, if it's Marco's French toast."

"Now you've piqued my curiosity," she admitted.

He took the eggs and milk from the fridge. "I'm going to need a bowl, a whisk, a spatula and a frying pan."

She gave him the bowl first, and he began cracking eggs while she gathered the rest of the equipment for him.

He opened a cupboard beside the stove and searched through the bottles of spices—adding a couple of dashes and sprinkles without letting her see what he was putting into the bowl.

She watched him work, his movements confident and competent. "You're a nurturer," she realized.

He turned on the element under the frying pan. "What are you talking about?"

"It's in your nature to take care of people," she explained. "You listen when they talk, you understand and anticipate their needs, and you try to fulfill them."

"You got all of that from watching me whisk some eggs?"

"Not just from the eggs," she acknowledged. "I've seen you with Renata and Craig, I've watched you with your nieces, I've heard you talk about your brothers, and I've observed your interactions with the guys at O'Reilly's."

He dipped the first slice of bread into the egg mixture. "Sounds like you've been keeping a pretty close eye on me," he teased.

"I guess I have," she admitted.

"Sounds like you might even like me a little."

She smiled at that. "I might. A little."

He dropped the bread into the hot pan, then glanced over at her. "And why does that worry you?"

To her credit, she didn't deny that it did. "Because I think you're looking for more than I can give you."

"Have I asked you for anything?"

"No," she admitted. "But I hear the way you talk about each of your siblings and their significant others, and I know you want the same kind of committed, long-term relationship that they've all found."

"That's true," he confirmed. "But I'm happy to take things one day at a time."

"I don't know that I can give you anything more than this one day."

"That's okay—because I do."

She huffed out a breath. "You're stubborn."

"I would have said 'determined,' but 'stubborn' works."

"It doesn't work for me."

He slid the French toast out of the pan and onto her plate. "Eat."

Because it smelled good and she was hungry, she picked up her knife and fork and cut into the bread, then dipped it into the small puddle of syrup she'd poured on her plate.

"This is really good." She popped another bite into her mouth. "What's your secret?"

"If I told you, it wouldn't be a secret, would it?"

"Cinnamon?" she guessed.

He just sat down across from her and cut into his own meal.

She savored another bite. "There's definitely cinnamon," she decided. "But there's something else, too."

"Eggs and milk."

"Besides the basic ingredients, I meant."

He just shrugged, refusing to give anything away. Jordyn decided to give up trying to figure out his secret and just enjoy it.

She couldn't remember Brian ever making a meal for her. Not even a sandwich for lunch—even when he was making one for himself. Of course, he'd been an only child—accustomed to fending only for himself. Marco had grown up with two brothers and a sister.

And why was she making comparisons between Brian and Marco? She'd been head over heels in love with her fiancé and planning to spend the rest of her life with him. She was twisted up in lust for Marco and planning only to spend the rest of the night with him.

"What are you thinking about?" Marco asked.

"What?"

"You suddenly got this really faraway look in your eyes," he told her.

She shook her head. "It wasn't anything important."

"You were thinking about your fiancé, weren't you?"

She dropped her gaze to her plate, swirled a piece of bread through the syrup. "Not on purpose."

"Well, I guess it's better now than an hour ago."

She winced at the slight edge in his voice. "Actually, I was just thinking how nice this was—having you cook for me, because Brian never did."

"It's only French toast," he pointed out.

"He never even made me regular toast," she admitted.

"You almost had chicken *piccata*," he reminded her.

She smiled. "I got something better...and *then* I got French toast."

"Something better, huh?"

"Well, not having experienced your chicken *piccata*, I don't really know for sure," she teased. "But I have no complaints."

He cleared their plates off the table and dumped them into the sink. "Let's go back upstairs and see if I can make sure you have no complaints again."

"Let's," she agreed.

Jordyn was in the kitchen, savoring her first cup of coffee of the day, when her sister wandered in.

Tristyn halted in midstride on her way to the coffee-maker, her glance shifting from Jordyn to the bathroom overhead, where the shower was clearly running.

"I was just wondering..." Tristyn began.

Jordyn lifted her cup to her lips, certain she knew where the conversation was going.

"...if *you're* here in the kitchen, and *I'm* here in the kitchen, *who* could be in the shower?"

"That is a good question," she agreed.

"Would it be safe to assume it's the owner of the SUV parked in our driveway?"

"I would think so."

"And since I've seen that same vehicle frequently parked behind Valentino's restaurant, I'm led to the inevitable conclusion that Marco Palermo spent the night in your bed."

"Wow, Sherlock Holmes had nothing on you," Jordyn said.

"So—" Tristyn took a bowl of strawberries out of the fridge and popped one in her mouth "—how was he?"

Jordyn was helpless to prevent the smile that curved her lips. "Spectacular."

Her sister grinned. "Well, then—good for you."

She shook her head. "Not good—spectacular."

"Hmm." Tristyn nibbled on another berry. "I wonder if that's a result of your extended period of abstinence or the skill of your partner."

"I'd have to vote for the partner," she admitted. "Because it wasn't just spectacular the first time but also the second...and the third."

"No need to sound so smug," her sister admonished.

"Sure there is."

"No guilt or regrets?" Tristyn asked gently.

She shook her head. "I'm just afraid that Marco might think it meant more than it did."

"So why don't you tell him what it did mean?" he suggested from the doorway.

"I need to...um...get ready to...um..." Tristyn gave up trying to complete the sentence and escaped with her mug of coffee.

"Hey," Jordyn said, forcing a smile as Marco stepped into the kitchen.

"Hey." He reached into the cupboard over the coffee-maker and located a mug, then found the Italian roast he wanted, popped it into the machine. When the coffee had finished brewing, he carried his cup to the table and sat down across from her.

They were sitting in the same seats they'd occupied the night before, when they'd shared the French toast that he'd made, but he seemed so far away from her now.

"So what did it mean?" he asked again.

"Do we really need to do this?"

"I think we do." His tone was unyielding.

She wrapped her hands around her mug. "Last night was...more than I imagined it could be."

"And this morning?" he prompted.

She wondered how it was that even after everything

they'd shared and done, such a simple question could make her cheeks flush. "This morning, too," she acknowledged.

He studied her, as if he could see everything she was thinking and feeling but didn't know how to put into words—or maybe didn't want to. After a long moment, he nodded. "Then I'd say that's a pretty good start."

Jordyn didn't expect to see him later that day.

She had to work until closing, and since Marco's days started early now that renovations on the new restaurant were under way, she figured he'd want to get to sleep early. But she'd just announced last call to the few remaining customers when he walked into O'Reilly's.

He asked for a cup of coffee—decaf—and sipped it while her customers finished their drinks and headed out.

"So what are you doing here?" she asked when they were finally alone.

"I wanted to see you."

She lifted a brow. "Think you're going to get lucky again tonight?"

"I was thinking of letting *you* get lucky."

She laughed, because she realized that she was lucky. She didn't know what the future would hold—she didn't want to look too far ahead. But right now, being with Marco, she felt very lucky.

She lifted her arms to link her hands behind his head. "You're too kind."

"I try," he said, and covered her lips with his own.

She melted into the kiss, her body already stirring with the memory of all the wonderful things he could do to it— and had done. Numerous times.

The stirring—the wanting—worried her. She'd been alone for a long time, and numb for most of that time. But now, with Marco, she was feeling things she hadn't thought she'd ever feel again. And wanting things she knew it was dangerous to want.

But the knowledge didn't stop the wanting, so she pushed her fears aside and focused on the pleasure he was giving her in the here and now.

Chapter Thirteen

Eight days later, Jordyn had no choice but to admit that she was fighting a losing battle against Marco's endless patience and relentless charm on one side and her own growing feelings for him on the other. But she was still reluctant to put a label on those feelings, still unwilling to admit the depth of her attachment to him.

They didn't see each other every day. She was still working four nights a week at O'Reilly's and he was occupied at his family's restaurants—both the original Valentino's and the new location, only a few blocks from her house. Despite their busy and often opposing schedules, they somehow found time to be together.

But it was never enough—and the more time Jordyn spent with him, the more she wanted to be with him. And as much as she'd resented Scott's sudden appearance on the doorstep of O'Reilly's, she'd recently begun to appreciate that his assumption of some of her duties meant that she was able to take more time off—even the occasional Saturday night.

On this particular one, Tristyn was away for the weekend at the race in Michigan and Jordyn was cooking for Marco.

Gryffindor was chowing down on his dinner. She suspected it was a throwback from his years on the street that he never took his time with his food. When he heard his kibble being poured into his bowl, he came running. And he devoured every last crumb as if, after seven years of regular breakfasts and dinners, he still couldn't be sure where and when he might find his next meal. Of course, he still knew how to fend for himself if necessary—as he'd proven the night of the disappearing chicken *piccata*.

Marco kept one eye on the cat—who seemed to be keeping his one eye on him, even while annihilating his food.

"Can I help you with something?" he asked Jordyn.

"Sure—you can open the wine while I go preheat the grill."

He ignored the bottle on the counter and followed her through the French doors out onto the back deck. "Are you trying to emasculate me?"

She opened the lid of the barbecue, turned on the gas and fired up the grill. "What are you talking about?"

"It's a man's job to barbecue."

"Is it?" she asked, not even trying to hide the amusement in her tone.

"It is," he confirmed solemnly. "Going all the way back to caveman days and the discovery of fire."

"So a woman who doesn't have a man in her life should be deprived of food cooked on a grill?" she challenged.

"Well, I guess it would be okay for a woman to barbecue if there wasn't a man around to do it for her."

She shook her head. "And for that sexist remark, you get to set the table, too."

Because she looked so fiercely sexy pointing her tongs at him, he went inside to comply with her directions.

He opened the wine and left it to breathe, then got out the dishes for their meal.

"Where are the place mats?" he called out to her.

"Top drawer of the hutch."

He reached for the knob.

"Bottom," she called out. "Place mats are in the bottom drawer."

But the top drawer was already open and his gaze was snagged by the glossy folder with the name *Jay Addison* elaborately scrawled on the front.

Intrigued, he pulled it out and opened the cover. He didn't know a lot about art—in fact, he could barely tell a pastel from a watercolor—but it was apparent even to him that whoever had created the pictures was incredibly talented.

"Ten minutes," Jordyn told him.

He set the folder aside and found the place mats, then finished setting the table. He was pouring the wine into two goblets when Jordyn came in with the platter of ribs in one hand and a bowl of potatoes in the other. Gryff followed closely on her heels, and if he'd had a tail, Marco was sure it would have been twitching from side to side in hopeful anticipation.

"You already had Seafood Medley," she reminded the cat when he wound between her feet, nearly tripping her up.

Gryff's one eye looked up at her pleadingly.

Jordyn just chuckled and shook her head.

"I found this in the hutch," Marco said, holding up the folder. "What is it?"

She set the food on the table and reached over to snatch it out of his hand. "Nothing."

Except that it was obvious to both of them that it wasn't "nothing," and he couldn't help but notice the color that flooded her cheeks. He didn't protest when she shoved the folder back into the drawer and closed it firmly, but he didn't forget about it, either.

When dinner was finished, they worked together, clearing the table and loading the dishwasher, and the whole time one question hovered on his tongue. When the cleanup was done and she'd emptied the last of the wine into their glasses, he finally just asked, "Is it his?"

She looked at him blankly. "What?"

"The folder of drawings," he clarified.

"His—who?" she asked.

"Your fiancé's," he said. He didn't care if it was. He didn't even care if she wanted to frame them and hang them on the wall—in fact, he'd feel better if she did. That the pictures were kept hidden away in a drawer suggested that they were too personal to be shared.

"The folder labeled 'Jay Addison'?"

He shrugged. "I figured it was a pseudonym."

"It is a pseudonym," she admitted. "But no—the drawings aren't his."

"They're yours," he finally realized. "'Jay' because it's the first letter of your name and 'Addison' because…?"

She sighed, mentally cursing herself for leaving the folder in the drawer where it could easily be found.

"Addison is my mother's maiden name," she admitted.

"I didn't know you were an artist."

"I'm not."

Once upon a time, it had been her dream, but a few college art courses had persuaded her to change direction. She'd loved to draw and paint and create, but there were so many of her own pictures and ideas in her head, she hadn't wanted to study or emulate anyone else's style—an apparently fatal flaw if she wanted an education in art.

"Jordyn, your drawings are amazing."

He sounded sincere, but considering that he was seeing her naked on a regular basis, what else was he going to say?

"Why aren't you doing something with your talent?" he asked her now.

She shrugged. "It's not a talent—it's a hobby."

"There was a contest flyer in the folder."

"Yeah. Tristyn picked it up from somewhere."

"Who's A. K. Channing?"

"A bestselling science-fiction novelist who's looking for an illustrator for a new series."

"Are you going to submit an entry?"

"I don't think so."

"Why not?"

Because she was uncertain and insecure, afraid to put herself out there and risk having someone else confirm what her college art teacher had decided—that she was a wannabe artist with a modicum of talent and even less desire to focus that talent into something real.

But all she said to him was, "There will probably be hundreds of entries."

"Possibly," he agreed.

"So the odds of my entry being selected—"

"It's not a lottery," he reminded her. "It's not about odds but ability. Maybe A. K. Channing is looking for a particular style and maybe it's not yours, but you won't know if you don't take a chance."

He was right, of course, but she remained paralyzed by her former teacher's harsh assessment of her work.

"You should do it," Marco said.

She set her glass of wine aside and reached for him. "Do you really want to talk about my childhood dreams?" she asked, working her way down the front of his shirt, slipping the buttons free from the placket. "Or do you want to live out my adult fantasies?"

He lifted her off her feet and into his arms. "Why don't we go upstairs and find out?"

She made him forget about the folder—at least for a while.

With Jordyn in his arms, he simply couldn't think of anything else, want anything else. She might have been teasing about her fantasies, but she really was his dream come true. She was everything he'd ever hoped for and wanted, and when he was with her, there was nowhere in the world that he would rather be.

She was snuggled against him now, her naked body sprawled over his, her heart beating in rhythm with his own. She'd lit the candles again, and their flames flickered and danced.

He stroked a hand down her hair, watched her lips curve in a slow, contented smile.

"You really are the most beautiful woman I've ever known."

She propped herself up on an elbow. "It's the candlelight," she told him. "Every woman looks beautiful in candlelight."

He trailed a hand down her side until it rested on the curve of her hip. "There was hardly any light the first time I saw you—just a quick flash of lightning—and still my heart stopped for three beats."

"*That* you're making up."

"I'm not," he promised. "It happened exactly like that, exactly that fast."

Her brows lifted. "What happened?"

"I fell in love with you."

The hand that she'd lifted to brush her hair away from her face trembled, the curve of her lips faltered. "Marco—"

"I know—I shouldn't have said it," he acknowledged, but he'd been holding the truth of his feelings inside for so long already, and they refused to be denied any longer. "I should have realized you're not ready to hear it."

The panic in her eyes confirmed that was true. "I can't—"

"I'm not asking for you to say it back," he assured her. "I'm just asking you to let me acknowledge my own feelings."

"You don't even really know me," she protested.

"Seven weeks ago, that might have been true. But even then, I knew that I would love you."

"You couldn't possibly know such a thing."

"I did," he insisted. "My grandmother always said that when I met the woman I was destined to be with, the realization would hit me like lightning."

"And you think—because you first saw me during an electrical storm—the lightning was some kind of sign?" she asked incredulously.

"When you say it like that, it does sound kind of farfetched. And maybe the lightning was just a coincidence, but my feelings for you are real."

"The attraction is real," she acknowledged. "I'm not convinced there's anything more than that."

"How can you say that after what we just shared?"

"One orgasm is hardly a foundation for forever."

He lifted a brow; she blushed.

"Okay—several orgasms," she allowed.

"You're deliberately demeaning what's between us because you're afraid to acknowledge that it's more than a physical thing."

"I'm not demeaning it," she said. "I'm just not turning it into something that it's not, and you need to accept that I don't want the same things you do."

"I think you do. You're just afraid to let yourself reach for them—afraid you'll get close only to have them slip through your fingers again."

"I like my life the way it is," she insisted.

He nuzzled her throat, felt her shiver. "Right now, I have no complaints, either."

"I don't want to hurt you, Marco."

"Which you wouldn't worry about if you didn't care about me," he pointed out, tracing the curves of her torso.

"Of course I care about you." Her breath hitched when his palms skimmed over her breasts. "I wouldn't be here with you if I didn't."

"Then I can be satisfied with that for now."

* * *

She let him convince her, because as much as she didn't think she would ever fall in love with him, she didn't want to let him go, either. She knew she was being selfish, and probably unfair, but she had no desire to change the status quo.

Because no one had ever touched her the way he touched her. No one had ever made her feel the way he made her feel. Except that couldn't be right. She must have experienced this same excited anticipation with Brian, but he'd been gone for more than three years now and she didn't remember. There had been a time when she'd wanted only to stop hurting, and then she'd felt guilty to realize that her memories had begun to fade along with the pain.

She didn't want to think about him now; she didn't want her memories to interfere with what she had with Marco. But then she realized there was no danger of that at all— she couldn't remember Brian; her mind and her senses were filled with Marco. Only Marco.

The realization terrified her.

She hadn't expected to feel so much so soon, for him to be so important to her. She enjoyed being with him, whether they were on opposite sides of the bar at O'Reilly's or snuggling on the sofa in her living room. She missed him when they weren't together and found herself looking forward to when she would see him again. And she knew that if she wasn't careful, she could fall in love with him, and that was too risky. She didn't want either of them to get hurt.

"Fun, Food & Fireworks" was the theme of Charisma's Fourth of July celebration, and the whole town got into the spirit. Buildings were decked out in red, white and blue bunting and the Stars and Stripes flew proudly on every corner.

The first major event of the day was the Independence Parade, which included high school marching bands and majorettes, equestrian riders and tumbling troupes. There were also pipes-and-drums bands, church groups, Cub Scouts, local sports teams, motorcycle clubs and service veterans.

The parade started at the college and finished at Arbor Park, where there was face painting and balloon animals for the kids, market stalls and homemade crafts for the shoppers, and food vendors offering everything from ice cream and popcorn to barbecue sandwiches with baked beans and fried okra.

For as long as Jordyn could remember, her parents and sisters had gathered together with all the aunts, uncles and cousins for a potluck meal in the park. Over the years, the number and composition of the family had changed. Many of the cousins that she'd played with when they were all kids were busy with kids of their own now.

The summer that she and Brian were engaged, he'd been here with her. She'd loved having him by her side, watching her cousins with their spouses and their children and counting the months and weeks until the wedding when she and Brian wouldn't just be engaged but actually married. Except that had never happened, and before the next summer, she was alone again.

She shook off the melancholy and glanced over at the picnic tables, where she spotted Lauryn and Rob in conversation. Lauryn must have asked him something, because Rob shook his head, then his wife shrugged and walked away.

"I'm craving ice cream," she said to Jordyn. "So Kylie and I are going for a walk to see if we can find some. Do you want to come with us?"

"Ice cream before dinner?" Jordyn feigned disapproval, then she winked at Kylie. "Of course."

They headed away from the family gathering.

"Rob didn't want ice cream?"

Lauryn shook her head. "He said if he starts catering to my whims now, I'll keep him running for the next seven months."

Jordyn clenched her jaw to hold back her instinctive response.

"He's not thrilled about the baby," her sister admitted, fighting back tears. "He says we can't afford another child right now."

Jordyn wished her sister's husband was there so she could remind him that Lauryn didn't get pregnant on her own—and then so she could smack him in the head for being such an ass. Since he wasn't there, she slid an arm across her sister's shoulder and squeezed reassuringly. "He'll come around."

"I hope so." She tried to smile, but failed. "After all, it's not as if I can take the pregnancy test back to the pharmacy and ask for one with only one line instead of two."

"And if you could?" Jordyn asked gently.

"I wouldn't." Lauryn responded without hesitation. "I want Kylie to have a brother or a sister—hopefully one that she'll feel as close to one day as I do with you and Tristyn."

"Do you know why two sisters are better than one?"

"Why?"

"One to help bury the body and the other to be your alibi."

This time Lauryn's smile came easily. "I'll keep that in mind."

Marco didn't think there was any chance his grandparents would change their plans for the holiday, so he wasn't just surprised but a little suspicious when they agreed that it might be fun to celebrate the Fourth of July at Arbor Park. Although there was some grumbling from

Salvatore—"we'll probably have to park so far away, we might as well walk from home"—but everyone seemed willing to check out the town's festivities.

Their acquiescence made Marco wonder if the big family celebration might be too much for the elderly couple—not that either of his grandparents would ever admit as much. And although his mom and aunts helped with the food, Nonna still did the majority of the cooking, and he was glad that, this year at least, things would be a little easier for her.

Because Renata didn't feel up to standing around in the heat for an hour to wait for the parade to start, Marco offered to go ahead with the girls so they wouldn't miss it. After the last float had passed, they turned with the rest of the crowd to head into the park.

They didn't make it far before Anna spotted the face-painting tent, and he let her drag him inside. There weren't too many kids waiting in line, but when it was her turn, she still hadn't been able to decide whether she wanted to be a butterfly or a kitty cat. Unexpectedly it was Bella who made up her mind first, going in a completely different direction and choosing to be painted like a dinosaur.

Half an hour later, he walked out of the tent with a grinning kitty cat holding on to one hand and a ferocious triceratops latched on to the other.

"Look, Uncle Marco—there's the lady from the shoe store."

He stopped abruptly, forcing others on the same path to move around him. He didn't know how Anna could have spotted Jordyn through the crowd, but she had. Jordyn was there, walking beside her sister, Lauryn, and a little girl who looked younger than Bella.

"Her name's Jordyn," he reminded his eldest niece, which she interpreted as an invitation to yell out, "Hi, Jordyn."

Jordyn paused in midstep and turned, surprise—and a hint of wariness—on her face when she saw him with his nieces. But she smiled as he guided the girls over.

He knew Lauryn, but he didn't know she had a daughter—and there was no doubt the toddler clinging to her shorts was hers. Jordyn introduced him to her niece—Kylie—then introduced the little girl to his nieces.

"Raarr!" Bella said, making a snarly face to show her teeth. "I'm a scawy twi-zair-o-sop."

"Triceratops," Marco corrected her.

"You are very scary," Jordyn said.

Kylie seemed to agree, as she hid her face behind her mother's leg.

"Are you a scary triceratops who eats little girls?" Lauryn asked.

Bella's eyes grew wide with horror at the possibility, and she shook her head vigorously. "I eats ice cweam."

"Well, it just so happens that we're on our way to get ice cream," Lauryn told her. Then she asked Marco, "Is it okay if I take them over?"

He nodded, grateful for the opportunity for a few minutes alone with Jordyn.

"I like this look," he said, his gaze skimming from her sandals to her short shorts and halter-style top, admiring all the smooth, tanned skin on display.

"It's hot," she said, just a little defensively.

"Very hot," he agreed, taking a step closer to brush a quick kiss on her lips.

"What are you doing here, Marco?"

"Celebrating the Fourth of July," he told her.

"You told me that your grandparents usually have a get-together at their place."

"Usually they do," he confirmed. "But this year, they decided to do something different."

"Just this year? Out of the blue?"

He understood her skepticism. After all, the last time he'd seen her—two days earlier—he'd asked her to celebrate the holiday with his family at his grandparents' house. Not surprisingly, she'd said no.

"Okay, I might have made the suggestion that played a part in their decision," he acknowledged.

"Why?" she asked warily.

He shook his head. "I don't know whether to be amused or frustrated by your deliberate obtuseness."

She frowned at that.

"I suggested that we come here because I wanted to spend the day with you and you turned down my invitation to go there," he explained patiently.

"I turned down your invitation because, while I'm sure your family is wonderful, I didn't want them making the kind of assumptions about our relationship that tend to be made when a guy takes a girl home to meet his family."

"What kind of assumptions are those?" he asked.

"Now who's being obtuse?"

It was an effort to hold back the smile that wanted to curve his lips in response to the frustration in her tone. "If you're worried that they'll assume you're important to me, you shouldn't—because they already know it."

"I feel so much better now."

"Good," he said, choosing to ignore her sarcasm. "Now I should get the girls and track down the rest of the family."

"And I need to get back to help my mom and the aunts get dinner set out."

"Are you staying for the fireworks tonight?"

"They're my favorite part of the day," she admitted.

"Then I'll come find you later so we can watch them together."

"It might not be that easy," she said. "It's a big park and there are a lot of people here."

"I'll see you later," he promised, and kissed her again before wandering over to the picnic table in the shade where Anna and Bella were sitting with Lauryn and Kylie, trying to eat their ice-cream cones before they melted away.

Chapter Fourteen

It turned out that she saw him sooner rather than later.

When Jordyn, Lauryn and Kylie returned to their usual picnic area, she discovered that Marco's family had somehow found their way to the same spot.

"This was a setup," Jordyn grumbled.

"If it was, I had nothing to do with it," Lauryn assured her.

"Tristyn," she decided. "There's no way he could have known where to find us unless she told him."

"You're probably right," her sister agreed. "But instead of scowling at her, you might consider saying thank-you."

"We'll see how this goes," she said.

Afterward, she could acknowledge that it had gone fairly well. In fact, with so many of each of their respective family members gathered together and everyone being introduced to everyone else, there was less of an emphasis on Jordyn meeting Marco's family and vice versa. Still, she didn't think it was a coincidence that his grandmother lingered to make conversation with her, or that her father cornered Marco for a chat. And when she saw her mother and his with their heads close together, she was more uneasy than reassured.

When it came time to eat, the two families pooled their culinary offerings so there was no shortage of food— quantity or selection. In addition to the standard potato salad and pasta salad, baked beans, fried okra and spicy potato wedges, there were trays of lasagna and penne with meatballs and green salad and crusty rolls. When everyone had their fill of those offerings, dessert was put out:

platters of fresh fruit, lemon squares, double chocolate brownies and cannoli.

"Marco mentioned that those are a particular favorite of yours," his mother commented when Jordyn put a cannoli on her plate.

"I would suspect they're a favorite of everyone who has tasted them," Jordyn said.

"They are a popular dessert at the restaurant," Donnaleesa acknowledged, smiling as Bella raced over to steal one from the tray. "And family gatherings."

"The way this family is growing, you're going to have to share that recipe and let someone help you with the baking," Renata chimed in.

"You're a good cook, but you have no patience for baking," her mother chided.

"I wasn't thinking of me, but Francesca."

Donnaleesa glanced around the gathering until she found her eldest son and his fiancée, then nodded. "Maybe I'll talk to her about it after the wedding."

"In the meantime—" Nata linked her arm through her mother's and began guiding Donnaleesa away, sending a conspiratorial wink over her shoulder to Jordyn "—maybe you can talk to Dad about the tree house he promised to build for his granddaughters."

After dinner and dessert were cleared away and the kids finally stopped running around, the parents of the younger ones started to round them up to take them home before the fireworks.

Renata and Craig tried to convince Anna and Bella that it was time to go, but the girls wanted to stay because Kylie was staying.

Jordyn took a seat on the top of the picnic table, with her feet on the bench. She'd pulled a hooded sweater over her head, more to deter the mosquitoes than to ward off any chill in the air. Marco sat beside her, so close that their legs were in contact from hip to knee, then he took her hand in his and linked their fingers. It was nice—sitting quietly in the dark, holding hands and snuggling close together. She almost felt like a teenager again, except that she and Marco had done all kinds of things she'd never dreamed of as a teenager.

Before the fireworks were over, her cousin Justin, an ER doctor, was paged to go into the hospital. Unfortunately, his car was blocked so Tristyn offered to take him, leaving Jordyn without transportation. She could have asked for a lift from any one of her relatives who were left, but she decided to take Lauryn's advice and be grateful for the opportunity.

"Any chance I can get a ride home?" she asked Marco. "My sister abandoned me—again."

"This is getting to be a habit," he noted.

"At least this time, she had a good excuse—she had to give Justin a lift to the hospital."

"I'd be happy to give you a ride home," he said. "Or back to my place."

"Are you inviting me for a sleepover?"

"You don't have to work early tomorrow, do you?"

"No, but I don't have my pajamas."

"That's okay—you're not going to need them."

With the renovations at the new restaurant in full swing, Marco started most of his days there. And though it was only a short walk from her house, Jordyn never ventured over to say hello or check on the progress they were making. Probably because there were always numerous and various other members of his family also on-site helping out, and, even after meeting everyone on the Fourth of July, she was still wary of being labeled his "girlfriend."

So he was taken aback when, a week and a half later, she walked over to the site.

"This is a pleasant surprise," he said, steering her to a quiet corner where they'd be out of the way of the painters.

"I got something in the mail that I wanted to show you."

He took the envelope she offered, noted the registered mark and the return address.

"You entered the contest," he realized, proud that she'd done so and a little disappointed that she hadn't told him before now.

She lifted a shoulder. "You made me believe I had a shot."

He opened the flap and pulled out a sheaf of papers.

Congratulations on being selected one of five finalists in A. K. Channing's "Search for a New World Design."

He couldn't have prevented the smile from spreading across his face if he wanted to—and he didn't want to. "And now you know that I'm not the only one who can see your talent. Jordyn, this is incredible news." He wrapped his arms around her and hugged her tight. "I'm so happy for you."

"I think I'll be happy, too," she said. "Once I get over the shock."

He chuckled. "What did your sisters say? Your parents? They must all be so proud of you."

"I haven't told anyone else yet—I wanted you to be the first."

That admission took most of the sting out of his earlier disappointment. "So what's the next step?"

"I've been given a short scene to illustrate, and I'm supposed to go to New York City to present my work to a panel of judges."

"What do you mean 'supposed to go'?"

She shrugged. "I'm not sure it wouldn't be a waste of my time."

"How can you say that? This is the opportunity of a lifetime," he told her.

"Is it an opportunity?" she wondered. "Or a pipe dream?"

"It's *your* dream—and you should go for it."

But still she hesitated. "I don't want to get my hopes up."

"You were chosen as one of five finalists out of—" he glanced at the letter again "—more than a thousand entries. Your hopes shouldn't just be up, they should be dancing and singing and throwing confetti. And *you* should be booking your flight to New York City."

"You really think I should go?"

"Definitely," he said. "And if you want some company... I've always wanted to visit New York City."

"You've never been?"

He shook his head. "You?"

"A few times," she admitted.

"Then you could show me around."

She nibbled on her bottom lip, obviously tempted but still resistant.

"Come on, Jordyn—you can't tell me it's your ambition to serve drinks at O'Reilly's for the rest of your life."

She'd almost managed to convince herself that it was, that she didn't need or want anything more. Until Marco had encouraged her to take this chance. He'd nurtured the seed of a long-forgotten dream and it was starting to grow in her heart. But the bloom was still fragile, tentative.

"I like my job," she said, just a little defensively.

"That's not the point."

She took the letter back from him and tucked it into the pocket of her shorts. "And I don't see how you can take off for a weekend with the opening of the new restaurant on the horizon."

"I can because this is important to you and you're important to me."

"You'd really go with me?"

"Absolutely." He kissed her softly. "Maybe we could even catch a Yankees game while we're in the city."

She smiled. "You sure know how to tempt a girl."

"I promise you—baseball tickets are only the beginning."

"I've decided on a date for O'Reilly's twenty-fifth anniversary celebration," Wade said to Jordyn when she arrived at the pub for her evening shift a few nights later.

"The first weekend in October is the twenty-fifth anniversary," Jordyn reminded him.

He shook his head. "Business is too slow in October."

"Which is what makes the timing so perfect—it gives us an excuse to do something big to bring customers out."

"I'm not sure we could do anything big enough to replicate the summer crowds," he told her. "So we've decided to do it the third weekend in August."

She knew the "we" was Wade and Scott, but that didn't bother her as much now as it would have only a few weeks earlier. Besides, it was the last part of his statement that snagged her attention. "The third weekend in August?"

"Twenty-five hours of food and drink specials," he told her, his voice filled with enthusiasm. "Starting Friday afternoon until closing Saturday night."

"That sounds great," she agreed. "But I'm not going to be here that weekend."

He scowled. "What are you talking about?"

"That's why I came in early—to ask for that weekend off."

"The answer is no," he said. "You know how busy summer is—there's no way I could manage without you for a whole weekend."

"And you know I wouldn't ask if it wasn't important."

"More important than O'Reilly's twenty-fifth anniversary?"

She huffed out a breath. "I need to go to New York—"

"New York City?" He waved a hand dismissively. "You don't want to go there in August."

"Actually, I do," she said. "There's—"

"You're my assistant manager," he reminded her.

"You have another assistant manager now. Remember? The one who's going to run O'Reilly's when you retire?"

"Is that what this is about? Are you still upset—"

"No," she interjected. "In fact, I'm glad Scott's here because I've realized I like having a life beyond the walls of this pub."

"Scott doesn't have either your experience or your knowledge of our customer base. I need you here, Jordyn. I can't do this without you."

She knew she was being manipulated, that her boss would say or do anything to get what he wanted. And while she was flattered by his claim that he needed her, it wasn't really true. Wade had enough capable employees to make it work whether or not she was around.

On the other hand, they'd been talking about this event for months. O'Reilly's twenty-fifth anniversary was a huge milestone and she wanted to be part of it.

But she also wanted to go to New York, to meet A. K. Channing and see how her illustrations compared with those of the other finalists, and to spend a few days—and nights—with Marco.

"…three o'clock tomorrow."

She realized Wade was still talking, having taken her acquiescence for granted.

"I'm sorry," she said. "What's at three o'clock tomorrow?"

"We're meeting to finalize the menu, drink specials and entertainment. You and me and Scott."

"You and Scott have managed to figure things out without me so far. I'm not sure what I could add."

"Look, Jordyn, I know you're still sore that I brought Scott on board, but what else could I do? He's my sister's kid, and she was worried about him in Vegas. He got into some trouble—gambling, I think she said—and she wanted a fresh start for him."

She understood that. She'd been looking for a fresh start, too, when she'd gone into O'Reilly's three years earlier after seeing the help-wanted sign in the window. And Wade had given her that fresh start. He didn't remind her of that fact now, but he didn't need to. They both knew it.

"I'll be at the meeting tomorrow," she promised.

Jordyn looked at the pages she'd finished only the night before and felt good about the work she'd done. She'd had more than a few doubts when she started the assignment. Old insecurities had reared up and made her question not just her abilities but her purpose.

Why was she doing this? Did she really think she was good enough to translate A. K. Channing's story into pictures?

She hadn't been able to shut those questions out of her mind, but she'd worked through them. She'd refused to let them undermine this opportunity. And when she was finally done, she knew that she'd nailed it. She'd created a strong cast of characters and an exquisitely detailed fantasy world. Although the villain didn't appear on any of the pages in the scene that she'd been assigned, she'd been given some background information—enough that she could picture him vividly in her mind. So vividly, in fact, that she'd had to sketch him out.

Now she closed the cover of the folder and tucked it away.

When Marco came by later that night, she told him, "I can't go to New York."

"Why not?"

"Wade has scheduled O'Reilly's twenty-fifth anniversary celebration for that weekend."

"I don't see why that's any reason to change our plans."

"He needs me here."

He shook his head. "Even if he does, you don't need him—or that job—enough to miss this chance."

"I *do* need that job."

It was the only one she had since she'd chosen to walk away from Garrett Furniture. She knew her family would find a position for her somewhere in the company if she decided that she wanted to go back, but she didn't. She was no longer haunted by memories of Brian; she'd just made a different life for herself. And even if she didn't want to serve drinks at O'Reilly's for the rest of her life, it was what she wanted to be doing right now.

"You need to follow up on this opportunity," Marco said. "If you don't, you'll always wonder 'what if.'"

"I'm not an artist—I'm a bartender."

"This is your shot, Jordyn. The chance to use your talent and do what you really want to do."

He was doing it again—nurturing the seed of a long-buried dream. But she'd had too many dreams trampled already to let herself believe this one would be different. She would rather tuck the tiny blossom of hope away in a dark corner of her heart than let it reach out. Even if that caused it to slowly wither and die, that was preferable to having it crushed by the heavy heel of rejection.

"We can go to New York another time," she told him. "Maybe in the fall, when the trees in Central Park are changing colors and the streets are a little less jammed with tourists."

"You think I'm upset that you canceled our plans to go away," he realized.

"Aren't you?"

"No. I'm upset because you're letting the opportunity of a lifetime slip through your fingers and you don't even seem to care."

"What opportunity?" she challenged. "The contest was probably nothing more than a publicity stunt designed to focus attention on his upcoming series. He probably already has an illustrator. The fine print gives him the right to choose another candidate if none of the entrants prove suitable."

"You're scared," he realized.

"I'm only afraid of wasting my time."

"One of five," he reminded her.

She looked away.

"Do you ever fight for what you really want? Or are you so afraid of failing that you'd rather not try? And what about us—what's going to happen if our relationship hits a bump? Are you going to put any effort into making it work or are you going to walk away?"

"Why are you doing this?" She felt tears burning behind her eyes, so many emotions churning inside of her. He was right—she was afraid to try and afraid to fail, and panic rose up inside her. "Why are you making this about us?"

"Because it *is* about us, and if you can't see that, then maybe that's the answer to my question."

She didn't know how to respond to that, what to say to make everything okay with him. So she said nothing.

After a long minute, Marco nodded. "Yeah, that's what I figured."

Then he turned and walked out the door.

Chapter Fifteen

She pushed aside all thoughts of New York City to focus on planning the twenty-five-hour event to celebrate O'Reilly's twenty-fifth anniversary, determined to prove to herself that she'd made the right decision in choosing to stay in Charisma.

But no matter how busy she kept herself, thoughts of Marco continued to intrude. And when she thought of Marco, she couldn't help but think about how much she missed him. But she was mad at him, too, for the unfairness of the accusations he'd thrown at her. He'd accused her of not being willing to fight for their relationship, but then he'd walked out on her.

She might have felt better if he'd slammed the door, but he hadn't. He'd simply pulled it shut so that it closed with a quiet *click*—an ending, like the period at the conclusion of a sentence. And when she thought of that quiet *click*, when she thought that it might well and truly be over between them, she felt cold and empty inside.

And when she went to bed at night, when she crawled between the cold sheets of her empty bed, she cried for what she'd had, and what she'd lost.

She wanted to make it right, but she still didn't believe she'd done anything wrong. It was *her* future, *her* choice, and *he'd* overreacted because he didn't like the choice she'd made. She held on to that conviction and her righteous indignation for almost a week. Then she swallowed her pride and went to Valentino's.

She stopped by early in the morning, when she knew that only the cooks would be there, getting the sauces and pastas ready for the day. The main doors were locked, of course, so she knocked on the one at the back designated for deliveries.

"Marco isn't here," Rafe said when he answered the door, his blunt tone leaving her in no doubt that he was aware of her falling-out with his cousin.

"I'm actually looking for your grandmother," she told him.

Rafe studied her for a long minute before he turned and yelled back into the kitchen, "Nonna, there's someone here to see you."

A few minutes later, Caterina was at the door. She seemed startled to find Jordyn there, then she said something to her grandson in Italian—a hasty string of words that succeeded in sending Rafe back to the kitchen.

When he'd gone, she smiled at Jordyn, and the kindness—both unexpected and undeserved—made her throat tighten.

"*Sì, cara*—what can I do for you?"

"I need a favor," Jordyn said.

Marco's grandmother had already set up in his kitchen when Jordyn arrived with the grocery bags containing everything on the list Caterina had given her.

The older woman had bowls and utensils at the ready. A handkerchief covered her braided salt-and-pepper hair, and a chef's apron protected her clothes. A pot on the stove was already boiling.

"I hope you don't mind—there were potatoes in the pantry, so I decided to get started."

"I don't mind," Jordyn assured her. "But I was supposed to do the work, following your instructions."

"Do you know how to peel and boil potatoes?" Caterina asked.

"Of course."

"Then you don't need my instruction and we're one step ahead."

She could hardly argue with that logic, so she only said, *"Grazie."*

The older woman smiled at her. "You're learning."

"Un pochino."

"It's the effort that counts," Caterina declared. "In languages, in cooking and especially in relationships."

Jordyn didn't know what to say to that, so she turned her attention to unpacking the grocery bags. Marco's grandmother arranged the items on the counter, setting them where they would be needed.

"What is this?" she asked.

Jordyn glanced over to see her frowning at the jar she held in her hand. "Sauce?"

"Are you asking me or telling me?"

She felt her cheeks flush. "It's sauce for the pasta."

Caterina turned the jar in her hand to read the list of ingredients on the label. "Not bad, but nothing is as good as homemade."

"I didn't think we'd have time to make homemade sauce."

"A basic red sauce doesn't take long," Marco's grandmother told her. "And you have what you need right here." She pointed to the area where she'd grouped together the necessary ingredients—a can of whole tomatoes, fresh garlic and basil, olive oil and salt.

"That's it?"

"Food does not need to be complicated to taste good." She drained the potatoes—using the pot lid as a strainer—then set the pot on a hot plate on the counter and handed a masher to Jordyn.

She obediently began to mash.

After a couple of minutes, Caterina told her to add an egg and mix it in.

"Now flour." She opened the bag.

"How much?"

"Sprinkle it over the potato and blend it together. Don't worry about the measurements—you need to *feel* the dough. If it's too sticky, you sprinkle in a little more flour. If it's too dry, you add another egg."

"How many potatoes do you use?"

"It depends on how much pasta you want to make."

Her logic was infallible, but it didn't answer Jordyn's question.

"How many potatoes did you peel?" she prompted.

"Four or five." Caterina put her hand into the bowl, squeezed the dough to check the consistency, nodded.

"*Buona.* Now—" she dusted a section of the counter-top with flour "—you make a shape—*un serpente*—like a snake."

She demonstrated, taking a piece of the dough and rolling it with the flat of her hand so that it formed a long, thin snakelike shape.

"Then you—*tagliare in pezzi*—cut it—" she sliced it into approximately one-inch pieces with a butter knife "—and finish it."

Using the side of her thumb, she pushed down on the small piece of dough, rolling it so that it now more closely resembled the pasta Jordyn had seen on her plate.

"*Tutto fatto.*"

"It's done?"

"*Sì.*" Caterina nodded. "Except for the cooking, but that only takes three to four minutes in boiling water."

She'd appreciated the lesson, but she couldn't imagine cooking like this every day. And Marco's grandmother did—not just for her own husband but for the restaurant.

Not by herself, of course. Jordyn had discovered that there were half a dozen women who worked side by side in Valentino's kitchen to make the various pastas every day, including Caterina's two daughters and two daughters-in-law.

"It's a lot of work for one meal," Jordyn noted.

The older woman shook her head. "Preparing a good meal is not work," she chided. "It is a labor of love."

Jordyn agreed with the "labor" part, anyway—and then she imagined the surprise, and hopefully the pleasure, on Marco's face when he saw the meal she'd prepared, and she was happy to have made the effort.

"And the sauce?" she asked now.

"I made it while you were rolling the gnocchi." Caterina gestured to the skillet on the back burner. "It will be ready before your pasta and can be left to...*cuocere a fuoco lento.*" She looked at Jordyn, to see if she understood.

"Simmer?" she guessed, more because it seemed to fit the context than because the words Caterina uttered sounded like anything she understood.

"Sì." The other woman nodded. "Simmer."

"That's it?"

"Well, you might want to clean up a little before Marco gets home."

Jordyn glanced down at her flour-dusted clothing. The apron Caterina had given her to wear had afforded her some protection, but there was flour dust on her feet and streaks of it down her arms—not to mention the counters and the floor.

"Thank you so much for your help," she said.

"È un piacere trascorrere del tempo con la donna che è amato da mio nipote," Caterina said sincerely.

"I'm sorry—I didn't understand a word of that."

"I said, 'it was my pleasure.'" Then she kissed Jordyn's cheeks—first one, then the other. "Now go—make yourself irresistible."

Thankfully, she'd had the foresight to bring a change of clothes and a few other things in addition to the groceries. After she'd cleaned up the kitchen, she borrowed Marco's bathroom for a quick shower.

Half an hour later, Jordyn was hovering near the stove, chewing on her thumbnail. She'd boiled the water for the pasta, then turned it off again so it didn't boil away. The slow ticking of the clock was making her crazy. Caterina had promised to send Marco home, but he still wasn't there. Maybe he'd decided to go out for dinner. Or maybe something had happened to him. Maybe—

The thought froze in her head when she heard his key in the lock.

He stepped into the apartment, his eyes skimming over the table already set for two, with candles lit and wine poured, before they landed on her.

"What are you doing here?"

She hadn't expected him to immediately sweep her into his arms and kiss her breathless, but she had hoped for a slightly warmer greeting. Neither his gaze nor his tone gave away anything of what he was feeling—if he was feeling anything.

The quiet *click* of the door closing at his back echoed in her head. Was it an ending? Had she made a mistake in coming here? No, she didn't—wouldn't—believe it.

"I made you dinner," she said.

"Why?"

It was the perfect opening, her chance to put her feelings out there, and she opened her mouth to do so. But at the last second, she balked. "Because you feed me a lot, so I thought I should return the favor."

He moved into the kitchen, frowned when he saw the tray of pasta waiting to be cooked. "Gnocchi?"

She nodded.

"From the restaurant?"

"No. I made it."

His brows lifted. "Where did you learn to make gnocchi?"

"Your grandmother taught me."

"Nonna—*my* nonna—taught you to make gnocchi?"

She nodded.

"Why?"

"Because I asked."

"Why?" he said again.

"Because it's your favorite. And—" she drew in a breath "—I wanted to show you that our relationship is worth fighting for."

And that simply, that easily, the anger and frustration he'd tried to hold on to melted away.

He understood what a big step this was for her. Not just big—monumental. It couldn't have been easy for her to swallow her pride and ask for help—to go to his grandmother and enlist her assistance with this plan.

The fact that she'd done so showed him more clearly than any words the depth of her feelings for him, and the pressure that had been weighing on his chest for the past six days finally eased.

"Are you going to say anything?" she finally asked.

"Sorry, I was just thinking about how hungry I am."

Some of the stiffness eased from her shoulders, and the corners of her mouth tipped up, just a fraction. "Dinner can be ready in five minutes."

"Give me ten," he said. "I need a quick shower."

Ten minutes later, he was sitting at the table with a plate of steaming pasta in front of him. He picked up his fork, eager to dig in. Across from him, Jordyn did the same, but she continued to watch him, waiting for him to sample and assess the meal she'd made.

She'd obviously gone to a lot of effort and was anxious about the result. He didn't blame her for her apprehension. He knew gnocchi could be tricky, and though it looked like his grandmother's pasta, it might be gummy or heavy or tough. But even if it was, he knew that he would eat every bite.

He pierced a piece of gnocchi with the tines of his fork and lifted it to his mouth. He chewed slowly, considering. The flavors—both pasta and sauce—were familiar and delicious. Not exactly like Nonna's, but impressive nonetheless.

He scooped up more pasta. "This is really good."

She finally sampled the food on her own plate, nodded. "I didn't think your grandmother would let me screw it up too badly."

"She might have," he said. "If she didn't already love you because I do."

She opened her mouth as if she wanted to say something, but he spoke again before she could.

"I didn't tell you that for any reason other than that I want you to get used to hearing me say it. Because I do love you, Jordyn."

She looked at him with fear and regret in her deep green eyes. A week earlier, that look would have slayed him because he would have believed that she regretted not feeling the same way. Now he knew the truth. She did love him—she was just afraid to put those feelings into words and risk having her heart broken again.

He shifted his attention back to his plate, surprised to realize it was empty.

"Do you want some more?" she asked.

He shook his head. "No, I'm good, thanks."

She stood up to clear their plates away. "Did you save room for dessert?"

"What's for dessert?"

She took the bowl out of the fridge. "Fresh whipped cream."

"On?"

She smiled. "Whatever you want."

He slid his arms around her waist and drew her close. "I definitely have room for dessert."

O'Reilly's twenty-fifth anniversary was a big hit with their usual patrons, and the advertising blitz had brought in an impressive number and assortment of new customers.

The regular menu was temporarily suspended as the kitchen staff was kept busy preparing trays of hot and cold hors d'oeuvres that the servers circulated through the crowd. And it was a huge crowd. In fact, Jordyn was relieved to see several members of the Brew Crew in attendance because she trusted they would ensure the crowd didn't exceed the capacity of fire regulations.

"This place is crazy tonight," Carl grumbled, not at all pleased to find that his usual stool at the bar was occupied by another customer.

"It's a party," Jordyn reminded him, pouring a pint of his favorite draft beer.

"Who's the guy behind the bar?"

"Phil—he usually works days but Wade brought him in to help out tonight."

Scott was supposed to be helping out behind the bar, too, but Jordyn hadn't seen him in quite a while. Wade, making the rounds through the crowd, didn't seem to realize that she was both overwhelmed and understaffed behind the counter.

She was working on a pint of Guinness and a pitcher of Murphy's Irish Red when Hailey squeezed past with a tray full of empties. "Can you tell Aaron that I need more garnish out here? Lime wedges and olives."

"Got it," the waitress said.

She grabbed her glass of water, swallowed a mouthful.

"Where the hell is Scott?" Phil demanded, reaching past Jordyn for the lemon zester.

"He went to drop off the bank-deposit bag."

"Almost two hours ago," Phil noted.

Jordyn exchanged a draft and a glass of wine for a twenty.

The customer winked at her. "Keep the change."

"Thanks," she said, as grateful that she wouldn't have to take the time to make change as she was for the generous tip. She turned to the next customer. "What can I get for you?"

"A bottle of Bud and a gin and tonic, extra lime."

She popped the top off the bottle, scooped ice into a highball glass. She'd never understood why customers chose to sit in an Irish pub and drink domestic beer when there were so many other options. Ordinarily she would have chatted with the customer a little bit and encouraged him to try something new. Tonight, she didn't question choices but focused on filling orders.

Hailey slid a plate of lime wedges and olives across the bar. "Thanks."

She squeezed two wedges over the ice, then added the gin and a squirt of tonic from the soda gun. She passed over the drinks and took the money, and when she glanced up again—Marco was there.

"You need an extra hand back there?"

"I could use a couple," she admitted.

He came around the bar, rolled up his sleeves, washed his hands and immediately got to work.

He didn't invade her space, but she was conscious of him there. Close enough that she could touch—if her hands hadn't been full of glasses and bottles and various garnishes.

Melody squeezed up to the bar. "I need six more tequila shots, a pitcher of Smithwick's, two G&T, one red, three white, a pint of Kilkenny, two Harp and your opinion of the blond guy in the closest booth."

"Bottle or draft?" Jordyn asked.

"What?"

"The Harp—you didn't specify pint or glass and we also have it in bottles."

"Oh." Melody huffed out a weary breath. "Let me check on that."

"Busy tonight," Marco noted.

"It's been like this since four o'clock this afternoon."

"Why are there only two of you behind the bar?"

"There were three," Jordyn told him. "But Scott went to drop off the bank deposit."

"Two hours ago," Phil interjected again.

Melody came back. "Pints."

Jordyn nodded. "The guy in the booth—did he ask for your number?"

"Yeah." The waitress's cheeks flushed.

"You card him?"

"Of course. He's twenty-two."

Jordyn, because she knew Melody had recently celebrated her thirty-fifth birthday, lifted her brows.

The waitress sighed. "He's just looking to take down a cougar, isn't he?"

"I think you need to consider the possibility."

Melody glanced over at the booth again as she lifted her tray. "What if I don't mind being taken down?"

Jordyn chuckled. "Your call."

It was almost 3:00 a.m. before they were able to get away from O'Reilly's.

As soon as she slid into the passenger seat of Marco's car, Jordyn kicked the shoes off her feet.

"I'm going to sue the salesman for false advertising," she grumbled. "He said things like 'arch support' and 'comfort sole' and enticed me to hand over a hundred bucks."

"No shoe is going to feel comfortable after ten hours on your feet," Marco said.

She glanced at the clock. "It was actually closer to eleven."

"Then you can't blame the shoes."

"But it was good, wasn't it?" she said.

"I don't think there's any doubt that the party was an incredible success." He pulled into her driveway and turned off the engine.

Jordyn looked at the shoes and winced, and he knew she couldn't stand the thought of shoving her feet into them again, even for the short walk to the door.

He went around to the passenger side, handed her shoes to her, then lifted her off the seat and carried her to the door.

"My hero," she said.

"Don't you forget it."

She unlocked the door and he took her directly to the sofa, setting her down so that her back was against the arm and her legs were stretched out on the cushions. Then he sat on the opposite end and lifted her feet into his lap to massage them.

"Oh. My. God." Her eyes closed, her head fell back and a low moan sounded deep in her throat.

Gryffindor, intrigued by the sound, left the comfort of his bed in the corner to come over and investigate. He hopped up on the sofa, demonstrating the agility Jordyn had told Marco about, climbed over her outstretched legs and settled against the back of the sofa, his single eye fixed on Marco.

She moaned again. "Seriously," she said. "Your hands are…magic."

"That's what all the girls say."

She summoned the energy to open one eye—an effect

that was eerily similar to the look Gryff was giving him. "*All* the girls?"

"Well, Anna and Bella, anyway," he said. "Because I can make quarters appear from behind their ears."

She smiled at that and her eye drifted shut again.

Marco massaged her feet for a few more minutes and she encouraged his ministrations with soft sighs and murmurs. Eventually even those sounds faded as exhaustion overcame her.

She would be more comfortable and sleep better in her bed, but he was reluctant to wake her, reluctant to leave her. So he stayed where he was and watched her sleep for a while. She was so beautiful—her thick, dark lashes casting a shadow on her creamy skin, her soft lips curved, just a little, as if she was having a pleasant dream. Her chest rose and fell in a steady rhythm.

But it was more than her physical beauty that appealed to him—it was her sense of humor and her quick mind, her strong sense of loyalty and obvious love of family. He loved every part of her and, despite what he'd said when he'd walked away from her that fateful day almost four weeks earlier, he knew that he couldn't let her go.

"Come on—let's get you into bed."

"Hmm." She struggled to open her eyes. "What?"

"You're falling asleep," he pointed out.

"Oh. Right." He lifted her feet off his lap, then stood up and helped her do the same.

In the bedroom, Marco undressed her, then found a nightgown in her drawer and tugged it over her head. The soft fabric floated over her skin, gently caressing her curves in a way that made him envy the silk and lace.

The week had been a busy one for both of them, and though they'd been together on Tuesday, that now seemed like a lifetime rather than only four days. His body ached with wanting her, but he could tell that she wanted sleep, so he tucked her into bed and touched his lips to her forehead.

"Sweet dreams."

She caught his shirt as he started to draw away. "Wait— where are you going?"

"Home," he said. "You're exhausted, and you'll sleep better if you don't have to share your bed."

She shook her head. "I sleep better with you here."

It wasn't a declaration of love, but it was more of an admission than he'd expected. "Really?"

"Stay," she said. "Please."

"Well, since you asked nicely." He stripped out of his clothes and slid under the covers beside her.

She immediately snuggled up against him. "What time do you have to work tomorrow?"

"Not until late afternoon."

"Maybe you could make your special French toast for breakfast?"

He brushed his mouth against hers. "Maybe I will."

She shifted closer. Her breasts grazed his chest through the thin silk, her nipples immediately hardening into twin points that caused all of his blood to rush south. Then she reached her hand between their bodies and into his boxers, her fingers closing around him.

"You're supposed to be going to sleep," he reminded her through gritted teeth.

"I'm not tired anymore."

"In that case…" he said, and proceeded to show her that he wasn't tired, either.

Chapter Sixteen

He made French toast for breakfast and, after they'd eaten their fill and cleaned up the kitchen, they went back to her bed and made love again.

Jordyn no longer denied that what they shared was lovemaking. She wasn't yet ready to put her feelings for Marco into words, but she'd finally stopped pretending that their relationship was purely physical.

They lingered in bed as long as they could, cuddling and talking, but eventually Marco had to head back to his own place to get ready for work. He was scheduled to be at the restaurant at four o'clock, and she didn't protest when he left. After the hours she'd put in at O'Reilly's over the weekend, she had no right.

But she found herself wishing that she had more time to spend with him. Both of them had demanding schedules, but while Valentino's closed at ten o'clock because it was primarily a restaurant, O'Reilly's didn't stop serving drinks until at least midnight—and not until 2:00 a.m. on Fridays and Saturdays.

She recalled Marco asking if she really wanted to serve drinks from behind a bar for the rest of her life. She hadn't given him an answer, but even then, she'd realized that the hours she worked would present a challenge for any relationship. She didn't doubt that she and Marco could work around the erratic hours because they had been doing it for several weeks already. But their relationship was still fairly new, in the early stages where everything was hearts and flowers. And it was only the two of them. She knew it wouldn't be nearly as easy to juggle their conflicting schedules and responsibilities when they had kids—

The thought had barely formed in her head when she dropped onto the edge of the mattress, her chest tight, her head spinning.

Kids? Where had that idea come from? What was she thinking?

Obviously she'd been spending too much time around people with children, because her mind didn't usually travel down the traditional path of marriage and children. At least, it hadn't in the past three and a half years.

Until Marco. He'd changed everything for her, made her want things she thought she'd given up on forever. The biggest question now was—did she have the courage to go after what she wanted?

Monday afternoon when she went into work, she found Wade staring at an array of receipts spread out on his desk. She didn't understand why he was frowning.

"Is everything okay?" she asked him.

"I'm not sure," he admitted.

Jordyn took a seat across him. "I think the weekend was a bigger success than any of us anticipated."

"The cash register receipts definitely bear that out," her boss agreed. "Unfortunately, the bank deposits tell a different story."

"What are you talking about?"

He showed her the bank deposit records indicating the amounts that were put into the account on Friday, Saturday and Sunday. The numbers were good, but not nearly as good as she'd expected.

"This doesn't make any sense. It's barely more than we take in on a regular weekend."

"I know."

"I don't understand," she said, because the one possibility that niggled at the back of her mind—that someone had skimmed money from the till—was one she didn't want to consider.

"Scott told me that he counted the cash but you double-checked each deposit before he took it to the bank."

"I did," she confirmed, still trying to comprehend the discrepancy. Her initials were on the deposit forms, confirming that they hadn't been altered. The only possible explanation was that the money had gone missing somewhere between the time it was taken out of the register and when she counted it in the back room.

And the only person who'd had access to it during that time was her boss's nephew.

She remembered Wade mentioning that Scott had left Vegas because of a gambling problem. Then there was the fact that Scott had been quick to volunteer to take the deposit bag to the bank, and he'd been gone a lot longer than that simple task had warranted. And when he finally did return, he'd had the gall to act all disapproving because she'd enlisted Marco's help behind the bar.

"Did you question Scott about the numbers?" she asked her boss.

"Of course," Wade assured her.

"Did he have any ideas about where the money might have gone?"

"He was as confused as me—but then he remembered that you had a customer helping out behind the bar Saturday night."

"Marco?" she echoed in disbelief. "You think Marco took the money?" She shook her head. "No. No way."

"It's the only explanation that makes any sense."

"It doesn't make any sense at all," she told him. "Marco isn't just a customer—he's a bartender at Valentino's. And there is no way he took ten cents from the till, never mind the more than ten thousand dollars that's apparently missing."

Wade scribbled *Valentino's* and *Marco* down on his notepad. "What's his last name?"

Jordyn had to curl her fingers into her palms to resist reaching out and tearing the page away from him. "Marco did *not* take the money."

"I'm sure he'd appreciate your loyalty, but I think, at this point, that's a determination for the police to make."

"Go ahead," Jordyn said. "Call the police. And when they come in to talk to me, I'll be sure to mention the fact that Marco was helping out behind the bar that night because your nephew, who was supposed to be working with me and Phil, was gone more than three hours when he went to drop off the bank-deposit bag."

Wade frowned. "If that's true, why am I only hearing about it now?"

"Because I didn't want to stir up trouble."

"Or maybe you're grasping at straws to protect your boyfriend."

Jordyn pushed her chair back and stood up. "If you really believe that, then you don't know me at all."

"I don't know what to believe," Wade admitted. "I've worked with you for almost three years, but Scott is my sister's son—he's family. Why would he steal money from me when he knows I would give him almost anything he asked?"

She understood his reluctance to suspect his nephew—she did. But it still hurt that he would prefer to suspect her. And pointing a finger at Marco was suspecting her, because she was the one who had asked Marco to help out. She was the one who had put him behind the bar.

"I'm not telling you not to call the police," Jordyn said to him. "In fact, I hope you do because I'm confident that they'll figure this out. I'm just suggesting that you ask your nephew some hard questions before you turn the investigation over to the city's finest." She moved toward the door. "I will, of course, answer any questions that they have, but that is the last thing I owe you. I'm done here."

"What?" He looked sincerely baffled. "What are you saying?"

"I'm saying that I quit."

"Come on, Jordyn—you're overreacting."

"I don't think I am."

"Don't do this. Please. You know how much I need you—"

"No," she interrupted. "I fell for that once. I gave up a weekend in New York to stay here because I believed you needed me. You don't. And I don't need to tie myself to a job that has already limited other opportunities for me."

She didn't even care that she'd missed out on the final round of A. K. Channing's contest, not really. She did care that she'd given up the chance to spend that time with Marco. She'd chosen her job over the man she lov—

She severed the thought, pulling herself back from that edge, not quite willing to take that final leap—even in her own mind.

It was Thursday before she saw Marco again.

Although they talked and texted every day, he was spending most of his time at the new Valentino's, overseeing all of the work that was being done there. So far, everything was on schedule for the planned soft opening in September. The new appliances had been installed in the kitchen and given Nonna's nod of approval, and Rafe was apparently as giddy as a kid in a candy store as he arranged pots and pans and worked on the menus.

But he wanted some feedback before any new recipes were approved, which was why Jordyn had been invited to the restaurant for lunch. Her stomach had been tied up in knots since her confrontation with Wade three days earlier and she didn't feel much like eating, but she wanted to help Rafe out. On her way to the restaurant, she got a call from her former boss, who wanted to apologize for the 'misunderstanding' after Scott confessed to the police.

When she walked into the dining room, she found Marco's enormously pregnant sister, Renata, supervising the hanging of pictures on the walls while her sexy firefighter husband, Craig, wielded the hammer. They bantered and bickered as they worked, but there was an obvious affection in their voices—and the smoldering glances they exchanged when they thought no one was looking.

She tore her gaze away from the couple to check out the decor. The ivory-colored walls contrasted with the dark wood floors to create a simple and elegant first impression. The chairs were padded in dark brown leather and the tables, bare now, would be covered in ivory linens.

Jordyn moved closer to the wall to examine the sepia-toned pictures that had already been hung. They were photographs, she realized, mostly of a vineyard, probably somewhere in Italy. A panoramic view of rolling hills covered with neat rows of grapevines; a simple stone farmhouse set deep in the hills; a gnarled hand inspecting the fruit; a barefoot child skipping between the vines. As Jordyn moved from one picture to the next, she realized that the photographs told a story—an enduring tale rich with history and tradition.

"Where did you get these pictures?" she asked Renata. "They're absolutely stunning."

"My brother Gabe took them when he and Francesca were in Italy in the spring," Marco's sister told her.

"I didn't know he was a photographer."

"Actually he's a lawyer, but he can take decent pictures when he's in the mood."

"What do you think?" Marco asked Jordyn, coming through from the kitchen.

"The whole place looks fabulous," she assured him.

"It's starting to come together," he agreed modestly. "There are some finishing touches to be added—including the fixtures in the bathrooms. And we're still waiting on the liquor license, but we're starting to sort through applications and do interviews for staffing."

"Do you need a bartender for the new place?"

"I've got half a dozen interviews set up for tomorrow afternoon," he told her.

"Want to see my résumé?"

"I'd love to see your... I'm sorry—did you say résumé?" She nodded.

"I think I missed something."

"I'm looking for a new job," she said, deliberately keeping her tone light.

"Why? What happened?"

"Wade questioned me about more than ten thousand dollars that was missing from the weekend bank deposits."

"Seriously?"

She nodded.

"He can't honestly believe you took it, if you needed the money...oh—not you," he realized, when her gaze shifted away. "He thinks *I* took it."

"Not anymore," she assured him.

"The nephew?" he guessed.

She nodded. "It was obvious to everyone but Wade—until he brought the police in and Scott finally confessed."

Marco shrugged. "Everyone wears blinders, to a certain extent, when it comes to their families."

"Maybe," she acknowledged.

"I can understand why you were upset," he said. "But are you sure that quitting your job wasn't a little hasty?"

"No," she admitted. "In fact, I'm pretty sure it *was* hasty. And impulsive. But I also feel that it was the right thing for me. It turns out, I don't want to work at O'Reilly's for the rest of my life."

"So what do you want to do?"

"I think I need to take some time to figure that out, but if you need some help here in the interim, I'd be happy to pitch in."

"Would you really want me to be your boss?"

"I think we could make it work."

He took a minute to consider her offer. "Well, my brother's the head chef at the original Valentino's and his wife is the hostess, and no one seems to have an issue with that. So maybe, if you agreed to marry me..." The words trailed off suggestively.

She knew he was teasing, but that knowledge didn't prevent her pulse from skipping. "You better be careful," she warned. "If you keep throwing out proposals like that, someone might surprise you one day and say yes."

"Is today that day?"

"No."

He pulled her closer and kissed her softly. "Okay, here's an easier question—are you hungry?"

Now that the mystery of the missing money had been solved, she discovered that she was. "Hungry and eager to sample whatever Rafe's cooking up in the kitchen."

"It was supposed to be homemade tagliatelle with porcini mushrooms."

"Has the menu changed?"

"Not changed but expanded," he told her. "In addition to the tagliatelle, he's trying his hand at pork medallions with a shallot-and-red-wine sauce served with baked apples and yams on the side, and grilled salmon with roasted root vegetables and asparagus spears."

"Mmm—everything sounds good."

"Those are just today's offerings," Marco said. "Tomorrow he's planning to serve osso buco with saffron risotto, roast duck with marsala gravy served with red-skin mashed potatoes, and lobster ravioli in a tomato-cream sauce."

"Am I invited back for lunch tomorrow?'

Marco chuckled. "Absolutely."

After they'd sampled all of Rafe's creations and deemed them worthy of inclusion on the new menu, Lauryn came by to get Jordyn so they could go pick out the paint for Kylie's bedroom.

When she was gone, Marco wandered back to the kitchen and found Renata scooping up tagliatelle with the fork in one hand and rubbing her back with the other.

"So everything's okay with you and Jordyn now?" she asked.

"Better than okay," he told her.

She nodded. "I hope so, because I've never seen you look the way you look when you're with her."

"I love her, Nata."

She touched a hand to his arm. "I know you do—but how does she feel?"

"She loves me, too."

"Has she said it? Has she spoken those words to you?" she asked gently.

"No," he admitted. "But I know it."

"Oh, Marco."

He rolled his eyes. "Don't say 'oh, Marco' to me in that tone."

"What tone?"

"That pitying tone."

"It wasn't a pitying tone," she denied. "It was a worried tone."

"There's no reason for you to worry about me."

"Don't get me wrong, I really like Jordyn—"

"That's good, considering that she's going to be your sister-in-law someday."

Renata sighed again. "How long are you going to wait for that someday, Marco?"

"As long as I have to," he told her.

The certainty in his tone must have convinced her, because her next question was, "Have you got a ring?"

"I've been looking," he admitted.

"Both of you?"

"No, just me."

"You can't pick out a diamond without a woman's eye," she told him.

He frowned. "I have to buy a diamond?"

She looked so horrified by his question, he couldn't help but laugh. "I'm kidding, Nata."

"I hope so."

"You want to go shopping with me—to help steer me in the right direction?"

She grinned. "I was just waiting for you to ask."

"So explain to me again why you quit your job at O'Reilly's but don't want to come back to the family business," Tristyn said.

It was the last Saturday in August and another spa day with her sisters. Jordyn leaned back in her massage chair while her feet soaked. "It's just not what I want to do at this point in my life."

"What do you want to do?" Lauryn asked.

"I thought I might look into taking some art classes, just for fun."

"You could *teach* art classes," her sister told her.

"Okay, let's put aside the career plan for a minute," Tristyn said. "I'm more curious about what's going on in your personal life."

"You know what's going on in my personal life," Jordyn said.

"I know that every time Marco tries to take a step forward, you push him two steps back. And that you had a big fight and then you moped around the house for a week. Then you got back together, and now you walk around the house singing and dancing all the time."

"I do not sing and dance," she protested.

"Sounds like love to me," Lauryn said.

"If you're waiting for me to deny it, you're going to be disappointed," Jordyn said. "In fact, I've decided that I'm going to ask Marco to marry me."

Tristyn's jaw nearly hit the floor. "*You're* going to propose to *him*?"

She nodded. "That's the plan."

"When?"

"Hopefully next week. If Marco can get a couple of days off, we're going to go to Braden's place on Ocracoke."

"You've really thought this through," Lauryn realized.

She shrugged. "I figured he's put his feelings on the line often enough, it's probably my turn to do the same."

Tristyn splashed her feet in the water. "I'm going to be a maid of honor."

"You will," Jordyn confirmed. Then she turned to Lauryn, "And you'll stand up with me, too, won't you?"

"I'd love to—depending on when you schedule the wedding and whether or not I'll be able to fit into a dress."

"Well, obviously that's something Marco and I need to discuss, but I'm thinking sooner rather than later."

Lauryn's eyes misted. "You really are ready. You're finally moving on."

"I really am ready," she confirmed.

With his sister's help, Marco had finally decided on a ring. The next step, of course, was asking Jordyn to marry him, but he hadn't yet figured out when or where that should happen.

The "when" was the most crucial question—he was eager to propose, not just to plan the wedding but the rest of their lives together—but he reminded himself to be patient. If he popped the question prematurely, he ran the risk of Jordyn saying no—and he was nervous enough about asking her without considering the possibility of that happening.

He also didn't want to propose when her future was uncertain. He didn't want to wonder if she'd said yes because she was at loose ends. No job, no career plan—why not get married?

He didn't doubt that she loved him, but even if she realized the depth of her feelings, she hadn't acknowledged them. At least not to him. So he had a ring in his pocket, but no definitive timetable for putting it on her finger.

Saturday morning, while Jordyn was with her sisters, he was meeting with the plumber to select bathroom fixtures for the new restaurant when his phone rang. A quick glance at the display screen showed an unfamiliar number. He was tempted to dismiss it, certain it was someone selling something, but the number looked vaguely familiar. Excusing himself, he stepped away to connect the call.

The second time the number showed up on his screen—Sunday afternoon when he was with Jordyn—he recognized it immediately and passed the phone to her to answer.

She gave him a questioning look but put the receiver to her ear.

Of course, he could only hear her side of the conversation, and he could tell that she was both skeptical and wary at first. He could also tell the exact moment when A. K. Channing managed to convince her of his identity and the purpose of the call, because her eyes went wide and when her gaze shifted to his, he could see that she was slightly panicked.

"I'm sorry," she said, sounding sincerely regretful. "But I don't think you're looking for me—I didn't submit any illustrations for the final round of judging."

Her brow furrowed as she listened to the response.

"I don't understand…" Her words trailed off as her gaze shifted back to Marco, and suddenly she did understand.

She talked—or rather listened—for several minutes more, responding with the occasional "yes," "okay," and "of course," before she said, "I'll see you then," and disconnected the call.

"You sent my illustrations."

He couldn't tell by her tone how she felt about that. It seemed apparent that she was thrilled to have spoken with the author, but that didn't mean she couldn't be upset with him if she felt he'd crossed some kind of line.

He nodded. "It was too big an opportunity for you to miss."

"Did you ask Tristyn to sneak my folder out of the house to you?"

"It wasn't anything that clandestine," he told her. "I just stopped by the house one afternoon when I knew you would be at work and asked her for it."

"I'm trying to figure out how I feel about that," she admitted.

"While you're figuring it out, why don't you tell me what Mr. Channing said?" he suggested.

"He said all of the finalists presented excellent work, but he was particularly impressed with my depiction of the villain based on the minimal character description we were given."

"So you won?" he prompted, because she seemed to take forever to get to that part.

She shook her head. "No."

He winced. "I'm sorry."

"I knew I couldn't," she told him. "The contest rules clearly stated that the finalists had to be in New York City to present their work. The gold ribbon and the check went to a seventeen-year-old kid from Spokane."

"So why did he call you?"

"Because he's coming to Charisma to meet with me," she said, sounding a little bewildered by the fact. "He actually lives in Virginia Beach, but he had the contest judging in New York City so that his editor and his agent could give their input. And they both agreed that my illustrations were right for his new series. Although I couldn't win the contest, he wants to meet me to be sure that we can work together and, if he thinks we can, he's going to hire me."

"So you're not mad that I sent your work to New York without your knowledge or approval?"

"I'm not mad." She lifted her arms to link them around his neck and draw his mouth down to hers. "In fact, I'm very...very...grateful."

He savored the sweetness of her lips and the softness of her body pressed against him.

"You know—when Wade refused to give me the weekend off to go to New York, I think I was almost as relieved as I was disappointed. Because if I didn't go, I could console myself with the fact that I hadn't actually lost without risking failure by putting myself out there."

"I knew you wouldn't fail."

"No one has ever believed in me the way that you do."

"You have a tremendous talent," he said. "You just needed a little nudge to seize the opportunity that was there."

"I've been scared for too long," she realized. "Afraid to go after what I really wanted, in case it was out of my reach. Or worse, afraid that I might actually hold it in my hands, and then have it snatched away."

"And now?"

She took both of his hands and linked their fingers together. "Now I'm ready to reach for what I really want."

It was the perfect opportunity for him to drop down to one knee. In fact, he was reaching into his pocket for the ring he'd been carrying with him for the last three days when his phone rang again.

Chapter Seventeen

Marco disconnected the call and tucked his phone back in his pocket. His head was spinning, trying to sift through all of the information his mother had thrown at him and latch on to the most important pieces.

"What's wrong?" Jordyn asked.

"There was a fire in an abandoned warehouse in South Meadows. Three firefighters were inside when the roof collapsed."

She immediately guessed the reason for his grim tone. "Craig?"

He nodded. "I don't know the details about what happened, I only know that he's been taken to Mercy Hospital."

"I'm so sorry," she said.

"My mom and dad want me to go over to my sister's, to stay with Anna and Bella so Renata can go to the hospital with them."

"Of course. Do you want me to come with you?"

He was surprised by the offer, and even more surprised to realize how much he wanted her with him. "I do," he admitted.

She took his hand. "Let's go."

Renata was waiting on the front porch when they arrived. Marco spoke a few words to her and hugged her tight—or as tight as he could considering the size of her belly—before she got into the backseat of her parents' car and headed off to the hospital with them. The girls were inside watching a video on TV, oblivious to the drama that was unfolding around them.

Despite the fact that it never chimed to indicate a message, he kept checking his phone every two minutes, desperate for word of his brother-in-law's condition. The rest of his family was at the hospital with Renata, but Jordyn could tell that he wished he were there, too. Not that he could do anything more than what was already being done, but families stood together in times of crisis, and it was obvious he wanted to be there for his sister.

They had dinner with the girls, made pictures with modeling clay, then Anna got out a board game, which they'd been playing for the past two hours.

"Agin," Bella said, when her token landed on the rainbow square to finish the game. "Wes pway 'gin."

Jordyn fought against a smile as she mentally translated Marco's youngest niece's words. "Marco?" she prompted.

"What?"

"Bella wants to play again," she told him.

"Oh, yeah, sure."

"I love Candy Land as much as the next person," Jordyn said. "But we've already played six games and I'm guessing that it's getting close to bedtime."

Marco glanced at the clock. "I didn't realize how late it was," he admitted.

"Is it bedtime?" Anna asked.

"Past your bedtime," he told her.

With a reluctant sigh, she started to gather up the cards to put the game away.

"No, Anna." Bella grabbed for the cards. "Pway 'gin."

"It's bedtime," Anna told her sister, tightening her grip on the pile of cards in her hand.

"No!"

"Bella," Marco said, a note of unmistakable warning in his voice.

"Pway 'gin," she insisted, yanking the cards with such

force that they flew out of her sister's hands and scattered around the room.

Anna gasped. "Bad!" she told her sister. "Bad Bella!"

Which, of course, made Bella start to cry.

Then Anna's lower lip started to quiver and her eyes filled with tears, too. They were both overtired and undoubtedly aware of the tension in the room, even if unaware of the reason for it. Renata, not wanting to cause them distress, hadn't told them where she was going, she'd only said that she had to go out and that Uncle Marco and Jordyn would look after them for a while.

Marco sighed. "Okay, girls, let's get this game picked up and get you into the bath."

Bella, sobbing theatrically, pushed herself between his knees to snuggle against his chest. He put one arm around her and kissed her forehead.

Anna approached more tentatively. "Is everything okay, Uncle Marco?"

He wrapped his other arm around her and drew her into his embrace. "It's going to be," he promised.

"I'll put the game away while you deal with bath time," Jordyn suggested.

"Sounds like a plan."

After the girls were bathed and dressed in their pajamas, they were given a snack before bed.

"Why don't you go to the hospital?" Jordyn suggested to Marco, while Anna and Bella were occupied brushing their teeth.

"Because I promised Nata that I'd stay here."

"You don't think I can handle two little girls?"

"I don't know why you'd want to," he admitted wryly.

She touched her lips to his. "Because it's the one thing that I can do to help you."

"They'll want a bedtime story," he told her.

"I do know how to read."

He managed a smile. "Are you sure you don't mind?"

"I'm sure." She squeezed his hand. "Go—be with your sister and the rest of your family. I can hold down the fort here."

And she thought she did pretty well with it. She read the girls a story—actually two. Since they couldn't agree on one story, she let them each choose a favorite book, but she didn't mind—especially when they sat quietly and listened attentively while she read.

It was only when she closed the cover of the second book that Bella ventured to ask, "Are you Unca Mahco's girfwiend?"

She decided that was the easiest explanation for their relationship—or at least the most appropriate one to share with his nieces. "I guess I am," she said.

"Are you gonna get married?" Anna asked.

"We don't have any definite plans," she hedged, though she hoped that would change soon.

"Uncle Gabe is going to marry his girlfriend."

"So I hear."

Bella chimed in again, "We's gonna be fwower girs."

"That sounds like fun."

"Mama says it sounds expensive," Anna confided.

Jordyn smiled. "It's probably that, too."

"Where is Mama?" Bella asked.

"She went out with your grandparents," she reminded them.

It struck her as both lucky and sad that because of the shifts their dad worked as a firefighter, they were accustomed to him being away overnight and didn't even ask about him.

She turned off the light. "Sweet dreams, girls."

"Jo'dyn." Bella's soft entreaty stopped her at the door.

"What is it, honey?"

"If Unca Mahco mawies you, could we be fwower girs 'gin?"

"I think you probably could," she agreed.

She was cleaning up the dishes from the girls' snack when her phone rang. Recognizing Marco's number, she snatched it up immediately.

"Hi," she said, then held her breath as she waited for an update.

"There's no news on Craig yet," he told her. "But Renata's water just broke."

Jordyn couldn't think of an appropriate response to the situation. She only knew that she ached for Marco— for his whole family. What should have been a joyous celebration—the impending birth of a new child—was now inextricably tangled up with grief and fear. Renata, she knew, had to be going out of her mind, not knowing if her husband would even live to see their baby born.

The tragic possibility made Jordyn's own throat tighten. "Is there anything I can do?"

"You're doing it," he said. "Taking care of Anna and Bella so the rest of the family can be here."

"I wish I could do more."

"You could pray."

"I've been doing that, too."

When she disconnected the call, she went to check on the girls and found they were both fast asleep.

Back downstairs, the house was quiet. Too quiet. She turned on the television for background noise while she thought of Renata and what she was going through.

Was it a blessing or a curse that the baby had decided to come now? How was Renata supposed to focus on bringing a new life into the world when her husband's life was hanging in the balance?

With everything that was happening, maybe it wasn't

surprising that Jordyn's mind drifted back to the hours that she'd spent pacing the hospital corridors, praying and pleading and waiting to hear if her fiancé would live or die.

Weddings and funerals; births and deaths. She wondered if it was a cruel trick of fate that so many beginnings and endings were linked. One day she'd been addressing wedding invitations, the next she was writing Brian's obituary and feeling as if her heart had been ripped out of her chest.

She'd loved Brian, but their time together had been a brief interlude. They hadn't had anywhere near the kind of history that Marco's sister had with her husband, but still Jordyn had grieved for a long time. She'd had family support, but she hadn't had to worry about anyone but herself. If Craig didn't make it, Renata had two little girls who would be grieving for and missing their father—and another child who would never know him.

No—Jordyn refused to consider the possibility that Craig wouldn't survive. He was young, he was strong, and he had so much to live for, so many people who were praying for him.

Jordyn added herself to that number.

Marco should have known that his sister was too stubborn to let something like the start of labor pull her away from the surgical waiting room.

Understanding her need to stay as close to her husband for as long as possible, her mother took the necessary documentation to Labor and Delivery to get her registered. Apparently the triage nurse was anxious for her to be checked out, especially since this wasn't her first child, but Renata kept insisting that there was time and that she needed to be with Craig.

"Your contractions are five minutes apart," he noted. "I really think we need to get you to Labor and Delivery."

"Not yet," she insisted. "I can't have the baby yet."

"I don't think you have much choice," he told her.

Tears spilled onto her cheeks. "Craig promised he would be with me when I went into labor. He promised."

Marco felt his own eyes burn. "Come on, Nata, you can't fall apart now. The doctors are taking care of Craig—he needs you to take care of yourself and your baby."

She shook her head. "I can't do it without him. I don't know how."

He knew she wasn't just referring to the process of labor and childbirth—she was thinking about the whole life she shared with her husband and the family they'd built together. He slid an arm across her shoulders and silently prayed that her claim wouldn't be tested.

Renata was in labor twenty-seven hours with Adrianna, nine with Isabella and only three with the son who was born at 11:49 p.m. that night, weighing eight pounds and eleven ounces and measuring twenty-two inches.

Marco had stayed with her throughout, a poor substitute for his brother-in-law but at least she wasn't alone. Not that there had been any shortage of volunteers—their mother, Nata's mother-in-law and Nonna had all offered to coach her through the delivery, but his sister had taken hold of his hand and refused to let go, conscripting him into service.

He got through it by focusing on her face, talking her through the contractions, and trying not to think about what was happening under the sheet that was draped over the lower half of her body. Then they placed the baby on her belly, all pink and slimy and screaming at the indignation of being naked under the bright lights.

"Nonna was right," Marco said. "It's a boy."

The baby was weighed and measured, then swaddled and given back to his mother. She'd barely settled him into her arms when there was a knock on the door and another doctor, dressed in faded hospital scrubs, walked in.

Marco recognized him before he was halfway across the room, and when the doctor paused, he realized Jordyn's cousin had recognized him, too, from the Fourth of July celebration in the park. Justin nodded a brief acknowledgment, then went directly to Renata's bedside. "Congratulations, Mrs. Donnelly."

"Thank you." Her response was automatic, her body already tensed for what was to come next.

"I'm not sure if you remember me, but I'm Dr. Justin Garrett," he continued in the same even tone that was no doubt intended to put patients at ease. "I was in the ER when they brought your husband in."

"Craig..." It was all she could manage, and that, barely a whisper.

"He's going to be fine," the doctor assured her. "He had a pretty severe concussion, which is why we'll need to keep him here to monitor him for a few days. Aside from that, he suffered some bruised ribs and a broken clavicle, so he's not going to be much help to you with the little guy for at least four to six weeks, but afterward, there's no reason he can't do his share of diaper duty."

Renata nodded as the doctor detailed the extent of her husband's injuries, but Marco suspected she hadn't really heard anything after the first words. A suspicion that was confirmed when the doctor left and she turned to him and echoed those words, "He's going to be fine."

Marco nodded.

And his sister, who had valiantly held herself together from the moment she got the harrowing call about her husband, who'd barely muttered any sounds of discomfort through labor and delivery, finally let go of her emotions and bawled like a baby.

* * *

Jordyn fell asleep on the sofa sometime during the fifth episode of a *Ryder to the Rescue* marathon she'd found on TV.

She didn't hear Marco come in, but she woke up cradled in his lap with his arms tight around her. It took a minute for her mind—clouded with worry as much as sleep—to clear enough to ask, "How's Craig?"

"He's going to be okay."

She exhaled an unsteady breath. "Thank God."

"Yeah," he said hoarsely. "We've been doing a lot of that."

"And Renata? The baby?" she prompted.

"She's good. He's good."

"It was a boy?"

He nodded. "Ethan Salvatore Donnelly."

"Has Craig seen his son?"

"Yeah. Renata was allowed to take the baby into his room for a few minutes."

She could imagine how emotional that scene must have been for all of them and felt the sting of tears in her own eyes.

He tipped her chin up. "You okay?"

She nodded. "Better now that you're here."

"It's been a hell of a day," he acknowledged.

She nodded again. The events of the past several hours had reminded her how quickly things could change, how fragile life was, and that it was truly a precious gift to experience and share love. She couldn't deny her feelings for him any longer, and she didn't want to.

She took a deep breath and, lifting her eyes to meet his, finally said, "I love you."

He stared at her, as if he couldn't quite believe what she was saying. "Can you repeat that?"

She framed his face in her hands and held his gaze steadily. "I love you, Marco."

"Is this one of those impulsive posttrauma, adrenaline-crash declarations?"

She felt a smile tug at the corner of her lips, because she understood why he sounded a little bit skeptical, a little reluctant to accept her words at face value. "Have you been the recipient of many of those?"

"No," he admitted. "I'm just trying to understand where this is coming from—why now."

"I had always planned to tell you tonight. Last night," she amended, when she glanced at the clock on the fireplace mantel and saw that it was almost 2:00 a.m. "I was just trying to find the right words—and the courage—to admit my feelings.

"When I met you, I didn't want to fall in love—to open myself up to potential heartache again," she admitted. "But your grandmother was right—the head cannot control what the heart wants."

"Nonna said that to you?" he asked, his voice rough with emotion.

She smiled. "Among other things."

He wondered about those 'other things,' but for now, for tonight, Jordyn's confession of love was more than he'd expected—and everything he wanted. "My grandmother is a wise woman."

"She is," Jordyn confirmed. "And she helped me accept that my heart wants to get married."

His own was pounding hard and fast inside his chest. "Are you making a general statement or hinting at something more specific?"

"I'm bungling this," she admitted.

"Bungling what?"

"My proposal."

His brows lifted. "Are you asking me to marry you?"

"Yes. No." She huffed out a breath. "I was planning to wait until next week, when we were at Braden's cottage in Ocracoke."

"*You* were going to propose to *me*?" He was stunned, flattered, thrilled.

"Well, I figured it was up to me since you'd most likely given up—"

He took a ring out of his pocket. "I didn't give up on anything—and I would *never* give up on you."

"Oh." The diamonds flashed in the light, almost blinding her. Or maybe that was the tears that filled her eyes again.

"*I* was going to ask *you* next week," he told her, "when we were in Ocracoke."

She laughed. "I would have said yes."

"Then say yes now," he suggested.

"You haven't asked the question," she pointed out.

In fact, none of this was at all how she'd imagined their engagement would happen—in the living room of his sister's house, in the early hours of morning, with two kids sleeping upstairs. She'd thought there would be candles and champagne, and maybe soft music in the background. Instead, there was only her and Marco—but she knew now that was all they needed.

"Do you want me to get down on one knee?"

She wasn't surprised that he was traditional enough to want to do so, but she was still cuddled in his lap. "No, I don't want you to let me go."

"I'm not going to," he promised. "Not ever."

"Prove it," she said, holding out her hand and wiggling her fingers for the ring he still held in his.

He chuckled softly as he took her hand and held the ring poised at the tip of her third finger. "Jordyn Garrett, will you marry me?"

"Yes, Marco Palermo," she said, pressing her lips to his.

"I will marry you and spend the rest of my life as your wife and the mother of your babies."

He grinned at the echo of the words he'd said to her so long ago, then he slid the ring on her finger.

For just a moment—not even a heartbeat—an icy trickle of fear slid down her spine, reminding her that she'd been here once before: full of love and hope and dreams for a future with the man she loved. Then she looked at Marco, and the love that filled her heart was stronger than any lingering fear, stronger than anything else she'd ever known.

Maybe love was a risk, but he was absolutely worth it.

And so were they.

Epilogue

They argued about when and where to get married.

After finally admitting the truth of her feelings for him, Jordyn was eager to get on with their life together. She suggested a quick and quiet ceremony with their closest friends and family around them. But Marco had waited for her for too long to cut any corners. He wanted a big wedding to celebrate with everyone they knew, and big weddings took time to plan.

In the end Jordyn got what she wanted, because Marco would do anything for her. And because she told him that she wanted to marry before the end of December, because she wanted to start the new year as Mrs. Marco Palermo, and how could he possibly argue against that?

So on the thirtieth of December, at seven o'clock, he was standing at the front of Saint Mark's with his brothers beside him. Anna and Bella came down the aisle first, wearing identical lavender dresses, walking side by side and scattering pale pink rose petals along the way. Lauryn followed close behind the flower girls—beautiful and elegant in a violet gown despite being eight months pregnant; then came Tristyn, wearing a slightly darker shade of the same color in a more fitted style. She winked at Marco, making him smile and helping to untangle some of the nerves that were knotted up in his stomach.

Then the tempo of the music changed and all of the guests rose to their feet, turning to the back of the church for a first glimpse of the bride.

His anticipation was greater than anyone else's, and when Jordyn finally stepped through the arched entranceway, she completely took his breath away.

It wasn't the dress—although the strapless design with the fitted bodice and long, full skirt was absolutely stunning on her. It wasn't the delicate veil or the bouquet of white roses. It was simply that she was Jordyn. His bride.

And as she made her way toward him, the love that filled his heart to overflowing shone right back at him from her eyes.

He'd waited a long time to find her, but he had no regrets about that now. Everything that had happened before was in the past—she was his present, his future, his forever.

* * * * *

MILLS & BOON®

Want to get more from Mills & Boon?

Here's what's available to you if you join the exclusive **Mills & Boon eBook Club** today:

- ✦ *Convenience – choose your books each month*
- ✦ *Exclusive – receive your books a month before anywhere else*
- ✦ *Flexibility – change your subscription at any time*
- ✦ *Variety – gain access to eBook-only series*
- ✦ *Value – subscriptions from just £3.99 a month*

So visit **www.millsandboon.co.uk/esubs** today to be a part of this exclusive eBook Club!

MILLS & BOON®

Cherish™

EXPERIENCE THE ULTIMATE RUSH OF FALLING IN LOVE

A sneak peek at next month's titles...

In stores from 18th September 2015:

- **The Tycoon's Proposal** – Shirley Jump
  and **A Proposal Worth Millions** – Sophie Pembroke

- **Soldier, Hero...Husband?** – Cara Colter
  and **Betting on the Maverick** – Cindy Kirk

In stores from 2nd October 2015:

- **The Baby Who Saved Christmas** – Alison Roberts
  and **The Good Girl's Second Chance** – Christine Rimmer

- **Falling for Mr December** – Kate Hardy
  and **The Boss's Marriage Plan** – Gina Wilkins

Available at WHSmith, Tesco, Asda, Eason, Amazon and Apple

Just can't wait?
Buy our books online a month before they hit the shops!
visit www.millsandboon.co.uk

These books are also available in eBook format!

0915/23